THE ELIXIR OF INHERITANCE

The Alchemist's Agent No. 2

E. M. BURNHAM

To my family, who encourage me, and my friends, who enable me

CONTENTS

I

Ibram fidgeted outside Lady Azadiya Hobon's closed—*closed*—office door in complete darkness, utterly unimpressed with his life. The sound of Ladyship's pacing suddenly ceased; he imagined he could hear the whoomph of her throwing herself down onto one of her cushioned chairs. He squinted at the diamond pattern carved into the wood before him, and raised one cautious fist.

"*I can see that!*" Lady Azadiya roared from within, and Ibram dropped his hand back to his side like it had been yanked. He stepped back.

"She can see that!" Attendant Zorion whispered excitedly to himself, somewhere to Ibram's right. "Ask her if her sight has been lengthened or if she's standing by the door!"

Several other folk Ibram couldn't quite see shushed him immediately. The Fourth Mentor of Yseult had been sent the last parcel of Attendants from Afsoun for evaluation just that morning, and already they had caused trouble. Inside her office, Ladyship groaned. Ibram pictured her, possibly draped over one of the overstuffed chairs, clasping her dark head in her hands and rubbing her temples. He could empathize with that image.

Every spring, the first day of the Festival of Sangrin kicked off that heady combination of learning and merrymaking that drew so many folk to live near the Sect of Seven Fires. The festival celebrated the creation of the Preceptory of Bedris and its devotion to education, and heralded the beginning of a twelve-day's worth of tests, exams, arguments-thinly-disguised-as-panels, and exhibitions of alchemical form. Each preceptory farmed its Learners and Attendants out between themselves to prove competent at their secondary specialization and then bade them return home covered in acclaim, glory, and not a little soot.

The celebrations, naturally, matched the alchemists' enthusiasm with equal fervor, spilling from village to village with bonfires and parties. The smell of rich dark earth just yielding from winter mingled with the scent of candied fruits. Stickums for luck flew through the air like flocks of real birds, trailing multi-colored sparks. Children fired off Orilindan candles and spun luminous green and blue Blooming Wheels for luck. The rich threw balls, and the less fortunate ran amok in street fairs, while circlers of every musical variety played in any village within walking distance of the sect—which was most of them. The four Mentors of Bedris dined at a dizzying succession of noble homes, and the evening courtyards bloomed nightly with Attendants flush with triumph or pale with despair, and ready to spend their stipends liberally.

Agents, in Ibram's opinion, reaped the best and the worst of the festival, trailing after Afsoun Attendants with buckets of fire sand, or netting Govan Learners before they tumbled down the living mountain. The work made for an entertaining story around the draughtshop —even a free pitcher of wine if the keeper laughed hard enough. As well, the trouble sect agents had to endure each year was in direct proportion to the superb ingenuity of the potions and gadgets that came out of the examinations. Ibram had looked forward to the little rewards for good behavior a sufficiently motivated agent might acquire, say, if someone tall and hardworking from Yseult managed to make a helpful bauble or three.

It wasn't a comforting thought, to be sure, in the dark of the tower. The usual cavalcade of agents, alchemists, and servants who bustled within the tower's confines had been exiled. Shutters had been drawn over every window. The servants had even silenced the gigantic central fountain, and the alchemically translucent roof had been extinguished with a resounding clang of metal shutters. Ibram took a cautious step to the right, where Hilbert Zorion was mumbling amongst his fellows, suddenly aware of the tread of his boot heels on the wooden floorboards.

He tried to pitch his voice loudly enough to be heard, but not too painfully.

"Is your head any better, Ladyship?" Ibram called out.

"Of course, it isn't," she snapped. "Not until this blasted infusion of Zorion's wears off."

"Well, it shouldn't be more than a day or two," Zorion said. "I mean to say, the herbs did steep a bit longer than usual, but—"

"And don't think this gains you a passing score, Hilbert!" Lady Azadiya interrupted him. "Incapacitating the judge was not mentioned in your submission!"

Ibram winced. No doubt if Ahksell had been standing with Ibram, instead of showing off higher up the mountain range in the Preceptory of Afsoun, he would have said something soothing at this point. The Attendants from Afsoun merely shuffled their feet against the wooden floor. Someone coughed. Ibram dimly remembered Ahksell remarking about how useful his friend Zorion's infusions were, but for himself, he wasn't seeing the possibilities for greatness here.

"Should I send for a tonic, Ladyship?" Ibram tried again.

Lady Azadiya was not tempted. "If I have to look at one more refraction of light, someone is going out the window."

"But my notes!" Attendant Zorion exclaimed. He made a sad noise, and was quickly hushed again by his compatriots, all of whose exams now hung in the balance. The other three mentors of Yseult already had their full complement of evaluations. If this batch were halted, then that was it for the rest of the year. Ibram shook his head.

Soft footsteps echoed along the hallway and drew closer at Ibram's left. He turned away from the door and peered through the gloom. He made out Amota Viran's stern face as the man patted Ibram's shoulder. Ibram stepped aside. As Lady Azadiya's longest serving agent and Ibram's titular 'uncle,' Amota Viran had precedence over everyone in the Fourth Mentor's tower except an actual alchemist, and even then, the Attendants and Learners soon knew better than to challenge him. Amota Viran took Ibram's place, and laid one hand against the door.

"May I come in, Damita?" Viran asked in his normal low speaking voice. Ibram tilted his head and glanced left and then right. There was truly so little light in the tower that Ibram strained to focus on the crowd around Ladyship's office.

"Attendant Zorion, what was in that infusion?" Ibram asked quietly, and something heavy hit the floor with a bang in the office beyond.

"We shall postpone the rest of the trials," Lady Azadiya announced, and then made a rough noise of discontent. "Until I am recovered enough to adequately examine the rest of this untidy lot."

The aforementioned lot made a great deal of shuffling noises, and pushed Attendant Zorion to the front. Ibram knew that because Zorion smelled like stale shay and old citrus peels; his nose wrinkled. In the darkness, he barely made out Zorion bowing to the door.

"Mentor Hobon, once again, I am very—" he began.

"I want everyone but Viran out of this tower by the time I count to ten," Ladyship said. "Go practice, or revise, or something of the kind. You've got all my agents out grazing the fields, let them manage you."

He could just see her waving them all away from her chair. Ibram swallowed down a chuckle. He heard the others' footsteps straggle quietly down the second floor to the broad staircase that led out of the tower and shifted his weight to follow. Amota Viran pinched the back of his arm, and stopped him.

"What?" Ibram whispered.

"Three," Ladyship threatened.

"What happened to one and two?" Ibram asked, and tugged on Amota Viran's grip.

"Ibram," Amota Viran whispered. "Hold your tongue! I have a job for you."

Ibram pointed behind himself. "I was going to make sure they none of them tripped and hurt themselves!"

"Six!"

Amota Viran pressed a curl of paper into his hand. "Take this and go to the Savoldyns' manor," he said. "I was supposed to go and oversee Lady Azadiya's order, but as you can see—"

"No, I can't."

"Nine!"

Amota Viran loomed out of the darkness, unamused. Ibram attempted to look repentant. He skittered back towards the stairwell.

"Our schedule will need to be changed," Viran called out as Ibram ran down the steps. "And take Attendant Zorion off the mountain, or Catha the Grey will have his bones by midday!"

◈

Lityen bustled in the sharp morning air, making all the day hum with energy as shops and stalls opened for the day's business. He'd managed to drop Attendant Zorion in front of a festive street caffa with promises to escort him back up the living mountain once Ibram had picked up Ladyship's order. It wasn't difficult. Even though Zorion should have been taking the time to refine his infusions, Ibram had yet to meet an Attendant who wouldn't choose relaxing in the village over examining their mistakes back at the dormitory. And if he wandered anywhere, Ibram could easily find Zorion again. Every traveling merchant caught between caravans had a stall out on the main road and every shop from Book Row to Weaver's Hive had hung painted banners that glimmered in the sun. Something had to catch Zorion's bespectacled eye, though if Ibram was being strictly honest, all the fluttering cloth and shimmering paint was starting to give him a headache. Still, the crowds were navigable this early; he kept his complaints to himself.

Ibram stared down at Amota Viran's list of sundries as he walked the last few feet down the alley off the main road to the door of the Savoldyns' manor. He'd never seen one of Lady Azadiya's goods orders before, they were usually handled by other agents. The number of bolts of cloth and spools of thread numbered far above what his own mother and father ever needed. Though, to be sure, as a Mentor, Lady Azadiya was required to provide for a portion of the Sect of Seven Fires' outlay as a whole. Strictly speaking, Ladyship wasn't allowed to maintain a personal household; her servants and agents were supplied by the sect, who ultimately employed them.

These orders for linen, silk and damasks, and cotton could be for her own use, of course, but then Amota Viran had marked 'senra' next to three items. Ibram frowned. Senra meant... He paused before knocking. What did that mean in Merrilian again? Special, perhaps. Reserved? No, that wasn't it. He scratched the back of his head. Ama had made sure he and Katka learned the Western tongue, but sometimes the details escaped him.

Nothing for it, though. Ibram grabbed the rope pull next to the tall wooden double doors and heard a bell toll from inside the manor. He let go and stepped back. The doors were clean of mud or traffic dust, with fresh dark paint over the swooping water birds carved into the panels. The Savoldyns had done well for themselves, rich enough to have a home within the village's limits, but still mostly disconnected even from its neighbors by narrow alleyways.

The doors opened silently, and in the gap stood a small, compact woman in a plain blue gown slashed at the sleeves to show white wool, and her blonde hair taped around her head with thick white ribbon. She had a thin, narrow face, but her skin had a healthy red flush to it, as if she'd been running. Ibram bowed politely.

"Good morning," he said. "I've come on behalf of Lady Azadiya Hobon, Fourth Mentor of the Preceptory of Yseult. I was told to look over Ladyship's order?"

The woman frowned slightly, showing a few wrinkles at the corners of her mouth. "We were expecting Master Kalmar."

Ibram nodded and held out his list. "My uncle Viran was regrettably detained, Mistress, or he'd be here. It's the festival, you know. Heavy work makes schedules run over their banks just as rains to rivers, to be sure."

Mistress Gatekeeper didn't seem as impressed with Ibram's turn of phrase as he felt, but then it did sound better in the original Merrilian. He smiled at her and popped his weight from his toes to his heels. Her rather wide eyes narrowed at Ibram's chest, where his freshly polished torch-shaped brooch marked him as an agent of the sect.

"And you are Master Kalmar's nephew?" she asked.

He was and he was not, but Ibram definitely didn't feel inclined to explain the finer workings of Westerner society today. The lady didn't seem inclined to listen to a detailed explanation, either. He gestured again with his list, and tilted his head.

"We have the same chin, don't you think?" he lied.

Her eyes narrowed, but she said nothing. Ibram pressed onwards, regardless. He brandished his list yet again.

"Now," Ibram declared. "Not that I am *not* inclined to stay at the gate and listen to your honeyed tones for a twelve-day, but Lady Azadiya's shopping awaits me. Do you think I might pass through, Mistress?"

"Dolman?" a woman's voice called out behind the door. "What are you doing? Who's at the door?"

The door wavered in Mistress Dolman's hand, and Ibram set his foot over the threshold, just in case. Mistress Dolman's entire face pinched, as if she'd tasted something sour; she half-turned from the door to face the newcomer.

"There was no need to run, Mistress," Dolman said through thinned lips. "I've things well in hand."

"And yet I sent for shay an hour ago, I'm certain. You know how it soothes him."

A woman of middle age stepped into view, broad all over, and stood there, breathing quickly. Her pleasant round face was dewed at the temples with sweat and her snub nose was a trifle red. She was finely dressed in a yellow wool gown and a blue kirtle pinned to her waist with golden clasps, emerald stones made the leaves. Her blonde hair, which she was in the process of patting with both hands, was caught back in a fine net held by a green velvet band, very much in the style of the river folk further south. She had rings on her fingers and a delicate silver chain around her neck, looped three times and then caught in the center by an enameled pendant in the shape of a spoked wheel. It wasn't as accomplished as Ibram's father's work, but it certainly appeared expensive.

"I beg pardon," the housekeeper said, "but shay was served to the master just as Mistress Ignalle requested. It's been no more than an hour, since."

"Then I'm sure the pot has gone quite cold, Dolman, and it would go much better for us all if someone brought in a new tray to refresh them. And who is this?" she asked, turning a polite face towards Ibram. The lady of the house—or one of them, perhaps—clasped her hands together in front of her chest and then twisted a ring on her first finger. "What brings a handsome stranger to our door?"

He hated to get in between two evenly matched combatants, but if he came back up the living mountain with only Attendant Zorion, he had the feeling his life would not be worth living. Ibram bowed more fully, putting his hands on his stomach, and then straightened. He held up his list again and opened his mouth.

"He says he's from Mentor Hobon up the living mountain," Mistress Dolman interrupted him, with a suspicious look. "But Master Kalmar handles all her goods."

"And I remember informing you that I'd been sent in his place," Ibram said.

The new woman chuckled. "Ah, he's been caught out because of the festival, hasn't he?" she asked and then flapped her hands in Ibram's direction. "Come in, come in! We've been expecting someone today, you know."

"But Mistress Savoldyn," Mistress Dolman protested. "Mistress Ignalle left strict instructions—"

"Nonsense." Mistress Savoldyn waved her off. "Business is business. Now, young master, you have your list? Good, good, come along!"

Ibram grinned and walked over the threshold, ignoring Mistress Dolman's sour look. He tucked his free hand behind his back; the door shut decisively behind him. The reception hall was long, but narrow, with oil lamps clamped to the whitewashed timbers. Air and a little light came in from an open window above. The blonde woman resettled her skirts and the dangling chain of keys at her belt.

"Ibram Ucalegon, at your service, Mistress," he said.

"And I am Yanna Savoldyn," she said and inclined her head with a smile. She had good green eyes set only a little too widely in her head. "Master Savoldyn's wife. Follow me then!"

Ibram felt his eyebrows raise entirely of their own volition. Married persons kept their family name unless required to give it up in the marriage contract, usually in exchange for a large settlement of coin or an equally large exchange of prestige. Mistress Savoldyn waved him to her side. It was always nice to feel welcome, to be sure, but he had a feeling she was hurrying him along for an entirely different reason than Lady Azadiya's account. She turned in a swirl of heavy skirts, and walked down the hall to a smaller entrance cut next to the larger double doors; he followed.

Ibram blinked as he crossed the threshold and hung back behind her half a step. The hallway had been richly appointed, but this was downright ostentatious. He turned at a cough from behind him; Mistress Dolman glared as she swept past.

"Don't be tardy," she scolded as she entered the public courtyard. Ibram huffed and then followed the pair of them inside. Dolman veered left down the terrace, but Mistress Savoldyn was already leading the way on Ibram's right. He hurried after her, and sneezed. Earthy, sticky pitchwood smoldered in fluted braziers; he could see the smoke drifting from almost every corner of the courtyard.

Ibram touched the back of his sleeve to his nose; Mistress Savoldyn seemed used to it. The public courtyard was full of artfully arranged profusions of fabric, and child-sized clothes suggested what buyers could fashion from Savoldyn's wares. No doubt, there were the latest southern styles, flowing, shimmering gowns that hung from shoulder clasps to float loosely at the waist, and belted kirtles with embroidered ribs at the bodice. There was even some from the deep garden provinces, where they wore exaggerated blowsy trousers in red and yellow and heavy smocked shirts. It was clear the Savoldyns knew their clientele well, supplying both means and vision in one fell swoop.

The public courtyard was dotted with heavy glass ornaments and soaring trees, the kind which only the best alchemist-affiliated glassmakers could create. Their tell-tale iridescence cast endless wavering patterns against the clothing samples as if they were caught in a crystalline spider's web. All this elegance and induced mystery was wasted, of course; the place lay entirely deserted—not that he could blame anyone running for an open window, but this was a showroom on an entirely different sphere from Father's pavilion. It was meant to be marveled at just as much as the cloths themselves. He felt the back of his head tighten. Where were the workers? The Savoldyns' servants? And where was that noise coming from? It sounded like two foghorns locked in combat.

Ibram looked up, taking note of the gigantic glowbulbs—worth thousands of gold picks—hanging by delicate chains from the ceiling. Instead of a public courtyard open to the air, the Savoldyns had enclosed the space in glass and covered the center with wood floors. The overcast sky darkened the place, but the lights made the expensive wares below glimmer in the center of the room, even on the large cobwebs strung between the chains. Ibram sniffed; he looked down at the list in his hand and then back up. Waist-high counters piled with fabrics of all colors and design were arranged in concentric rows where typically folk erected garden pavilions.

He sniffed again and then sneezed into his shoulder. Pitchwood was second only to dragon's blood sap when it came to noxious yet useful substances to burn. Pitchwood was supposed to open the airways and calm the anima. Possibly, it reduced stress in any area because so few folk stayed around to smell it. If they could afford an entire glass ceiling, they might have considered opening a panel or two to let the fresh air in.

"Oh, apologies, Master Ibram," Mistress Savoldyn said. She waved her hand at a brazier as they walked past. "It protects the wares, and you know, you do become used to the smell."

Ibram nodded. "To be sure, Mistress. The best defense is a strong attack."

Her face briefly twitched, wrinkles appeared at the corners of her eyes before they smoothed away. Mistress Savoldyn led him past three closed doors—presumably store rooms—along the right-hand path. The noise of the foghorns grew louder and finally separated into two distinct voices, raised in anger. Ibram glanced around himself; that certainly answered any question about where the rest of the household was. He was surprised the door wasn't hanging off its hinges with the force of whoever was making that racket.

"Would you for once in your stubborn life listen to *reason!*" a woman loudly demanded from behind the door.

"Reason?" a man sneered. "Greed, more like. You and that husband of yours—you'd drain my coffers dry if you could!"

Ibram scratched the back of his head and then tucked his brown hair behind his left ear. It was getting a little long again, not so much curling around his earlobe, but dropping below almost to his shoulders. The order list crumpled in his other hand. He cleared his throat.

"As though we need your money!" the woman shrieked.

"Why else even come here today? I didn't invite you!" The man chortled loudly, and even Ibram winced.

"Stubborn *tarmap!*" the woman yelled. "How long can you keep up this pretense? Let me see—"

"You'll not touch those shelves!"

Something heavy screeched and then thudded against the floor.

"Mistress Savoldyn, perhaps we should go over this list together," Ibram said.

"Oh no, no, this is just what we need," Mistress Savoldyn assured him with an overly firm pat on his back.

"How dare you speak to me this way?" the man Ibram was very much afraid was Master Savoldyn bellowed from behind the door. "You wanted nothing from me! You'll get nothing!"

"This isn't about me!" a woman yelled back. "I told you when she was born that I—"

Mistress Savoldyn knocked loudly on the door, and the argument's volume lowered to unintelligible noise. She smiled at Ibram, and placed her hand on the door handle.

"Einar?" She called out as she opened the door. Ibram leaned forward to see over her shoulder.

"We are busy," the elegantly dressed woman inside the room snapped. Her loose purple and orange robes, caught low at the waist by a chain belt as they did in the south, flowed about her as she whirled towards the door. Her gleaming brown hair was curled into cascades of ringlets held up and around in braided gold rope. Ibram wavered under her hawklike stare; it was rather early in the morning to weather that amount of derision.

Mistress Savoldyn ignored her completely and addressed herself to the florid, thickset man sitting behind a frankly ostentatiously large desk. "Lady Azadiya's agent has arrived, my sweet," she cooed, with the kind of melting look Ibram had last seen featured on a player's stage. "He's here to assess the goods she ordered last season, I believe."

"Is he," the man barked, making it less a question than a statement. He sighed, and raised himself up with both hands on his wide desk. Ibram noted the carpet beneath was crumpled; it must have been the desk he'd heard moving.

Einar Savoldyn squinted. "You're not Master Kalmar?"

"Master Ucalegon, actually," Ibram said, and bowed. "I have Ladyship's list right here."

"Shouldn't be too hard to find then, young master." Savoldyn didn't seem too unhappy to be interrupted, but he didn't seem glad of it either. The color was high in his cheeks and across the bridge of his nose. He grunted deep in his throat, and slurped from a small cup of shay at his elbow. He grimaced and set the cup down with a clatter, and then fell back into his chair. "Send for Hilo, Yanna."

"There was no need for her to burst in at all," said the other woman, whom Ibram presumed to be the aforementioned Mistress Ignalle. She crossed her arms over her chest and gripped her own arms tightly. The trio of bracelets on her right wrist clacked; they looked like a matched set of gold-flecked glass. Ibram blinked, that sort of thing had gone out of fashion years ago. Most folk who had them kept them as family heirlooms, and simply passed them to the next generation without actually wearing them.

Mistress Savoldyn seemed to have a gift for ignoring what she didn't want to see, but it was clear she had no more wish to be in the room than Ibram had. She patted the wheel pendant on her neck, and backed away. "I'll just see about the shay, Einar," she said and exited the room.

"Now that's a proper woman," Savoldyn muttered as he drank from his cup again. Mistress Ignalle huffed and turned her face away from him. "Listens when you speak. Works for the good of the family."

And whatever settlement had been worked out in their marriage, Ibram hoped it was extravagant. Ibram was beginning to wonder if Amota Viran had passed this task on to him for his own amusement. Surely, no fabric was worth this encounter. He crossed to the front of the office, and stood with his weight on his heels. No reason to make either party feel like his own good humor hinged on their approval.

"She's after the samite, I suppose," Savoldyn said with a grunt. "This Western lady of ours."

"As its use is strictly at the Imperial family's discretion, I'm sure she is not," Mistress Ignalle retorted. She had retreated to her own smaller wooden chair, next to a low table. She had no shay of her own, Ibram noted. Only the master of the house seemed allowed to have a drink.

"Are you still here, Elene?" Master Savoldyn inquired with narrowed but blurry eyes. "I wonder at that."

"Oh, I don't mind," Ibram said. Better than being alone with the old crank. "But I believe Lady Azadiya is mostly concerned with wool and silk this season."

"We have it all, of course, even those pieces she ordered specially. Who else would make that treacherous journey?" Savoldyn asked. He spread his hands and almost met Ibram's eyes. He appeared to be having trouble focusing, and the flush on his face was spreading from his nose across his forehead. He patted his chest irritably and readjusted his high, tight collar. "We stock—" He coughed. "The best fabrics—" He cleared his throat. "—from the Red Coast itself, not that *anyone* is grateful for our trouble."

"Father, *enough*," Mistress Ignalle hissed.

Ibram's eyebrows twitched. "If it's talk of coin, Master Savoldyn, I'm sure Lady Azadiya's purse is more than deep enough for the commission."

Savoldyn's face reddened further, and sweat shone on his brow. "It's respect!" he barked and slammed one bulky fist on his desk. "There is no respect left in this misbegotten village, none to be had!"

Ibram frowned and stood taller. He clasped his hands behind his back, crumpling the list. "Then I should be off as soon as possible, to be sure," he said. "And trouble you no more."

Savoldyn didn't appear to hear him, but simply patted his own face again. The office had no windows, but the room was in fact rather cold. Light came from glowbulbs molded in the style of braziers but without any heat or smoke to mar the expensive tapestries on the walls. The pitchwood smell wasn't so bad as outside; he could see a few pertinent charmed tiles set above the door lintel. There was even an Isconian carpet on the floor, depicting some kind of sea battle. The entire place reeked of coin, but the atmosphere made Ibram's skin prickle with distaste.

Was this truly a more pressing issue than herding the Attendants? Surely someone in their first year of trials was up a tree or needed to be fished out of a pond by now. Ladyship had more than enough clothing, and so did everyone she was obligated to provide clothing for. Ibram's mouth quirked up at the corners, and then fell again. He glanced down at the row of flat wooden buttons strung diagonally across his chest, opposite the leather strap, on his new twill gambeson. It was dyed green now, and woven with tilted, interlocking t-shapes in black along the front and along the lower hems where it split to allow him to move freely. He looked more like a horseman then a door guard, but he'd needed a replacement after the incident with the Learners on bonfire night. It might be he should grow his hair past his shoulders like a Valantin and complete the image.

Mistress Ignalle cleared her throat and then frowned at her well-shod feet. Ibram glanced between her and Master Savoldyn. There was a marked similarity in their features, especially about the eyes and brow and the resentful mannerisms. Neither appeared to truly take notice of him, but they both kept the other in the corner of their respective eyes. The door opened, and a slim man in a plain rust brown tunic and trousers came in, followed by Mistress Dolman carrying a small tray upon which rested a pot of shay.

"Your refreshment," she announced and marched past Ibram to the other side of the desk.

"You sent for me, Master Savoldyn?" the man asked, and stood with his hands clasped before him. He had long brown hair and a high-peaked forehead, and was dressed incredibly plainly for a fabric merchant's servant. Ibram leaned his weight on his heels. This would be the Savoldyn's Marshal Steward, in charge of directing the house-hold and lands. He certainly didn't dress as well as other marshal stew-ards of Ibram's acquaintance, but that didn't always follow.

"Yes, yes," was the reply, though Master Savoldyn seemed distracted by Mistress Dolman. "All these interruptions. No time for a man to conduct his business! This man"—He pointed in Ibram's direction—"wants something for that—that—"

Hilo coughed loudly and obviously. "The Fourth Mentor of Yseult," he interrupted with the ease of practice. He smiled politely at Ibram. "I expect Mistress Yanna is already wrangling with the porters, Master."

Ibram lifted his chin. "I have the order right here," he said. "I hope Ladyship hasn't put you to too much trouble."

Savoldyn waved his hand. "He—oh deal with him, Hilo! I've contracts to go through!"

Ibram ground his teeth. Mistress Dolman banged the new shaypot on the desk. She grabbed the older shaypot and set it down on her tray, and then stood, holding the tray in both hands.

"Did Marit make it hot enough?" Savoldyn asked. "Last cup was cold as water."

"She drew the kettle directly from the coals," Mistress Dolman said. "Will that be all?"

Master Savoldyn waved her away. Mistress Ignalle stepped forward. "Yes, thank you, Dolman," she said. "I believe I'll walk out with you."

"As you say, Mistress Ignalle," Dolman said after a sharp glance about the room. She bowed to Master Savoldyn.

Ibram watched Savoldyn ignore the room in favor of carefully pouring himself a cup of shay. He blinked heavily as he drew the cup to his lips, and tossed the liquid down his gullet. Savoldyn's nose wrinkled as he drank and smacked his lips.

"Never hot enough," Savoldyn mumbled.

Mistress Ignalle cleared her throat. "Good day, Father," she said to the air above his head. "I hope to return to this house in a kinder hour."

She swept past Ibram with a flutter of cloth and a lingering smell of lillia blossoms. Mistress Dolman traveled at her heels, tray carried in both hands. Hilo bowed slightly with his arm outstretched. "Shall we?" he asked.

"Hate to outstay a welcome," Ibram said. "I'll ensure Lady Azadiya is fully informed of the trouble her order's put your house through."

He bowed slightly to Master Savoldyn and then left the man to his contracts and fresh shay. Hilo closed the door firmly behind them both, and then turned to Ibram. Now that they stood closer, Ibram could see his clothes were of a finer weave, but some of the sewing seemed clumsy, as if they'd been remade to fit him without much attention paid to Hilo's measurements. Hilo had an air of apology about him, but the set of his mouth and dip of his head was too practiced to be effective. Ibram settled his free hand around the hilt of his sica, and jerked his head backwards.

"I've got a pile of cloth to inspect," he said, side-stepping whatever words had been about to tumble from Hilo's mouth. "Where do you keep it?"

Hilo paused and licked his lips, before straightening up and gesturing out across the enclosed courtyard. "We keep the special orders across the way," he said. "If you'll follow me, Master..."

Ibram nodded stiffly. "Ucalegon."

"This way, then," and Hilo walked to the stairs leading down into the courtyard.

Ibram followed him through the laden tables and past the expensive mirror stand, glancing up at the pale sky through the glass paneled ceiling. The clouds were rolling in down from the mountain, promising rain they most likely would not disburse. Still, he hoped Attendant Zorion would remember to stay under canopy; he seemed a forgetful sort.

Hilo cleared his throat. "I hope you will not take the master's word against him too much," he said, stepping aside to gesture Ibram up the short staircase again.

Ibram tucked his brown hair behind his ear. "You mean, you hope Lady Azadiya won't take them to heart, I think."

Hilo cleared his throat again and added a short swallow. "No, well, yes," he said. "But truly, he doesn't mean anything by it. He's a blustery man, but there's no real harm in him."

Ibram paused on the pathway, waiting for Hilo to indicate which direction in which to turn. "To be sure," he said.

"The Hobons have traded with this house for so many years—the account is our most lucrative, you see," Hilo continued as he walked to the right. "The Savoldyn house has no reason to think they've been treated ill in their dealings, and I'm sure Master Einar would tell you the same, it's—oh, here. It's in here."

He skirted around Ibram with an apologetic smile and a dip of his chin, and opened a plain wooden door marked with a finely painted number three. Ibram walked through to be greeted with crates of materials pushed to either side of the small room, dominated by an array of fabrics set out on a wide table. A glowbulb hung from the ceiling by thick chains. He looked at the now much crumpled piece of paper and held it in both hands. Ibram frowned. He should have brought something to mark items off the list.

"As you can see," Hilo said. "We have everything well in hand." He moved to the laden table and began fussing with what looked like a pile of handkerchiefs. "Usually Master Kalmar only takes the samples with him for Ladyship's approval, and arranges for the rest to be brought up by cart. Will that arrangement still meet with Lady Hobon's approval?"

Samples. *Senra.* That's what that meant! Ibram eyed a bolt of glass cloth, linen so tightly yet finely woven it looked as gossamer as a spider's web even wrapped up. One yard of the stuff cost the yearly rent of an entire town.

"Ah, yes! Yes, I'm sure that would be fine," he said, and flicked the edge of a carefully folded red felt. Everything laid out before him was of the finest quality Merrilian weavers could construct, fit for the royal palaces of the south in true Vissilia. The cost to transport these goods alone was a princely sum. "Not that Ladyship will be able to check it over now."

"She won't?" Hilo asked, his voice sharpened. His high forehead creased. "Why not?"

Ibram felt the back of his head tighten. He hadn't meant to say that out loud. Amota Viran would send to him to muck the stables if he let people know Lady Azadiya was indisposed by one of the sect's own Attendants.

"It's the festival," he answered quickly. "She's got a whole troop of them out of Afsoun, and one of them already set fire to a copse of withy trees."

It was even true, which was how Ibram preferred his lies. Attendant Burlen's first attempt at a portable sundial had been deeply counterproductive. At least it meant the gardeners had a new project.

Hilo's face relaxed. "Ah well," he said. "That's alchemists for you, I suppose."

Ibram nodded. "It's never dull, to be sure."

Hilo laughed and picked up the stack of fabric samples. "I shall have these wrapped up for you," he said. "If you'd like to—"

Ibram might have liked several things, but a woman screamed, and Hilo's offer was never repeated.

"Dolman! Dolman!"

Hilo was out the door first with Ibram hard at his heels, only he made for the pathway and Ibram jumped the railing. Across the courtyard, Mistress Savoldyn ran screaming from her husband's office with her arms raised in front of her. She knocked into a bowl full of bluecaps, and sent it crashing to the floor in a flood of water, flowers, and glass. Ibram drew his sica with his left hand and switched it to his right as he ran; no point in being surprised by misfortune. By the time he had reached the second balustrade and climbed up over onto the terrace, Mistress Dolman had burst out of some narrow passageway and caught her employer by the elbows in mid-flight.

"Mistress!" Dolman shouted over her. "Mistress, calm yourself! You must breathe!"

Mistress Savoldyn dragged in a gigantic, shaking gust of air, and Ibram took the opportunity to slip back into the office and close the door. He turned on his heels and took quick stock of the room. Strictly speaking, this wasn't his affair, but if—

Oh hang it, the man was dead.

$$\text{❧} \quad 2 \quad \text{❧}$$

Ibram sheathed his weapon and crossed his arms across his chest. He stepped away from the door, and held his breath. As a growing boy, Ama had impressed upon him the need to observe the setting before becoming a part of it. The air was clear and there were no candles or lamps—only glowbulbs—so he had no fears of poisonous smoke. The temperature in the room was as he remembered. He took a cautious sniff: nothing out of the ordinary.

Master Savoldyn sat slumped in his chair, arms dangling below the desk where Ibram couldn't see, and his great red face gaping at the ceiling. Ibram glanced about himself. The room had no windows, and the inset bookshelves lining the walls were as full of bound papers, books, and stacked scrolls as they had been when Ibram had left. He sniffed again, and walked closer. He bent down with his hands behind his back. This close, he could smell the body, but nothing else. A trail of thick pinkish spittle hung from Savoldyn's mouth; his tongue was a deep vermillion red.

Ibram frowned. He leaned in and took a third sniff, right over the corpse's face and then ducked away with a violent sneeze. Savoldyn reeked, something pungent and a trifle sweet yet without a real identifying scent. Alcohol? Ibram turned his face to the desktop; Savoldyn had been fooling with a ledger. His broad shaky penmanship scrawled over the carefully written numbers; the stylus was still clenched in his fist, dripping ink onto his fingers. The shay had been overturned, as if he had dropped it in a rush to clutch at his stomach where his other hand sat clenched in the velvet of his tunic.

Well, that explained the eyes and the loose tongue during this morning's introduction. Ibram's skin prickled; he shook his head and tucked his hair behind his ears. He felt his belt pouch, where he kept his dice and soundless bells, and then stepped back. Ladyship would have to be informed. A hard day's work suddenly loomed on the horizon, but at least it wasn't packing handkerchiefs. Had Master Savoldyn taken his alcohol in shay? Why hide it in his own home? He leaned over for a closer look, and the door banged open.

"Master Savol—what are you *doing*?" Hilo demanded. Ibram twisted around and upright, and stepped into Hilo's path. He caught the man against his chest and held him off, digging his heels into the Isconian rug. "Let me go!"

Ibram shook his head and got a mouthful of Hilo's lank brown hair for a reward in the struggle to keep the man off the scene. He spit the hair out. "No, don't touch him! Cool your heels, damn it." He threw Hilo off and pointed back to the door. Hilo stumbled and made a break for the desk, and Ibram caught him again. He put real force into his shove on the second attempt.

"Who's his household divinity?"

Hilo rocked backwards with a gaping mouthed gasp. "What?"

"Someone needs to tell his small gods! You know how they get when they're not kept informed. Who should be swinging a wheel or striking a flint for the pyre?" Ibram pushed him back another step, with both hands on Hilo's shoulders. "There's business to be done still."

Hilo gaped at him, a fine sweat broke out over his face.

Ibram walked forward and blocked him from circling the desk. Hilo had a good three inches on him, but nothing like Ibram's own strength. "Come now, didn't you see your own mistress out in the hall? Leave Master Savoldyn be."

He pushed him and cajoled Hilo all the way back out onto the terrace and then shut the door firmly behind himself. Hilo's demands for information had sputtered into incoherence. He stared past Ibram at the door and turned a pasty yellow-green.

"What's gone wrong?" Mistress Dolman asked in a voice like the bell before a burial. "Let me in to the master at once!"

She stood in the center of the hall with Mistress Savoldyn shaking at her elbow. Her thin arm was wrapped around her waist as if the lady of the house would sink to the floorboards without the assistance. Judging by how she swayed in all her finery, Ibram wasn't sure Dolman was wrong.

"Master Savoldyn is dead," Ibram said, and Mistress Savoldyn covered her mouth. Her pleasant face was drawn and pale.

"I told you," she mumbled behind the hand clenched before her mouth. "I told you it—"

"Are you certain?" Mistress Dolman interrupted. Her eyes narrowed; her jaw clenched.

Ibram nodded. "I've seen my share of corpses."

Mistress Dolman steadied herself like a captain at the wheel of a battleship. Mistress Savoldyn moaned and hid her face in her shoulder. Dolman's lips disappeared into a thin line. She nodded once, firmly.

"I see, Master Ucalegon," she said. "We shall—we shall arrange matters from here."

Ibram raised his eyebrows. "Is that so?"

"Yes, of course," she said. "We shall send a girl to the Navigator's Ark, but I'm sure you have no need to listen to me prattle on." She turned to guide her mistress back down the walkway, presumably to a more private sitting room. "Hilo will pack Lady Azadiya's usual samples at once. I apologize for your inconvenience, and hope you will convey our regrets to your employer."

"To be sure," Ibram said, and then frowned. "Was Master Savoldyn such a great drinker, then?"

She paused, almost as if she had forgotten him as soon as her back faced him. "He liked his tolnic of a morning," she said. "But no more than was natural."

Ibram pressed his lips together. The polite thing would be to hold his tongue and let the day play itself out. He wasn't a keeper of the public peace, after all, but on the other hand, he was already in place as Ladyship's representative.

"He has been sick for days," Hilo said. "I—we should have sent for a healer, at least."

"Perhaps the message to the Navigator's Ark could be sent at a slow pace, Mistress Dolman," Ibram said. "Bury in haste, hang at leisure, after all."

Mistress Dolman halted immediately, but did not turn around. The only sound was her crying mistress and Hilo's labored breath. Ibram waited patiently.

"I shall see to it," Dolman said finally.

Mistress Savoldyn sobbed loudly, and Dolman resumed her slow walk. Ibram considered himself dismissed. He settled himself against the closed door and hooked his thumbs through his belt. Hilo cleared his throat next to him.

"Shall you come with me, Master Ucalegon?" Hilo asked.

Ibram paused, and then let himself smile. "Ah, no, I'm fine where I am, Master—do you know, I only know your given name?"

Hilo swallowed; he looked ill. He touched his sleeve to his sweaty temples. "Kenes, sir."

"Master Kenes, you'll forgive me for holding up this door for a bit, won't you? It's a shocking thing to see a body so early in the morning."

Hilo's chuckle was more a hiccupped ripple of air, but his shoulders climbed down from his neck. "I suppose it is," he said. "I never—well, I didn't expect to see him like that. But if you'll follow me, you can wait for your packages in a better setting."

Ibram nodded slowly. "I appreciate the thought, truly, but I think it's better I stay here and look after everything, don't you think? Just in case."

"In case of what?" Hilo asked. "You don't really—you can't think he was..."

He didn't seem able to say it, and so Ibram didn't force the issue.

"Oh, as to that," Ibram shrugged. "It's a Western affectation, really. Someone must always be with the body until the clerics can protect it."

"But Master Savoldyn was from the riverlands—"

"And I'd hate not to pay one of Ladyship's favorite merchants the same respect she'd expect to be shown a corpse in her own house," Ibram spoke over his protests. "After all, I was first in the room with the late master."

Folk put store in such things; Ibram certainly did, and would have even if this had been his first corpse. Hilo chewed his lower lip. He glanced all about himself before resting his gaze on the door over Ibram's shoulder. Ibram held still and relaxed against the door.

"Of course, I wouldn't wish to upset Lady Azadiya," Hilo said. He backed away from the spot with his hands scratching against each other. "I'll leave you here, then?"

"A sound idea," Ibram said. "I'll be ready to go when those packages are wrapped up for the porters. You could take over for me, then!"

Hilo gulped and then turned around swiftly. "Yes, yes, of course," he muttered as he walked away.

Ibram unhooked his thumbs and then rubbed the back of his neck, directly where his skin prickled. He listened until he heard the sound of a door closing, and no footsteps thereafter. He surveyed what he could see of the empty showroom before him; all those impressive stands of fabric could hide a burglar in their midst, but he couldn't imagine Mistress Ignalle hiding amongst them as a child as he and Katka had played with Father's display cases. Those braziers of pitch-wood would most definitely hide any kind of new smell, but the smoke wasn't enough to disguise movement.

He dug his fingers into the nape of his neck and then let his hand drop. Ibram frowned. A drunkard dying of drink was not unheard of— to be expected almost—but the smell of alcohol had been strong and pure. Tolnic was spiced. He opened Master Savoldyn's office door and stepped inside. No, he didn't like it one bit.

Nothing had changed, of course. Savoldyn remained sagging in his chair, and the shay cup was still overturned. Corpses were the strangest things. Folk always said it looked like they were sleeping, but Ibram had never found it so. The dead...deflated in a way no one with the animating force still within could mimic, the absence was too profound. Ibram skirted around the desk, with one ear out for Hilo's return.

He flexed his hands as he walked to the shelves where Mistress

Ignalle had stood. Nothing looked disturbed, though he wasn't certain he'd have been able to tell in any case. He scanned the remaining shelves, but they were full enough that any item taken would have been noticeable by a hole or a shift in the pyramid of scrolls. There were even texts of bound wooden slats; the sect used those for their official records, but they'd been the fashion for noble garden tales and poetries since the time of Her Gracious Majesty's grandmother. He raised his eyebrows at a small decorative alembic bracing two stacks of papers on either side.

Lots of minor houses and prosperous merchants kept those about, fairly useless objects that mimicked the working models the alchemists used. He leaned down; the still pot had a patina of cracked white film at the bottom. He looked at the receiver, which appeared clean, but there was no tube connecting the two. Ibram straightened immediately, and looked towards the corpse. He sniffed the air again, but smelled nothing out of the ordinary.

Yilka the Green was laughing at him, he could hear it as sure as the rattle of dice in a cup. Ibram glanced at the empty doorway, and quickly withdrew a handkerchief from inside the neck of his gambeson. He wrapped up the still pot and shoved it inside his belt pouch; it just about fit. The papers immediately began to shift and shuffle from their perch. He bent down and braced them, and tsked to himself.

"Worst thought, Ib-la," he muttered to himself. "You're stealing from a dead man."

Ah well, if his behavior was anything to go by, the spirit of Einar Savoldyn was too busy explaining himself at the Crossroads to worry about a bit of petty theft. He pushed the papers back into their place, and then grabbed up the receiver with its tight-fitting cork as well. A door closed somewhere in the distance. Ibram went to the shay pot, and ripped the cap off the alembic's receiver. He poured what was left of the shay, leaves and all, into the glass, careful of drips, and plugged it closed. He palmed it, and then smacked his hand against the nearest glowbulb, agitating the charm and darkening the luminescent sand. He ran about the room repeating the gesture as footsteps began to knock against the wooden walkway outside, and swirled outside the door.

"Master Ucalegon?" Hilo asked.

Ibram shut the door and twisted on his heels to face the man. He held his right hand behind his back, squeezing his hand around the receiver. He cleared his throat.

"Master Kenes," he said. "Just turning off the glowbulbs, you know. I'm sure Master Savoldyn needs no light where he's off to, aren't you?"

Hilo carried a basket filled with tied rolls of fabric. He was still whey-faced and wide-eyed. "Yes, of course," he said. 'I'm sure, but—"

"Is everything stowed away for Lady Azadiya?" Ibram asked quickly. "The porters have her address? Is that for me?"

He pointed. Hilo held out the basket automatically, and Ibram grabbed it with his left arm. He tucked the basket into his elbow, and shuffled right. Hilo tracked him with a distracted air.

"I thank you for your help today, Hilo," Ibram said and sketched a short bow. "I think it's your turn to stand guard over your master, don't you? I'll head up the living mountain now."

"Yes, young master," Hilo said. He swallowed. "I should show you out."

"No, no, I wouldn't feel right leaving unless you were there, *exactly* there," Ibram said, already backing away. He turned and stuffed the sloshing receiver deep down into the basket. "It's a Western duty, remember? I shall send Ladyship your regards."

⁂

There was no one to see him out, which troubled him, but also allowed Ibram the opportunity to let a carefully wrapped bundle fall to the floor in the receiving hall. Once the outer doors of the Savoldyn manor house clanged shut behind him, he let himself relax, though he kept the basket tucked protectively at his side. The house would be closed in mourning soon, he would have to hurry. He tapped the side of his thumb against its woven handle as he walked towards the noise of the crowds on the street ahead of him.

Ibram pursed his lips briefly in thought. He hadn't seen a single person except for Hilo, Mistress Dolman, and the Savoldyns in the entire place. Porters had been spoken of, but never shown, and his had been the only unfamiliar face. Well, except for the daughter, but that didn't count.

He paused at the mouth of the alley for a wheeled cart full of braided grass belts and woven bags swaying down the street. The daily market further on down the road had spilled its banks and flooded the village as far down as Butcher's Block. Ibram tightened his grip on the basket, and stepped into the cart's wake. The sun made him squint.

The sun wasn't much farther progressed across the sky than it had been when he'd stepped inside for his appointment. Could that have been why the place was empty? Amota Viran represented an important client, the Savoldyns might have wanted to create an atmosphere of exclusivity. Though why they'd waste that impression on a mere agent was a mystery.

No, he'd have to—he sidestepped a fellow pedestrian and scuttled into a free spot next to a bubble man—he'd have to report back to Ladyship, if she was well enough by the time he returned. If not, then he'd have to tell Amota Viran and see what he could make of the matter. Ibram reached into the basket and brushed his fingers over the cork stopper in the alembic's receiver. He might even be making much out of nothing, but he'd learned to his cost that no one liked a complacent sect agent. Better to maintain an active and suspicious imagination.

Ahead of him, an automaton of a four horse carriage careened across the tops of a connected set of toy stalls, whinnying and striking purple and yellow sparks along their tracks. Every time it slowed, the woman below it howled for the crowds to clap if they loved the empress, which generated dutiful enough rounds of applause to propel the horses around again. It also distracted a pair of patrolling warders to the delight of the little urchins by the candied fruits barrels.

Festivals drew all sorts. Ibram sidled and bullied his way up the street through the crowds, and kept his eye out for a familiar green uniform. A few Attendants were to be found in and amongst the crowd, though most of the sect would still be hard at their trials. At the bend where the spinners' workshops gave way to the basket weavers, he fell into step behind a parading group of drummers and pipers, Merrilians from closer to the border who processed in an ever-bewildering weaving walk that never missed a beat nor failed to confuse the eye. One of the players in a long grey wool surcoat held closed by elaborate clasps winked at him. Ibram felt his own footsteps pick up to match the rhythm and hurriedly turned right between two stalls before anyone noticed a sect agent with dancing feet.

He pushed forward into the throng down closer to Book Row, and walked straight into a wobbling iridescent bubble. It popped in his face, and he shivered to a halt, and then sneezed. Lemon and flowers and soap scented the air before a stray wind blew the scent of roasting onions past his nose, and overpowered the bubbles. He rubbed soap out of his face on his left sleeve, conscious of a laughing crowd. He cleared his throat, and took a look around himself.

There in the little square carved out of the village by a large roasting kitchen and an attached caffa, sat a dozen or more plank tables lined with a crowd of caffa drinkers, arrayed in their festival clothes, beneath a much repaired canopy of tattered rugs. Roast mouflon and cheese on platters of bread pranced by Ibram as servers ran from the street kitchen. He moved out of the way and turned his head at a roar of laughter. Off by the bubbling, boiling drips all yoked in dark wood cases, stood Attendant Zorion, balancing on the edge of the caffa stall's counter with his face in the top of the nearest grinder.

"All right, try it now," Zorion called out.

The grinder made its noise and a bracing scent of lemon bloomed in the air. A gigantic bubble grew from its open funnel and floated away across the crowd. They clapped. By their clothes, Ibram saw it was a higher society of youngsters out with their maids and minders, easy to entertain. Ibram didn't groan aloud; dismay in the face of an Attendant behaving badly was only encouragement to them.

"Pardon, beg pardon," Ibram called out as he made his way through the crowd to the wayward alchemist. They parted with good nature, too entertained to worry about a man intent on a drink, as it no doubt seemed to them. He held the basket before him, and rested it on the bar by Attendant Zorion's feet. He was a tallish sort of man, dark-skinned, supple and thin like a withy tree. How had he climbed up on so narrow a perch?

Ibram tugged Zorion's trouser leg. Zorion left the grinder, and blinked down at him. His glasses were fogged over and his thick braids stuck out at odd angles around his dark face.

"What did you put in there?" Ibram asked, very peaceably he thought. This was Ahksell's friend, after all, and Amota Viran had put Ibram in charge of Zorion's welfare. Well, he'd been instructed to get him out of the way, at the least.

Attendant Zorion's shoulders were rounded in a perpetual scholar's hunch. He removed his glasses and rubbed them on his green gambeson. He replaced them on his face, and smiled.

"Master Ucalegon! Is it time to go?"

"It will not be," the woman behind the bar interjected. She set a small wooden cup onto the grate of the caffa drip before her and opened the spigot. Dark, bitter, rich caffa poured over the rock of sugar balanced over the cup by a slotted metal ring. "Not until Master Alchemist here fixes my best grinder."

"But it will work so much better now, Mistress! And the leavings will be cleaner." Zorion made a strange waving gesture, briefly lost his balance, and then steadied himself again. "This is Mistress Grouvan's establishment, did you know that?"

The smell of lemon was overpowering; Ibram wrinkled his nose. Around them, the caffa drinkers and their servants made a happy crew. Folk were always pleased to see an alchemist in Lityen. The owner, of course, was not so happy, and unhappy shop owners often made official complaints. He sighed. Perhaps it was his fault; he'd left Zorion to make his own entertainment, and this *was* a man who had blinded Lady Azadiya, possibly forever, in the name of passing his examinations. Or...if not blinded, then seriously inconvenienced. To put a point on it, Ibram wasn't supposed to allow those sorts of situations to occur in Ladyship's life, even if they were in the realm of an examination.

Attendant Zorion shook the hopper on the grinder, and dipped his arm inside. He came up with a small flask that looked like it had been mangled. Ibram tapped thoughtfully on his belt, just above the purse where he kept his dice. Yilka the Green's second face was luck, perhaps his being stuck with Zorion was a happy turn after all.

"I did know she owned this counter," Ibram said, and angled his head to see the woman more clearly. "Good morning, mistress. Has this one gotten you in trouble?"

An older woman with short grey hair and a neat cloth tied around her waist raised one silvery eyebrow at him. Her hands moved through the motions of closing the caffa spigot; she revolved the mug to the left on the little circle of metal beneath it with one finger and removed the slotted ring with her other hand. She tossed the ring into a bucket of water.

The woman next to Ibram took the mug and was off with a jostle to his elbow. He righted the basket in front of him. Attendant Zorion opened his belt pouch above Ibram's head; he ducked out of the way of its dangling traces.

"I'm only trying to help," Zorion said. "It's not my fault the grinder needed cleaning."

"So you have been fiddling," he frowned and Zorion scoffed. Ibram settled his weight against the counter and tugged at Zorion's pants leg again. "You'll come down now, Attendant. Mentor Hobon won't like word of further meddling."

That did seem to give the man a moment's reflection, but Zorion soon shook his head cheerfully and peered deep into the grinder. It stood waist height, there was no need to clamber over the counter. Ibram tsked. Ahksell never fiddled with merchants' stalls when they were out together. Why did other preceptories have to be so difficult? Yseult was not ranked highly in the Sect of Seven Fires, but they at least knew how to get a caffa in public.

"What's to do?" Ibram asked with a sigh. "Is it the bubbles or the smell?"

"I wanted my usual," Attendant Zorion answered, as he secreted away his ruined flask, and dug into his pouch with a frown. "Mistress Grouvan makes the best caffa—I found her soon after you left on your errand—and I merely wanted to accentuate the delightful fruity acid in her roast."

Mistress Grouvan glared at her equipment. "He turned my grinder into a sideshow, that's what he did."

Zorion tilted his head; he seemed a little hurt at the implication. Both of his hands tightened on the lip of the grinder's funnel. Ibram rested one arm on his basket and took a slow look looked about the crowd underneath the open canopy. "Doesn't seemed to have hurt your trade," he said. "People like a bit of a show."

"They like to drink in peace," she countered.

Ibram rubbed the back of his head and tucked his hair behind his ear. The bottled shay in his basket was growing cold as cold as the corpse he'd found it next to. Still, he had his standards when dealing with layfolk.

"Now," he said, loudly. "What's this special drink you desire, Attendant Zorion?" He looked up into Zorion's startled spectacles, and then briefly glanced out amongst the sundry bored rich children in the crowd. "Does it make you fly?"

Zorion seemed incredibly confused. "How would it possibly do that?"

"Well and who knows what an alchemist's infusions might do?" he said, keeping his voice up. From the corner of his eye, he saw several young Tyal scions inch closer.

"Certainly not that," Zorion said, and crinkled his eyebrows. "No, I just wanted a summer coffee."

Ibram shook his basket back and forth and considered his options. Did poison go bad? If it even was poison. "And what's that when it's at home?"

Zorion's face cleared with enthusiasm. "It's cold."

"Is that all?" someone called out. They sounded young and disappointed.

Zorion looked about himself. Ibram saw he had one of those cold charms they made in the north dangling from his fingers. "Well, it's got sugar," he said, "and lemon juice and water."

"Lemons?" Mistress Grouvan scoffed. "Grown out here?"

"No, from my family's orchards in Bastilat," Zorion said.

Ibram's eyebrows hit his hairline, and maintained position. Family orchards in an ancient garden city such as Bastilat? It appeared Attendant Hilbert Zorion had hidden depths, or at least, a family vault or two. He whistled, and the crowd murmured.

"That's what in your grinder, a distillate of juice. The bubbles are just for fun."

Ibram winced. "Was that supposed to go in the grinder, Attendant?"

Attendant Zorion shook his head. "No, I tripped getting up on the counter and spilled."

"But its contents were all the way from Bastilat?" Ibram said as he reared back to cover. "Mistress Grouvan, that's a princely drink order. Lemons and sugar! In caffa!"

"I was attempting to add sugared peel."

"Is it really for royalty?" one of the larger Tyals got up the courage to ask.

"Well, I don't see why they wouldn't drink it," Attendant Zorion said. He tugged on a large green bead in one of his braids. "Why do you ask?"

"A cold drink for clear eyes and a thoughtful mind!" Ibram cut in swiftly. They needed to leave, after all. "Healthy for sailors, I'd expect. And devotees of the Navigator! What prince or princess of Vissilia wouldn't have such a drink as that? Surely, the Attendant should have his order. It's the festival after all."

A swell of general agreement washed across those assembled, even the ones who still had their own drinks. A few of the servers walked past with water pitchers sent over from the roasting kitchen. As she eyed the crowd now at her counter, it appeared the good mistress was revaluating her attitude.

"I'm sure he'll need the energy," she said. "May the Wheelmaker set his hand to the Preceptory of Bedris."

Incorrect on many levels, but Ibram supposed not everyone could see the neck tab of a scrub jay on Zorion's gambeson. Still, a worthy effort. Ibram nodded.

"An excellent thought," he said and then shouted. "A summer coffee for our Attendant! To speed him up the living mountain!"

The crowd cheered, and finally Attendant Zorion jumped down from the counter. Ibram hooked the cold charm out of his hand, and slung it over the nearest caffa drip. He smiled at Mistress Grouvan. "We'll keep the cup, and be back for the charm at end of day, shall we, Mistress?"

Mistress Grouvan ignored him, but she did grab a mug.

❧

Apart from the lead up, Zorion's concoction didn't take that long to make. In fact, had Ibram been allowed a bet on it, he'd have wagered it took only half as much time to chivvy his charge up out of the square and back up the living mountain. The relay systems were all working, instead of being constantly down for repairs, and this time of the day, crowds weren't too much of a problem. He simply propelled the Attendant before him to cut whatever line might be forming, and then tucked Zorion in a corner of the aerial gondola so that he might not escape.

"Do you do this to Ahksell?" Zorion asked, and wiped cold, citrusy caffa from the corners of his mouth.

It was a low blow to remind him of better, more amiable Attendants. Ibram kept the basket on his left arm blocking Zorion's escape route, and leaned his right arm against the wall of the gondola as if he was tired and needed the support. It would have been as well to say that Ahksell had never needed Ibram to do anything to him, but he let the temptation pass through him. He had wrangled Zorion's freedom, won him the admiration of a crowd, and managed not to say anything about what bad manners it was to incapacitate a man's employer. Ibram counted these as victories, and not even Zorion would spoil it for him.

"He never mentioned the herding aspect of your work," Zorion continued, and gestured slightly with his cup. "It's really very efficient, but I don't know if I like the feeling of being impelled."

Ibram smiled politely, and swayed with the jostling group of servants and agents at his back. As he'd gotten on, he'd spied a few Learners as well, no doubt out on a daytrip; it wouldn't do to be impolite. He readjusted the basket, and then had a thought.

"What's your concentration, Attendant Zorion?" he asked, and then risked a quick look out the window. They were on the last run before the station outside Yseult's walls. His gut rebelled as they climbed higher, but Ibram was the conqueror of his own stomach. "Is it all potions and potables for you?"

"I suppose you could say so." Attendant Zorion readjusted his glasses. "I make infusions. Mentor Tikari says they're quite extraordinary!"

"Lady Azadiya certainly found them unique."

Zorion winced. "Yes, sometimes testing can be a little...unpredictable."

Ibram snorted, and then glanced behind himself at the rest of the passengers. The gondola was swaying into the hands of the servants at the station, preparing to stop. He turned back and lowered his voice.

"What was it supposed to do, anyway?"

Zorion's mouth opened and closed on a puff of air. He shook his head and looked briefly out the window. He wasn't as tall as Ahksell (who could be?) but he was of a height enough that it made his braids something of a hazard when Zorion shook his head.

"It's intended to mimic the same changes made possible by a lifelong study of the human body in Yseult," he said. "Sharpening the eyesight, in effect."

"Don't they make spectacles for just such an occasion? Or those water bottles cobblers use for magnification?"

Zorion adjusted his glasses. "Metal frames can be a trouble in my line of inquiry, and wood can often debase the lenses with ephemera. I hope to create a potion which will eliminate the need for glasses entirely."

Zorion's dark eyes caught on Ibram's for a moment, before he quickly looked away. It sounded a bit like cheating—counterfeiting all that effort Attendants of Yseult put in to gaining the smallest modicum of control over their bodies; Ibram approved. He nodded. "A worthy effort, Attendant."

The gondola swayed to a stop with a jerk of the hauling rope's machinery. Ibram heard the crowd surrounding them sigh and shuffle forward in a dozen busy footsteps. He stepped back and Attendant Zorion took a sip of his summer coffee.

"You'd do well to savor that," Ibram said. "I think we might need to wait a few days before we're welcomed back in that particular caffa."

"I do," Zorion said. "It reminds me of home."

"I see."

He did, more's the pity. Bastilat was as old a city as you could find in the Empire of Vissilia, covered in the soft golden light you only found down south, where the temples were only eclipsed by the imperial palaces. He'd spent a summer drenched in sweat there, drinking wine chilled by charmwork, and trying to remember which manor Lady Azadiya wanted a report back on. There had been a family there all the way from Merrilia, directly from the Red Coast. Their store had smelled like home, same spices and flavors, and he'd eaten handfuls of small brined fish with flatbread dripping with oil and herbs. The master of the house boiled down asajika so thick and red that it could make a man spit fire and thank them for the privilege. It was a city that lingered in all six senses.

Slowly, the other passengers disembarked. Ibram turned aside when there was room, and they walked out of the gondola onto the station's platform. Above them, the sky had turned a bright blue heavily threaded with wooly clumps of cloud. Ibram gestured the Attendant through the little roofed station with its small benches and waved at the woman in the back kitchen, where the relay servants took their meals.

The stone stairs down to the walkways around the mountain were wet. They took them down side-by-side, and Zorion didn't spill a drop. Ibram held the basket in both hands, and clenched so hard the smell of withy tree wood rose up in the air.

He had the thought, still, in his mind that Master Savoldyn was a murdered man, and though he knew it was based on very little but a strong scent and a sudden demise, it still seemed more likely than a drunkard's innards giving up his ghost just at that specific moment. He frowned.

He shook his head and rubbed his eyebrow with his thumbnail. Around them, the day-to-day crowd of folk who lived and worked in the Preceptory of Yseult, as well as those from the surrounding preceptories, made their way, laden with goods or pulling carts. Some of the larger carriages were out and about; the ponies were good hill stock, and navigated the curves and ramps carved into the mountain with little trouble.

Ibram resettled his basket. He glanced up at the sky and then back down to the green and yellow scrub beside the road. The problem was that his thoughts tended to circle if not given some kind of an outlet, and there was no one here inclined to play 'worst thoughts' with him. He couldn't very well make his case to Amota Viran while still arguing it with himself.

"I don't suppose you know how to kill a man, Attendant Zorion," he said.

Attendant Zorion laughed sharply. "Very well, I expect!"

Ibram looked up. "You do? I didn't think they went in for weaponry up in Afsoun."

"Of course not!" Zorion drank the last of his summer coffee and then held the cup down at his side. They turned up the road towards Yseult's gates. "We're much too far from the capital to be allowed any kind of permit for offensive constructs. But we all know the principle of the—the transmutations. At their heart, making up survival equipment and glowbulbs and weaving some wire nets... Well, it's the sort of common knowledge every sect has."

Ibram nodded and raised his arm to guide Zorion down the left side of the road, out of the way of a passing cart. Zorion handed him his empty cup; Ibram pinched his lips together briefly. He tossed the dregs out into a nearby bush, and then placed the mug in his basket.

"And you're from Bastilat, besides," Ibram said, glancing up at the thick stone walls as they passed through the inner gate. For a brief second, it almost seemed like one of the massive lodestones clamped to the outside of the walls sparked with blue lightning. He shook the afterimage from his eyes, and squeezed his eyes open and shut quickly.

"Which is why I know my infusions best," Zorion said, and grinned. He peered about the open courtyard with a polite interest. "The university there always has a great need for something a little out of the reach of ordinary folk."

"Then maybe you could answer a question for me," Ibram said, and flicked his thumbnail against the basket handle.

Zorion laughed. "Yes? About infusions? Or killing a man?"

"How easy would it be to poison a cup of shay?" Ibram asked.

Attendant Zorion looked forward and then down at his feet; his smile turned thin. They walked onward down the narrow, winding cobblestone pathway that led through the main administrative courtyards towards the practice fields and laboratories. The mountain air was crisper than down at the base in Lityen and stung the back of Ibram's nose when he breathed. He cleared his throat.

"I don't—why would you want to know that?" Zorion asked.

Ibram shrugged. "I'm only a simple agent," he said. "They taught me how to bow correctly, not recognize when a man's been poisoned. I'm not what you call a man of violence."

Zorion turned his face just enough for Ibram to be certain he was staring pointedly at the wickedly curved knife belted at Ibram's hip. Ibram resettled his basket and continued walking. It wasn't his fault the world sometimes required a poke or two in order to run smoothly in the proper direction.

That direction, of course, being towards whatever spot Lady Azadiya desired. Ibram's employer was the fourth mentor of the Preceptory of Yseult, after all. They had to wrangle with all manner of unpleasantness from the outside world that the other six preceptories of the Sect of Seven Fires cheerfully ignored. Still, Ibram wasn't a murderer.

"Attendant?" Ibram prompted.

Zorion looked up sharply and chewed his lower lip. "Yes, yes," he said, and then took off his spectacles to give them a cleansing swipe along his sleeve. "Well, it would depend on how you took your shay, wouldn't it? There are all sorts of nasty concoctions you can dump into someone's breakfast, but they'd change the taste or the texture immediately."

"And people do tend to notice that sort of thing," Ibram said. "If your soup is runny one morning and like cold honey the next, no one's waiting around for a second bowl."

"You eat soup for breakfast?" Zorion asked.

Yet another delightful askance look from his most recent charge, as if Ibram had upended a bowl over his head, rather than used an example. Ibram opened his eyes wide. He felt his mouth twitch dangerously upwards, and controlled his smirk.

"Why? Don't you?"

Zorion blinked at him and then shook his. "The kitchen in the dormitory just serves quash."

If Ama had been by his elbow, Ibram would have been forced to offer the Attendant a seat at their dinner table. She might no longer be a working member of Lady Azadiya's coterie of sect agents, but her opinions on the sect's kitchens were more than well-known, they were infamous. As it was, Ibram nodded and hummed something politely, and together they walked down the tree-lined road that lead to Lady Azadiya's tower.

Around them, business was continuing as usual. The Learners were excused from morning classes due to the festival, but by now they were out in the field practicing for their evening exhibitions. They weren't to be judged, of course, but every alchemist worth their salt was born with the innate desire to show off. Already, he saw huge wobbling pink bubbles drifting away from large glimmering portable pools, and just past that, at least six Learners attempted to remove—through a variety of means—a series of rings from atop a course of elevated poles. The training grounds themselves were already showing heavy scorch marks.

Ibram nodded to a charred fence post; the acrid stench of a burnt substance overpowered the lingering hint of woodsmoke. "It appears we missed something lively," he said.

"What?" Zorion looked up and then over. "Oh, yes. I think there was to be a sticky fire demonstration today."

Ibram raised his eyebrows. "Sticky fire?"

"No need to worry," Zorion said. "You won't be allowed access to it for some time."

Ibram inclined his upper body shortly and straightened immediately. "I'm grateful for such restoration of my courage, to be sure."

"To return to your question," Zorion began and tucked both arms behind his back. "There are several ingredients you could put into someone's shay without them noticing. Most of them would make you sicken immediately, if not kill you outright. Are you wishing to murder anyone in particular?"

Ibram shook his head. "I wouldn't even know where to find a murderous impulse, Attendant. Ladyship keeps me far too busy."

Zorion laughed, suddenly, as if he'd been startled into it. "Well, for future reference then, an animal toxin might do—fish from the deep seas and the like—or a plant such as nightshade. Mentor Hobon has fragrant Myristica in her stores, as I recall."

Ibram tilted his head and tugged his hair back behind his ear. "And would those sorts of things show up? If you could, perhaps, test for them?"

"Of course, I could test for them!" Zorion scoffed. "It's simply a matter of isolating the substances. If something is present in the liquid, then it will be present once searched for."

"That's very reassuring," Ibram said.

They continued down the rest of the way in silence. Ibram noticed the branches of a tree shaking as they passed. He made note of it; the wind was up this high on the mountain, of course, but trees didn't shake like that when buffeted by a stiff breeze, nor did they do so alone. He resettled his basket by switching arms; his biceps was beginning to ache. Sometimes the servants avoided the main pathway in favor of a footpath just behind the trees, but he hadn't seen anyone, and the underbrush wasn't that dense. Still, Attendant Zorion hadn't noticed. It was no doubt better for Ibram if he took this moment to plan out what he was going to say to Amota Viran.

❅   3   ❅

When they arrived at Ladyship's tower, the grounds surrounding its great squatting bulk were covered in canopies and tents that buzzed with the same kind of startled agitation as a beehive following a strong kick. Agents, servants, and alchemists dove in and out of the makeshift structures. A small flock of older Learners on the cleared ground to the left, those who might be the Attendants under examination next year, were being dutifully led through their paces with practice gars by sect agents. Those few of Ibram's amitai—his uncles and aunts—who had no pressing duties had taken up residence around an open fire, and lounged on low benches.

Ibram sighed. "I don't believe your potion has worn off yet, Attendant."

"No, I don't think it has," Zorion replied with a zest that Ibram hoped was merely professional pride.

Ibram gestured in the direction of the main tent. "We should inform Master Kalmar of your arrival," he said.

Amota Viran would want to know they'd returned. And he'd probably have someone available to pass Attendant Zorion off to, most likely a ranking Attendant who could help him work on Ladyship's eyesight problem. Ibram looked over the assorted crowd of displaced persons. Plenty of Attendants hung about the open tents, but they were all attached to Lady Azadiya's division. Ibram suspected he would be in need of the ones from Afsoun quite soon.

He guided Zorion down the road towards one of the half-circles of low benches where some of the other sect agents sat around the blue and red fire. They were passing a flask amongst the group, and seemed quite tense. As he approached, he smelled roasted meat and fresh bread.

"Can anyone tell me where Amota Viran is?" Ibram asked as he came to a stop with Zorion at the end of a bench. "Attendant Zorion needs a new date for his examination, and I've got a package to deliver."

He waved the basket at the group, and then winced. One of the women closest to him was Amita Sarrha, who was not usually found caught in the act of sitting down. Her leg must have been hurting again, though she never admitted to pain.

Amita Sarrha slung her arm over the back of the bench and leaned far over to her right. She peered up at him, wrinkling her broad face, and idly scratched the side of her head, just behind the tightly wrapped braid of her hair. The other women and two men sitting around the fire looked at him, blank-faced. Well, Amota Berac looked encouraging, but then, he nearly always did. A short, but expectant silence developed.

Ibram sighed. "Hello, Aunt Sarrha," he said. "How are you today?"

"Why Ib-la," Amita Sarrha exclaimed. "How kind of you to ask."

Ibram felt his right eye twitch. He didn't mind the existence of an affectionate name in the Western tongue, but his entire soul rebelled at the thought of one that made him sound like some kind of sickly dessert wine. His objections never carried much weight with his elders or his betters, sadly. It was his own fault for growing up amongst them.

"We're all doing very well," Amita Sarrha continued. "Waiting on Viran to stop his hand wringing and put us to work. Berac's got an order in for a brace of duck's eggs to burn for Kivan the Red; might get Lady Azadiya's sight back in time for the rain tomorrow."

"It's not going to rain," Attendant Zorion pointed out. "The meter-pool in Afsoun is lower than expected."

Amita Sarrha's entire face smoothed into polite incredulity. "The pool does what it does, young Attendant," she said, "but my knee says otherwise, and if an agent cannot trust her own body, then what can she trust?"

"Your knee predicts the weather?"

She grinned, gap-toothed, and it highlighted the thin scar down the right side of her cheek. "Only the part the Isconian pirate didn't slice!" she declared and slapped the side of her leather and steel leg brace. "Kivan the Red sent me the gift in way of compensation."

Ibram blew out his breath. It had seemed odd that Amita Sarrha was sitting down, usually she was out on the hills shouting folk out of their wits. He ducked his head low, but brought it up again when Amota Berac snorted loudly. "What are you all still doing here?" Ibram asked quickly. "Did Ladyship roust out the kitchens as well?"

"Lady Azadiya's ordered everyone out of the tower," Amota Berac said, in his deep bell-like voice. You could hear the man across two fields and down a hillside; Ibram knew that for a fact. "She started talking about restructuring her foundations, and said we needed to go be useful elsewhere."

"After she melted a glowbulb," Amita Sarrha said.

"Ladyship melted a glowbulb?" Ibram asked.

"It's merely a touch disfigured," Amota Berac said, elbowing Amota Tono when he laughed. "It still functions well enough, to be sure."

"We're to await further instructions while Viran gets the house in order," Amita Dervla said while holding her pale hands to the fire.

Amita Sarrha tsked. "How can a potion for sight cause this much upset?"

"It's possible," Attendant Zorion sighed, "I used too much dilli."

A short pause ensued, and then as one Ibram's amitai swiveled their faces to eye Attendant Zorion much as a pack of manor hounds evaluated their feast day's treat. Ibram widened his eyes at Amita Sarrha. She was in charge of corralling the newly appointed Attendants before the sect allowed them out to wander. Surely, she could understand that Attendants made mistakes and Ibram didn't deserve the extra trouble of hauling Zorion out of danger at home as well as down the mountain. Amita Sarrha blinked innocently back at him.

"The dilli?" she repeated, while Ibram began to count backwards from seven. "Didn't you measure, Attendant? This is an important examination after all, and a smart young man such as yourself is expected to know the difference between a handful and a pinch."

Ibram tugged on the back of Attendant Zorion's jacket. The standards of hierarchy being what they were, an Attendant flatly outranked a mere agent, but Aunt Sarrha was a *training* agent, who taught Yseult's alchemists survival when all their clever tricks failed. The torch brooch pinned to her green woolen tunic was bronze, where Ibram still had his silver buckle. Her authority over anyone below the rank of Attendant was absolute, and above that, a body had to eclipse her in age by a score of years before she would admit they deserved more than a correctly performed bow.

"It doesn't really matter, in regards to a concentrated infusion, I don't think. It's stabilizing properties for hearing might have interfered with the wimberry tincture," Zorion continued in the face of all good sense.

"Doesn't really matter," Amita Sarrha echoed.

"Well, I know it *matters*," Zorion said, "I measured exactly, but—"

"Which is what we shall tell Amota Viran, just as soon as we can be brought to him," Ibram jumped into the conversation. "He'll want to know about our progress in regards to the, uh, the current problem. I also have this delivery to make. To him. I need Attendant Zorion's help with that."

Amita Sarrha raised an eyebrow. Ibram held his basket in front of him and lifted it high. From the corner of his eye, Ibram saw Attendant Zorion open his mouth. He calmly, and without looking, stepped on the man's toe, and Zorion's lips sealed themselves shut.

"Viran's out in the main tent," Amota Berac took pity on him. He grinned and stroked his dense black beard. "Blue canopy, yellow sides. We used it last when Ladyship went on tour in the lowland north. You can't miss it, it's got a big patch on the front, repairing the damage from the bonfire."

"What bon—I mean, thank you, Amota Berac," Ibram said, already walking backwards. "Come along, Attendant!"

He took hold of Zorion's elbow lightly, but firmly, and didn't let go until they had stepped back onto the road and were firmly ensconced in the safety of its light traffic. Together, they moved on towards the tower at a distinct pace. Ibram glanced left and right, and saw a fair crowd of the usual folk who worked and lived in the tower. He also spotted Attendants with collar tags embroidered with scrub-jays, phantom cats, rachtbears, and far more sun eagles than he really thought necessary. Did the Preceptory of Mariae have so little to do this Festival of Sangrin?

"Is she really your aunt?" Zorion asked, and Ibram's attention was shattered.

He turned his head. "I'm sorry?"

Attendant Zorion shrugged and pulled his arm out of Ibram's grasp. "You called the agent back there 'Aunt Sarrha'."

"Ah, well," Ibram shrugged. "She's a close friend of my mother's. In Western terms, it makes her a sort of kin."

"I've heard of a lot of Western terms since I arrived here."

"We're close enough to the border. There are many here."

Zorion nodded. "She was about to be angry with me, wasn't she? My training agent had the same look around the eyes whenever I made a mistake."

Ibram weighed his words. "I believe she was about to point out some flaws in your research," he said, finally.

Zorion resettled his glasses on his face and squinted ahead of him. "Sangrin has been very exciting this year."

Ibram chuckled. "Festivals are never boring, to be sure," he said. "Ah, here we are."

By chance, a hole opened in the crowd, and Ibram and Zorion ducked through it without treading on anyone's toes. The blue and yellow tent was the closest to the tower, only a short walk's distance, really, and it did indeed have a large panel of fabric that was clearly more recently sewn than the rest. The front panels were tied open, and within, Ibram could see a large rectangular table. At its head sat Amota Viran, his dark head bent over a double stack of loose papers. At his elbow, lay a travel writing set. Next to him on Viran's right, a runner was just straightening up from a bow with a small box carried in both of his hands.

Ibram walked straight into the tent, and Zorion followed him. Zorion sat down in a chair near the middle of the table, and Mila, one of Ladyship's maids, darted towards him with a pitcher and cup. Ibram bowed quickly, and held out his basket. Amota Viran waved him to one side of the tent, and then turned back to the runner.

"You may inform the First Mentor, that Fourth Mentor Hobon is grateful for her concern while she is indisposed," Viran said, "but she is not insensible and we expect her return to her duties shortly."

The young man held out the box in his hands. He was very neatly put together, not a blond hair out of place, and his green tunic sleeves were slashed to show a yellow blouse beneath. "First Mentor E'garcid would also like to remind the Fourth Mentor that her reports on the examinations she held before the... unfortunate experiment are still outstanding. While Mentor—"

Amota Viran smiled as he interrupted the runner. "Ladyship's duties are of the utmost importance to her, as they are to all who serve in her division. You may return to the manor." He turned back to the stack of papers in front of him, and picked up the stylus from his writing kit. He paused, and then pointed to the wooden table. "Leave the box."

The runner looked about himself with a faintly awkward air. He glanced towards the top of Amota Viran's bent head, and then to Ibram. Ibram shrugged and sat back on his heels. The runner's mouth pursed. He blinked at Attendant Zorion, and then straightened his thin shoulders.

"I should think," he began.

"I'm sorry to interrupt," Attendant Zorion said. He turned a cup of wine in both hands. "But I do need Master Kalmar's attention right now."

The runner flushed a lovely shade of strawberry. He set the box down on the table stiffly, and then bowed with both hands precisely over his stomach, and a sense of dignity denied.

"Good day, Attendant. Master Kalmar," the boy said, and then marched himself out of the tent.

Ibram blew out his breath. Amota Viran gave him an exasperated look as he raised his head, and tossed his greying braid over his shoulder. The buckle on the inside of his right leather bracer caught the light for a moment. Ibram stood up straighter, and held the basket down by his side.

"What can I do for you, Attendant?" Viran asked. "Has your trip down the mountain given you fresh eyes on Mentor Hobon's dilemma?"

Zorion shook his head. "No, I thought about it, but I was a bit distracted," he said. "I was wondering if there had been any change in her condition?"

"As far as we can tell from outside the tower," Amota Viran said, "there has not."

Ibram tightened his grip on his basket; the handle creaked. His gut turned sour. It had been hours since that she'd taken that potion. Amota Viran looked grim.

Zorion drank from his cup. "Hasn't anyone been in to see her?"

"She threw a rock out of a tower window about an hour ago," Amota Viran said with a sigh. "It was wrapped up in one of her shawls, and she'd written out a few choice instructions on it. She's allowing one of the medicinal corps in to discuss her symptoms now, and they've been studying your application for examination as well as what's left of your preparations."

"My notes?" Zorion startled so hard he sloshed wine from his cup; it dribbled down his fingers, and he cast about himself before unearthing a handkerchief from his left leather bracer to sop the mess up. "There's no need to go prying like that, I'd have been happy to share my observations."

"They have already spoken with the other Attendants who were present, but they needed the exact formula to begin to understand the predicament you've placed the Fourth Mentor in."

"She could have gotten someone else to drink it," Zorion said. He frowned and set down his wine glass next to his crumpled handkerchief. "I'd asked Lydie to demonstrate."

"Attendant, you know you aren't allowed to provide your own test subjects," Amota Viran said.

"Still, to just take my formula like that," Zorion protested. Outrage had animated him, he seemed more focused than at any other time

Ibram had witnessed before. Which was to say, Attendant Zorion was sitting bolt upright in his chair and creases had formed on his forehead. He was even, by this point, beginning to flap his hands a bit. "It's not right, not even in an emergency should a fellow alchemist fiddle with another's work!"

Amota Viran took a slight breath and then set down his stylus. "I realize it comes as a shock, Attendant Zorion, but the Fourth Mentor of Yseult's incapacitation outweighs your right to professional courtesy."

Zorion sighed, and then sat back in his chair. He crossed his arms and then uncrossed them to fiddle with his glasses. He took them off and put them back on again. "This was much easier when I was only dosing myself," he said.

"It always is," Ibram said, breaking into the conversation. He pushed his hair back behind his right ear. "I wonder, Attendant, if perhaps you should find the doctors in charge of Lady Azadiya's condition, and make sure they're accurately investigating your infusion?"

He might need to find the man again, but it would be a relatively easy task. Zorion and his cohort from Afsoun were assigned to Yseult for the duration of the Festival of Sangrin. They couldn't hole themselves up in their own preceptory for quite a while yet. Besides, nothing could be done about his suspicions concerning the Savoldyns without speaking to Amota Viran first, as Ladyship's representative. Ibram shifted his weight from his left to right foot.

Zorion turned his face to look up at Ibram. "That's a very good point, Master Ucalegon," he said.

"Water skitters on a hot plate occasionally with Ib-la," Amota Viran said with a wry look.

Zorion's eyebrows furrowed. "Surely that happens all the time?" he asked.

Hang it. "It's merely a figure of speech," Ibram said. "Where are the doctors keeping themselves, Uncle?"

Amota Viran's mouth quirked upwards. "By the outdoor kitchens, of course," he said. "In the pavilion with the red border."

Attendant Zorion stood away from the table, and bowed shortly.

Ibram's eyebrows raised. He glanced at Amota Viran, who seemed equally surprised. They both bowed as well to cover their expressions.

"I'll go directly," Zorion said. "Thank you for the wine, Master Kalmar."

They waited until Zorion had left the tent and walked a ways down the path. Amota Viran leaned back in his chair and hooked his arm around the back. He nodded at Ibram's basket. "I expect that belongs to Ladyship," he said. "Did the old hammer-tongue get the order right?"

Ibram snorted. "All present and accounted for," he said. "Including the samples."

He set the basket down on the table, and then stood at his leisure. Ibram rolled his right shoulder; it ached from being in one position for so long. He stared down into the packages of fabric. How to broach the topic correctly?

"Was Master Savoldyn always such a grump?" he asked.

Amota Viran paused in the act of dragging the basket towards himself. "He's always had a rough way about him," he replied and narrowed his eyes. "But nothing sordid or inexcusable. His company does good business with the Hobon weavers."

Ibram hummed in agreement, and nodded. He reached out and tapped the side of the basket. Amota Viran frowned, and then sat back.

"Mila."

Mila stepped forward to Ibram's left with her tray of wine. "A drink, Master Kalmar?" she asked.

Amota Viran shook his head. "A pot of shay would do well for me," he said. "Go and fetch two cups, there's a good girl."

Mila bobbed her bow and left. Ibram watched her go, and then turned back. Amota Viran swirled his first two fingers in the air.

"All right," he sighed, and rubbed the side of his head. "What's Savoldyn done to earn your displeasure."

"Nothing," Ibram said with a shrug. "Rude as a thorn in Cangsa, which seems like it should put a cap on his income."

"Ah well, we don't pay caravanners for their charms. Is that all?"

"The housekeeper and I nearly came to blows, but I don't mind a good wrestle now and then."

Amota Viran laughed. "Mistress Dolman? She's a regular bear, isn't she?"

Ibram nodded. "I could see her swiping fish from the stream, if that's what you mean, but my current problem with the household, Amota, is that Master Savoldyn is dead."

Amota Viran sat up in his chair. "Dead?" he barked.

"Incredibly so," Ibram said. "Died just after our first meeting as well."

"How did this happen?" Viran asked. He leaned forward and clenched his hands into fists on the edge of the table.

Ibram shook his head, and pointed to a chair. Amota Viran gestured for him to sit down, and Ibram did so. He pushed the basket a little further down the table with his left hand.

"I arrived during an argument between him and his daughter," Ibram said. "Dresses like a Southerner. They don't seem to get along."

"His daughter was in the house?" Viran asked. "That's quite a surprise."

"Why?"

Ibram looked up to the front of the tent at the sound of a cough. Mila stood at the end of the table, carrying a loaded wooden tray. Ibram half stood to grab the fabric basket, and set it down at his feet, so that she could lay out the tray. She settled it between them with the shaypot facing in Ibram's direction. Next to the two small cups lurked a small basket of nut-filled pastries. Ibram licked his lips. He hadn't eaten since the early morning.

Amota Viran shook his head. "It was during your time away," he said. "She ran off with a clerk from the Bureau of Commerce." He looked up and smiled. "That will be all, thank you, Mila."

Ibram poured them both shay, and set the first cup in front of Amota Viran. He took the plate of pastries off the tray, and set it between them. Then, he waited while his uncle dosed his own cup with three largeish honey drops and enough cream to make the liquid slosh dangerously against the ceramic rim. Viran wrapped his hand around the cup rather than taking it by the handle. He nodded at Ibram.

"Yes, sorry." Ibram blew across the shay, and took a quick sip for politeness' sake. Being younger than Amota Viran, it was his privilege to eat first in the Western custom, but it never did to keep folk waiting. Then, Ibram added one honey drop and enough cream to smooth the smokey woodfire taste of the shay. "Why did she run away? There can't be too many parents upset at gaining influence in the imperial bureaucracy."

"She is—well, she was—her father's only heir," Amota Viran explained. "He wanted her to marry someone who would take their family name and preserve the business. He was furious when she ran off to the Wheelmaker's Workshop in Delbrite with a man who already had a profession."

Ibram frowned. He picked up one of the pastries and popped it in his mouth. Treeka nuts and cinnaks and honey filled his mouth as he chewed. "How'd she manage that?" he asked around his mouthful.

Viran reached out and flicked him in his temple. "Manners, you dog," he said.

Ibram grinned and swallowed. "I can't help if I'm dog-hungry," he said.

"Of all my aneptai, you are the worst, anefa," Viran said. "But to answer your question. She paid the marriage fee. In full."

Ibram blinked. He picked up another pastry and nibbled on one flaky end. "That," he said. "Is a very rich woman."

"So the Savoldyns are rich," Amota Viran said. He drank his shay and set the cup down again. "Rich and stubborn, which I suppose must go hand in hand. Because when her father found out about the marriage, he cut her out of the will entirely."

"He did?" Ibram licked crumbs from the corner of his mouth.

"It was the talk of the province for months," Viran said. "He drew up an entirely new settlement and re-married within the year to the woman you probably met... Yanna?"

He said her name oddly, a little hesitance in his voice that Ibram wasn't used to hearing from Amota Viran. He made note of it in his mind. That was what his stint in Amota Evren's clutches down in the archives had taught him, how to make notes in his head that stayed in the places within his mind where Ibram'd thought them.

"A lovely, if young, mistress," Ibram said, and watched Viran out of the corner of his eye while taking a drink of his shay. Did his uncle's tan face just flush? "She seemed very upset at her husband's death."

Viran nodded. "She's a woman of sentiment," he said. "Very open with her feelings."

Sounded tiring, to be honest, but Ibram had to agree with Viran's words if not the gentle tone of his voice. He watched his uncle drink for a moment, and then asked, "So Mistress Savoldyn became her husband's heir?"

Viran raised his eyebrows. "Not at all," he said. "Master Savoldyn's will was quite clear. He was very impressed with it, actually. The amount of times I had to sit and discuss it with him, I'm surprised he didn't have copies printed for distribution. No, his daughter by his first wife receives nothing. Yanna receives only a widow's portion for her lifetime, and a farm somewhere south—Itol, I think. He gave all the rest, his money and business, to either his grandchild, or his first child by Yanna, whichever came first."

Ibram sat back in his chair. "What kind of a fool's race is that?" he exclaimed.

Amota Viran snorted, and ate a pastry. "The kind that ended when Mistress Ignalle gave birth to a healthy baby girl. The whole matter's been settled for years now."

Ibram opened his mouth to ask what happened if Yanna Savoldyn suddenly found herself with a baby, and then closed it again. He could hear a bell when it rang, after all. It wasn't, perhaps, the right time for that question. He took a breath.

"Well, that's all right then," he said. "Since he's dead."

Amota Viran nodded. He chewed his food and frowned down at his paperwork. "I suppose his heart finally gave out," he said. "He could become absolutely wild when his daughter was mentioned, and she has his temper. Her actual presence would have incited a worse rage."

"I'm told he'd been sick," Ibram said.

Amota Viran sighed into his cup. "Well, there you are, then."

Ibram's foot nudged against the basket at his feet. He winced. In light of what Amota Viran had told him, it might... He sighed. Better to speak up and be a fool, than closemouthed and condemned.

"I don't know about that," Ibram said, and then cleared his throat. He spoke louder. "What I mean to say is, it's true an old and angry man might shout himself into oblivion if given sufficient provocation, to be sure, especially a sick one. But it's in my mind, Amota, that Master Savoldyn was taken out of this world with a great deal of help."

Amota Viran choked on his shay, and set the cup down with a thud. He swallowed and wiped his mouth with the back of his hand. Ibram cleared his throat, and tried to look competent and assured beneath Viran's incredulous stare.

"You think someone killed him?" Viran asked.

"I do," Ibram said.

"Murdered," Viran said flatly.

"It seems like."

Viran leaned back in his chair and breathed in deeply; he rubbed his temples again. His mouth thinned as he stared at Ibram. Ibram held up both hands, palms-forward.

"I know," Ibram said. "I realize it sounds foolish, but for a man to die so suddenly? For what? He wasn't an invalid, was he? No, he was up at his work desk, going over the accounts. Didn't have those attacks of bile the healers all warn us about? He seemed sturdy enough to me."

"And me as well, the last I saw of him," Viran said, frowning deeply. "But—"

"And he dies all of a sudden?" Ibram pressed onwards. "Just like that?"

"It's just as likely a time as any for someone to die," Amota Viran said. "We don't get to choose."

"Ah, but murderers do," Ibram said. "Hear me, please. I entered the building in the middle of a fight. Mistress Savoldyn specifically requests me to enter—though Mistress Dolman is against it—so that my presence might sooth the savage screamer."

Amota Viran made a face. Ibram amended himself. "Not that the good lady used those words. But when I entered Savoldyn's study, the man was not himself."

"How would you know that?" Viran asked. "You've never met."

"His eyes wouldn't focus," Ibram said. "Every time he spoke to me, he seemed to find me just a little to the left or right of my actual location. He sweated, was red-faced and intemperate with his words."

"And so he was in life," Viran said. He shook his head. "Perhaps he was tired."

"Or perhaps he was drunk," Ibram said. "When I examined the body, I smelled alcohol, pure spirits."

"Did you?"

"And," Ibram said. He dug into his pouch and lay the still pot with its patina of cracked white film in the bowl down on the table. Then he reached down to the basket and retrieved the receiver full of shay. "I found this in Master Savoldyn's bookshelves."

Amota Viran stared down at the pieces of the small alembic. He breathed out and crossed his arms over his chest. Ibram nudged the receiver.

"This is what he drank the entire time I was with him," Ibram said. "Mistress Dolman said he had a pot of shay and then she brought him a new one. If this is all he drank, then how did he come to be smelling so pungently of alcohol? And why does this alembic look as if it has seen use?"

Slowly, Amota Viran nodded without looking away from the table. "You suspect poison, then. Have you told the family?" he asked.

Ibram shook his head. "I wanted to test the shay first," he said. "In case, I was wrong."

Amota Viran caught his eye and held it for the space of two breaths. Ibram firmed his jaw. Caution was all well and good, but not when folk died for too much of it. He'd crack an egg for Yilka the Green and roll her dice later.

"If that is the case," Amota Viran said. "Then we shall test the shay. A common table of poisons should do."

He stood up from the table, and grabbed the still pot and the receiver in both hands. Ibram scrambled out of his chair as well.

Amota Viran nodded sharply. "We'll have to petition one of the Attendants not taking their examinations."

"Yes, of course," Ibram said. "What—I mean, shouldn't we make a report to Lady Azadiya?"

"Not yet," Amota Viran said. "Let us see what comes of our tests first."

With that, he left the tent and Ibram followed. In the chilled sunlight outside, the normal sounds of the camp scraped at his ears. It made sense to keep vague suspicions from Lady Azadiya when she was already dealing with so much, but still, the way Amota Viran's voice had curled around the name of Yanna Savoldyn stayed with Ibram.

$$\text{❄}\quad 4 \quad\text{❄}$$

I f Lady Azadiya's tower, as solidly built example of Merrilian architecture as could be found outside of the West, could be said to operate in a state of perpetual and controlled chaos, then the tent encampment which had sprung up outside of it was the aftermath of an explosion. Firepits had been brought out, chairs and tables drug from the building to provide the tower denizens room to work. Ibram thought every tent, canopy, and pavilion in the Sect of Seven Fires must have been hauled out of storage for Lady Azadiya's use.

He worked his jaw, suddenly aware of how tense his face felt. The Learners and younger Attendants were cavorting about as if it were a grand adventure. They ran in and out of the temporary buildings and some even attempted to climb the larger anchoring ropes holding the tents together. Ibram ducked as a little girl dressed in a green smock with her hair in flying braids tumbled past him along the split rail fence.

"Careful, Imriska!" shouted Amota Viran, and the girl slid down the rail to the grass, barely stopping her speed.

"There seem rather more folk about today than usual," Ibram said as he walked at Amota Viran's right shoulder. Ahead of them, a small group of Attendants were bent around a portable firepit, over which bubbled a cauldron of something that smelled horrifically like fish and tree sap. Ibram coughed, and turned his head away. "They haven't stopped the examinations, surely?"

Amota Viran walked by the firepit without changing expression. He shook his head. "They have been postponed for a time, which is the reason we have so many curious guests," he said.

"The merchants will protest the loss of trade if we hoard all these Attendants for ourselves," Ibram said.

"The evening courtyards will be absolutely furious," Amota Viran said, and sighed.

They turned down the beaten footpath and took a right past a group of servants calmly doing their daily mending. Ibram raised his hand towards Dihya, Lady Azadiya's housekeeper, where she sat in the servants' midst, examining an enormous pile of clothes. Amota Viran guided them down the righthand path at the fork where the road split into cart tracks up the mountain towards the higher preceptories and a shell path which led down and then around again to the back of the tower, where a small kitchen garden lay. Ibram glanced right and saw Amota Lakum in the small stables Ladyship kept near, leading the palfrey on a rope around in a circle.

Amota Viran guided them down the shell path, lined on one side by a dense thatch of imported thorny whin bushes and cleared ground on the other. The bushes thrashed a few times as they walked past. Ibram frowned and squinted, stopping directly. He bent his head at a now completely still bush, but the small green leaves and bright yellow buds were so tightly packed, the cause of the disturbance could have been anything from a Greater Uplands Wyvern to a Bog Wren.

"Ibram, keep up!" Viran called from further down the path.

Ibram glanced behind himself and then faced front. The wind blew lightly, but he saw no one else on the shell path except for Amota Viran, who didn't seem bothered. He sighed and got himself moving again.

Well, not bothered by the feeling of being watched, anyway. His face was certainly pensive, and several times he looked down at the alembic pieces he held in his hands and sighed heavily. Though, whether that was because Ibram had brought him disturbing news, or simply added to his workload, Ibram couldn't say. Lady Azadiya's agents were expected to be adaptable, precise, and above all, sufficient to any task required of them. There were none of them she depended on more than Amota Viran.

"Stop sticking your chin out like that," Amota Viran said. "You look like you're about to duel the glass apple tree."

"I'm not sticking my chin out," Ibram protested. "I'm merely aware of my surroundings."

"Be less aware and more attentive."

"How would that work exactly?"

Amota Viran sighed. Around the back of the tower, the bushes stopped behaving oddly, and the shell path widened into the entrance to the kitchen garden. He could smell something sweet and a little soapy in the air. Ibram's feet crunched down on a freshly strewn patch of freshwater mussel shells as he followed Amota Viran into the garden to the bell tent set up near the well at its center.

"Our troubles are more than adequate for the moment," Viran muttered. "Must you recruit insolence onto the roster?"

Ibram winced. "Sorry, Amota."

Viran sighed and patted Ibram high on his shoulder. He looked like a man dearly wishing for a strong cup of ale and a quiet moment; it was a pity that Ibram could not supply it. Ibram glanced up at Ladyship's tower, and stiffened his spine. They were paid to be vigilant and suspicious, after all.

The bell tent was a proper travelers' tent, meant for a large party, made of stitched together hides and supported by poles. The front panel of the opening was rolled up and tied to one side, and within, Ibram could see a round table set right up against the center wooden pole, filled with all the usual alchemist array of equipment, double basins and alembics, and cauldrons placed above the two portable burners, one lit and glowing merrily with heated coals and one unlit. A small wheeled catapult lay just outside of bell tent with a pyramid of rocks beside it. The Attendants must have carried the lot outside from the basement laboratory themselves.

Ibram looked up and to his right, where Lady Azadiya's tower loomed. The long, narrow screens of wire cloth had been removed from one of the windows. Well, no. Ibram winced. The screens were on the ground by the row of Sleeping Roses, half-in and half-out of the beds, trailing bits of framework and long metal strings. It looks as though they had been torn from their hinges. Had she done that when she'd sent her message? Ladyship was usually more precise, but if she couldn't see where she was aiming, perhaps she had thrown her rock through the screens and this was the result.

He rubbed the back of his neck and stretched his jaw again. Lady Azadiya was up there just now, no doubt snapping the heads off the doctors as they tried to perform their jobs. The last time she had caught a winter's chill, she'd been unbearable for a seven-day. Ibram pressed his lips together. If he could just go inside and tell her his concerns, it would solve every problem from his suspicions to Amota Viran's increasing work duties. He glanced at his uncle, who was approaching the entrance to the bell tent, and then back over his shoulder. The huge greying wooden doors that led inside the tower were firmly shut, as was the gate in the garden wall that marked the way to the bakery and kitchens. The heavy locks in the center of each door snapped with a flash of lightning over their lodestones. Whoever had done that meant business.

Ibram sidestepped the catapult as they walked up to the front of the tent. Amota Viran paused at the tent opening, and cleared his throat. He bowed shortly and with his hands on his stomach, but didn't wait for her to make the appropriate gestures to call him back up. As Lady Azadiya's marshal steward in all but title, Amota Viran's position in the sect was nuanced in relation to the rest of the Sect of Seven Fires, especially in regard to the alchemists. Ibram rocked forward onto his toes and saw Attendant Abele stand up from her camp chair. He fell back and bowed, and then Abele waved him back up.

"Good day, Master Kalmar," Abele said. "Is there any news from Mentor E'garcid?"

"I'm afraid not, Attendant." Amota Viran stepped inside the tent, with Ibram on his heels.

"Nor from our vantage point," she said and shook her head. Abele was the only person inside, though there were chairs for six more folk and two tiered bunks for four. Abele was an Easterner, one of the Valantin horsefolk. She stood tall and wiry in body, with a rough length of stick straight brown hair partially tied away from her face. In her height, she came to only a little below Amota Viran's hairline, which still put her above Ibram's head by five inches. Ibram sighed and nudged a loose stick of wood back over to its pile with his boot. The world was not built for people more sensibly grown in relation to the ground.

"Is Master Ucalegon known to you, Attendant Abele?" Amota Viran asked.

She smiled politely and nodded. "Yes, of course. He showed me around the preceptory when I arrived."

"It was my pleasure, Attendant," Ibram said.

"Good, good," Amota Viran said, even though his tone lacked any kind of relation to approval. "Has Ladyship sent any other message from the tower?"

"Not since I got here," Abele said. "That was just after breakfast." Her tear-drop shaped eyes had bags underneath them. She shook her head, and tugged on her left earlobe. "An hour ago, we fired off the request for entrance by the medicinal corps, but her morning's missive was the last we heard from her."

Amota Viran's broad shoulders sagged, but he mastered himself quickly. Ibram made a circle of the work table. There was a small woodstove in the back of the tent, with a crackling fire inside. The atmosphere made him long to undo his collar. He put his back to the stove.

In truth, Ibram had expected to speak with one of the Attendants in the medicinal corps. They were sheltered within the Preceptory of Yseult, and largely exempt from festival examinations due to the timely increase in their workloads. Where were the healers, the doctors? Lady Azadiya surely would not allow all of them into the tower if her entire division was forced to camp outside of it.

He couldn't ask Amota Viran that, of course, now that he'd made the offer to Attendant Abele. Perhaps he had thought a doctor or two would be lurking in this tent. Judging by the catapult it was the main communication hub, after all.

"If we're all still waiting," Ibram said, "then I would think you'd have a moment to provide your expertise, Attendant?"

Abele blinked at him and smiled. She was a kind woman, maybe three years younger than Ahksell, and usually too tied up in her work with long-distance messaging to need much in the way of guarding, escorting, or fetching, which ordinarily Ibram found attractive in an alchemist. Now, he almost wished she had a standing order for hot shay at midnight or something like that, just so he could know whether or not they stood a chance of getting her aid. Delay would not help his case, and if they had to run through their store of available Attendants, Savoldyn's corpse might already be out of reach in the Hall of Tranquility.

"My expertise?" she repeated. She quickly touched the owl embroidered on her collar. "I hope you aren't suggesting we look for someone to help Mentor Hobon outside the sect? I've never gotten one of my messages out past the imperial border and really, I don't think it's appropriate to bother another sect before at least Second Mentor Stadat has a chance to weigh in on the subject."

"No, no, not to worry," Ibram assured her, and patted the air with both hands. "It's another matter entirely. Say, you don't have one of those wire things, Hessele's Cages, do you?"

She smiled, a trifle bemused. "They have all been loaned out for the examinations," she said. "and Fourth Mentor Hobon locked the unfinished arrays in the storage cupboard. Master Kalmar has the keys, of course, but..."

She twisted to the right and held her hand out in the direction of the tower. Ibram nodded. Cangsa, of course they were. He tilted his head.

"I don't suppose we might roll out the catapult again?" he asked.

"I don't think we need to go so far just yet," Amota Viran said.

"Fire a rock with a note tied around it up to her and ask Ladyship to send one out?" Ibram asked.

"Ibram," Viran snapped.

"Apologies," he muttered.

"I don't suppose so, Master Ucalegon," Abele said. "But perhaps I might help? Why do you need an array for consequent affinity?"

Amota Viran frowned at him, but he did not say anything. While Ibram knew it was perhaps indelicate to reply 'because it is useful to know if a man has been murdered or merely suffered from acute gastritis,' it was the first reply that came to his mind. Still, an agent had to be courteous in his approach. Instead, Ibram pointed at the separate alembic parts in Amota Viran's hands. "Then can you tell if one—or both—of the substances in those glass bottles was used to kill a man?"

She turned pale about the mouth immediately. Ibram's eyes widened. Abele shuddered as if in a cold wind. She was so surprised she took a physical step backwards.

"I beg your pardon?" she asked, as if the problem was her own hearing.

"What Ibram is trying to say, Attendant Abele, is that we need to know the content and composition of these substances." Amota Viran held out the still pot and receiver. "Do you have the equipment necessary to make sure a test?"

"I..." Abele swallowed down whatever sour thought had first made her nose scrunch up, and then took a calming breath. She licked her lips. "Yes, I believe I do." She stared at the bottles, but made no move to touch them. "They're not... I mean to say, they're not *from* the body, are they? The liquids?"

"Never in life, Attendant Abele," Ibram said. "I poured the shay direct from the pot, and whatever lies within the still pot was present when I touched it."

She nodded and smiled tightly. "I more properly belong in Baran, you see," she said. "I concentrate on the effect of Atlavian and Bredis on the ability to read the wind. The true study of the body is a bit outside my range, really."

Ibram nodded politely, though he only had a vague idea what she meant. They were eastern gods or goddesses, probably. Easterners worshiped a fair few deities dedicated to nature, as he recalled it. Something to do with the shape of the world and the treeless spaces.

"And we in Yseult welcome your study with us for however long you need before returning," Amota Viran said. He walked forward and lay both the still pot and the receiver on the work table. "If perhaps you still feel equal to the challenge, we can leave these items for you?"

Ibram dug the toe of his boot into the ground at his feet. The tent was set up on a wide expanse of shell path, but no one had laid out a rug to make the place more comfortable. His boots were already acquiring a layer of white dust.

Abele reached out and laid her hand on one of the cold cauldrons. "Of course," she said. "We can start with the residue left in that still pot. Master Ucalegon, would you mind fetching me some water from the well?"

He bowed. "Of course not," he said.

Ibram walked behind Amota Viran and out the tent. The sun was still warm in the sky, but the air was chilled. It felt good against his heated skin. He walked over to the well, which operated on small version of a perpetual wheel. A metal belt with rectangular wooden buckets continuously revolved, set in motion by a crank wound each morning. The crashing water and creaking apparatus made enough of a racket that Ibram wondered why Lady Azadiya hadn't ordered it stopped for the day.

He crouched low to pick up the bucket discarded at the base of the well; a stick snapped. Ibram bounced to his feet and looked about the kitchen garden. Nothing moved but the desiccated tendrils of pea shoots still strung on their frames from summer. To his right, one of the several clingstone trees growing against the stone wall wavered. Ibram frowned, and grabbed the hilt of his sica.

Puzzle him once, more fool thrice, as the saying went. Trees did not move without cause, and though he hadn't seen anyone, that didn't mean Ibram wasn't being watched. He'd been rolled by bandits once on a lonesome night in Thrunibrite, for lack of awareness. The lesson had cost him his purse and his good cloak, and if Ibram hadn't jumped into the river and let the current have him, the junkers might have taken his life as well.

He looked down at his feet, but all he saw were cracked white shells. He hadn't touched any of the plants, and the noise of a small twig breaking wouldn't have been heard over the burbling well. Slowly, he put down the bucket and drew his sica. The long curved blade caught the sunlight, and cast a wicked shadow.

It could be nothing, to be sure. They were in the mountains, sometimes animals got into the gardens, or invaded the midden. He stepped lightly around the left side of the well, and then approached the middle path between the raised beds. His boots crunched along the broken shells. He winced, and paused.

Ibram turned his head slowly, eyes sharp along every shrub and fruit tree, poised to strike towards any flicker of movement. The wind blew lightly. The air smelled like greenery and woodsmoke.

A small brown fenek, all legs and belly with its tufted ears pointing right and left, hopped out of the leek bed and onto the path.

Ibram waited a breath more, and then stood up straight. He slammed his knife back in its sheath. The fenek startled and ran across the garden into a syah berry bush.

A damn fenek was big enough to break a stick, but the trees were planted against the garden walls, nowhere near the leeks. And there had been no one on the path with Amota Viran, nor by the tree when he walked past with Attendant Zorion. And none of the Savoldyn household had the temerity or, more importantly, the skills to follow him up the living mountain.

Ibram grimaced. Yilka's *megrims*. If he was alone, then at least no one else had seen that display.

He turned back to the well, and grabbed the bucket up from the ground. He held it under the nearest upending trough, filled the bucket halfway, and marched back into the tent. Amota Viran and Attendant Abele looked up at his arrival.

"That took a little while," Attendant Abele remarked. "Is everything all right?"

"Yes, Attendant," Ibram said as he plopped the sloshing bucket on the table. "Just a little run-in with a fenek."

She nodded, and then looked away to gather up a stir-stick and a pile of roughly cut cloth. Amota Viran frowned at him while her back was turned; Ibram held his hands up and shrugged.

He crossed his arms over his chest, and waited while Attendant Abele scrubbed a portion of the white residue out of the still pot and into a ceramic bowl. She added half a ladle of water, and swirled the bowl in one hand. She cocked her head to the side, and glanced up at him and then Amota Viran. Ibram tensed; he leaned forward on the balls of his feet.

Abele's mouth twitched. She sniffed the bowl, and then set it down again quickly. "It's natron," she announced.

Ibram's heels smacked back down to the dirt floor. "Natron?" he repeated.

"I see," Amota Viran said. His eyes narrowed in Ibram's direction.

"Oh yes," Abele said, somewhat amused. Her eye held a definite twinkle. "You can't mistake that smell. No doubt someone was cleaning the still pot and didn't dry it very well. Happens betimes when the Learners are first being taught to care for their equipment. You see, the cleaning solution gathers in the bottom and once the solution dries, it leaves this film."

"What sort of blend is it?" Ibram asked.

Amota Viran frowned at him. "Oil and natron," he said. "Honestly, Ibram."

Ibram shrugged. Attendant Abele held the still pot out towards Ibram, bowl-first, in explanation. Ibram smiled and nodded. He dropped his arms from his chest and hooked his thumbs into his wide leather belt.

Amota Viran bowed shortly to her. "I apologize on behalf of my colleague for wasting your time, Attendant Abele," he said. "We realize you have more important work to do."

"Oh no," Abele said, much more relaxed now that the first possible 'poison' had been eliminated. "As I said, I'm willing to help. I can still test the shay, if you'll help me narrow down what I should be looking for. What were the symptoms?"

Ibram took a step closer to the work table, but kept Amota Viran in his peripheral vision. "Loss of focus, red face, slurred and loose speech, and sweating," he said. "Also a very sharp odor of alcohol."

Abele nodded slowly. "Well, I am not an expert," she said, "but I can certainly help define what is not present in the shay. Leave it with me, and I'll send a runner for Master Kalmar when I've finished."

Ibram bowed, taking his hands out of his belt to fold them properly over his stomach, and she waved him up. Abele turned to a side table stacked with pots. She opened the nearest round clay jar and removed a ribbon of cloth. Then she picked up copper beehive saucer, and returned to the work table.

"Would you pick up that spirit lamp for me, Master Kalmar?" she asked as she adjusted the base of a tall metal clamp. She secured the clamp to the table, and then set the beehive saucer on its extendable arms.

"Of course." Amota Viran retrieved the small thick copper bowl from another side table, and placed it between the legs of the metal clamp. He pinched its braided rush wick to aim the flame upright, and then gestured at the little flask on the work table. "Shall I pour?"

"Yes, that would be very helpful," Abele said and brushed down the sleeves of her green tunic. She drew her hair back over her shoulders with both hands, and then tied the entire dark mass into a horse's tail with a length of braided fabric.

Amota Viran uncapped the flask, and Ibram's nose twitched. He sneezed. Attendant Abele offered him a handkerchief from her sleeve.

"Oh, no, thank you, Attendant Abele," Ibram said and sniffed. "That's the same odor as what I smelled in the—" Amota Viran frowned at him and shook his head quickly. "It's similar to what I smelled in connection with our poison," Ibram finished. "But not really. There was something sweet about it as well, if that helps."

"It might," Abele said, as she felt in every single one of the small pouches attached to her belt. "And he'd only been drinking shay? How curious... Flint, where is my flint..."

Amota Viran cleared his throat. "We shall leave you to your efforts, Attendant," he said. "Ibram and I have still other business to attend to."

She made an acknowledging noise, and waved them off. Amota Viran smiled thinly at her downturned head, and then made sharp shooing gestures at Ibram. Ibram backed out of the tent with his arms raised to his chest.

They walked out past the well. Amota Viran's face was set in narrow lines; his eyes as sharp as the displeasure in the cast of his mouth. He sighed through his teeth and shook his head, coming to a stop between the raised beds nearest the garden wall. Ibram faced him, putting his back to the entrance. The space between his shoulder blades twitched in discomfort.

"You come all this way, crying murder," Amota Viran said in a quiet, but no less intense tone of voice. "And it reveals itself to be nothing but a common salt!"

"What need does a non-alchemist have for an alembic?" Ibram countered. "Certainly nothing good!"

"Are you proffering a charge of alchemastery?" Amota Viran asked. "In response to what very well may be nothing but an overly zealous maid?"

"No, Amota, I am not," Ibram said, and sighed. "I doubt very much anyone in the Savoldyn manor knows the least aspect of alchemy, much less would practice it unlicensed."

Amota Viran paused, then, and let his forehead briefly crinkle in worry. Ibram wavered. He cleared his throat, and Viran's face returned to its usual polite authority.

"Master Savoldyn's death is very shocking, Ib-la," he said, a bit too gently for Ibram's liking. "And I understand its suddenness might surprise one so young as yourself, but if Attendant Abele does not find anything untoward in that shay, you must admit your suspicions rest on very thin evidence."

Ibram looked up at the tower, and the back to the tent. He flexed his jaw. "I do not admit that," he said. "You yourself told me he was involved in scandal. A farm and a stipend sound like a fair future to me. Perhaps Mistress Savoldyn doesn't care about the business if his death secures a return to freedom again?"

Amota Viran's face hardened; his spine snapped straight. "That's too heavy a charge!" he exclaimed. "Mistress Savoldyn is not the sort of person inclined to murder."

Ibram pointed at the sky. "Then I should speak with her again in order to clear her of the suspicion!"

"You are the only person accusing her of anything!"

"And yet I have spoken it to the open air with a witness, and Kivan the Red will have answers," Ibram said. "That's what it says in the Codex of Conduct, is it not?"

Amota Viran's silence weighed heavily upon Ibram's conscience as they stared at each other. Most of Lady Azadiya's agents—those from the West, anyway—were dedicated to the god of fair justice and mercy, Kivan the Red. Ibram was the only one given to Yilka the Green, the three-faced goddess of skillful hands, but that didn't mean he didn't make full use of the Merrilian pantheon upon occasion. He might even bake rose cake for Catha the Grey if it pried Ladyship out of her tower a day sooner.

"You may proceed with your investigation," Amota Viran said finally, and Ibram breathed a touch more lightly. He nodded as Viran continued, "but if Attendant Abele finds nothing in that shay but honey and milk, then you will set aside these notions of yours."

"Absolutely, Uncle," Ibram said, and grinned.

"And you'll do a seven-day twice over patrolling the south Learners' Dormitory to make up for not helping the rest of us during the festival."

Ibram groaned inwardly. The south Learners' Dormitory was built by a natural cave the preceptory used for its communal baths, and near a small waterfall that fed a stream. Anyone patrolling there inevitably went home with wet feet and sore legs from hauling the children up and down the pathways and out of the water. Regardless, he nodded and accepted his fate.

"Thank you," Ibram said. "I promise—"

"You will be polite, and most of all, subtle," Amota Viran interrupted him with a wagging finger. "That house has done business with the Hobons for three generations. I won't have that contract disrupted because you trod on someone's toes. Do you hear me?"

"I hear," Ibram said. "I obey, I under—"

Ahksell Solari peered out from behind the clingstone tree directly opposite, and then ducked back behind its green, thorny branches.

"*Cangsa*," Ibram snapped.

"What did you just say?" Amota Viran said. His eyes widened. He took a step back and to the side, twisting to follow Ibram's line of sight.

"Nothing!" Ibram declared loudly. He grabbed Amota Viran firmly by the shoulders and drew him around in a spiraling circle, firmly whacking at Viran's sleeves and then his sides. "A spider! Big as ever I saw one," he babbled with his head firmly fixed ahead of him and not the gigantic lump hiding in the trees. "One of those awful ones, black with a striped carapace, you know the kind. Here, let me do your back."

"Yes, very well," Amota Viran said in a bewildered tone as Ibram turned him to face the entrance to the garden. "A striped back? Black and yellow?"

"Exactly so, yes," Ibram raised his voice. "They should stay in the hedgerows where they belong!"

He heard rustling and grit his teeth. He gave Amota Viran's broad back a thorough brush down, hoping the distraction would be enough. No one enjoyed spiders, not even in theory. He kept smacking at Amota Viran's shoulder and biceps, and then slammed his bootheel onto the shell path and ground it down. Ibram quickly kicked more mussel shards over the hole in the ground as he walked around to face Viran so that his uncle's back was firmly presented to the tent and the clingstone trees.

"All done," he said. "No need to worry."

"Did it bite you?" Amota Viran asked. "Show me your hands." Ibram presented them, palms-up. Viran frowned as he examined Ibram's fingertips and knuckles. "It's not venomous, but those kind often pack a sting."

"No, no," Ibram said and took his hands out of Viran's grasp. "I'm quite well. Yourself?"

"I think I'm fine." Amota Viran examined his right sleeve and then his left. He looked up at Ibram and frowned.

"That makes me very happy," Ibram said with a wide grin that made Amota Viran's eyes narrow. "Well, I'm going to the relay station now, Amota Viran. Where are you going?"

Amota Viran studied Ibram for a moment before replying. "I'm expected at the doctors' tent," he said. "To learn more of Lady Azadiya's progress when they make their report to the First Mentor's representative."

"That is very important," Ibram declared.

They stood, staring at each other in silence. Ibram licked his lips. This was not working. Any moment now, Ahksell was going to sneeze or trip over a root, and then it would be like that time he and Ahksell and Katka had tried to hoard jam tarts in a water barrel all over again. Amota Viran glanced at the gate to the garden.

"Shall we walk together?" he asked.

Ibram didn't startle, but only because he had made up his mind to walk to the well. He did so while shaking his head. "No, I thank you," he said. "I'm a little thirsty. I think I'll take a drink before starting my journey. No need to wait for me."

"All right," Amota Viran said slowly. He took a measured look from Ibram to the tent and then outwards towards the raised beds of the kitchen garden. "But mind you leave Attendant Abele to her work. We've interrupted her long enough."

"I promise," Ibram said.

He stood by the well, and then reached out, cupping his hands together to catch the overflow from the rising buckets. He pulled his dripping hands towards his mouth, and watched as Amota Viran left the garden. He counted to ten and then ten again, and drank; the water did feel good on his dry throat.

Once he figured Amota Viran was far enough away down the path, he dried both his hands on his trousers and ran down the shell path towards the clingstone tree.

"All right, out!" Ibram hissed as he neared the wall. The tree's leaves rustled as Ahksell slid out from behind them. He stood tall from his previous hunch, and stretched his arms out to the side. The top of Ibram's head came to about Ahksell's shoulder; it was a perennial injustice.

Ahksell grinned and brushed leaves and moss off his green gambeson. "That was quick thinking," he said. "I thought Master Kalmar might have caught me otherwise."

"Yilka's *feverish* megrims!" Ibram pushed him with both hands; Ahksell's back thumped against the wall. Ahksell laughed, and rubbed leaves off the sides of his dark-skinned head and out of his closely shorn black hair. He had a new ring on his middle finger, a thick silver band with a green bezel. Ibram pointed at him and then up to the sky to wherever a doubtlessly amused goddess concealed herself, and then back again.

"You!" he said, trying to both yell and whisper all at once. "What are you doing here? You're supposed to be getting examined up in Afsoun!"

Ahksell looked at him as if Ibram had said something amusing. "I can't take an examination right now with Mentor Hobon locked up in her tower."

"She isn't locked up in her tower," Ibram countered. "She ordered everyone else out. You can't be locked away if you did it yourself."

"I still want to see how I can help, regardless," Ahksell said. He emerged once more from the clingstone tree and stepped onto the path. Leaves and twigs stuck to his arms and legs. He crouched to brush them all off. "I don't suppose you'd lend me a hand, too?"

"Oh, you saw that, did you?" Ibram asked and crossed his arms.

"Some of your finest work," Ahksell said, as he rose up again. "Well? What's to do?"

"Was that you?" Ibram asked. "Shaking the trees and snapping twigs like a raw walker in the dense forest?"

Ahksell winced. "I wasn't that bad at it," he said. "You thought I was a fenek."

"I knew I was being watched!" Ibram raised his hand to his shoulder and flicked his middle finger in Ahksell's direction. Ahksell laughed and then caught himself, and stifled his noises behind one hand. He ran his other hand down the diagonal length of buttons holding his gambeson closed and tugged on the end to straighten it beneath his belt. Ibram rolled his eyes, and Ahksell sighed loudly.

"I simply thought that if I wanted to know what was happening, then I could just seek you out, then follow you a bit and find out what I needed to know. Then I could return to the guest rooms in Afsoun with all the news," Ahksell said. "You won't believe what those wire twisters up the mountain are saying about us all. Only now I hear that Attendant Abele is helping you in your work? What do you need her for? Has someone broken their household altar?"

Ibram stared at him. Ahksell cocked his head. Ibram sighed. "You didn't withdraw your place, did you?" he asked. "You'll have to wait another year complete, if you did."

"I know that," Ahksell said, "and no, as a matter of record, I did not. I simply changed places with Frimula. She's very nervous and wanted to get her examination over with."

"And her place was?"

"Oh, last," Ahksell said. "Or nearly anyway. She got so anxious she almost missed the sign ups completely, but then she drank one of Hilbert's infusions and scrawled her name on the lists at the last second."

Ibram sighed, and pinched the bridge of his nose. "Wonderful," he said, and then dropped his hand.

"So we have a little time," Ahksell said. "Well? Where do we start?"

"We cannot start anywhere, to be sure," Ibram said, as he poked Ahksell in the shoulder. "You can return to Afsoun and let the rest of the Attendants know that Lady Azadiya is perfectly well and unseasonably chipper, considering her circumstances."

Ahksell made a small gesture with his first two fingers, and Ibram's hand smacked out to the right all by itself. He shook his wrist out and glared at Ahksell. Ahksell's great shoulders hunched a trifle closer to each other.

"Is it true Mentor threw her desk out onto the training grounds?" he asked.

"Do you see a large hole in that wall?" Ibram said, and threw his arm out in the tower's direction. "They had to build the tower around that damned thing just to get it inside."

"Well, those wire screens—"

"It was a stone wrapped in a shawl," Ibram interrupted. "And as you can see, we have everything well in hand."

"Are we communicating with her by way of Master Housgan's *catapult?*"

"Ladyship is fine," Ibram said firmly. Behind his back, he mimed ringing one of Yilka the Green's clapper-less bells for luck. "She's just fine."

Ahksell's mouth twisted. He rubbed his hands together. He looked up to the tower windows, and swallowed heavily, and then turned his wide eyes towards Ibram.

Ibram stood tall; he was unmoved. Ahksell had made the same face when he was twelve and Ibram was seventeen and the last cup of the summer cider was at stake. Ahksell's shoulders came down; his face grew a tragic resemblance to a hero off to sacrifice himself on the altar of his vocation. Ibram sighed.

"I don't suppose you have a Hessele's Cage?" he asked. If he wanted to help, the least Ahksell could be was useful.

Ahksell wrinkled his nose. "Why would I have need for one of those?" he asked.

"Never mind." Ibram shook his head.

"I've got my pendant?" Ahksell offered, and touched a pouch on the side of his belt.

"Your pendant?" Ibram held out his right hand and wiggled his fingers. "Your introverted pendant?"

"My *introrse* pendant," Ahksell corrected. "And yes."

Ibram tugged on the hair at his nape. In the absence of aid, Yilka the Green often sent unexpected boons, after all. He pointed. "And you're certain you're in no danger of missing your examination?" he asked. "I'll not have Ama railing at me over dinner as the cause of all your woes. I've already got a seven-day of Learner duty ahead of me."

Ahksell grinned. "May I never speak again, if I'm lying."

Ibram breathed in deeply, as if a great weight had lifted from him. He'd convinced Amota Viran, and now with Ahksell, the case for Ibram's suspicions held water. "I'm for the relay station, else I've lied to my uncle."

"Well, we can't have that," Ahksell said without a lick of guile in his voice. "I'll chaperon you, just to make certain."

The sun was shining, and the wind was bracing, but tolerable. Ibram grinned. They'd take the servants' footpaths and stay out of sight from the rest of the preceptory; Ahksell would be back in no time at all. Ibram clapped Ahksell on the shoulder, and pulled him down the garden path.

The trip down the living mountain to Lityen was relatively empty, the larger flood of Attendants and staff released on their liberty was a few hours off. Ibram filled Ahksell in on the particulars of what he had observed in the Savoldyns' house, but he kept Amota Viran's odd behavior to himself. There was no need to tell fire tales before sunset, after all.

The markets were as rowdy as ever, almost all of them maintained a presence until well after dark during the festivals and feasts of the alchemical calendar. Their entire section of the province of Vanima was dominated by the Sect of Seven Fires economically, after all, even as the sect itself was restricted from the rest of the province by imperial decree. A body could make a lot of coin providing the villages surrounding the sect with the little privileges their neighbors to the east, west, and south enjoyed.

Ibram was careful to walk at Ahksell's side, but a half-step away. It was easier in a crowd, and also what folk expected to see when an alchemist walked with a sect agent. The merchants certainly eyed Ahksell up like he was a lone mouflon, separated from his flock.

"Are your parents out in this?" Ahksell asked, as he stepped out of the way of a passing baker's apprentice.

"Only Katka," Ibram said. He breathed in the warm scent of the ring cakes' salty and sweet glaze as the baker escaped into the crowd. "They're offering private appointments at home, and letting her get a feel for the marketplace."

Ahksell nodded. A flock of automated birds in bright dyed chicken feathers flew towards his head above the crowd; He raised his right hand, palm out, crooked his first finger and thumb and swept his hand to the right, as if he were drawing a flowing line in the air. The birds flew straight up and then twisted over themselves mid-air, tangling their lines, and falling back towards their seller's stall. A fair few villagers who noticed the display laughed and clapped.

"We should say hello if there's time," Ahksell said as he twisted through a break in the crowded street.

"To Katka or my parents?" Ibram asked.

"Well, your parents are nearest the stove..."

Ibram laughed. "Is the food so different up in Afsoun?"

"Bread is bread," Ahksell agreed, "even if the flour is milled a little more finely."

"And yet..."

Ahksell shrugged. "And yet it tastes different at Mistress Ucalegon's table."

Ibram snorted. "Leech."

Ahksell laughed, and Ibram shook his head, grinning. They passed through Preserved Corner, where the salt and sugar traders worked, and then up along past where the Kilk clothiers hung up their banners, and finally down past the stables to where the Savoldyns lived. Ahksell looked up and down the street. It was more quiet here, almost like one of the minor noble houses further outside Lityen, but the space given to the Savoldyns' manor was only on four sides, leaving two walls connected to the next merchant's home. They had a laden cart out in the packed earth street and a stall decorated with doll's sized clothes to demonstrate their quality materials. The line of contractmen in front of them meant word of an Attendant's visit would spread perhaps almost as fast as news of Savoldyn's death.

"They're a bit quick," Ahksell said with a nod in the cart's direction.

"If my nearest neighbor died and his entire family had to cease work for even an hour," Ibram said, "Katka would be outside with a barker before you could snap your fingers."

He cocked his head. Now there was a thought.

"Oh now," Ahksell said. "It's not the entire month, is it? When your grandfather took passage to the Crossroads, your father began work again after a twelve-day."

"He worked," Ibram said absently, still thinking as he led Ahksell down the alley to the door. "He didn't sell anything. And we weren't allowed out to the village for another twelve-day complete."

If Master Savoldyn had been as mean as they said he was, then perhaps his neighbor and competitor might have seized the opportunity of revenge. A few days out of business beginning on the Festival of Sangrin—which itself heralded a great many festivals to come—meant many contracts might die on the vine. Custom could always return, of course, but the winds of commerce were fickle.

"Ah," Ahksell said. "I don't believe we'll be getting inside today, Ibram."

Ibram brought his attention back to the house it belonged with. They'd somehow gotten to the front gate while he'd been thinking. It had been tied with five dried rushes in the pretense of a rope, signaling the death in a family. Ibram sighed.

"What if we just lit the rushes ourselves?" he asked. "Surely they need some fresh air."

Ahksell smacked him in the arm. "Don't be rude," he said. "They wouldn't be at home to vandals any more than visitors."

"Fine," Ibram said. He bounced on the balls of his feet, and then looked up and down the alley. "Come along then."

He turned and made for the street at a fast pace, forcing Ahksell to scramble behind him. He grinned even though Ahksell's long legs easily caught up to him. At the street, he led Ahksell further down the opposite end, skirting the manor's outer wall.

"Where are we going?" Ahksell asked.

Ibram waggled his eyebrows at him. "Even mourners must eat," he said.

Ahksell wrinkled his forehead. "I thought you said you only saw the housekeeper and that, uh, Hilo Kenes."

Ibram shrugged. "A place this large? They must have a cook, at the least. No one's such a skinflint they'd forgo a good meal."

"Addeus E'grum ate only quash," Ahksell began to chant under his breath. "Addeus E'grum saved all his—"

"Children's rhymes are beneath you, Attendant," Ibram muttered. "Now hush yourself! Where there is a cook there is a kitchen, and where there is a kitchen, there is a door for deliveries. Now, we're here."

Honeycomb manors, popular in the garden provinces, generally had smaller servants' courtyards in the back to protect the main family areas from fire or cooking smells. Ibram couldn't remember a home inside the village that didn't have at least one connecting wall, and some even shared their cooking areas with their neighbors. In this, the Savoldyns were no different. They had arrived at the end of the alley and now faced two wooden doors on either side of a joined seam. Above them towered a shared stone chimney with sparkling fire suppression tiles affixed at regular intervals. Ibram knocked on the door to their right and then stood back, clasping his hands behind his back.

Ahksell frowned down at him. "I am not here, am I?" he asked.

"How philosophical," Ibram said. "Shall we lose you to a university next Festival of Sangrin?"

Ahksell knocked his elbow into Ibram's side. "Strictly, officially, speaking, I mean."

Ibram shrugged and smiled as the door opened to reveal the distrusting but young face of a servant. She didn't smile back, in fact her frown deepened, but she let go of the door, and patted the escaping whisps of her hair back from her forehead with both hands. Her dull smock was tied up at the waist and her wide-legged trousers ended sharply at the ankle above her simple cloth shoes, which were damp. From behind her, came the sounds of feet rushing and pots bubbling, and a woman's sharp tones.

"Good day, mistress," Ibram said, and bowed his head.

"This is a house of mourning," she said sourly, with an unsettled look at Ahksell. "I—I'm not to admit folk."

"Oh, indeed," Ibram said and very carefully did not address himself to Ahksell lest he overplay his hand. "And, to be sure, I would never think to intrude at such a delicate time. In point of fact, I was here earlier, picking up Mentor Hobon's order."

He patted his sect brooch on its length of leather across his chest. The servant flushed a little at that, and the door she still held in her hand wavered. She looked behind herself into the kitchen, and then turned back with a pursed mouth. Ibram kept his face polite and his body language open; Ama had had a lot to say on posture and composure when he had been in training.

"And what's that got to do with me?" she asked.

Ibram sighed and showed her his open palms. "It's my own fault. I was on the premises when the terrible event occurred, and in my haste to make room for the grieving widow, well... I'm afraid I left behind part of the order somewhere in the house. Do you think we could just take a quick look around, perhaps see if we might find it?"

Her eyes widened. Perhaps she was a bit younger than Ibram had first assumed, a maid-of-all-work, rather than a house servant. "Oh, but we can't, I mean to say, Mistress Dolman has already tied the rushes!"

Ibram sighed. "I know it," he said and shook his head slowly. "But you see, they've sent me back down the living mountain and Attendant Solari came with me. May I make you known to Attendant Solari, Mistress?"

The girl's entire face blushed; her frown dropped away as if it had never appeared. Her head whipped around to peer up and up at Ahksell, who had taken to fidgeting. Ahksell cleared his throat.

"Attendant Ahksell Solari," Ibram said. "Be known to..."

"Jara Whaite," she mumbled, and suddenly remembered her manners. She bowed with her hands on her stomach; the door swung lightly onto her upper arm. She stumbled a little, but recovered.

"And I'm Ibram Ucalegon," Ibram said to the air above her head.

Beyond Jara stood two women, a boy, and Hilo Kenes, all now staring Ibram's way in shock. The long table which bisected the small group was piled high with bowls and platters, and steaming dishes. The light from the flameless torches bracketed on the walls was steady and golden, and Ibram could smell dilli cream sauce.

Ibram waved. No one returned his pleasantry, but then sad folk never responded as they were supposed to. Before Ahksell waved Jara back up, he saw Hilo Kenes frown. Ibram refocused on the servant girl.

"That's why we came around the back way," he said. He heard footsteps, and spied Hilo on his way over to them. "So as not to excite comment. I mean, you know what— Good day, Master Kenes."

"Good day," Hilo said. "Jara, what's to do here?"

"Oh no need to mind her," Ibram said. "As I was just explaining, in my haste to leave you to your grief, I didn't realize I'd left one of Mentor Hobon's packages behind. I thought I might just see where I could have dropped it?"

Hilo frowned. "Back to your duties, Jara," he said, and waved the girl out of his way.

She retreated to the large preparation table, angling her head for a last glimpse. The older woman, tall with a hunch to her shoulders, picked up a large knife and began loudly chopping a pair of carrots. She frowned and bent forward, as if she was having trouble seeing them clearly. Hilo Kenes moved, and blocked Ibram's view of the other two servants.

"My apologies for this," Ahksell said suddenly and a bit too loudly. "Ibram's so clumsy, you understand. Loses things all the time."

Ibram spread his hands in a helpless gesture. "I was just so startled, you see. To be in at the death is a shocking experience!"

"No excuses," Ahksell said, and actually waved his finger under Ibram's nose. Ibram had to look away and bite his lip. "Mentor needs that, uh, that package for her research."

"She does," Ibram nodded. "To be sure, she does."

"Which package was it?" Kenes asked. "Perhaps we could send it up to her?"

"I'm not at liberty to say," Ibram said.

"Mistress Savoldyn is not at home to visitors," Hilo said. "I don't think it right—"

"Well, the problem is," Ibram interrupted. "Is that Mentor Hobon is quite busy right now, it being the festival, and she doesn't feel she can wait for the entire two days. Her calculations are precise in these matters."

Hilo's resolve wavered. He glanced over both shoulders towards the other servants, most probably on the lookout for the appearance of Mistress Dolman. Ibram stepped forward with both feet on the threshold of the door. He was going to owe Yilka the Green so many rose cakes for this escapade.

"Lady Azadiya Hobon is like the rest of her family, you understand," he said with a lowered voice. "Alchemists and nobles don't like to be kept waiting, and Ladyship is *both*."

Hilo took a step backwards, and then another. Ibram followed him inside the kitchen with Ahksell at his heels. He nimbly skirted Master Kenes and bowed shortly to those assembled at the table.

"Good day all," he said. "My most sincere apologies for your loss and our disturbance."

His nose had not failed him. The splendor of an early harvest lay on the kitchen table, no doubt ready to be served. An entire caskfish, plump as a berry, lay smothered in dilli sauce on a round platter. In its mouth sprouted a sprig of the same leafy herb, and to either side lay dishes of roasted leeks glimmering with butter and cubed potatoes covered in a white sauce flecked with peppercorns. There was a pickled salad crusted in treeka nuts and an elaborate salt dish shaped like a river mussel with a tiny spoon sticking out of it.

"I did not think we were interrupting an occasion," Ahksell said at Ibram's left side.

The woman across the table bobbed up and down in a bow, polite except she did not wait to be ushered upwards. She shook her head and set her knife down, and then handed her carrots to Jara, who ran to the large crackling fire in order to add the vegetables to a cauldron. The young boy of perhaps twelve years had both hands on either end of the salad tray.

"Not at all, Attendant," she said briskly. "I'm doing no more than I was ordered—nor more than any of us here, mind! Midday's meal was arranged before our sad event, and Mistress Savoldyn wants waste no more than I do."

"I commend her household economy," Ahksell said.

He even sounded as if he meant it—probably did, if Ibram knew his own friend. He looked up and down the kitchen and let his hands hang at his sides. The place was sparse, but functional. Two doors on either side of the room no doubt led further into the servant's courtyard. In the country, they would have an outside door to lead to the laundry or a bread oven. In Lityen, there wasn't space for either such luxury. The size of the kitchen boded well for the servers, a short walk to the family's dining room meant hotter food and fewer complaints. Still, this was a confusingly small collection of staff.

Further to his left, Hilo Kenes stood, shifting his weight from one foot to the other. "Now Marit," he said. "Don't go wasting the Attendant's time."

She snorted, picked up a large grass whisk, and began spinning it in a bowl of something that quickly turned frothy. "You'll mind your tongue in my kitchen," she said. "I'll talk to who I want, no matter that it should be mine own time that's precious, and not this one." She looked at him from the corner of her eye, squinted, and kept whisking. "Begging the Attendant's pardon, of course."

"Oh no, I quite agree," Ahksell said. "If you don't time that dressing correctly it will break, after all."

She did him the honor of turning both eyes to look up at him, and raised a reddish eyebrow to boot. "Do you know dressings, Attendant?" she asked.

"I know only what I like to eat," Ahksell said with a smile.

In the light from the torches, he looked exceptionally boyish. Ibram felt himself begin to smile and restrained the impulse. He frowned down at the kitchen table instead. The young boy looked up at him.

"All this for the widow?" Ibram asked. "I hope she feels generous later."

"Oh, she always does!" the boy piped up. "We always get what's left if there's any—excepting the master's tolnic of course, but *sometimes* during the festival we get a whole half of small beer and a nip to take home!"

Ibram widened his eyes. "A whole half?" he echoed. There was a large cask set up on blocks by the wall, next to a case of small empty clay pots. There must have been no space for the empties in the under-croft. Most houses made their own beer, but tolnic was usually another matter. "How kind."

"She is," Marit interjected. She placed the bowl of dressing on the salad tray and jerked her head to the right. Her reddish curls bounced off her forehead. "What she saw in that old hammer-tongue, none of us know. Off with that, Tawrit. Don't dawdle!"

She seemed unconcerned by a death in the house, but from Ibram's vantage point none of the servants appeared too fussed. Tawrit oblig-ingly ran off with his tray, leaving Ibram to smile at the final unnamed person in the room, a young woman with blonde hair caught in a net of fine-spun linen and a gown of blue cloth with mouflon fur at the collar. Clearly, this one had access to her mistress' castoffs. Everyone else was in rough russet wool. He smiled and bowed.

"May I be known to you, mistress?" he asked.

She dimpled and set down the small pewter cup she had been holding on the table. "Liepa," she said.

"Mistress Liepa, good day," Ibram said. He inhaled and gave a great sigh. "I see Master Savoldyn's house is not as empty as I first thought! Master Kenes, you should have told me such worthy folk worked in this courtyard."

"Yes, this is what's left of us," Marit said, wiping her hands on a rag. She slapped the cloth down on the table. "Save for the porters, but they're housed in the village."

"That seems like a lot of work," Ahksell said. Ibram turned to look at him and saw that, somehow, he had been given a small bowl of stew. He frowned. Ahksell widened his eyes at him, and deliberately slurped. "This is delicious, Mistress Marit, I thank you."

Why did everyone they meet become seized with the need to feed Ahksell? He was already the height and breath of a second living mountain. Surely, no one could look at him and believe the sect starved him. Perhaps it was the wide eyes. As a child, Ibram had learned to grow wary of every innocent gaze turned his way; he was inevitably blamed for whatever nonsense that ensued. Ahksell made a small revolving gesture with his spoon. Ibram made a face. Just because the man had bought them a little time in the kitchen didn't mean Ahksell wouldn't be hearing about this later.

"You don't get such up the living mountain?" Marit asked. Her hands never stopped their work, passing ingredients off to Jara and then stirring something in a copper bowl on a bed of ice.

"Nothing so spiced," Ahksell said. "I think the sect's cooks believe salt sustains a man enough."

She laughed. "Well, it does," she said, and patted back her red curls. Her bun was a little worse for wear. "But nothing like a strong khrin to buck up the blood. Young men need that." She spared a glance for Hilo Kenes as well. "Indeed, so do old men."

"Master Ucalegon, you did say it was urgent," Hilo said. He seemed to be sweating a little, near the heat from the fire. "I have no wish to be impolite, but Mistress Savoldyn should not be disturbed at this time."

"Oh, I would hate it, too," Ibram said. "Mistress, may I ask, is that a cask of tolnic I see?"

He pointed to the far side of the kitchen, just to the left of Mistress Liepa's elbow. The entire kitchen paused. Ibram simply continued.

"My Ama makes her own, you know," he said. "Spiced as an Isconian's—"

"Ibram," Ahksell muttered.

"Your pardon, Attendant," Ibram said, and sketched a bow in Ahksell's direction. He winked as he came up, and saw Jara's face color as she bent over the kettle nearest the fire. "Merely a Merrilian's love of a fine drink."

Marit appeared confused. "She has a still, then, your..."

"My mother," Ibram clarified. "Do you make your own?"

Marit shook her head. "We do not," she said. "It's sent for from the House of Tarsis, but the mulling is my own recipe."

"Really?" Ibram asked. "That's quite a large cask. It must take you all day to mull."

Jara snorted. "More like we go through it in a day," she muttered.

"Jara!" Marit snapped. "Sour words curdle quash."

Ibram leaned forward over the table and lowered his voice. "I don't suppose I might be able to taste it? Just as a fellow enthusiast, you understand."

Marit's smile turned sly. "And let a youngster such as you loose in the courtyards afterwards? You'll not be fit to be seen."

"As strong as that?" Ibram affected surprise.

"Stronger, even," Mistress Liepa said. She swayed closer. "Marit has the deft touch with rock sugar, you know. She can make it taste like nothing so safe as posset and then next morning you wake up under the table!"

"Liepa," Kenes said sharply. "That will do. Mistress Savoldyn doesn't pay you for prattle."

Mistress Liepa bristled. "I no more prattle than you! And there's nothing wrong with a warning about strong drink, is there? Master Ucalegon and I are young enough for it to matter."

Marit coughed a laugh into her arm. "Just as you say," she said. "Though nothing I make needs a warning."

"Oh, but," Liepa protested. "What about that time with the green citrus? It had to be sieved!"

"That will do," Marit said and slapped her rag down on the table again. "Go and see if Mistress needs anything for her dinner. Tawrit has served and should be on his way back."

Mistress Liepa colored rather prettily, but Marit would have none of it. "Off!" she repeated, and off Liepa went.

Ibram and Ahksell glanced at each other. Ahksell was nearing the end of his bowl of stew. They would have no recourse but to move on soon, despite Ahksell's attempt to delay.

"The Marshal Steward must be in your debt, Mistress Marit," Ahksell said quickly. "It must be difficult to manage a household staff and a business. Is it not, Master Kenes?"

Hilo's long face turned wooden and stiff. He tugged once on the low tail of his thin brown hair. "I have not that honor, Attendant," he said stiffly. "I am merely Master Savoldyn's—I mean, I am Mistress Savoldyn's man of business."

Ahksell paused in surprise, and then set his empty bowl down on the table. It was quickly taken away by Jara. Ibram crossed his arms over his chest. Now that was a way to stay in business, a marshal steward cost a household far more in pay than a mere servant. It explained the plain clothes as well.

"My apologies, Master Kenes," Ahksell said finally. "I did not mean to strike a nerve."

"Not at all, Attendant," Kenes said, and Marit made a face at her copper bowl. "Master Savoldyn was a shrewd man who kept a tight hand on his household. He preferred a more hands-on approach than other houses in the region. And, please, call me Hilo."

"Hilo," Ahksell said with a nod and polite smile. "I thank you."

There was a lull in conversation then, and Ibram took a chance on gaining a slice more of information before they were forced to leave the kitchen. He made a show of looking around, and then bounced on the balls of his feet. Hilo—for if Ahksell could name him such, no doubt Ibram could continue as well—took on an air of strained patience.

"Mistress Dolman is not about, is she?" Ibram asked. He shuddered deliberately, and the turned an ingratiating eye towards the ever busy and helpful Mistress Marit. "I wouldn't wish to get in her ill graces again—our first meeting was fraught as it was."

Marit's face turned knowing. "She's got a bite on her could kill a tarmap," she agreed. "But you'll find no one more devoted than her to the household. She's at her meal with Mistress Savoldyn; the mistress hates to eat alone."

Ibram nodded. "She shows an admirable loyalty."

"Indeed," Hilo said before Ibram could ask his next question. "But I do think we should go and find your lost package now, don't you, Master Ucalegon? Seeing as how your mistress has such an urgent need for it?"

"I agree, Hilo," Ahksell said. "Let's go, Ibram. Where, uh, where do you think you dropped it?"

Back in the reception hall with his own good sense, sadly. Ibram shook his head. "My apologies, but I have no idea, Attendant. Perhaps we should retrace my steps?"

"An excellent idea!" Ahksell turned to Hilo. "Which door leads to the family's courtyard?"

Hilo looked taken aback and cleared his throat. "This way, Attendant," he said, "and if I may, Master Ucalegon, please remember to keep your voice down. I wouldn't want—"

"Silent as a crane in a pond," Ibram said, and held his finger diagonally across his lips as he spoke. "You won't have to worry about a thing."

Hilo opened the door and jumped aside as Tawrit pounded through. "She wants the alegar!" he announced. "Says there isn't enough bite."

"Well," Marit began in what was certainly to be a fine tirade, but Hilo and Ahksell had already left the kitchens, and so Ibram did as well.

Hilo led them out into the open air servants' courtyard, where a small kitchen garden and a wooden drying platform sat out in the center, and down the terrace to the great doors that marked the entrance to the family's courtyard. Ibram frowned as he counted the closed doors on the floor about them.

"I had no idea the Savoldyns kept a three courtyard manor," Ahksell said, as if he had even heard the name before today. "How do they manage it with such a small staff?"

"Ah, no, Attendant Solari," Hilo said. "There is only the family courtyard and then the public space. They live in the upstairs apartments in both buildings. The ground floors are where we of the household sleep, and for their business."

"Still, it seems rather big for only you five," Ibram said. "Tawrit isn't one of the porters hauling Ladyship's freight up the living mountain, is he?"

"The porters keep to their own arrangements in the villages," Hilo said, shortly. "Master Savoldyn—we used to have a larger complement of staff, of course, but for some time now, we have been reducing to essentials."

"Cuts back on allowances, I suppose," Ibram said.

"The more stock you have to sell, the more money," Hilo said. He shrugged his shoulders, and once more the rather cheap weave of his tunic caught the torchlight.

It wasn't unheard of for a rich man to bear his minimum responsibility to his estate. Not everyone, after all, was lucky enough to enjoy direct access to the Sect of Seven Fires, which had a reputation for lavish care, and a resulting influx of loyal servers. Ibram even had a set of brigandine in his rooms back home to wear when Ladyship traveled outside the imperial boundary. Still, it seemed odd that a fabric merchant wouldn't use his servants as living advertisements for his available wares. Mistress Marit might not need such fripperies as a busy cook, but Mistress Liepa seemed the only one to enjoy her mistress' castoffs.

He tilted his head to the left as they walked through the doors, and into the public courtyard. It was much darker, of course, with its enclosed ceiling, but the glimmering alchemically strengthened glass radiated just enough light to aid the irregularly lit glowbulbs on the upper floor. The glowbulbs and pitchwood incense reminded Ibram even more strongly of a stuffy old temple in Delbrite. One of the ones dedicated to the Advisor where no one was allowed to speak until they'd published at least three treatises on Her Gracious Majesty Soliya IV's use of lawful execution and four anti-Isconian pamphlets of unusual size.

Ahksell whistled quietly. "Those glass trees must have cost a fortune," he said. "And the vases! I've never seen such quality outside..."

His voice stuttered on an embarrassed cough. Ibram waggled his eyebrows at the floor. Ahksell only spoke the truth, after all. Most merchants, no matter how successful, couldn't afford the purity and precision of such quality workmanship. This spoke of close ties up the living mountain, or a deep familial concession.

"Master Savoldyn's first wife came from a family of artisans," Hilo said. "I believe the pieces were part of her wedding negotiations. There used to be more, but upon her death, the remainder went to her daughter."

"Master Savoldyn could not touch it?" Ibram asked. He noted that someone had cleaned up the bowl of flowers Mistress Savoldyn had knocked to the ground.

Hilo shook his head, but made no reply. He paused at a familiar door. "This is where I showed you the samples Mentor Hobon ordered."

Ibram nodded, and then shook his head. "Ah, but you didn't give me them packaged until later!"

"Where was that?" Ahksell asked.

"Master Savoldyn's office," Hilo answered sourly.

Ibram grinned. "Hilo obliged me in a Western custom, Attendant Solari," he said. "And allowed me to stand guard over the body."

"That was very kind of you, Hilo," Ahksell said. "Shall we go there now?"

The glowbulbs strung from the ceiling remained strong enough that Ibram could see how little Hilo wished to go back to his employer's office, but nonetheless, he didn't resist Ahksell's polite request. It would have been a much longer conversation if Ibram had tried that alone. In fact, he might have had to pretend to search any number of apartments, and risk gaining unwanted attention.

Their footsteps slapped against the wooden walkways. Ibram glanced upwards to the second level. Where might a grieving widow and her irascible housekeeper feast together? And wasn't that interesting to think on as well. He'd first thought they didn't get along at all. Perhaps death in the household had joined them in a united front of grief.

He raised his eyebrows as they passed a table covered by a rough tarp. Or perhaps, if it was murder, they had pretended to hate each other in order to secretly work together! They were certainly eating heartily while the body chilled somewhere. Of course, that would only hold true if they stood to gain from Savoldyn's death, and to be sure, Ibram had no evidence of that either way. Amota Viran's impression of the will was that it didn't go too well for the mistress of the house, after all.

"Has Master Savoldyn been moved to the Hall of Tranquility?" Ahksell asked, with a glance out of the corner of his eye towards Ibram.

Hilo shook his head. "No, Attendant. Mistress Dolman had him moved to the root cellar. We have sent messages to the Navigator's Ark, but none of the Navigator's pilots have arrived yet."

Good, that was good. Ibram looked out over the covered materials in the courtyard, and then up to the second floor again. One of the doors was ajar; he could see light spilling out from the crack. He nodded to the office door, marked now by a flat board hung from the door handle. It had The Navigator's compass painted on it.

"Mistress Dolman's not taking any chances, is she?" he murmured.

Hilo's laugh died an inch from escaping his mouth. "She never does." He reached out but didn't touch his hand to the door. "This is it."

"Thank you, Hilo," Ahksell said.

"We'll look in the office," Ibram said. "Why don't you retrace your steps? You wrapped Lady Azadiya's packages, didn't you?"

"I don't..." Hilo trailed off, and then sighed. "Yes, of course."

He bowed to Ahksell and then took off down the right hand side of the walkway, brushing past Ibram a bit roughly. Ibram rocked onto his tiptoes to avoid Hilo, and then turned raised eyebrows up at Ahksell. Ahksell shrugged back. Ibram settled himself with a sigh. Some folk had fewer manners than they ought.

Ibram put his hand on the door handle; a spark jumped from the center of the wooden board to his palm. Ibram's wrist seized. He jumped back with a yelp, and grabbed his hand, before pressing it against his mouth to block further noises. He breathed hard through his nose. Ahksell rocked forward with his hands out. Ibram made a shaking fist and brought it down to hold against his stomach.

"Itchak!" he swore under his breath. "Who put that there?"

"Are you all right? Ahksell left the door and crowded Ibram for a better look at his arm. "Keep your voice down!"

"I am keeping my voice down!" Ibram whispered. "You try keeping quiet when a door bites you!"

"It didn't bite you," Ahksell said, and grabbed him by the elbow.

Ibram winced, and growled. He jerked out of Ahksell's hands. The shaking had traveled up his forearm; his skin shrunk with cold. He pressed his lips together and then shook his head.

"He didn't warn us about that."

"No," Ahksell said. "And he should have."

He frowned and reached for Ibram's arm again. Ibram's hand spasmed, but he held steady. He turned his head at the sound of hinges, and then ducked back under the overhanging balcony. Ahksell followed him.

"Did you hear something, Dolman?" Mistress Savoldyn asked. Her voice was faint, but clear.

"I thought I did, Mistress," Dolman said, by the sound much more near. She must have walked out of the dining room.

Beside him, Ahksell huffed. He shuffled to the side, turned, and dropped his hand down in between them. Ibram looked down and saw Ahksell's ring on his middle finger turned so that the green stone faced the board with the Navigator's compass. He clenched his fingers in a pulling gesture and slowly drew back. Something like fire bubbled up from the middle of the compass, the fire grew into thin strands too fine and regular to be called lightning which wavered like seagrass after Ahksell's hand as he drew them forth.

Ibram tore his gaze from the sight, and looked upwards towards the second level again. From their position, he couldn't see into the next floor up, but then neither could Mistress Dolman. Her footsteps moved to their left. They had a reason for being in the courtyard, of course, but Ibram had a feeling this would not reflect well on him with Amota Viran if Mistress Dolman saw he and Ahksell just then.

"I think it was nothing, Mistress," Dolman said, finally. "A trick of an old house."

Ibram slumped back against the wall, and clenched his shaking arm. It felt as if pins and needles were rolling up and down his skin, pricking him in an endless wave. He turned his attention to Ahksell, and grimaced.

"What is that?" he whispered.

Ahksell shook his head. He slowly revolved his fingers, gathering the strings of light like they'd used to roll yarn for Ama as boys. Then, he whipped his arm out and behind him, and flung the vibrating mass out into the air. It unraveled immediately, floating on nothing and dissipated without a sound.

"Come on!" Ahksell opened the door and darted inside, with Ibram on his heels. Ahksell shut the door and then leaned his forehead on it; he breathed deeply. The office was dark and quiet.

"Did you just defuse a lightning lock?" Ibram asked.

Ahksell straightened up from the door with a sigh. "No," he said. "I temporarily drained a religious ward."

"Who has the authority to put one of those on a door in this house?" Ibram asked.

Ahksell shrugged and shook his head. "We should hurry. I don't think it has anything to do with keeping folk in the office, but you never know."

Ibram rubbed his tingling arm and stretched out his wrist. His fingers shook, so he hid them in his fist. He felt along the walls with his good hand until he stumbled upon on the braziers holding the glowbulbs. At his touch to one, they all lit.

"How's your hand?" Ahksell asked. "Here, show me."

"It's fine," Ibram said, and stuck his arm behind his back. It was growing slowly numb. "I'm already getting feeling back."

"The Navigator has an interest in property," Ahksell said. "I'm sure it wasn't offensively meant."

Ibram nodded.

"Really, are you sure I can't have a look at it? The medicinal corps rated me very highly at my last survival training."

"No," Ibram said. "They said you were tall at your last medical examination. There's a difference."

Ahksell rolled his eyes. "Are you at least unburnt?"

"I'm as raw as an oyster," Ibram said. "Now, unless you're too tired from your little exhibition, what can you tell me about this office?"

Ahksell blinked at him for a moment's breath without moving, and then abruptly crossed his arms and stood straight. He surveyed the office from the built-in shelves to the Isconian carpet to the small painting of a rachtbear on the wall Ibram hadn't noticed before. He huffed.

"It's well appointed," Ahksell said.

They were alone, and so Ibram wasted no time in leveling the sort of look at Ahksell a comment like that deserved. Ahksell grinned.

Ibram flung his non-deadweight arm out, and then turned to point at the spot on the shelves where he had removed the alembic.

"Didn't you tell me you saw emanations?" Ibram asked. "You said you had to drink something foul and then you saw the fabric of reality."

"It wasn't foul," Ahksell objected. "It was merely...thick."

"Truly, thank you," Ibram said. "But I have told you I think Master Savoldyn was poisoned, so I ask again: Is there anything you can...see in here that would support my thought?"

"All right, all right." Ahksell's head waggled left and then right. He frowned at the shelf. "This is where you found the alembic?"

"Yes," Ibram said with a sigh. He pointed at the hole its displacement had left in the shelves' stock. "It held a silvery residue in the still pot that made me suspicious."

Ahksell hummed in agreement. "We should find out what that is," he said.

Ibram cleared his throat. "Attendant Abele ran a test," he said. "It was natron."

Ahksell snorted.

"It's still strange!" Ibram protested. "What non-alchemist needs to use an alembic, much less clean it?"

"No, you're right," Ahksell said, and then held both hands out in front of him. "And judging by the space, the apparatus would have been too small for anything but personal use. Mistress Marit did say they don't have a distillery on the premises."

"Exactly," Ibram said. He walked to the desk and moved behind the big chair. He set his good hand down on the chair's back, and stared out at the office. The view from Savoldyn's erstwhile throne was not illuminating. He took a breath and stretched out his hand over the desk, ignoring its trembling.

"The shaypot was here," he said. "Savoldyn sat here, and there was naught but papers elsewhere. The daughter..." He pointed out to Ahksell's right, where the little table and chair stood. "She was there."

"Mistress Ignalle?" Ahksell asked. "You didn't mention that."

"Does everyone know this family but me?" Ibram asked, and tugged on his hair in the back of his head.

Ahksell laughed. "You know what gossip does to a small village," he said.

"Small village," Ibram muttered. "Might as well live on the same street for all the privacy."

Ahksell turned to the low table. "And she drank as well?"

Ibram rubbed his opposite thumb into his palm, trying to massage some feeling into his hand. "She did not."

"I suppose their relationship was bad enough," Ahksell said, "but that seems a bit too rude not to offer her something."

Ibram paused. "Not if she were uninvited." He thought back, angling himself so that he could picture the office as it had been only this morning. In his mind's eye, he saw Mistress Ignalle's short fingers and square palm reach out. "I didn't see another cup."

"So, if it was poison," Ahksell said, "only Master Savoldyn had the means to drink it. Could she have put something in the pot?"

"Would he have let her fiddle with his shay in the first place?" Ibram frowned. "Or she arrived after he had been served, and was simply not offered any. After all, I arrived late in their argument; her cup might have been on the way from the kitchen."

Ahksell played with the ring on his middle finger in thought as he looked about the office. Ibram pointed at it, and then let his hand drop. It still tingled, making his fingers feel almost as if they were about to cramp.

"When did you get that gewgaw?" he asked. "It's handy."

"Hmm? Oh, this," Ahksell replied and showed Ibram the ring. "I took one for my exam from Mentor's storeroom just in case my locating light overloaded again."

Ibram winced. He'd acted as Ahksell's testing subject while he developed his work for the exams. Many agents did so, especially as victorious Attendants often passed on the spoils of victory as a reward for their help. Ahksell's little button shield had gone through several variations before he'd landed on a rechargeable beacon.

"How would that help?" he asked. "And why was I not allowed one?"

He turned his back, and began to check over the bound books and stacks of scrolls in their nests on the shelving. He pulled one thin volume down and flipped open the cover. It was merely an old ledger, not even from five years ago; he returned it to its place. The second was a more recent accounting of a trip down the river Sig to the port at Junibrite.

"It's an active energy exchanger," Ahksell said, behind him. "You have to be able to align the fluorospar with the nucleus of containment, and then..." He made the pulling gesture again. "It takes practice."

"Well, then why didn't you have one during your experimenting?" Turning, Ibram put his hands on his hips, and then immediately dropped them. When had he become his father? "I was seeing two of you for a twelve-day!"

"Runner's corns, I didn't know I would need it!" Ahksell spread his hands. "And I wouldn't have been prepared except for, you know, when that happened to you."

"How glad I am," Ibram said, "to sacrifice for alchemy."

"They used to be standard issue for all of us," Ahksell said, and frowned down at the ring. "But there hasn't really been a need since the last alchemaster cabal was thrown down."

Ibram considered the empty space where the alembic had stood on the shelf. "Let's hope your keeping that on you was a happy accident."

"Anyone can buy an alembic," Ahksell reminded him. "They're quite fashionable to have in the house these days, you know. I'd say most folk with a hefty enough purse could afford to buy them."

"I will admit that natron by itself is not suspicious," Ibram said. He flexed his hand. "If you'll admit it's a strange household with one maid of all work who still takes the trouble to clean out an object which supposedly has never seen any use."

Ahksell raised his hand up. "We don't know it was even cleaned recently! The alembic could have been washed years ago, and simply left upon the shelf." He sighed, and looked around the room again. "Really, I don't know what I should be looking for, in any case."

"What does a Hessele's Cage do, exactly?"

Ahksell paused, and then tilted his head. "It accesses the weave of causation and targets disturbed threads of correlation."

"Well," Ibram said. "Do that."

"Just be a Hessele's Cage?" Ahksell asked, and snorted in disbelief. "Why not just apply for my mentorship now? I'm sure no one will be surprised at my ambition."

"Oh, it can't be that hard, to be sure," Ibram said. "Look at the size of you! You're brimming with alchemical verve."

"That is not how alchemy works!"

"Just look for a warped thread, or a knot, or something!"

Ahksell rolled his eyes. "How can you have gone all through the Bedris school and yet know so little?"

"My talents were required elsewhere," Ibram said. "Now please take a closer look at the fabric of reality."

Ahksell groaned. He took his introrse pendant out of his belt pouch and strung it by the end loop on his left middle finger, letting the iridescent trimstone arrowhead hang down on the braided copper length. He closed his eyes and took a deep breath, and then slowly began rubbing his palms together. The pendant twisted in the air. Ibram had seen Ladyship do this before; it was a common centering position before a training drill. Usually, it heralded some kind of tumbling formation. The air grew hot.

Ibram shrugged and tugged on the neck of his gambeson. He grabbed a tightly bound scroll up from the nearest tray, and sneezed. He frowned, and then sniffed the air. He sneezed again. Kandrilat cedar? And something else, a jellied scent like lillia, but more sickly.

Ibram considered the scroll in his hands. It wasn't paper after all, now that he had hold of it, but a spiral of delicate wooden slats bound in silk and tied closed by a length of leather cord. The blue wax seal on its knot was broken, and bits crumbled underneath Ibram's fingernails.

"The threads around the desk are stretched thin," Ahksell said. "But there's nothing demonic in it, nor divine for that matter. I would say he was troubled by something, but I have rarely met an untroubled merchant."

Ibram chewed the corner of his mouth. Not many secular folk had bound slat scrolls, since paper worked perfectly fine for their sort. Alchemists were the ones who often found their formulae and treatises dripping off the parchment as the ink refused to dry, or moldering in vellum half a day following the first transcription. Still, it didn't have to mean anything. There had been a fashion some years previous to bind poetry and songs in slat scrolls with tassels and ribbons on the ends. Some of the Vissilian pantheon used them as well, like the Speaker. Ibram couldn't remember if the Navigator was one such deity, however.

But Master Savoldyn had not struck him as a poetical man, nor a religious one. Ibram pursed his lips. Mistress Savoldyn was, as Amota Viran had said, a woman of sentiment. Perhaps it was hers? The ledgers he discounted, even though the trip to the river Sig had ended as a loss, according to the figures. As expenses went, a man with this many bound books was not likely to be in financial trouble, even this close to the living mountain. Still, the records keeping tallied with a man of business. He unrolled it, and wrinkled his nose immediately.

"What do you have there?" Ahksell asked from behind him.

Ibram coughed as he rolled the scroll back up again. "Nothing much," he answered. "Caravan romances. I think Master Savoldyn thought of himself as a poet."

"Any good?"

"Not at all," Ibram said. He thrust the scroll back on the stack and turned about. "Barely a limerick, and not even funny."

Ahksell stood with his head tilted, unblinking. He held both of his hands in front of him. Ibram frowned. The air twisted in the center of Ahksell's palms, like fabric revolving upwards beneath the trimstone arrowhead pulling the copper braid taut. No, not the air—Ibram felt no wind—but the light turning in on itself as if in the center of a kaleidoscope. He swallowed heavily.

"Find anything?" Ibram repeated and leaned casually away.

Ahksell nodded and looked past Ibram to the bookshelf. "May I?"

"Are you certain you wish to stop...whatever it is you're doing?" Ibram asked.

"No, not really," Ahksell said. "But I believe the real..."

Ibram waited, but Ahksell had fallen silent and still. Ibram glanced about the empty room, and eyed the door; no telling when they might be interrupted. He cleared his throat loudly, and poked Ahksell in the shoulder with two fingers.

"There is intent here," Ahksell announced, abruptly. "A weave of a particular color, like copper when it rusts... I think there is a lot of effort in those bookshelves."

Ibram paused. "Of course," he said. "What's that supposed to mean?"

Ahksell took a step forward, crowding into Ibram's space, and shook his head. Ibram obliged Ahksell and stood aside. Ahksell approached the bookcase, wavered by the little table, and then lowered his first finger. The pendant curled upwards as quick as a striking snake, and wrapped itself twice around the furthest end. The arrowhead shifted restlessly, up and down the shelf with the stack of scrolls.

Ahksell tugged his left hand, and the pendant reluctantly uncurled. He snapped his pendant back into his palm, stepped back, and took a deep breath as if he were surfacing from deep water. He nodded, mostly to himself, and then caught Ibram's eye, still not quite present.

"We should see about that," he said.

"As you say," Ibram said. He frowned down at the little pile of slat scrolls. "What do you mean when you say 'effort?' Is it Savoldyn's anima, or something?"

Ahksell smiled. "Yes," he said. "He's placed a lot of time and energy in these objects. They have become a part of his energetic sphere."

"Must be fading by now," Ibram said.

"Oh, it is," Ahksell nodded. "And something—a strong impression, but a recent one—is decaying quickly, too. But he died amongst his belongings, and thus..."

"They have resonated for longer, as does anything else directed to him."

"Lucky you brought me to the office quickly enough to perceive the connection."

Ahksell was grinning; Ibram frowned. "I do remember my lessons," he said, and smacked Ahksell's arm. "Stop making that face."

"I'm merely pleased to know you were listening!"

Ibram smacked him again, but Ahksell refused to change the

expression on his face. Ibram huffed and tucked his hair behind his ears.

"I remember it well enough!" he said. "Lead may not become gold, but alfrin and copper might marry to produce it. The focus of reality describes its presence."

Ahksell's grin became a proud beam. Ibram narrowed his eyes and glared.

❧ 6 ☙

Ibram turned back to the half-emptied bookshelf. "Yilka the Green is laughing at me with all three of her mouths," he said, as he poked the stack of scrolls.

"There must be thirty such things here," Ahksell said. "It's a small fortune."

Ibram waved the open ledger in his left hand. "And him with a lost ship out past Layaline Harbor."

"Indeed?"

Ibram gazed down at the ledger in thought. A ship with all its crew and cargo meant a significant outlay for a merchant. A success could herald two years of high living, but failure should have meant penury. Perhaps it was not so odd that the household was reduced to a skeleton crew of servants. Ibram shifted his attention down to the rest of the scrolls. He gathered them up one by one, tucking them into the crook of his elbow until their tray was empty, and then piled them in Ahksell's arms.

"The rest are mixed in with vellum," he said, and stared at the next stack of scrolls, obviously constructed of delicate wooden wands and silk. Their tassels were tangled together. Yilka's megrims, were they all Savoldyn's work?

Ahksell sat down on the floor, cross-legged, and dropped the scrolls before him. He picked one up and unrolled it; holding the parchment before him. Ibram's attention snapped to him, caught by the movement. He watched as Ahksell's face slowly slackened in astonished horror as he read; his lips moved, Ibram hadn't noticed that before. He chucked the ledger to the floor.

"You're right," Ahksell said, at last, as he tossed the scroll behind him. "This is tripe."

Ibram chuckled. "Is it too spicy for you, Attendant?"

"I don't mind spice," Ahksell retorted. "But this poem is nothing but salt and fat."

Ibram's mouth curved upward, but he directed most of his attention to the bookcase. "I doubt he performed them," he said. "A man of business in the street for coin?"

"Maybe he just wrote them for himself," Ahksell said.

Ibram heard the sounds of another scroll being revealed before Ahksell tossed it aside just as quickly. "I don't know," He jerked his head towards the other wooden slat scrolls. "It's a lot of money to throw after something so personal."

"If you have the money, it might not seem so much of an expense," Ahksell said. He picked up another scroll and frowned down at it. "An ode to coupling," he muttered, before tossing it aside. "And he wasn't spending anything on his daughter."

"Or his household," Ibram said. "I'm going to take on a few more of the ledgers."

Ibram pulled three thick cloth-bound books from the shelf and settled opposite Ahksell. He glared down at the stack, while Ahksell snapped his copper and trimstone pendant into his palm. He clenched his fist, and then stuck it out over the scrolls on the floor.

"They heat up," he muttered, "but nothing resentful. More studious."

"Well, he liked himself, clearly," Ibram said.

Ahksell sent his equipment swirling over the stack of bound wooden slats again, and the air crackled. Ibram's back crawled. He cracked open the ledger on top of his own stack, and drew his finger down the splotched figures. It began neatly enough, but as the figures continued the lettering became a messy affair, with blots and trailing lines in the margins. Savoldyn had dated the pages clearly at least; they stood from a twelve-day ago.

"These are contracts for the next shearing season in Hobilat," he muttered. "But it's a very bad hand. Do you think we shall find the cost of the scribe in here?"

Ahksell pulled the ledger out of his hands. Ibram leaned back, frowning. Ahksell ignored him, and held the ledger in his left hand with one of the scrolls on his right. He shook his head.

"No, it's the same writing," he said. "Here."

Ibram leaned forward as Ahksell tilted the book and scroll in his direction. "Did this one heat up for you?" he asked.

"It's about alembics," Ahksell said with a crook in his smile. "He must have been inspired."

Ibram frowned. "How so?"

Ahksell let go of the ledger and turned the scroll towards himself. He cleared his throat. "On my travel so I saw two still pots disordered/no frail rope to tether their use—Well, how could there be? You connect still pots to the condenser with a lyne arm."

"I think he was being poetical."

"You can be accurate *and* poetical."

Ibram laughed. He looked over their pile of scrolls and breathed out through his nose before settling back on his heels. Ahksell dropped the scroll, and then rubbed his temples like he was fighting off a headache.

"There can be an innocent explanation," he said. "For the handwriting, I mean."

"But if he was being poisoned over time," Ibram said and pointed at a particularly mysterious symbol in the ledger. "Then this could be proof of his deterioration."

Ahksell's face turned a bit grey. "It's a heavy sentence," he said. "It's death, they'll question the servants, and the lady of the house, and how much money did he make anyway? It's no doubt a job for the warders—"

"First," Ibram said, cutting Ahksell off and staring up at him until

Ahksell began to focus. "It's me who will be questioning the servants, and you know I am the soul of discretion."

Ahksell's mouth widened in a sudden grin. Ibram pointed at him. "That was a different matter," he said, quickly. "And I thought we agreed never to discuss it."

Ahksell nodded with a jerk of his head. "Nothing even crossed my mind."

Ibram squinted at him severely, but Ahksell only blinked placidly back. "Secondly, Savoldyn was rich, but he wasn't noble. The warders won't even notice he's gone until we send them a notice for the official records."

"But if he's very rich," Ahksell said, "then they'll have to get involved on behalf of the guild."

Ibram shook his head. "To that point, I don't think he was that rich. If these ledgers are correct—and the penmanship says more than Savoldyn's figure were off—then I think our merchant may have gone down with a few of his transport ships."

Ahksell's mouth pinched. He nodded. "We should look at the rest of the books in this office."

Ibram felt the back of his head begin to ache. Figures had never been his favorite occupation. Oh, he could add and take away with the best of them, but the time it took to make sense of the economies Ama and Father dealt with in the family business had always made him itch for the outdoors. It was just as well he'd been born first; had he been Father's heir instead of Katka, the family would be suffering. He left the first book to Ahksell and settled the next ledger in his lap. This one marked the trading expeditions Savoldyn had sponsored overland, which then gave way to river barges and ocean-vessels. They were all of them moderately successful. How then the lack of servants? Ibram frowned.

He flipped through the next pages, which featured more of the same numbers, and then came to a page with the corner folded down. By the date, it had been written out at the start of the Feast of Wain-shollow, during the deep rains when the rivers flooded their banks. Savoldyn had financed a brace of caravans—no surprise, there—but the distances over time began to shrink.

Ibram's skin prickled with chill. That didn't seem correct. He turned the next page, and saw Lady Azadiya's name, marked in red ink, and connected to the longest travel period. The next six expeditions for trade were no farther than Delbrite, and some represented strings of smaller journeys that made up a full tour.

"Lityen to Lityen-by-the-Blue-Hole," Ibram muttered to himself as he dragged his forefinger down the list. "Thence to Othy, Othy to Itol, Itol to Fontis, and then all the way to Polia, but neither Nyarribrite nor Delbrite. Yet Delbrite down the river to Pocaris." He looked up. "Does that sound right to you?"

Ahksell glanced up from his own ledger. "What?"

"What is the longest journey recorded in your ledger?" Ibram asked. "On the—choose the most recent page."

Ahksell cleared his throat and flipped to the back of the ledger. He studied the page for a moment, and Ibram saw him counting off on the knuckles of his right hand. Ahksell blinked and then stared at his palm. He counted again, and raised his eyebrows.

"Speak, please," Ibram said, "My feet are falling asleep on this floor."

"You could have chosen a chair," Ahksell said. "I wouldn't have stopped you."

"Oh yes," Ibram said. "A dead man's seat sounds lovely."

Ahksell shrugged. He dropped his counting hand into his lap, and nodded. "The Red Coast," he said. "It's Mentor Hobon's shipment."

Ibram waved that aside. "But besides her."

Ahksell counted again. "It would be...I would say twenty miles."

"Twenty miles," Ibram repeated. "A merchant with contracts worth hundreds in gold from the Red Coast, who can't send out a caravan so far as Delbrite?"

Ahksell frowned. "That does not sound correct. Do they all have to do that?"

Ibram waved one hand in a negative. "Not at all," he said. "When I was working my way by caravan, the folk in charge held operating permits for entire regions of the empire. The only time I've seen smaller trade permits is when a local merchant wanted to hitch their wagon to our larger one for protection."

"Perhaps a business rival snaking his contracts?"

Ibram snorted. "Where did you learn that term?"

Ahksell jabbed the air between them, and Ibram's left shoulder rocked back from an invisible blow. Ibram grinned. "No, I don't believe that accounts for the permits," he said. "Ladyship's contract is untouched."

Ahksell nodded. "She would be an expensive catch."

Ibram rubbed the back of his head. "It is strange that—oh." He stopped and then winced. "Amota Viran."

Ahksell wrinkled his forehead. "What about him?"

Ibram pictured Mistress Savoldyn up in her dining room with Mistress Dolman. She had seemed truly overwrought at her husband's death. Had she known about the decreased trips? Had anyone else? The day-to-day functioning of Vanima province within the imperial boundary around the sect belonged to the Fourth Mentor's division. Someone knew about it up the living mountain.

"I don't think Amota Viran is so quick to dispense with a trusted merchant," he said, and kept the rest of his thoughts to himself. They wouldn't be going anywhere until he had proof to connect them, anyway. He set down the ledger, and picked up the lone wooden slat scroll left untouched. It was tightly rolled and dusty at one end, where it stuck out from the shelf. Clearly, it had been placed there and forgotten for some time. Ibram undid the leather strap holding the scroll closed and unrolled it in both of his hands. He tilted the contents up to the light, and felt his eyes widen.

"This will do quite nicely," he murmured.

A quick knock on the door made Ibram jump. Ahksell reared back and twisted towards the door, still clasping a scroll in one hand. The rapping occurred again.

"It's Hilo, no doubt," Ahksell said, and swallowed.

"Indeed so," Ibram said. "We should clear up."

He stood, and staggered back a few paces while his ankles protested the change in position. Quickly, he rerolled the wooden slat scroll he held and shoved it up underneath his gambeson, caught in the inner flat belt that held his tunic in place. Ahksell opened his mouth to scold and Ibram windmilled both hands at him.

"I will explain later," he whispered. He swooped down and grabbed the stack of ledgers, while Ahksell gathered the scrolls. They piled them back onto the shelves, and then Ibram strode to the door and pulled it open. Hilo Kenes startled, and dropped his fist, caught in the middle of knocking.

"Master Ucalegon," he said, recovering himself. "Have you been searching Master Savoldyn's office this entire time?"

Ibram forced himself to speak normally. He smiled. "Alas, our search was slowed, Hilo," he said, and caught the flicker across the man's face at Ibram's lack of honorifics. Ibram held up his hand. "I suffered an unfortunate mishap with the Navigator's ward on your door."

Hilo's mouth dropped. "My apologies," he said. He looked down at the door and then back up. "I had no idea, Master Ucalegon. We use them for freight on long sea voyages, but I did not know they were carrying a charge."

"Why do you have them in the house, then?" Ibram asked.

Hilo swallowed. "I suppose...it's been some time since we've had call to use them," he said.

"Then why affix it to the door?" Ahksell asked from behind.

Hilo bowed and Ibram blinked. He cast his eye behind him towards Ahksell. Ibram wrinkled his brow. Ahksell came up behind him, and made a beckoning gesture to Hilo, who stood.

"Mistress Dolman," Hilo replied, "had me place it there. Master Savoldyn was a patron to the Navigator, and she thought it would be a good idea to keep the other servants out of the room until—" He swallowed. "—until it could be cleansed."

"Wonderful thought," Ibram said.

So Savoldyn was dedicated to the Navigator, the Vissilians' god of the sea and—more important in this case—navigation. Some merchants merely donated to the nearest Ark for business purposes. After all, the pilot and crew who sailed under the Navigator's banner had a vested interest in properly caring for their souls, before releasing it to the Crossroads. Ibram made a dim note of the facts in his mind as he propelled himself out of the office. Hilo fell back before him, growing alarmed.

"Master Ucalegon—Attendant Solari, what is the meaning of all this haste?" he asked, too loudly.

A door opened above them. "Hilo?" Mistress Dolman called out sharply. "Who are you speaking to? What's all this noise?"

Hilo stopped and looked upwards; his mouth hung open. Ibram motioned Ahksell to stay inside the office, and stepped out near the railing. He angled his face up and to the right. Mistress Dolman's thin face sharpened with outrage.

"Master Ucalegon," she snapped. "What are you doing back in here? This is a house of mourning!"

"Dolman?" Mistress Savoldyn called out, faintly. She seemed to be still in the dining room.

Dolman took a half-step back from the railing to address her mistress. "It's nothing," she said, with a glare in Ibram's direction. She quickly shut the dining room door and returned. "I will—"

"I've lost one of Lady Azadiya's parcels!" Ibram shouted over her. "Master Hilo was kind enough to retrieve it for me from your reception hall!"

He kicked Hilo in the ankle, and made a significant gesture with his head in that direction. Hilo gaped at him. Ibram widened his eyes. Surely the man wasn't this dense.

"Ye—yes," Hilo stammered and backed up. "Yes, I will just —I'll go."

He turned and ran down the hallway, back towards the front of the house.

Dolman leaned over the railing. The heat from her glare could had stoked a foundry furnace. Behind his back, Ibram gestured for Ahksell to make his way down the opposite hall to the kitchen.

"How *dare* you," she snapped. "This is insupportable."

"Dolman, who is it? Is it—oh!"

Mistress Savoldyn appeared at her side; she gripped the banister with both hands, and bent over it. She had not regained her color since last Ibram had seen her, and the white cap which covered her hair was plain and unadorned. She had dressed for dinner, if not completely for mourning. Her mouth moved soundlessly, but soon crumpled into such an anguished bend that Ibram feared tears were imminent.

"And yet I fear you will have to bear up," Ibram said, speaking loudly to cover Ahksell's great galumphing footsteps. "Kept your employer on the ice cantrips, have you? I'm so glad you took my advice."

"I am willing to entertain the notion that you have unsavory experience which I lack, Master Ucalegon," Dolman said. "But my respect for your position only goes so far. We have tied the rushes to the gate! The only folk allowed inside these walls are the Navigator's consecrated pilots. I will not—"

"Oh, I have the best of reasons," Ibram said, and patted the air in front of him reassuringly. In the corner of his eye, he could see Ahksell at the entrance to the kitchen. The door opened; Ibram cleared his throat to cover the sound of the hinges.

"What could they be?" Mistress Savoldyn asked. She pressed her hand to her Wheelmaker's spoked pendant which lay on her chest, and shook her head. "I thought—goodness, I thought it must be robbers!"

Ibram blinked up at her. "Why?"

Mistress Savoldyn stared at him, and then shook herself. She touched her fingers to her trembling mouth. "I am a widow now," she said, with a shake in her voice. "It leads one to think terrible thoughts, Master Ucalegon. If Einar can die so quickly...oh, anything might happen!"

Ibram nodded. Mistress Dolman glared down at him, but her eyes flicked scorn in her mistress' direction quite clearly. "As you can see," Mistress Dolman said. "We are not yet prepared to receive guests."

"I'm not a guest, I am but a humble customer," Ibram said. "Here on business, to be sure. Mistress Savoldyn, I agree that your husband's death was awfully sudden."

Mistress Savoldyn raised her head in a gasp. "You do?"

"Of course," Ibram said. "If you tell me it was too quick, than who am I to gainsay you?"

She nodded quickly and dabbed her eyes with her sleeve. "It was," she said. "It was so very sudden. Oh, he had pains in his side and bad eyes and he liked his drink, but that's nothing much, when you put it along his health."

"Rude with it, I suppose?" Ibram asked.

"Master Savoldyn was a man of exact standards," Mistress Dolman said. "Body and soul, the anima in conjunction, as you folk up the living mountain might say."

"He sailed a tight ship," Ibram said. "But I suppose old age slows us all."

Mistress Savoldyn rubbed tears from her cheeks and then nodded into her hand. "I hate this yelling," she said, letting her raised arm drift back to her side. "I've always hated it. Come up, Master Ucalegon. There's food enough for all."

She turned from the railing and disappeared back into the dining room. Ibram's mouth opened and closed; he raised his eyebrows at Mistress Dolman, who shook her head in one sharp motion, and then followed her mistress. Ibram looked down the hall to where Ahksell had disappeared to freedom, and then up to where Hilo Kenes had absconded. He sighed. Well, if the mistress of the house wished for company, who was he to deny her?

He climbed the stairs up to the second floor and quickly walked around to the dining room. It was of a healthy size, with oil lamps bolted to the walls and a line of half-melted candles down the center of the large table stuck in the middle. Ten sturdy chairs, no doubt used for family gatherings or work parties in the past, were grouped at its sides. Now, it sat Mistress Savoldyn at its head, the furthest from the door, with Mistress Dolman to her left. Ibram took the chair to Mistress Savoldyn's right.

"If you must wait while Hilo finds Lady Hobon's package, then you might as well rest yourself here," Mistress Savoldyn said. "I know you agents of the sect are run off your feet during this festival season."

Ibram settled himself into his chair, and left his hands in his lap. "I —yes, Mistress," he said. "We often are, thank you."

He looked out over the table. It had been set with white clay trenchers instead of wood. The salad tray he had seen the boy, Tawrit, carry out of the kitchen lay next to the jug of wine, with a serving spoon stuck out to one side. The slivered treeka nuts and parsel greens had been divided amongst the two women. Ibram could smell sawge, garlic, and chybollus in the air as well as mint and purslary. A loaf of bread lay broken on a platter with a trail of crumbs across the table.

The wine jug lay closest to Mistress Savoldyn, though both ladies had goblets. This close, he could tell by the redness of Mistress Savoldyn's lips that she had already indulged herself in a cup. If she was faking her grief, then it was a well-made performance; Ibram hated to unravel it. She had a smaller life ahead of her, no doubt, but Ibram could not say if that was an unhappy thought. The fight he had interrupted was of long standing, after all. Maybe an end to that fruitless aggression was enough of a reward.

She smiled at him, and gestured to the wine jug. "Would you like a cup?" she asked. "I—Dolman can send for another glass."

Ibram shook his head. "No, I thank you, Mistress," he said. "I'm not so thirsty."

She nodded and raised her heavy goblet to her lips. The wine sloshed in the blue glass. They made glass like that only in the southern cities, near the capital city; they were expensive to import. Mistress Dolman had its twin in front of her, though the wine in her goblet was much higher than Mistress Savoldyn's. So either they had been purchased in happier times, or Master Savoldyn's fortunes were still strong, despite the claims of his ledgers.

"I'd ordered the meal before—" Mistress Savoldyn cleared her throat. "—I mean, we always celebrate the closing of a contract such as Lady Hobon's. It's all of Einar's favorites, except for this." She gestured to the wine jug and then set down her goblet. "I suppose it's good that we hadn't decanted the tolnic before dinner."

Ibram smiled encouragingly. "Tolnic for every meal?" he asked. "Master Savoldyn was a man of indulgences, I suppose. My own mother keeps our supply under lock and key."

A smile attempted to climb her mouth, and then stalled at the bow of Mistress Savoldyn's upper lip. She shook her head. "He wasn't really," she said. "The ruckus he might raise over the smallest thing! I remember—don't you, Dolman—when we tried to stock the larder before the Feast of the Sundered Legion, and he quibbled over the price of salt? Salt of all things, as if I had placed an order for ice in summer!"

She sat back in her chair and shook her head. She reached up and rubbed the wheel pendant around her neck; her wide eyes drifted into the middle distance. Mistress Dolman pursed her lips and glared across the table at him

"Master Savoldyn was very set in his habits," she said. "A sudden upset tended to throw him greatly off his mark."

Ibram nodded. "Oh indeed," he said. "I can see how that might be. I have an uncle—"

"Yes, Viran," Mistress Savoldyn said suddenly, and then colored. She sipped her wine. "Master Kalmar, I mean to say."

Ibram blinked. "Yes," he said.

"He's been such a—a good customer," Mistress Savoldyn said. "Always prompt and—and there's something very soothing about a man who knows just what to say, isn't there? As a customer, I mean, your uncle has been very good to us."

A sudden image of Amota Viran sitting at this very table, halfway between Master and Mistress Savoldyn flitted into Ibram's mind. Viran was used to mediating disputes, and Mistress Savoldyn had shown herself quick to diffuse the situation between Einar and his daughter when given the chance. Perhaps their first conversation had been exchanging tips of conflict resolution. He glanced at her red-rimmed eyes and then her blushing cheek, and felt the corners of his mouth turn downward in thought.

"Master Kalmar is a very good man," he offered. "I am glad to pass such compliments onto him."

"Oh!" Mistress Savoldyn picked up her goblet and then set it down again. "No, there's no need to do that."

"Master Savoldyn often commented that Master Kalmar was wasted on the living mountain," Mistress Dolman said, with a quick glance in her mistress' direction. "He believed everyone with half a brain should be in trade."

"Sharp partners make good business," Mistress Savoldyn said, with the air of someone quoting a phrase she'd heard too often. "My own father said the same. He's in the transport trade, you know, it's how we were introduced."

"Really?" Ibram asked.

She nodded. "I think they're both wrong. It's all down to manners. How you treat people. I like—you Merrilians have the right of it, I think. Master Kalmar never says a cross word, but he still finds success."

Amota Viran had once personally dangled a petty bauble seller off a roof by his ankles for trying to sell him glass disguised as carnelian, but Ibram nodded anyway.

"You're too right, Mistress," he said. "He's a very calm sort of man. Soothing."

Mistress Savoldyn drank her wine. "We could have used more like him around here."

"Was Master Savoldyn often in a mood, then?" he asked.

She scoffed. "Often," she repeated into her glass. "And at everyone's expense, but his own."

Dolman leaned over the table. "Mistress," she muttered.

She set down her wine goblet and shook her head. "He was quick to think himself ill-used," she declared. "And I won't pretend otherwise, for sometimes he was ill-used, and by his own family! It made him suspicious, and—and cross. And now it's killed him."

She looked at Ibram and set her hands on the table. "That's what's happened, isn't it?" she asked him. "He lit candles for the Navigator before every journey. He had rose cake baked and laid at the Ark's altar on every feast day, and none of it mattered in the end. He turned his back on family and lost his way, regardless."

Ibram sat back in his chair. "Do you think so?" he asked.

She sniffed, and ran her thumb beneath her watery eyes. "It's what I worry about," she said. "There were too many arguments. He could never lay the past to rest."

Mistress Savoldyn stared at nothing for a long moment, or perhaps she had cast her mind back to a memory she now saw with new eyes. Ibram took the opportunity of looking at the fine plate and serviceware on the table. It was very well made; he was certain if he lifted up the platter, he'd see the makers mark of the silversmiths in Rutlilat, towards the eastern hills. There was an iridescence to the embossing that spoke of high quality metal and equally fine alchemical unguents applied to it. The salt cellar in the shape of a large mollusk with its little silver spoon was grand, but worn with time. Still, if that went missing while he was in the house, Dolman would have the warders on him before they searched the maid's pockets.

"Ours wasn't your usual marriage, Master Ucalegon," Mistress Savoldyn said so abruptly that Ibram jumped.

"Mistress," Dolman said again, with a furtive glare in Ibram's direction.

"No, the whole village knows it's true," Mistress Savoldyn said. She breathed in shakily. "Einar married me in anger, and I married him in— well, to better my lot in life, and neither of us bothered to ask if good travel companions made good spouses. You thought him rude, didn't you, Master Ucalegon?"

"I had that strong impression, yes."

"Well, he was," she declared. "But I was his wife, and I plan to keep up my end of the bargain. I'll see it through until the keys are handed over." A crooked, sad example of a smile bent her lips. "I like to think he wouldn't know how to feel about that. His little girl come into her own at last, even if it's only until her own daughter grows of age. He'd be terribly upset, of course, but you know...it does wipe the slate clean."

A man cleared his throat by the other side of the room. Ibram whipped his head around, and saw Liepa perched on the threshold with a large platter held before her. Over her shoulder, Hilo Kenes loomed. Mistress Savoldyn sighed.

"Here we are," Liepa said, and jiggled the fish platter.

"That is not how you announce the—oh never mind," Mistress Dolman snapped. She stood away from the table and gestured sharply. "Put the fish there, girl, quickly."

Liepa bobbed automatically, and stepped inside the dining room. She laid down the platter, and then stood back from the table. Mistress Dolman shook her head.

Ibram stood as well. Ahksell was probably pacing in the alley by now; it wouldn't do to keep him waiting out there any longer than he already had. He bowed to Mistress Savoldyn.

"I'll take my leave now, Mistress," he said. "If you don't mind. Should I pass on any message to my uncle? On behalf of you and your husband, of course."

Mistress Savoldyn stared up at him for a telling second, and then breathed in sharply. "Tell him," she stopped and then started again. "Please let Master Kalmar know how sorry we are that a package was lost on its way up to the tower, and that we—I hope he will not look upon us too harshly. It has been a trying day."

"Of course," Ibram said. "We all understand what that is like."

She smiled tightly, and then looked down at her lap. Ibram left her to her thoughts, and nodded to Liepa as he passed her on to the way out of the door. She dimpled at him. Mistress Dolman met him at the threshold.

"Why do you ask us such questions?" she asked quietly. "Has there been a charge leveled?"

"Nothing so dire," Ibram said and made himself grin. "I'm only performing my duties, same as any."

Mistress Dolman sniffed. "I don't know about that," she said.

"Then let us say, that I do for Lady Azadiya what you do for your mistress, after all."

It wasn't the politic most choice of words, but this house nagged at Ibram. The horrid master, the overwrought mistress, the housekeeper who alternately scolded and coddled, even Hilo Kenes had his irregularities. She should feel lucky he wasn't simply calling her a murderer to her face. Amota Viran couldn't despair at his diplomacy if he were speaking to criminals, after all. Dolman shook her head; her hair gleamed, tightly bound around her head. Ibram could see the tense line of her mouth falter.

"Do you," she said with a crack in her stinging voice.

"Indeed, Mistress Dolman," he said. "You might think of me as her courser."

He saw her visibly bite back whatever she had been about to say. Dolman breathed in deeply through her nose. She jerked her head to the left, and gave a quick nod.

"Hilo has returned with your package," she said. "How delightful that you knew just where to look. Good day, Master Ucalegon."

Ibram held out his hand without looking away, and clenched his hand around the bundle of cloth which Hilo had passed to him. He nodded to Mistress Dolman, and bowed shortly to Mistress Savoldyn.

No need to refuse an opportunity for a graceful exit, after all. He had an Attendant waiting for him in the alley way.

⚜

They didn't pause to discuss the situation; the day was getting on and they needed to reach Lady Azadiya before the body went to the Navigator's Ark. Once off the relay system, they made for the Preceptory of Yseult in all due haste. The circle of tents and canopies was unchanged as they walked down the mountain path towards the Fourth Mentor's tower. The mood had that quality of a fair which had gone on too long, half-expectant and half-anxious. A squad of sect agents corralled a pack of Learners, running after them with hoots and hollers and plucking the more advanced out of the air before the students flipped too far into the underbrush. The children's shrieks made Ibram's head throb.

"Just let me do the talking," Ibram said.

Ahksell startled. "What? What do you mean?"

"Let me speak with Amota Viran," Ibram said. There was not so much traffic about now, and they were quickly approaching the command tent. "That way we can say what I found curious in the ledgers, and you can merely be there as an interested party."

Ahksell looked at him askance. "And why should I want to do that?"

"Because you're supposed to be up a tree in Afsoun, pretending to be lost in a forest with nothing to signal your rescuers but that little light of yours."

"Don't be ridiculous," Ahksell said, lowering his voice and ducking his head.

"Don't be so quick to get out of your examination!" Ibram gestured out at all the rest of his amitai and the alchemists bustling about. "They'll think you don't take your work seriously."

Ahksell rolled his eyes. "Many folk don't participate in the exams."

"How many sign up and then fall away to sneak into a dead man's rooms?"

"We might not have to mention that," Ahksell said, and wrinkled his nose.

He kept walking, leaving Ibram to gape at the air for the sheer *gall* of the man. Ibram raised his hand and stabbed the air in front of him, and then ran to catch up with Ahksell before he ducked away into the crowd.

"For the official record, Attendant Solari," he said as he ducked around Amota Berac, and twisted through a crowd of exhausted, but jubilant Attendants. "Far be it from me, a humble agent of the sect," Ahksell snorted; Ibram ignored him, "to ever open my mouth before I am bid by my—"

"Oh, Ibram, you know I appreciate your advice," Ahksell said, and sighed. "But I think this murder more serious, don't you?"

"Of course, I do," Ibram said. "But you are supposed to attend to your studies, not my troubles."

"Even when you ask me along?"

Ibram looked to the sky. "I don't know what you're talking about," he said stiffly.

Ahksell laughed. They walked towards the biggest tent, where Amota Viran was no doubt back at his work. Amita Sarrha was on her chair near the fire again, watching them as they passed. Ibram grunted, finally, and Ahksell shook his head.

"So it is serious," Ibram said. "It's sect business, to be sure. That makes it mine."

"We can't just say that you went there alone," Ahksell said. "The servants saw me."

"You are too interested in other folk, that's your trouble," Ibram said.

"And you aren't?"

"I have a professional interest, thank you."

Ahksell shrugged. "I am still involved. At the very least, I am a party to theft."

"Would you keep quiet?" Ibram asked. "People will get the wrong idea of me."

Ahksell snorted. "Are you even going to tell me what you found?"

Ibram shrugged. The folk around the tents were mostly going

about their own business, but it suddenly dawned upon him that an open work area was perhaps not the best place for this conversation. The command tent loomed before them, its poles shivering in the wind.

"All I ask is that you follow my lead," Ibram said as he rubbed the back of his neck, and pulled lightly at his hair. He ducked his head as he entered Amota Viran's tent behind Ahksell. Amota Viran was indeed back at the head of the table, a plate of bread crusts and the remains of a wedge of cheese at his elbow. He was drinking out of a wooden goblet and reading from a ledger. He looked up as Ahksell's cough, and his eyes widened.

"Attendant Solari," he said in surprise, and stood up. He bowed from the waist, with his hands on his stomach, and came back up with a slight frown on his face. "I understood that you were still up at the Preceptory of Afsoun. Has something happened to delay your examination?"

"Oh no," Ahksell said. "Not at all, I'm not even up in the rolls yet. I've got at least another day, I should think."

"Really?" Amota Viran arranged his face in polite disagreement. "I recall the Fourth Mentor drawing up the lists to send to her Afsoun counterpart distinctly. Did Ibram send for you?"

"No, of course not," Ahksell replied.

"You know Mentor Tikari," Ibram interjected at the same time. "She has this way of creating chaos from order."

"You cannot draw the Attendant away from his work on a whim." Amota Viran pinched the bridge of his nose. "And don't speak ill of a mentor, Ib-la."

"I merely report from observation," Ibram said. "Anyway, I need— we need—to speak with you on a matter of greater importance."

Amota Viran dropped his hand and returned to his seat, weighted down by the heaviest sigh Ibram had ever heard, and Ibram had been sighed at by Amota Viran an awful lot. He leaned back against the high wooden back, and pursed his lips. Ibram opened his mouth again, and he held up his hand for silence.

"You should know," Amota Viran said. "That Attendant Abele has finished her examination of the shay you brought in."

Ibram blinked. "Oh," he said. "That was fast. What was in it?"

"Shay," he said. "A little goat's milk and some honey that she found interesting, apparently, for personal reasons, but nothing poisonous." Amota Viran's face stiffened into sharper lines. "So I will not be allowing you back down the mountain to bother the Savoldyn household again. Mistress Savoldyn is no doubt deep into her mourning, and doesn't need the additional stress of your presence at her table, I'm certain."

Shock rippled through Ibram like someone had tossed a rock in the pool of his stomach. He shook his head. "That's impossible! The man reeked of—"

"And it is quite possible that those very same excessive habits of Master Savoldyn's are the reason behind his demise," Amota Viran said. "Now, I'll hear no more of this, Ib-la. You have made your claim and been refuted. The spoken charge is appeased." He eyed the ledger in front of him. "I'm merely happy you didn't kick over a wasp's nest in the process."

"That's not entirely true, Master Kalmar," Ahksell said, and moved behind and around Ibram to approach the head of the table. He patted Ibram's back as he passed.

"I understand you two are friends," Amota Viran said. He sounded as disappointed as when he'd found them both as boys, up a tree tossing clingstones down to Katka in Ladyship's garden. "but I cannot condone your involvement in this matter, Attendant Solari. You will not progress unless you attend to your studies, and while Mentor Hobon is indisposed it falls to me to ensure the proper functioning of her tower, and all who dwell therein."

"I thank you for your concern," Ahksell said. He glanced behind himself at Ibram and twisted back again. "I have always been grateful for the care shown me at the tower, but that's not what I mean."

"We came to ask you if you knew that Master Savoldyn had been paying out for shorter and shorter trips."

Amota Viran settled back against his chair with a sigh. "Such is the life of a merchant, I would think," he said. "One must adapt to the needs of trade."

"But his notes—which have become worse over time, just so you understand—show that Lady Azadiya's order was the longest caravan or water traffic he provisioned," Ibram said. "His business was shrinking."

"So I have heard," Amota Viran said. "But how did you?"

"The information is available in Master Savoldyn's office," Ahksell said.

Amota Viran's attention shifted to him; his eyes narrowed. "How did you get in there?" he asked. "They would have tied the rushes to their front gate by now."

"Oh, I have my ways," Ibram said.

Amota Viran's face turned ashen. "You didn't break in, did you?" he demanded. "Ibram, you cannot violate the sanctity of a mourning house!"

Ibram scoffed. "You can if there's been a crime."

Amota Viran pounded his fist on his armrest for emphasis. "There has been no crime!"

"I went along with Ibram," Ahksell cut over him loudly. "Because I came down to learn more of Mentor's welfare, and insisted on tagging along. Once we went inside, I tested the office for any kind of disturbance in the fields of affinity."

"And did you find any?" Amota Viran asked.

Ahksell shook his head. "Nothing unnaturally so."

"Death is very natural," Ibram allowed.

Amota Viran sat back in his chair. He stared at them both.

Ibram cleared his throat and stood straight. "I request permission to speak with Ladyship," he said. "I feel a further inquiry is needed."

Amota Viran's head snapped towards him so hard, Ibram feared he'd cracked something. "Go to Lady Azadiya?" he exclaimed. "Out of the question!"

Ahksell's mouth dropped open, and though it was unattractive, Ibram feared his expression was no better. A knot twisted into life in Ibram's gut; he had a horrid suspicion of what Amota Viran was about to say. He certainly knew they weren't going to be pleased by it.

"Surely, the best thing is for Mentor to be informed," Ahksell said.

"Though she will be sad to hear of his passing, Ladyship has no need to hear you speak of Savoldyn's money troubles. She is in no condition to do anything about this," Amota Viran said. "The healers sent for the doctors, and the doctors have sent for that fool—" He took in a deep breath and then stood to breathe out. He put his hands on his broad leather belt. "As the fault belonged to Attendant Zorion, so too has he been given the task of remedy. Your Mentor requires a filtering mask, and he has been removed from the examinations so that he might prepare it. Until then, when she is able to leave the tower and return to her duties, there is no need so great that we need to call for her involvement."

"She won't like that," Ibram said, testing a theory. "Ladyship hates it when the other mentors interfere in her work."

"Third Mentor Nieminen is in charge of this division until such time as Ladyship is well again."

"Mentor Nieminen doesn't stop to smell a rose unless it's from a noble greenhouse!" Ibram exclaimed.

"Do not speak of a mentor in that tone of voice!" Amota Viran barked. He jabbed his finger at Ibram's face. "Because of her festival duties, she has left me in charge in her stead. I will send word to the Third Mentor, and when she sends for Attendant Solari, he will explain himself to her."

"Yes, Master Kalmar," Ahksell said, subdued.

Amota Viran tucked his hands behind his back and inspected them both with his dark gimlet eyes. Ibram tensed his jaw and stared back. This was ridiculous. Ladyship was just in her tower. Ibram could simply shout at her through that window she'd broken.

"And no attempting to contact Lady Azadiya without my express permission," Amota Viran said, pointing at Ibram. "I know you young folk believe her invincible. So did I at your age, to be sure, but she is ill. I will not have her disturbed. In point of fact, I don't want a word of this spoken—to anyone—until we have informed the Third Mentor. The festival is only beginning for some of the folk around here—and the merchants in the villages below don't need their own trade interrupted by a sad, but easily understandable state of affairs."

Ibram ground his teeth, but nodded. He carefully pressed his arm against the scroll tucked against his side. The Festival of Sangrin and its parties were the furthest from his mind that they'd ever been. Who cared if a few evening courtyards were deprived of their nightly income?

"Your word, Ibram." Amota Viran's eyes bored into him. "Out loud."

Ibram cleared his throat. He worked his jaw to loosen it. "Consider it given," he said.

Amota Viran relaxed back onto his heels, and nodded. "All right," he said. "Then we shall put this behind us. Thank you for bringing the matter to my attention, Attendant Solari. I am sure Mentor Nieminen will send for you up at the Preceptory of Afsoun when she has been apprised of the situation."

"Indeed, Master Kalmar," Ahksell said. He stepped back. "I think I shall get something to eat now. Ibram?"

"Ibram will need to return to his duties for the remainder of the festival," Amota Viran said. "The younger Learners have need of him by the whispering pool."

"Oh, but we've hardly eaten all day," Ahksell protested. "Surely a meal wouldn't hurt? Before I return, I mean? They never care about food up there; I can't get a bite to eat that isn't day old bread and last night's sausage."

Amota Viran laughed, something a touch relieved in his face now that no one had apparently been murdered, and Ahksell accepted his upcoming reprimand. Ibram ground his teeth. His stomach took the opportunity to rumble at that moment, as luck would have it. He hadn't had anything since breakfast, after all. He pressed his mouth together in case his voice reminded Amota Viran he was displeased with him.

"I'm sure we can find something for you," Amota Viran said. "We can't have you fainting at your examination after all. Ibram, the kitchens set up trestle tables by the withy trees to the south. Why don't you escort Attendant Solari to the midday meal? There should be more than enough left."

He bowed at Ahksell and then sat back down at his table, and picked up a travel writing set. He opened the inkpot and began dripping water onto the small cake of ink inside. Ibram raised his eyebrows, and met Ahksell's eyes. He jerked his head towards the tent opening. That was certainly them, dismissed.

They made their way outside, and Ahksell immediately opened his mouth. Ibram shook his head, took him by the elbow, and led him down the right side of the tent. A series of temporary lanes had developed, which meant that the view from the road was blocked, but there were folk walking all through the area no matter where Ibram looked. He paused behind one of the smaller canvas bell tents and reached beneath his gambeson. Someone in a nearby alley whistled, and Ibram shot them the filip without looking. Ahksell immediately peered up to the sky. Ibram rolled his eyes, and pulled out the wooden slat scroll.

"Food and then explanations," he said, holding it between them.

"Agreed," Ahksell said.

Ibram paused to adjust his clothes, and Ahksell snatched the scroll from his hand as he marched off, leaving Ibram to catch up. Quickly enough, their noses led them to the smells of roasted onions and baking bread. They passed an open tent where six servants were slopping enormous stacks of wooden trenchers into soapy water, and emerged in the midst of a feast.

The cooks who worked at Lady Azadiya's tower didn't really have a kitchen space, since most of the rooms had been given over to work, storage, and living quarters. They were more properly housed in separate outbuildings nearest the kitchen gardens, but clearly they had taken everyone else's decampment as an opportunity to expand their own operations. Open air canopies had been erected over a series of preparation stations, while several apprentices stoked a pair of large cooking fires, and another tended an absolutely staggering example of a pot-bellied chimney stove with a griddle on the top the size of a grown man's shield. It was entirely possible the cooks had decided to view this as an examination period for their own apprentices, as well as those they served.

Ibram loosened the knotted button that held the neck of his striped gambeson closed. Across from him, an entire contingent of Attendants out of the Preceptory of Mariae plowed through a tray of shay and stuffed buns. The heat in the outdoor dining hall was palpable, made worse with all the folk crowding the tables, and that was before Ibram spotted an entire mouflon roasting on a spit, being basted with the wine marinade in the pan below collecting its melting fat.

"You could smell those chilis in Delbrite," Ahksell said, and sneezed. He tucked the scroll under his arm.

Ibram cleared his throat; the smoke was getting a bit thick. "It's not so bad," he said.

"It's like your courtyard when Kholdo makes that red sauce you pretend is edible."

"Asajika," Ibram reminded him absently. He spotted a line of Learners being herded down once side of a trestle table by Amita Sarrha. "Come on."

"They should hand out masks when they do that," Ahksell said as they joined the line behind a small girl.

"Hand out masks for what, Solari?" Amita Sarrha asked.

Ahksell's spine stiffened so quickly Ibram thought he heard the vertebrae snap. He ducked his head and smiled down at his hands while he picked up a wooden trencher from the stack and handed one to Ahksell without looking. Ahksell grabbed it from him.

"Just the smoke, Mistress Pariamua," Ahksell said, and cleared his throat. "It sticks in the lungs, you know. Not healthy."

"Nonsense," Amita Sarrha said briskly. "A bit of smoke never hurt anyone. Don't the seers use it all the time? Never saw one of them dead past one hundred."

Ibram opened his mouth, and then paused. He wasn't absolutely certain that made sense. He shook his head and let the line carry him forward; he'd had enough of his amitai for one day's work. Unfortunately, Amita Sarrha kept pace.

"I see you've switched Attendants again, Ib-la," she said. "Aren't you supposed to be doing your Mentor proud at a higher elevation, Solari? I've got a bet on that flashing light of yours."

"I was," Ahksell said, and cleared his throat. "I have to go back."

"Ah," she said, and Ibram saw her nodding in that way of hers, that said she already had her opinion and if the Attendant wasn't careful, she would soon give it.

"It's a fine light," Ibram interrupted, as he glanced back at Ahksell and then Amita Sarrha. "It's an aid to rescue. A traveler would be wise to have one."

"Do they work for any old traveler, then, to be sure?" she asked. "I thought they were only for alchemical use."

"No, I've gotten mine to hold a charge," Ahksell said, and sounded more sure of himself. "The button shield has enough for a limited interaction with the external world. Then it needs to be refreshed."

"Hopefully after its bearer has been found alive," Amita Sarrha said.

"May the Runner's hounds be swift," Ahksell said.

"Wonderful!" Ibram exclaimed. "They've made ancasis, even Ahksell can eat that."

He leaned over and admired the tower of herb-stuffed flatbreads, so thin that he could see the glistening greenery bundled within the fried dough. Ancasis were old garden provinces fare, market day treats rolled into huge fat columns, and then whacked into portions with cleavers. Ibram twisted around and grabbed Ahksell's trencher. He held them both out before him, and the server laughed. She placed a heavy parcel onto both trenchers and then waved him off down the line.

"They've set you on the Learners, then?" Ibram asked. He glared down at the open sauce pots. "Examinations make for hungry alchemists, don't they? We won't keep you. Ahksell, come along, you've got the arm's reach here…"

Ahksell obligingly leaned forward and puddled sauce on both trenchers, goat's yogurt with dilli for himself and soured chilis for Ibram. They moved on to the platter of cheese.

"There's been a confusion of schedules since Ladyship has been indisposed," Amita Sarrha said. "And where have you been? I could have sworn to my own small gods that you were due to be patrolling the equipment shed with Tomika."

Ibram winced. His face was pitiful enough the next server added an extra inch to his hunk of cheese. Ahksell flexed his right hand in a drawing gesture; four glass apples lifted from their bowl and found a home in the crook of his elbow.

"I've been on a special assignment," Ibram said. "Ask Amota Viran about it."

"Oh, I've no need," she said. "Viran works in a tent now. All one has to do is linger by the side of the fabric."

Ibram paused; Ahksell stepped on the back of his boot. They wavered in line for a moment. Ibram glanced upward diagonally, and Ahksell shrugged with his eyebrows. Ibram frowned. She hadn't said she had heard anything, merely that it was possible. And wouldn't Amota Viran know that? He was a cautious sort of man.

"To be sure," Ibram said finally, and stepped away from the table. There was a cauldron of fish soup and another of quash ahead of them, and more than enough bread, but his stomach hadn't the mettle for more food just then. Let the children ahead of him have it all.

He ducked out of line and twisted to face Amita Sarrha. She crossed her arms and fingered one of the ribbons tying her sleeves back at the elbow. She cocked her head at him; he smiled.

"Your Learners are running for the jam instead of the carrots," he said. "Best catch them."

She frowned and glanced over her shoulder, and then rolled her eyes. "That they are," she said and clapped Ibram on the shoulder hard as she walked past. "I still want a word with you," she muttered.

Ibram breathed in and cleared his throat on the exhale. Ahksell took back his own trencher, and together they walked to an open spot by on the trestle tables the furthest from the roasting mouflon. Ibram sat down facing into the dining canopy and Ahksell took the opposite side. The scroll landed on the table, and the glass apples thudded between them. He plucked a fork from a bowl on the table and drew his eating knife.

Ibram grabbed the pitcher, found it pleasingly heavy, and sniffed at its mouth. "Water," he said. "Share?"

"Well enough," Ahksell said, and stabbed his flatbread. It crackled beneath his knife as he sliced off a mouthful.

Ibram raised his eyebrows. "No need to be so brutal," he said. "It's not going to fight you."

Ahksell savaged his pile of yogurt and dilli with a vicious swipe of his ancasis. "I did nothing wrong," he said. "And neither did you!"

"And neither did I," Ibram agreed. He looked about himself. It was mostly the Learners eating now, with a smattering of agents and a few attendants at the back. He cut a strip off his own meal with his eating knife. The herbs were laced in oil and vinegar, fresh and peppery beneath the tender flatbread. He chewed carefully, and then lowered his head.

"It's not poison," he grumbled. "If it's not poison, then what is it? I'm sure the man didn't die naturally. Not smelling as he did."

"I believe you," Ahksell said. He looked around them in a manner Ibram was sure Ahksell believed to be subtle. "But there was nothing in the shay."

Ibram sighed, and poked his knife into his cheese. "There was nothing in the shay."

"So what is this?" Ahksell asked, and used his chin to point at the scroll.

"A copy of Savoldyn's will." Ibram wiggled the knife until a small chunk of cheese parted from its wedge, and then cut that in half. His stomach grumbled. He prodded one piece across the trencher and then into the herbs within the flatbread.

Ahksell choked on his food, and coughed into his elbow. He shook his head, and stared over his arm at Ibram. *The will?* he mouthed.

Ibram nodded. "It might be a handy reference. Ladyship's always talking about those."

"In her library," Ahksell said hoarsely and coughed again.

Ibram set the water pitcher nearer to him. "It's only a temporary removal," he said. "I want to know the particulars—more than what Amota Viran told me, anyway."

Ahksell gulped his water and then groaned. "If it is not helpful," he said. "We are about to be in such trouble."

Ibram shook his head. "No, no," he said. "It's only me. You were never there."

"The kitchen staff know I was there, even if I did not stay to speak to Mistress Savoldyn," Ahksell said.

Ibram shrugged and ate more cheese. "It's like as not they forget all about it. This can't be the only copy of the will."

"Why not?"

"Wealthy people always have more of the same thing," Ibram said. "Ladyship does."

Ahksell opened his mouth, and then paused. "She does, doesn't she," he said in a wondering tone.

Ibram shrugged again.

"But is Savoldyn wealthy?" Ahksell asked. "The ledgers say no."

"They say perhaps," Ibram said. "He could still afford all the comforts of life, even if he had no use for them."

"Are you going to read it here?" Ahksell asked.

Ibram shook his head. "Later, we should find some place more out of the way."

They ate in silence for a moment, attending to their meals. Ibram let the din of the other eaters sink into the back of his brain. The situation was strange. Amota Viran was never the reckless kind, but he wasn't a man who shied away from trouble. Ibram's suspicious mind came mostly from Ama's tutelage, but a good third of the responsibility lay at Viran's feet as well. A bad feeling was rising from the outer banks of Ibram's mind, like a sordid mist. He didn't like it.

"Worst thought," Ahksell said, swallowing another bite.

"He died naturally and this is all a horrid coincidence," Ibram said immediately.

"He died unnaturally and someone in that house is plotting to do away with the widow, next."

"The widow murdered him and is even now running off to Delbrite with her husband's money chest in his best carriage."

Ahksell snorted. "That's not very likely."

Ibram waggled his head loosely on his neck and groaned. "Third Mentor Nieminen will want nothing to do with a merchant's house, even in such a case as this, and send it up to Second Mentor Stadat." He tore a bite free of his ancasis and wiped the oil from his mouth with the back of his hand. "And because he is in charge of the medicinal corps—who are all far too busy to care what happens here—he will dragoon Third Mentor Nieminen and yourself—and possibly me, if he remembers I was sent there or that I exist—into a conference and send the entire report to First Mentor E'garcid."

"And *she*," Ahksell sliced his ancasis into thirds and then fourths, "will call for Mentor Hobon, who by that time will be fully recovered, to deal with it all. And Master Kalmar will still insist the matter is beneath her notice."

Ibram tapped his finger and knife together as if the knife were a bell, just in case Yilka the Green's lucky third face chose to smile down on them. There were breaks in the clouds above, after all. He licked his fingers, and considered his trencher of food again.

"And by that time," he said. He ate some of his flatbread and spoke while he chewed. "The house will be out of mourning, Savoldyn's body burned, his soul remanded to the Crossroads, and whoever killed him unavailable for conversation."

"Cangsa," Ahksell said primly.

Ibram sputtered with laughter, and Ahksell's nose wrinkled in disgust.

"Cover your mouth at least," he said, and plucked up the water pitcher from the table.

"Your pardon, young lordship," Ibram said, covering his mouth with his palm. "I have never heard such words before."

Ahksell kicked him under the table; Ibram jumped in alarm. He tucked his feet under his seat for safekeeping. Ahksell drank directly from the pitcher.

"Have you picked up any other charming bits of Merrilian I should know about?" Ibram asked. "Who's been giving you lessons?"

"You say it enough that if I didn't know the meaning of that word, you'd accuse me of ignoring you," Ahksell said.

"Oh, well, forgive me," Ibram spread his hands. "I had no notion I was attended to so closely."

"It's in the title," Ahksell said. He set the pitcher down on the table.

Ibram groaned. Ahksell grinned at him, though it was a fleeting expression, there and then lost to the furrowing of his eyebrows. He put both elbows on the table and leaned in closely.

"What if you are wrong, though," he asked.

Ibram hunched his shoulders. "You just said you believed me."

"And I do!" Ahksell raised his right hand between them and held it flat. "But, I still think...what if you're wrong?"

Ibram scratched the back of his head and tugged on his hair. "To be sure."

"Well?"

Ibram sighed. "It's not enough to suspect," he said. "I know it, and so do you, but I cannot doubt what I saw in that office, nor what I examined in the body. Even if it turns out to be nothing, Ladyship would not stop investigating until she was satisfied, and—and nor will I."

Ahksell nodded slowly. "So we will continue to investigate. But what if you are wrong?"

"Then..." Ibram shrugged. "Then a man has not been murdered, and is that not wonderful?"

Ahksell snorted, and resumed eating his meal. He shook his head and grinned almost unwillingly. "Yes, quite wonderful."

"Besides, what else is there to do? Festival assignments are always dull. Not one Learner attends to reason until the Attendants themselves calm down, to be sure. And this festival? We are all of us unmoored." Ibram jerked his head in the direction of Ladyship's tower, and then bit into his sandwich.

"You were there, after she drank Hilbert's potion, weren't you?" Ahksell asked. He lowered his voice; the subject hung above the entire encampment like a dark cloud. "What happened?"

Ibram sucked herbs off his teeth, and drank from the water pitcher. He cleared his throat. Ahksell's mouth twisted. His big dark eyes widened.

"Stop, it wasn't so bad as that," Ibram said. He shrugged his shoulders; the space between them ached with tension. "We were on the training grounds. Ladyship thought Attendant Zorion's proposition had merit. He explained himself, she listened..." Ibram waved both hands in the air. "Amota Viran handed her the bubbling thing, which she drank in one swallow and then...it came on gradually."

He could see the moment still, as vivid in his memory as if it were still happening. The capped glass bottle full of viscous brown sludge, a rainbowed oil streak in its bubbling center. Amota Viran had held it in one hand by the long neck of the bottle as if it were too hot to handle for long. Lady Azadiya's hands had been sure and swift as she took it from him, and then the endless horrid shudder that had ripped through her body before she tossed the bottle away. Ibram shook his head; his neck crackled in strain.

Ahksell's face crumpled at the mouth. He had been so clearly marked for Yseult in his Learnership that Bedris had let him run wild in Ladyship's tower as long as she gave him permission. Amota Berac had marked his height on a linen closet until he'd outgrown it.

Ibram shrugged one shoulder and attended the remains of his meal. "It began as a headache," he said shortly. "And it quickly grew until—"

"They said she collapsed."

"She never!" Ibram looked up quickly. "She walked into the tower under her own power."

Staggering, but Ahksell never need know such things. She had been running, and Ibram had been the only one able to keep up. Until, of course, Lady Azadiya had breached the communal area by the central fountain, and in a voice like the crack of thunder, ordered her tower emptied. She'd jumped three stories upwards in the midst of the resultant chaos, and had already closed the door of her rooms by the time Ibram and the rest of the sorry bunch offered from Afsoun had stepped foot on the stairs.

"She was up and angry about it by the time Amota Viran sent me to the Savoldyns," Ibram said. "And if she were really so poorly off, then the medicinal corps would not have let her stay alone in the tower."

Ahksell breathed in and out deeply, a steadying breath just as they taught in the Bedris schools. He rolled his eating knife under his hand over the table, and then caught it up again. He bit his lips together, and then shook his head.

"What?" Ibram asked.

"I know Master Kalmar is right to be cautious with her health," Ahksell said slowly. "But I feel…I don't mean any offense by it, but—"

"Worst thought," Ibram said and did not wait for Ahksell to answer. "I think he is delaying on behalf of the new widow."

Ahksell's eyes widened. "Why do you suspect that?"

Ibram glanced about them. Most everyone around them were paying more close attention to their meals, or making sure none of the learners tossed food at their friends. Amita Sarrha was watching them from her spot by the clay oven, but she was too far away to hear.

"He was the one who sent me to gather Ladyship's order from the Savoldyns. He has been doing business with them for quite a while. And...he called Mistress Savoldyn a 'woman of sentiment'."

Ahksell raised his eyebrows. "A woman of sentiment?"

Ibram nodded.

"What does that mean?"

Ibram let his head wave left and then right. "I think he might..."

"No," Ahksell gasped. "Master *Kalmar?*"

"She's a lovely woman." Ibram leaned back and popped another sliver of cheese in his mouth. He glanced about them again. "I say we tell Ladyship what's going on," he said, quietly.

Ahksell glanced up from his own meal, and licked yogurt from a corner of his mouth. "You swore not to tell anyone!" he whispered.

"How can such an oath exclude my own employer?" Ibram asked. "Am I supposed to stand mute before Third Mentor Nieminen as well?"

"That's splitting hairs," Ahksell said.

"Besides that, you didn't swear to anything," Ibram pointed out and ate another mouthful. He scooped a greenish-red chili into his mouth and sucked in air after it. The burn cleared his senses like water to the face.

"I did—I think it was implied," Ahksell said. He swiped the water pitcher and drank from it. "How could we even get a message to her?"

Ibram took it out of his hand, and drank. He set the pitcher down between them.

"We can use the catapult in the kitchen gardens," he said.

"And Abele is just going to let us do this? Or whoever is on duty there now?" Ahksell cut off a piece of cheese and popped it in his mouth. "Neither of us have even fired a catapult before."

"It's just a slingshot you fire from the ground, how hard can that be?"

"What if we aim wrong, and strike the tower?"

Ibram chewed his ancasis for a moment, and carefully swallowed.

"Then she will have to come out to yell at us, and we can tell her afterwards."

Ahksell scoffed. "We'll be dragged off by Master Kalmar before we get a word out."

"Do you have a better idea?" Ibram asked. "Else we might as well get a bowl of quash after this, because we'll be sitting here all the day."

Ahksell shook his head. "No, you have to fish Learners out of the pond again."

Ibram rolled his eyes. "I'm not doing *that*." He sighed. "There's work to be done, I know it."

"Figuring out what sort of poison was used?"

Ibram nodded. "We have to get our hands on a Hessele's Cage. Then we can use it on the corpse—assuming it hasn't been claimed yet—and bring some actual evidence to bear."

"You mean, I can use it," Ahksell said.

Ibram spread his hands, and then licked oil off his fingers. "Can I help requiring the aid of my more knowledgeable friend?" he asked. "I'm but a poor arm-for-hire, attempting to fulfil my contractual obligations."

"You're nosy, that's what you are. You cannot stand to let an unfinished puzzle lie."

"Which is also in my contract."

Ahksell rolled his eyes. Ibram grinned.

"I can see about the equipment laboratory," Ahksell sighed. "They might have older ones for testing." He frowned and shook his head. "Not here, though. You recall the cave-in last seven-day? When Mentor Stadat's upper fifth session attempted to free climb upside down?"

"And brought down the entire ledge instead?" Ibram snorted. "It was all they spoke of at The Blinded Seer for a full two nights."

"I cannot believe you drink there," Ahksell said. "It's an evening courtyard."

"The draughtshops aren't on my way home, now are they?"

Ahksell shook his head, but continued, as if Ibram had not pulled him out of an evening courtyard a night or two as well. Usually it hadn't been Ahksell's idea to go, to be sure, but he had shown up. Ahksell poked the table in between their trenchers for emphasis.

"They'll have them in Afsoun," he said. "They're always overflowing with items and forgetting where they put them—"

"Until something degrades and then it blows up," Ibram interrupted.

Ahksell continued speaking over him. "And I'll lay three faunts on my examination panel having a Hessele's Cage they don't actually have a use for yet."

Ibram whistled. "Three whole faunts?" he asked. "Attendant Solari, you are far too free with your copper."

Ahksell ignored that, as was his due. The Runner took a dim view of gambling, and Ibram had never been able to cajole Ahksell higher than five faunts on a market race. "Look, even if—"

A large, meaty hand clamped down on Ibram's shoulder from behind. Ibram stiffened immediately. He cocked his head to the side and Amota Berac swung into view above him. He beamed down from behind his great black beard.

"Ib-la! There you are," he said. "Viran has asked me personally to walk patrol with you today."

Ibram's mouth dropped open. He straightened up slowly beneath Amota Berac's hand. "He did?" he managed. He looked to Ahksell; their glances caught and then slid away. "Why would he interrupt your busy schedule for such a small task as that?"

Amota Berac laughed. "Oh, not so little," he said. "Not when there's so much work to be done. Wouldn't you say, Attendant Solari?"

Ahksell coughed around a mouthful of food. He swallowed and wiped his mouth with the back of his hand. "I—I would, Master Comoros. Yes."

"Festival of Sangrin's a busy time for us all," Amota Berac continued cheerfully. He slapped Ibram on the back; Ibram caught himself against the table, wincing. "Now then, all done with your food, boys?"

Ibram met Ahksell's eyes. Ahksell shrugged, and Ibram couldn't help but agree. He could see Amita Sarrha watching them from over Ahksell's shoulder. "Yes, uncle," he muttered.

"Then will you join me?" Amota Berac asked.

Ahksell laid his hand on Savoldyn's will, and dragged it closer to his plate. It was a fair thought, no one would question an alchemist with a scroll under his arm. Ibram crammed the last of his ancasis into his mouth and spoke as he chewed, wiping oil from the corners of his mouth. "I will."

Ahksell wrinkled his nose. Ibram raised his hand to him as he stood away from the trestle table. Amota Berac waited patiently, like a stone in a high wall, by his side.

"We'll talk again," Ahksell said. "About the thing."

"So you will, young Solari," Amota Berac answered before Ibram could open his mouth. "Once Ibram's work is done. Now, good luck on your examinations."

He bowed with good grace, and then turned away, putting his hand on Ibram's back to guide him out of the makeshift dining hall. The sky above was turning heavy with dark grey clouds. Ibram wrapped his hand around the hilt of his sica, angling so that the blade stayed tucked against himself as they made their way through the incoming crowd. Patrolling would take up the rest of his day, no doubt on Amota Viran's orders. If he was summoned to the Third Mentor before he got a chance to examine the body, Ibram had the sinking thought that Master Savoldyn's body would be beyond his reach.

It was two full days of patrolling before Ibram managed to slip out from underneath Amota Berac's thumb. On the third, a Learner added too much resin of amber to their calming incense during a practical lesson and put the entire laboratory to sleep; the resulting disturbance sent Ibram racing up and down from the equipment buildings to Amota Viran's command tent, very obviously doing his part for Ladyship and sect. By the afternoon, Ibram was up and patrolling before he'd even had more than half an hour's chance to look for Ahksell amongst the returned Yseult Attendants. Some six or seven of them were milling about looking like ducks in search of a pond, but Amota Viran had sent him to the north training field instead. Three of the Govan Attendants had been found up the tallest tree in that corner, attempting to map the transmutation of red clouds to white clouds. Since that made less sense than usual, it had been decided that Third Mentor Nieminen's examinations timetable would have to be accelerated to provide the visiting Attendants with enough stress to focus their attention. It also meant Ibram had to guard the ladders.

Finally, at late midday, he was allowed his liberty for a meal. Four relays and a brisk walk later, he arrived at the Preceptory of Afsoun without any major mishap and discovered Ahksell amongst a group of picnickers outside the walls. He had his carry-all with him again, the leather strap slung diagonally off his left shoulder, and stood away from his friends as soon as Ibram had caught his eye. Folk abroad in the sect were buzzing, as they always were. Who was marking whose examination. Which Mentor found five Learners in the observation cave with a handful of Glow-In-The-Nights. Of course, no one discussed Lady Azadiya, nor her tragic affliction, but a great many conversations suddenly ceased once their participants recognized Ibram or Ahksell himself.

As the second most important preceptory, Afsoun had its reputation to maintain amongst the class of folk who relied on their business. The walk up to the outcropping that housed the main buildings was well maintained, better in fact, than the roads leading to Yseult with a profusion of carefully fanciful landscaping. They approached through a tangle of withy trees with their multitude of trunks arching over them in a canopy of spring greenery. Even Ahksell seemed a little put off by the display.

If anyone had ever bothered to ask Ibram what the distillation of a sect of alchemists would look like, he would have been able to supply them with all the necessary ingredients without once consulting a Bedris treatise. For all that the goal of any branch of alchemy was the refinement of reality towards its most perfect aspect, most of Vissilia would probably agree that, at heart, alchemists made things. Wonderous things, to be sure, but objects nonetheless.

As such, the Preceptory of Afsoun was a confection of a castle, spun from the beleaguered daydreams of its founder, constructed with every single architectural development borrowed from every corner of the empire. Its southern spires, painted in a deep vermillion, stretched far past a height which any respectable tower would tremble to grow, its northern-framed sharp-roofed outbuildings bore the patches and repair that spoke of decades of enthusiastic but absentminded experimentation, and the central western cupola that housed First Mentor Gaeild was the color of the sun itself. Ibram stood on the far side of the stone bridge which crossed its interior lake, and glared past its open gilded gates. The Attendants and Learners in their green wool gambesons looked like dolls in an enormous playhouse.

"They don't bite," Ahksell said, and clapped him on the back as he passed by.

Ibram cracked his neck to the side. He adjusted his leather belt wrapped around his blue gambeson and brushed his hand down his sect brooch, flicking lint off the seven poles in its torch. Then, he made sure his sica and belt pouches were in the correct position.

"Absurd creatures," he muttered.

He walked forward quickly to catch up. The sun was sinking lower behind the clouds, frosting the sky in pale silver. The walls surrounding the main buildings were awash in some kind of reflective scales which stung the eyes. He squinted.

He smacked Ahksell on the elbow and pointed to two Attendants in a tasseled dinghy, throwing laden sacks into the lake. "They have more money than Her Gracious Majesty, and they spend it on this."

Ahksell shushed him like a school teacher. "Don't say things like that! You know very well that could have a direct benefit for one of the others testing today."

Ibram rolled his eyes. "Attendant Lysisa still trying to breath underwater?"

Ahksell raised his chin and stared off into the central courtyard. "Perhaps."

They passed through the gates with nary a shiver of interest from the tiled wards on the floor. A squad of sect agents attached to Afsoun watched them from a trestle table stationed beneath an elaborate wooden awning. Ibram raised his hand in their direction, and the oldest one nodded her head back at him.

"And so where do we look?" Ibram asked, and tucked his hair behind his ears.

"Ah." Ahksell stopped, and looked hard to the east and then the west. He frowned. "Right, I think."

Obligingly, Ibram headed off to the right of the octagonal court-yard. A rumbling emanated from the First Mentor's manor, but no one else walking about seemed anxious. Ibram decided to ignore it. He frowned and glanced to his left.

"It's over here?" he asked. "Or are we sending a message to someone?"

The buildings ahead of them were decorated to within an inch of their lives with carved stone effigies and a mural of a winged messenger bird, only partially reconstructed. The Scribe's Bureau for Afsoun was larger than the one in Yseult, and boasted its own warder guard, lined up nicely on either side of the doors in their purple and black striped uniforms and decorative obsidian polearms. Ibram was most definitely sure neither of those two worthies kept a Hessele's Cage on their persons. In fact, he wouldn't lay fair odds on their ability to spell it.

"It's down that stairway," Ahksell said and pointed to the awning-covered break between the buildings.

Ibram groaned, but followed. The stairs had been carved directly from the mountain rock, at least, so they didn't squelch beneath his boots. A fine drizzle, not quite mist and not yet fog, coated his face and the backs of his hands.

"It's out of the common way," Ahksell said, "but I'm sure the other laboratories will be accounted for."

"So this one is beneath notice?" Ibram asked.

Ahksell laughed. "I wouldn't say that, more she doesn't wish to be bothered," he said. "Attendant Dakreia is—"

"The woman they assigned to tutor you?" Ibram interrupted. "Didn't you say she made you yearn for the days when Amita Sarrha dropped you down Frolik's Forest and left you overnight?"

Ahksell shuddered, but his voice remained cheerful. "She's a woman of intense standards."

Ibram shrugged. The air smelled of greenery, refreshing and just that side of sweet. Ahksell stepped down quickly, surefooted as ever, and Ibram made do in his wake. His stomach grumbled at him, protesting both the lack of a guard rail and the precipitous drop waiting for the unwary just beyond the low wall carved out at the height of his shins. Ibram kept his head angled to watch his boots. When he did look up he could see the next peak over for the love of the Speaker's voice. The crags and deep trench below were not beckoning in welcome.

"My folk came from the plains, you know," Ibram muttered. "None of this stairways nonsense, just a proper road."

They passed another tiny plateau, again with its own small cottages carved out of the sheer rock. This one had Snapping Euphorbia growing by the windows.

"Hmm?" Ahksell asked, over his shoulder.

Ibram pointed ahead of them. "Face front!" he demanded. "If you fall, I'll not go down after you."

"Oh, it's not so bad," Ahksell said and jumped down three steps entirely.

Ibram narrowed his eyes. "You've got your hands out," he said. "Levitating yourself is cheating."

"So says the little lordship," Ahksell turned on his heels and grinned. He stuck his right foot out behind him and bent his left leg as if preparing to jump. Ibram's mouth went tight and flat; his jaw clenched. He put his hands on his hips and then dropped them again.

"Don't you dare," Ibram said. "Who's going to let me into the equipment laboratory without you?"

He walked down to the step above, so that they were more or less at a height. Ibram grabbed Ahksell by the shoulders and turned him around; he gave a little push. Ahksell resisted for a moment, so firmly planted that he had to have been using whatever it was called in alchemy to affix himself to the world around him, and then began to move forward again. His bag slapped against his hip. Ibram rubbed the back of his neck.

"Did you read it?" he asked. "The will?"

Ahksell looked back over his shoulder, and patted his carry-all. "I did. I have it amongst my things."

Ibram rolled his head on his neck. "Do you plan to tell me what was in it?"

Ahksell shrugged. "Mostly it was as the gossips said at the time. Mistress Savoldyn takes with her everything she came into the marriage with, as well as a house in Itol—sounds nice enough, there's two wells—and the business goes to the daughter's child."

"Nothing about what happens if he died and the child was too young to take control?"

"I don't recall," Ahksell said. "How old is the child?"

"I don't know. Something to look into, I would think." Ibram shook his head. He'd look it over himself when they had a chance.

They passed a ledge occupied by a hut carved out of the rock, with empty gaping windows and a doorless opening facing out. All the preceptories had such places, either as areas to experiment or places for storing dangerous ingredients. This one had scorch marks on the rocks surrounding the building and oddly glimmering lichen. Ibram kept moving.

"What is it about you folk and stairs?" Ibram asked as they descended. "Is it a test of character?"

"Most of us know better than to fall," Ahksell said.

"And so the answer's yes, I'm thinking," Ibram said.

Ahksell laughed. "I suppose it's best we're here, then," he said, and stepped off the stairway to yet another road, this one of good beaten earth. The track led them to a small canyon wherein stood a short roundhouse encased overtop by a large natural cave, white smoke poured out from vents in the roundhouse's roof. There were no plants to be found amongst the rocks and gravel, nor anything like a bird or even an insect flying through the air. The acrid tang of the reagent the alchemists used in developing some of their more esoteric potables stung the back of Ibram's throat when he breathed.

He walked at Ahksell's elbow as they approached the leather curtain covering the space where the door should be, and knocked on the lintel. Ahksell's smile turned bemused. Ibram stood back and tucked his hands behind his back.

"Attendant Solari to see Attendant Dakreia," he called out. He heard metal clank from inside the building, and then thudding footsteps, heavy enough to make the ground shake.

"You don't have to do that here," Ahksell whispered.

"An impression made is never lost," Ibram whispered back.

No one would know it from him that agents for Yseult couldn't behave themselves in another preceptory. Unless it was for Ladyship's benefit, or down the living mountain, Ibram was under strict instructions not to be particularly noticed. His employment was, after all, a bit of a gray area in imperial law.

"Yes? Yes?" called a rather high voice from within the roundhouse.

The leather curtain was shoved aside, and a small, well-muscled woman with her hair wrapped in a protective cloth, and glowing baubles in her ears stood before them. Her high forehead was dotted in two lines of small gold tattoos at either temple, marking her as one of the fisherfolk from the Summer Sea. She wore a full leather apron, and beneath it a green dress drenched in sweat. She put her hands to her hips and frowned. Ahksell bowed shortly with his hands on his stomach, and so Ibram did the same.

"Up, up," the woman said in as thick a Southern burr as Ibram had ever heard. "I have little patience today, there is too much to do."

Ibram obeyed after making sure Ahksell rose before him. "Good day, Ladyship," he said. Always best to start off with a high title; it made little folk feel big and bigger folk believe their nobility simply exuded from them like perfume.

"Day?" she repeated. She blinked at him and then abruptly thrust her head out of the door, forcing Ibram to lurch out of her way. She peered up at the sky in severe distrust, and wiped sweat from her copper colored skin. "Suppose it to be, after all. And I am no lady, young master," she continued as she fell back into the roundhouse and wandered away from the door. The curtain fell.

Ibram thrust it back again, and stepped inside. The blast of heat from all sides was staggering; sweat immediately bloomed beneath his gambeson. The air smelled terrible, sour and smokey. His throat tightened, but Ibram refused to cough.

"Attendant Dakreia," Ahksell said behind him as he poked Ibram out of the way. "We wanted to know if you have a Hessele's Cage we might borrow?"

Attendant Dakreia lifted an awl and a large hammer from a tray of tools on her low work table, and began lightly smacking holes into a large square metal frame. Every time she made a hole, the frame sparked with a flare of red light. She didn't appear worried, and so neither was Ibram.

"Dowsing with that pendant's good enough for that gewgaw you made," she said without looking up from her work.

"I'm not—I don't need one for my locating beacon," Ahksell said. "I just—need one."

Ibram held his sleeve to his nose, and tried breathing through it. Dakreia finished one side of the metal frame, and unclamped the square to change angles. She began to punch holes in the next portion.

"What for then?" she asked over the racket.

Ahksell opened his mouth, and then closed it. He turned to Ibram.

Ah, yes. They'd forgotten that bit, the part where they asked for equipment without explaining its intended purpose. If they told her—and she even agreed rather than refusing simply because Amota Viran hadn't seen fit to give them one... Well, there was a thought and a half. Ibram ran through everything he was supposed to know of alchemy, which was not much, and all the bits he most definitely did not know, which was quite a bit. He dropped his sleeve from his nose, and shrugged.

"As you know, Attendant," Ibram began. He slid his right foot forward and came closer to her, and sadly, the smell. "Our own Fourth Mentor Hobon is indisposed with an affliction."

Dakreia grunted. "She's laid up because of that damn fool Zorion, you mean. What is it to you, though? You one of her rattling mob of operatives?"

Ahksell looked ready to protest, but Ibram had been called worse. "I am, to be sure," he said with as much cheer as anyone could muster while boiling alive. "Ready and able for all such tasks as is required."

"Never understood why we didn't just tag you all the same way we do ourselves," she said with a shake of her head to get a few stray wisps of hair out of her eyes. "Make it easier to see who is escorting and who is rambling where he ought not."

Ibram maintained his cheer. "Ah, but you know Attendant Solari," he said. "It's that fear of heights he has. I'm along to play guard rail."

"He's too tall to fear heights."

"He's a determined fellow."

"It's the insulating properties!" Ahksell blurted out.

Dakreia stopped her hammering and twisted in his direction. "The what?"

"I need a Hessele's Cage to insulate the examination table when I do a first run test of my locating beacon," he said. "The Helping Hand has been burning through the wood again."

She shook her head, and left her tools on the table to pick up a laden paper cone. She returned to the frame and held the cone's smallest end over the metal. "I told you the charge was too highly set."

Ahksell nodded. "You did."

"You'll never surpass your limitations if you keep ignoring the small details which create a complex whole," Attendant Dakreia said. She ripped the point of the cone open, and a fine trickle of sand flowed down as she maneuvered it around and around the punctures. She tossed the funnel to the ground and picked up a long lit taper. "The refinement of reality by necessity demands sacrifice. Don't breathe, duck."

He smelled something acrid. Ibram held his breath, hit the floor, and then covered his head with his hands. Ahksell slammed down after him, and Ibram twisted at the waist to make sure he had his hands up and over his neck. He didn't; Ibram knocked their elbows together, forcing Ahksell's left arm to slid down and cover his nape. The air above them burst into violet flames, translucent and smokeless. Ibram began to count backwards in his head from ten; his throat convulsed at three, trying for the merest hint of air. At one, the searing heat doused itself as quickly as it had ignited.

Ibram flopped onto his back, and shuddered. This was why he hated coming up to Afsoun. Yseult might be a preceptory of stubborn tarmaps without the sense to come out of the cold after a midnight soak, but Afsoun couldn't be trusted not to light a match in a flour mill. He grit his teeth, and kept Ahksell in the corner of his eye. Ahksell had his head pressed to the floor; the back of his gambeson was sizzling with small singed flames. Ibram slammed his bootheel against the wooden planks twice.

"Hmm? Oh, you can breathe again," Attendant Dakreia said in an absent-minded tone.

Ibram gasped and coughed. "Why, O' Great Masters, does everything you make smell like rotten swamp gas?"

He sat up and smacked Ahksell firmly on the back with the flat of his palm until all the tiny little fires were put out, and then rolled to his feet. And why wasn't he carrying those wonderfully handy little shield buttons the alchemists affixed to every itinerant Attendant they sent out around the province? Surely some clever bauble should be able to find its way into his pocket, possibly after falling from the pack of some merchant's mule.

Ahksell slowly moved his knees beneath him, and then pushed up from the ground with both hands. He stood, and struck dust from his gambeson and wrapped trousers. His chest heaved on an inhale. Ibram raised an eyebrow at him, but Ahksell waved him off.

"So, you see, Attendant," Ibram said, while Ahksell brushed cinders from his sleeves. "The Hessele's Cage is rather important for Attendant Solari's future development."

He dared to walk closer to her workstation. The frame was now imbedded with a fine, scrawling line of what looked to be brass all down the center of the metal, swooping elegantly around the punched out holes, which glittered as if they contained a clear gem. It looked rather like a filtering array, but of course Ibram would not officially know that unless he was told.

She looked up at him, and Ibram made himself look agreeable. He tilted his head. "Ladyship would have given him one, of course," he said. "But she is, as you say, indisposed."

"They're always drinking what they should not down there," she said. "And concerning themselves with what they should ignore."

"Not so, Attendant," Ibram said. "Attendant Solari—"

"Would be better served had he not switched places twice in his examinations," she finished for him. "He'll never gain a placement if he continues to disrespect his teachers."

Ibram frowned at him.

"Now, I never did so," Ahksell said, with a cough. "I am just as grateful for my lessons with you as I am for my place in Yseult. I simply need a little extra help this Festival of Sangrin."

Attendant Dakreia sighed, heavily. She turned around, dismissing Ibram from her side with a wave of her hand, and stumped towards her work table again. It was cluttered with all manner of tools and devices, a double basin bubbled in the center above a portable furnace. She hovered both hands over the table and wiggled her fingers. Something jingled on the table, but nothing arose.

Ibram looked at Ahksell from the corner of his eye. Ahksell shrugged. Attendant Dakreia dropped her right hand and held out her left. With a thundering frown, she crooked her first two fingers and thumb and drew them up in the air sharply. A bundle of wires wrapped up in red and yellow yarn flew into the air and smacked her palm. It dropped just as quickly, but she clutched a thin, waving tassel and caught it; the jangling mass swung in the air.

"This," she said, "is a crutch." She dropped the Hessele's Cage to the table and crossed her arms over her chest. "If your button shield cannot be used without it, then you will fail your examination and deserve to do so."

Ahksell cleared his throat. "I only need it as a diagnostic tool," he said. "If anything, the recent fuss has proven we need enhanced safety precautions during these examinations. I wasn't intending to—"

"No, these are excuses," she interrupted and turned back to her work. "Go and use your agent as a stand in. He'll be able to tell if it's too hot to use."

Ibram neither rolled his eyes, nor glared. He'd stood in for worse experiments down in Yseult. Instead, he bowed as politely as he was taught, and moved back to where Ahksell stood, quietly fuming. Ahksell's mouth pursed; he shook his head at Dakreia's back.

"It's no use," Ahksell said quietly, leaning down to Ibram's ear. "She's always so stubborn."

Ibram shrugged. "Ah well," he said in a normal volume.

There really was nothing for it. Ladyship was very clear on what constituted a narrowing of options, and what she required of him in terms of forcible expansion. Finesse and creativity were called for. He turned around to consider Attendant Dakreia. Her back was to them both. She had her awl in hand again and appeared to be counting holes with it. He bowed with his hands on his stomach, and tilted his head to the left.

The leather curtain flew open, and Ibram froze. From the corner of his eye, he saw movement, a man in green and grey. An additional person did not mean matters had become complicated, necessarily. He still couldn't lift himself unless ordered to by his betters, after all.

"Hello Hilbert," Ahksell said in the most disapproving tone Ibram had ever heard directed at someone other than himself.

Ibram grinned in the direction of the floor.

"Hello Ahksell," Attendant Zorion said. "Have you been relegated to the furnace, too?"

"No, I have not," Ahksell said and Ibram heard him moving across the floor. "Nor have I been poisoning other people's mentors!"

"Oh, I didn't do that," Zorion protested. "Not really, anyway. And I'm doing my best to make up for it."

"How, exactly?" Ahksell said.

"He's grinding the ingredients for your mentor's filtering mask," Attendant Dakreia said. "At least he's precise in *that*."

"And you're making it?"

"I am," she said. "Who else has the fine control to make something as delicate as Sugwari's Distillate?"

"What kind of mask are you proposing?" Ahksell asked. "If it was simply a matter of covering her eyes, Mentor would have done so already."

"It's a recursive field," Zorion said.

"You have both lost the value of my time spent tutoring you by this gross inattention to your studies," Dakreia said. "If Ahksell fails as well, I wash my hands of you."

Ibram had no idea what that meant, but if it freed Lady Azadiya from her confinement, then he was all for the effort. He glanced up and around from his bowed position. They'd forgotten him. Dakreia was making Zorion recite every pigment he'd been grinding for the lenses they were about to fit together for Ahksell's benefit. Ahksell, for his part, was still explaining to Zorion—in between agreeing that smoked quartz was best for resetting and yes, the glass needed a base in iron—that he should have tested his potion on volunteers other than himself before handing it off in his trials. While he waited to be waved out of his bow, Ibram put out his left hand and plucked the Hessele's Cage off the work table.

He slid it up and under his padded gambeson, which naturally fell to his knees, and back beneath the belt of fabric that kept his tunic smooth; it really was having an unusual workout these days. The thing might stick out, but he could cover it if he didn't move his arm too broadly. He smoothed down his clothes with his palm, and coughed, discreetly.

"Oh," Ahksell said. "Uh, Ibram. Up you get!"

Ibram rose smoothly, and pulled down his sleeves. He let his arms fall naturally to his sides. The three alchemists looked at him in mild surprise; he smiled.

"Thank you, Attendant," he said.

He'd never been able to tell when Ahksell blushed, but he definitely knew when the man was embarrassed. Ahksell coughed and pulled on his left earlobe. Beside him, Attendant Zorion frowned.

"Why are you here?" Zorion asked. He held a small plump linen bag in his hands. "I thought there had been a murder?"

Attendant Dakreia flinched. *"A murder?"*

"Inquiries are proceeding," Ibram said. "It's more theft of assets, currently."

Zorion's eyes widened behind his glasses. "Someone stole the body?"

"No! No, nothing like that," Ibram said.

"Master Kalmar has it well in hand," Ahksell said quickly. "Are you making the lenses yourself, Attendant Dakreia?"

"I am," she said with a curt nod. "It requires a greater grasp of the distillate components than Zorion has evidenced."

"That's not fair," Zorion said. "I was up all night making that potion."

Knowing the younger Attendants, that meant he had been up at his work for a grand total of four hours and spent the rest in slumber underneath a table. Ibram rested his weight on his heels, and eyed the door. He couldn't leave unless dismissed, but he was certain he'd carry the stink of the fires in this laboratory for the rest of the day unless he got an airing soon. He needed to be down the living mountain and back at the Savoldyn's manor. He'd already offended their sensibilities once, no doubt they'd survive another outrage. He frowned.

"And look what comes of those who will not attend to their duties in a timely fashion?" she asked. "You fall behind and commit costly mistakes in a paltry attempt to make up for it. Now, give me that bundle, I'll need to examine it before we begin."

Zorion handed over a small bag, and then readjusted his glasses. Ahksell crossed his arms over his chest.

"It really should have been steeped and not boiled down," Ahksell said.

"This isn't even your area of artifice!" Zorion said. "You make..." he waved his hand up and down at Ahksell's front, which featured all the button shields a traveling alchemist usually wore on the imperial roads.

Ibram glanced towards the trio of fires burning along the wall, and the iron contraptions surrounding them. The air stifled him; he pulled on the front of his gambeson, and ran a finger along the inside of his collar.

"And yet Attendant Solari excels at his shield buttons," Ibram said, and smiled politely when Dakreia turned to him, incredulously. "He has so many talents at his disposal, after all. Indeed, the other agents and myself are in a continual state of awe at his prowess."

Ahksell's forehead wrinkled. "That's not exactly how Master Kalmar sees it, I think."

"Ah, but Amota Viran is a man of depths," Ibram said. "Very deep ones."

"Deep depths?" Zorion asked.

"Ah, he's your uncle is he?" Attendant Dakreia said with a look of sudden understanding. "This close to the border, I suppose it's unavoidable. You Westerners have such large families."

"We're a friendly lot, to be sure," Ibram said. "Now, with your permission Attendant Dakreia, I'll be taking Attendant Solari off to prepare himself mentally, as ordered. He's got the pride of Yseult at stake, after all."

She waved her free hand. "Yes, yes, take him away."

Ahksell took a step behind him. "Oh, but Attendant Dakreia, about that Hessele's Cage, I would—"

She jerked a red hot poker from out of the center fire, and clanged it down on a small anvil. With her left hand outstretched, she coaxed a hammer slowly through the air and into her grip. Zorion went to a sack of glittering rocks and began plucking small pieces out onto the work table.

"I'll not change my mind," she said. "If you were truly committed to your secondary concentration, you would have no need of such items."

Ibram stifled a groan, and went quickly to Ahksell's side. He poked him in the back; Ahksell jumped and twisted to glare at him. Ibram went to the doorway and held open the curtain.

"After you, Attendant Solari," he said with widened eyes.

Ahksell's mouth twisted into what Ibram generously refused to call a pout. He blew air out of his nose, and then nodded jerkily.

"Good day," he muttered as he exited the laboratory.

Ibram let the leather curtain drop with both of them in the somewhat clearer air. Ahksell was already on the stairs leading back up to the courtyard. Ibram looked up past the overhanging trees and leafy bushes heavy with dew from the chill mist. The alchemist who invented a personal relay system for these outbuildings would be taken up into the heavens, directly, by the Advisor herself. He let Ahksell stamp ahead of him, and then ran to catch up.

☙❧

"And I am not Attendant Dakreia's Learner, I am her junior pupil," Ahksell said for the third time as they breached the courtyard of Afsoun. "I belong to the Preceptory of Yseult."

Ibram nodded agreeably, as he had done since Ahksell had opened his mouth, halfway through their march up the mountain. Far from enjoying the fresh air, Ahksell had instead chosen to circulate his grievances instead.

"And I am most happy there!"

"And they are happy to have you," Ibram said, and kept his left hand curled at his side. The walk made the Hessele's Cage he'd borrowed jingle against his body. The noise might be noticed.

"The Festival of Sangrin isn't even important to Yseult," Ahksell grumbled. "It's a *Bedris* fancy."

Ibram made a noise of agreement and guided Ahksell down the alley by the Scribe's Bureau. He nodded politely to the dozing warders as they passed. Warders. They'd have to be informed as well, more was the pity. Lady Sebbina would no doubt insist once she was informed.

"Mentor's insistence on practical secondary specialties is just silly," Ahksell declared with a savage blow to the air with the flat of his hand.

He stopped in the middle of the cobblestone courtyard and scoffed audibly at the nearest delicate spire as it disappeared like foam into the air. "Study *here?* How?"

Several lounging Attendants began to take notice of them. Ibram cleared his throat and slid in front of Ahksell. He peered upwards.

"Now, you all have to learn them," Ibram said in a soothing tone. He waved Ahksell onwards with both hands. Ahksell rolled his eyes but continued onward. "And you yourself said you never have to stay."

"You know their dormitory is like a cell," Ahksell said. He allowed himself to be herded, as Ibram guided them to the front gate. Clearly, his time in the examinations coupled with his worry over Lady Azadiya had unseated his reason. "They carved their beds out of the very rock."

"And at home you chop down the trees for your bunks with your own two hands," Ibram said. "We all know."

"And as if I need a Hessele's Cage!" Ahksell continued. "I am the soul of care!"

He stopped immediately, forcing Ibram to step on his heels, and revolved in place like a distressed top. His shoulders hunched; Ibram leaned back. Ahksell glanced around them in what he no doubt considered a subtle act.

"I forgot!" he whispered. "How are we going to get one now?"

Ibram restrained a sigh and made a shoving gesture towards the front gates. "I'm sure one will fall into our hands," he said. "but time marches on, and so must we."

Ahksell put his hand on Ibram's shoulder. "Wait, what if we tried the Learners' Pavilion? It's open all day on account of the festival. We can be in and out without a mutter from the Bedris folk."

"A wonderful idea," Ibram said, "if only you had thought of it sooner—"

"You didn't think of it either."

"Yes, a fair point, but we must be going, Ahksell." He could see two Attendants begin to stroll towards them. Ibram recognized Gregur and Lazul from Yseult. He slid his foot in the direction of the gate. "All will be well! But we should be getting you back to your examinations."

"You can't really think to drop me off at a time like this," Ahksell said.

"Ahksell, you've returned!" Gregur exclaimed. She bounced to his side and stood there, practically vibrating with nervous energy. Even her hair seemed—No, it was sticking up straight. Someone had let her near the lodestones again. Attendant Gregur was particularly susceptible to them.

Ahksell pinched the bridge of his nose, and turned to face her. "I'm back," he agreed.

"Well?" Lazul demanded gruffly. "Is Mentor in pieces like they're saying?"

"No, she is not!" Ahksell declared with a frown. "Really, how do you keep falling for this baseless gossip? Mentor Hobon is no more in danger than we are. She's simply indisposed."

Gregur, at least, had the grace to appear abashed; Lazul, merely suspicious. They were younger than Ahksell by a number of years; Ibram had been tasked with their supervision during their trial by vigil. This was their first official examinations, and if he recalled correctly they were still feeling out the exact parameters of their dignity.

"What do you know about it?" Lazul asked. "You had the tremors just like the rest of us when the runner came up with the news."

"Ladyship is well enough to communicate," Ibram said. If he let them stand around all day, then he'd never get his chance at the body. "She's been in to see the medicinal corps."

"Oh, we know all that, Ibram," Gregur said, without looking away from Ahksell. She had a thin pale face, but blotches of red stood out on her cheeks. "What we want to know is if he really melted the eyes out of her head."

"Did he struggle much when Master Kalmar booted him from the tower?" Lazul asked.

"He'd have to do a damned bit more than crush pigments if Attendant Zorion had managed that," Ibram said. "And you know very well, Master Kalmar would have locked him up for the First Mentor at the slightest sign of violence."

Lazul narrowed his rather wide-set eyes at him, but nodded. "Suppose you would know."

"Suppose I would, young master," Ibram said. He lifted his chin and faced them both, as he might have done had they still been

Learners out of bed. In truth, any alchemist might clean the floor with him, but as long as they themselves didn't think so, Ibram was content to overlook reality. "He was with me down in Lityen while our betters assessed the damage. And where are you two off to? Is the examination list so far completed, you have your hours free?"

Gregur shifted on her feet. "Not...strictly," she said. "But when Ahksell went off to see what had happened, the rest of us had to restructure our study plans."

Ibram crossed his arms. They were but barely Attendants, after all. He might not be Amota Lakum, or even Amita Sarrha, but they were still young enough to think he had the power to send them off to run punishment laps.

"When did you last spend an hour in study?" Ibram asked. "Or have you been playing in that whispering pool they have up here, trying to drown each other?"

Gregur's face slowly flushed red from her cheeks outward. "Not all day," she said.

Ibram nodded sharply. "Then you'll have no trouble going off and relearning patience by running through your drills on—" He shifted his eyes towards Ahksell.

"Both of you are weak on purifying gold through glass," Ahksell said quickly. "And you know they'll ask about it. You've based all your efforts on telescoping arrays to promote plant growth."

"Well—"

"No," Ibram interrupted Lazul before he could start. The boy looked like he'd been lured from a cave with a hunk of raw meat like a hibernating rachtbear, but he had a fast mouth. "Not another word. Ladyship shall receive all your care and best wishes for her recovery, and there's an end of it."

He pointed off behind him, in the vague direction of the administrative buildings housed along the courtyard. Gregur and Lazul looked at each other uncertainly, and then at himself and Ahksell with a dull resentment, but they each bowed and made their grudging good-byes, before stumbling off. Ibram had no doubt the rest of the displaced Attendants were about to be subjected to quite an earful.

Ahksell pinched the bridge of his nose. "Runner's corns," he muttered. "What are we going to do?"

"Well," Ibram said. The sun was sinking behind a thicket berm of cloud cover rolling in from the other peaks that formed the Emerald Mountains. If they didn't make it in time, then the body might not even be available for viewing, much less investigation. "If we hurry you can make use of this Hessele's Cage, I've found."

"*What?*"

⁂

Ibram frowned, and a man drawing a handheld cart rattling with wooden dolls swerved out of his way. The sky above was darkening, rain coming down off the Emerald Mountains in a growling splatter of drops. The wider squares in Lityen were unrolling their canopies, but that left the side streets choked with villagers and merchant folk seeking shelter.

"I cannot believe you," Ahksell hissed. His shoulders hunched against the weather as they walked through the crowd.

"The longer you speak of this," Ibram said in as quiet a voice as he could manage and still be heard in the throng of people surrounding them, "the more quickly we will be found out!"

"You stole from Attendant Dakreia!"

"I borrowed a necessary piece of equipment," Ibram corrected him. "And please keep your voice down. People will gain the wrong impression of me."

"She said we couldn't have one!"

"She said that you were not allowed to take one, but there was nothing in her refusal about myself."

"That's only because she never thought of you."

Ibram shrugged. "Then she should have been more explicit," he said. "We've had a lot of trouble lately with alchemical imprecision."

"You can't even use it!"

"Which is why I invited you along," Ibram said.

"I invited myself along, thank you," Ahksell said.

Ibram shrugged again. They had been over and over this already on the trip down. There was no point in bothering Amota Viran about events until he'd had a chance to speak with Third Mentor Nieminen; he'd said so himself. It made far more sense to do a bit of investigation on their own recognizance, and then present the facts in full measure when called upon to make their report.

"It could be that this device makes the strongest case for murder, and that leads us directly to the—" Ibram glanced about them, "—the *person* who did it."

"And what about this?" Ahksell asked, and gestured up and out at the sky. He was tall enough that no one about even thought of ducking. "A storm will keep the rest of us penned up in our dormitories. They might not have even sent for Mentor Nieminen yet."

"The festival will continue regardless," Ibram said. "No farmer's going to be put off his entertainments on account of the weather. And besides, when we prove he was murdered, Mentor Nieminen will have no grounds upon which to censure you."

Ahksell grunted and crossed his arms. A few of the more skittish villagers made ample room about him, creating enough space that he and Ibram could almost be said to be strolling at their leisure. The smell of damp wood was high in the air.

Ibram twitched his head in Ahksell's direction. "Should we take the left near Book Row?" he asked.

"No, I can see the printer's cart is caught in the mud," Ahksell said.

Ibram shifted his weight on his heels and veered to the right instead. They ducked under the awning that crossed between a shay shop and the green apothecary. Ahksell caught him by the shoulder, and propelled them both across the wider road and up onto the wooden walkway just beyond the two buildings, where the little sundries warehouse lurked.

"A little warning next time?" Ibram shook himself free and swiped water from his shoulders.

"I thought you were trained in the art of noticing things."

Ibram leaned left and elbowed Ahksell in the side. Ahksell sputtered, and pushed him off with a laugh. Ibram glanced up at him diagonally and saw Ahksell rub one hand down his face. Ahksell's chest heaved a great sigh.

"Brace up," Ibram said, "We shall be proven right."

Ibram pressed his arm against his side, where the Hessele's Cage hung beneath his clothes. It was a light bundle, at least, but Ibram had had to step carefully to avoid dislodging it. There had been no opportunity of hiding it in one of his belt pouches; the Attendants released on their liberty had stuffed the relay system to bursting in an attempt to beat the weather.

Ahksell stepped up onto the wooden walkway, and scraped mud from his heels on its ledge. The streets in Lityen were properly made things, good packed earth around the imperial stone roads with well-dug ditches on either side, and thick wooden planks set to get the walkers away from the wagons. For now, down this street, it seemed the weather was not proving an obstacle to travel, but Ibram heard the crack of distant thunder. He tucked his hair behind his ears.

"We should be quick," he said. "Don't want to be out all night in this weather."

"Give me the cage," Ahksell said and held out his hand, low at his side, as he put his back to the street. His wide chest blocked most folk's view.

Ibram glanced around the sides of him. The mass of people about them were more concerned in staying out of the wet. He paused and glanced up at the overhanging roof. The Wyvern shaped gargoyle carved above them spat water down to the street.

"The mews is just ahead, I could pass it to you over there," Ibram said.

Ahksell held out his hand a bit higher. "Just hand it over," he said. "The faster I can deploy the array, the faster we can be done with this, and return to the preceptory."

Ibram curled his fingers around the hem of his gambeson. "You do still believe me, don't you?"

"Why do you even ask me that?" Ahksell quickly looked behind himself, left and then right. "I'm not studying, am I? I'm not at Master Kalmar's side telling him all about your bright idea to steal an alchemical artifact on the eve of discovering a—"

"All right, all right." Ibram held his right hand up, and dug under his clothes with his left. The loose thread of the Hessele's Cage had become wrapped around the string that held up the tiny flat emergency stash of coin he kept under his clothes. He worked it free and handed it over.

Ahksell closed his hand around the bundle with a relieved sigh. Quickly, he opened the top flap of his carry-all and shoved the cage inside. He closed the bag again and held it close against his body.

"That's better," he said, as he redid the clasp. "We should get some white yarn. Do you think that stall will still be there outside the neighbor's?"

"I suppose," Ibram answered, and crossed his arms. "Why white?"

"For poison," Ahksell said.

"Can't you find that out without it?"

Ahksell shook his head. "It's old, only has the red and yellow strings. At most, I can tell you if something within the body was disturbed unnaturally."

"Death's natural," Ibram said.

"When we are more at our leisure, I will explain all about the different resonances of death, but for now I think we should get to the house," Ahksell said and shook his head. "We can ask to view the body without overplaying our hand, don't you think?"

Ibram took the lead as he walked further down the path. "I don't see why not," he said. "Mistress Dolman might not...be best pleased with me currently, but she had no idea you were even inside the house. Surely, if we come to the kitchens and ask for an audience with Mistress Savoldyn with you..."

"Expressing my most sincere condolences," Ahksell added.

"You even sound sorry," Ibram remarked as he glanced over his shoulder.

Ahksell frowned. "I am sorry!"

"Ah well, all to the good, then," Ibram said as he turned around. They turned right at the end of the warehouse and then ran across the next street to the shelter of the next building's roof. Thunder cracked overhead; Ibram hunched his shoulders.

They hurried further into Lityen, past the impromptu concerts that had sprung up from the various circlers who drifted at festivals. The vielle and citole players were tuning up a jig, even though there was barely enough room to dance. The audience clapped along, regardless.

"Here, turn here," Ahksell called out behind him, and Ibram skirted the revelers down the next side street. Ahksell caught up to him at the mouth of the alley, and they walked next to each other for the rest of the way down to the Savoldyn manor.

"We should make sure we talk to that little servant, the cook's girl," Ibram said. "She seemed impressionable."

"Jara was a lovely girl," Ahksell said. "There's no need to call her impressionable."

"Did I say anything?" Ibram asked with his arms outstretched. He grinned. They were close enough that he could already picture the pair of them inside the manor. Ahksell could do whatever it was he did with that cage, and then Ibram could begin to ask Mistress Dolman some highly pertinent questions. A few subtle hints of imperial notice would doubtless open her stiff jaw; the warders always loved to find trouble in Lityen.

Ibram heard jingling ahead of them. He stepped out onto the darkened road before the Savoldyns' home, and stopped immediately. Ahksell followed a step behind, and hissed between his teeth.

In front of the half-open house gates, still tied up with the rushes, stood a pale workhorse of twelve hands roped to a simple wooden cart covered in a thick layer of straw. Two broad fellows dressed all in yellow were shoving a large wooden box up into the wagon bed. A figure in a rough robe, also the color of spring butter, sat atop the driver's bench with their hood over their head in the rain.

Ibram dragged his fingers back through his damp hair and gripped the strands tightly. "Oh, *hang*."

The robed figure turned their head up to the darkening sky, and Ibram saw it was an old man, severe in his eyes and the depth of his wrinkles around his mouth. Ahksell dragged Ibram back into the alley they had come from. They were too blasted late; the Navigator's pilots had come to take the body to the Ark. Ibram's soul wasn't going to be fit for oblivion at this rate; he'd be too busy working off his debt to Yilka the Green, scrubbing cups in Catha the Grey's halls in Cangsa.

Mistress Dolman clearly had waited on Ibram's suspicions long enough.

They watched from the alley's confines as the two other men scrambled up into the cart. The driver cracked the reins, and the work-horse shambled forward. Ibram slumped against the damp wall, and rubbed the back of his neck. The Savoldyns' front gates clanged shut.

$$\text{❦} \quad 8 \quad \text{❧}$$

Ibram threw back the heavy bronze latch on the front gate and marched up the short road. Ahksell loped beside him, easily fitting his lengthy strides to Ibram's own quick pace. The blasted rain had turned into a coating mist, the kind that drenched a body faster than a simple downpour and left only the smallest inches of fabric nearest the body dry; they itched against his chilled skin.

Ibram ducked his chin into his chest. Savoldyn's corpse was on its way to the Navigator's Ark, it would take a day to prepare the body for proper burning, and perhaps another half-day to assemble the required mourners. His death being so sudden, it would take at least that amount of time to draw folks from their festival duties or even simply to notify the tiny Office of Residence that someone had died. They still had a little time left to gather the information he needed to present, either to Mentor Nieminen, or more importantly, Lady Azadiya, but how to get to her? And then there were the rushes on the Savoldyn's gate, *and* Amota Viran in some kind of mood about Mistress Savoldyn the Overwrought.

There was only one avenue left to take, and Ibram knew it.

The door opened soundlessly as he and Ahksell stepped up to the porch, and Kholdo bowed. Ahksell hunched his shoulders a little and waved him quickly back up.

"Welcome back, Attendant Solari," Kholdo said, as he rose.

Ahksell shook his head. "I keep telling you that isn't necessary, Kholdo," he said. "I've known you since I was thirteen!"

"And I know what's due to you, young master," Kholdo said with a chuckle. "What's this lazy one gotten you into now?"

He blessed Ibram with the resigned amusement in the careworn lines of his face that he had featured when Ibram had been young and apt to sneak cinnak cookies from the baking tray when Kholdo's back was turned. Ibram smacked rain from his sleeves and grimaced. He supposed he would take Kholdo as a housekeeper over Mistress Dolman, but there was never any arguing with a man who carried you on his hip for the first three years of your life.

"I am not lazy," Ibram rallied, none the less. "I am situationally motivated."

"You're dripping on the floor, is what you are," Kholdo said. "Get out of those drenched things, the pair of you, and hand them to me."

Ibram sighed, but whipped the tongue out of his leather belt. Ahksell grinned at him, already undoing the buttons that held his green gambeson closed. Ibram began to undo his own clothes.

"Now, these can dry in the kitchen with me. Looks as if your tunics are good enough to air out where they are." Kholdo took possession of both gambesons in his arms, and then frowned.

Ibram rewrapped his belt around his waist, and then shook out the damp sleeves of his undyed linen tunic. "What?" he asked.

"You've split the seam on your shoulder," Ahksell said.

Ibram squinted at his left, and then his right shoulder. Indeed, a loose thread hung from the seam nearest his neck. It looked small enough. He shrugged, and then eyed Ahksell's own fine white linen tunic.

"I hope you also made as careful a study of all that lovely red embroidery on yours," he said. "Else those protections will fail at a crucial time."

Ahksell opened his mouth, but Kholdo clapped his hands, and long habit kept both of them silent. "Now, I'll not have two thunderclouds inside as well as without," he said. "Come into the courtyard and warm yourselves."

Kholdo led the way, and since they could not stay in the vestibule all day, they followed. Ibram's family home was only two courtyards, the larger public one for Father's customers and Ama's guests, and then the family courtyard where they spent most of their time. Father's workshop was back there, where he designed jewelry and small devotional objects for select clientele, as well as the garden and living quarters. As Ibram was not Father's heir, he had never spent much time in the public courtyard beyond the necessary social courtesies. It was an empty space, with a lawn that cost too much money and a pavilion that only strangers used. Crossing from the former courtyard to the latter always felt like traveling through someone else's home to get to his own.

"Is anyone at home?" Ahksell asked, with a glance in Ibram's direction.

Ibram set his hand on his sica to keep it from whacking him in the knee. He drew in a deep breath and let it drift out of his open mouth. The Savoldyns had closed their courtyard's ceiling; here they let the rain and weather inside. Cloth needed more protection than gold and silver, presumably, but it was still an expensive measure. Savoldyn had known how to spend money, certainly.

"Yes," Kholdo said, and nodded as they walked down the right hand terrace to the large doubled doors on the other side of the courtyard.

"Both of them?" Ibram asked. "Are they alone?"

"Your parents are eating a small meal in the dining room," Kholdo said, with a touch of exasperation in his voice. He pushed the entryway door open and stepped inside, holding the door in one hand. "Katka and the young apprentices are still down at the trading stall. They're expected for supper, but not before. Did you need to see them?"

Ibram shook his head, ducking it as he passed by Kholdo. His hair swung against his face and tickled his nose. He sneezed and tucked the offending lock back behind his ear.

"Just Ama, I should think," Ibram said. There was a grim tension lurking in the base of this throat, like a prickling vine seeking purchase around his neck. Mistress Dolman could have ordered the corpse moved, but it was more likely that the widow had sent for her husband's clergy. He touched his hand to the wallet on his belt where he kept his bells and dice for Yilka the Green. He didn't like to rely on his goddess overmuch. After all, it took a lot of need to make a voice heard all the way up to the heavens in the Celestial plane, and one small murder wasn't bound to catch Her attention.

They walked through the public courtyard, and into the family apartments. The smell of wet greenery and turned earth floated from the kitchen garden in the center of the space, and Ibram breathed with a little more ease. Kholdo left them at the door, turning left down the terrace for his small workroom/sitting room. Ibram and Ahksell took the right-hand path that led to the little room where Ama and Father usually held family meals. Without Katka and the apprentices making a racket, the only noise came from the sound of his and Ahksell's boots on the wooden planks.

Ibram drummed his fingers against the door lintel as he entered the dining room, and found Ama and Father seated across from each other, sharing a pile of mixtus between them on a wooden trencher. Ahksell came in close behind and Father chuckled lightly. Ama's eyebrows drew together.

"Ibram?" she asked. "Ahksell? What are you doing here?"

"We're sorry for intruding, Mistress Ucalegon," Ahksell said, and bowed shortly. Strictly speaking, Ama and Father should have been bowing to him, but after running about the place since childhood, Ahksell had never gotten comfortable with the idea, and Ama had never been able to break him of the habit. Somehow, they struggled through the breach in etiquette.

"I'm not," Ibram said. "I am here on purpose."

Ama raised one eyebrow. "What happened to your clothes?"

Ahksell coughed his discomfort, and rearranged the open collar of his tunic. Ibram shrugged. "Kholdo took them to dry out," he said.

"Were you that wet?" Father asked. "It was only misting when we came home."

Ibram lifted his hands to show his palms. He walked over to the table, and pulled out the chair next to Ama, and threw himself down into it. She swatted him on the shoulder.

"You've ripped your tunic," she said. Her long greying brown tresses swept over her shoulder, loosely held by the filigree chain clasps she wore to secure the pin that held up half of her hair. She was in her house clothes, a long, patterned robe fronted by heavy embroidered clasps, and loose pants, but Father had oiled his beard and made an attempt to unrumple his blue tunic. He'd even rolled down his sleeves, and Ibram smelled the distinct odor of rosewater in the air.

"I'm a growing boy," Ibram replied, and cocked his head. "Are we allowed to the feast, or is this a private affair?"

Ama sighed, and shook her head. "If I wanted sauce with my meal, Ib-la," she said. "I would have asked the seller for mustard."

Ahksell laughed, and Ibram shrugged again. "You were the one taught me to ask questions even if I didn't want the answer."

"Oh, Ahksell, sit, sit," Father said, waving him to the table. "You know the way."

Ahksell smiled, and took up residence in the chair nearest Father. He sat properly, in the Vissilian way, with his back straight and his right arm on the table. Father patted him on the back.

"And what does Kholdo think of street food appearing on his dining table?" Ibram asked. "You've got enough to feed a battalion, here."

"There's nothing wrong with eating festival food during a festival," Ama said. "Ahksell, the cider pitcher is to your right. Pass out the cups, would you?"

Ahksell leaned over to the tray of clay bowls and the tall, wide-mouthed pitcher. He poured four measures, and then handed round the bowls. Ibram took his from Ama, gripping it by the rim to set it on the table. Ama handed Ibram one of the fried bits from the trencher; he held it before himself with two fingers. A two-pronged wooden stick lay on the table; the other resided in Father's hand. Ibram flicked the remaining stick in Ahksell's direction. Ahksell picked it up, and stabbed something small that crunched. He ate it and set down the stick again. Courtesies accomplished, Ibram popped his fried morsel into his mouth and chewed. He grimaced. Onion. He washed it down with cider, tart and smooth.

"What brings you back so soon?" Ama asked, as she picked up another unidentifiable fried bite. "Not that it isn't lovely to see you again, Ahksell."

"How is Lady Azadiya?" Father asked.

Ama made a face at him, and Father smiled back. She shook her head. "You know very well she has not come down from her tower," she said. "The filtering mask has not yet been prepared."

She hadn't been up the living mountain in a year, but this was why an investigation usually came down to Ama, or at least deliberately brushed past her. There was no one in the whole of Lityen—or its various outposts—who knew more about its goings-on. As an agent for Lady Azadiya, she had grown a healthy crop of informants, and as Father's partner in the business, she had a coterie of noble and wealthy ladies eager for shay and gossip. Sadly, Ibram's voyage out into the empire had left him decidedly lacking in recent history. He had quite a ways to go before he had his own circle of informants, or even people silly enough to see the brooch on his chest and think him the soul of discretion. He sighed heavily, and let his head roll on his neck, before reaching out and snagging himself another piece of food. It turned out to be potato, this time.

"I need information," he said around his mouthful. He dipped the steaming end into the pile of salt on the trencher, and finished off the fried potato.

"You should be patrolling," Ama said.

"I'm sure your mother can give you a strategy for dealing with the children," Father said, and speared his next bite. He dipped it in the small pile of salt on the rim of the trencher.

"No, on a separate matter," Ibram said. "And I do very well with children."

"It's a murder," Ahksell said, and fiddled with his wooden stick. The prongs hovered between two lumpy, breaded mounds of vegetable, before he stuck the right one. "Nothing to do with the Learners."

"The Wheelmaker spins us all home," murmured Father.

"A murder?" Ama asked. She sipped her cider delicately, thumb on the base of the bowl and her first two fingers balanced on the rim. "Has someone interesting besides Master Savoldyn died recently?"

Ahksell glanced up at Ibram; he shrugged in return. He turned in his chair rested his chin in his hands. Ama continued eating.

"No, in point of fact, it concerns Master Savoldyn," Ibram said. "I think he was poisoned."

"How so?" Ama asked, and licked grease from her thumb.

"He smelled like a barrel of preserved eels," Ibram said. "You don't get that from a morning cup of small beer."

"He was a sot," Father said, and pointed his wooden stick up in the air. "We used to see him at the common guild house, completely squandered in a corner after a feast. Or even before it, come to think."

"We're working on it," Ahksell said. He gulped his cider, and shuddered, and then placed the empty bowl on the table.

"Who better to murder than a man no one is surprised to see dead?" Ibram asked at the same time.

"Then what are you here to see your poor mother about?" Ama asked. The corners of her dark eyes crinkled in amusement. "What couldn't wait until the evening meal?"

Ibram sucked his teeth. "I need to know about the daughter," he said.

"You think she could kill him?" Ama asked.

Ibram shrugged. "They share a temper, and if one could disown his child for getting married, then who knows what drastic measures the other might go to?"

"You heard about that, did you?" Father asked, and shook his head. "A sad business."

"Amota Viran told me," he said.

Ama made a very neutral noise. So impartial, in fact, that Ibram immediately knew she was aware of something concerning the Savoldyn household. He leaned forward on his resting arm.

"I don't like to think it," Ibram said, "but—"

"It is a habit of a suspicious mind," Ama finished for him. She patted him on the cheek. "I'm so glad you're finally cultivating one."

Ahksell snorted, and shook his head. Father nodded ruefully, while Ama leaned back in her chair. She interlaced her fingers over her stomach and thought for a moment. She had been born in the inland area of Merrilia on the edge of where Lady Azadiya's people camped, though not at the same time, and shared her coloring, which she in turn had imparted to Ibram, the pale bronze skin and dark hair. Most especially, they shared a love of knowing more than the person next to them. When Ama had been an active agent for the Preceptory of Yseult life must have been very interesting up the living mountain.

"It is true," she began slowly, "that Mistress Ignalle paid the whole of the marriage fee—that was, as I recall, the bulk of the scandal. Her husband was newly arrived to the area and his prospects were seen to be middling at best. When it was discovered that she took his name instead of the reverse, the general consensus was that Savoldyn saw it as the final insult."

"Which it was," Father interjected.

She nodded. "Not even a chance of reconciliation between them. The marriage contract was barely a page."

Ibram blinked rapidly. His parents' contract was kept in their wedding box; it was as thick as a brick and heavy as a full water jug. "How did they manage with so little?"

"I sometimes think it was the lack of forethought that insulted Savoldyn even more than the elopement," Ama said. "How could you trust your business to someone so flighty?"

Father raised his hands palms up over the table. "They are very much in love."

"There is love, and then there is marriage," Ama said. "One does not save the other."

Father nodded. "Very true, my dear."

"I suppose the disinheritance helped then," Ahksell said.

Ibram selected a fried circle, and ate it only to discover a carrot, mushy on the outside and hard in the middle. "How so?"

"Well, if neither of them had much to bring to the marriage anymore there wasn't much to work out in the contract."

"You believe Mistress Ignalle anticipated her father's disinheriting her?" Ama asked. "In order to put herself on the level of her husband?"

Ahksell shrugged and wrinkled his mouth at the corners. "I don't know," he said. "The thought merely struck me."

Ibram turned that line of inquiry over in his mind, still chewing his carrot chunk. He swallowed. "Is it known how well off they are now?" he asked.

Ama shook her head. "He has his pay from the imperial bureaucracy... Some small position. He can afford their living, but nothing extravagant."

"Nothing they might have afforded if Mistress Ignalle had remained her father's heir," Ibram said. "How old is the child?"

"Must be walking by now," Father said. "A little girl, I believe."

"She is at most five or six years old," Ama said. "They ran away after you did, and the birth followed months after they returned for his job."

He had not run away, he had left to see the empire and find work on his own, but it was an old argument. Ibram settled on merely rolling his eyes, rather than chewing over the details again. Instead, he contemplated Ahksell's shoulder, where the strap of his carry-all dug into the gambeson, and nodded slowly. Ahksell frowned at him.

"Do I have a crumb?" he asked, and raised his hand before his mouth.

Ibram shook his head. "No," he said and reached out over the table. "Hand me the scroll, would you?"

"What scroll?" Ama asked.

Ahksell's eyes bulged. "What? Here?"

"Who will they tell?" Ibram asked. "Ama was probably a witness."

"Oh, for..." Ahksell grumbled beneath his breath, but rearranged himself to paw through his bag. He flipped up the top piece of leather and muttered at its contents until he withdrew the wooden slat scroll. Then, he popped the will on the table next to the pile of mixtus and sat back. "I want it noted that I didn't take this."

"No, Ahksell merely holds my stolen goods," Ibram said as he unrolled the scroll.

"Ibram," Father said, with a raised eyebrow.

"And here we are!" Ibram declared. He showed Ama the writing. "The Savoldyn will."

Ama made an approving hum, and took the scroll from him. She held it out before her, blocking Ibram's view of Father. He heard the resigned sigh well enough, though.

"Pour us out some more cider, Ahksell," Father said. "I have a feeling it will be required."

"He was remarkably indiscreet," Ama said following a minute or so of silent reading. "It's all as he said during the last feast at the common guildhall."

"He was positively jellied then, as well," Father said, and slurped his drink. "It's a shame, really. It was his final chance, too."

Ibram leaned to the right. "Final chance?"

"For what?" Ahksell asked.

"He'd not been paying his dues," Father said. "The members censured him twice over, but he remained delinquent. They had to vote him off the rolls."

"Maybe he was spending the coin on his poetry," Ahksell said. He revolved his cider bowl in both hands.

Ama lowered the will. "He wrote poetry?"

Ibram shook his head. "Only if you squinted."

"To be sure," Ama said. "Murder has been committed for less reason."

"And Savoldyn's will—regardless of who anticipated what—is still important," Father pointed out. He stroked a hand down his beard, and pinned Ibram to his chair with a softly disappointed stare. "It should be returned to his family."

Ibram cleared his throat. "I'm sure they have another copy."

Ama hummed in the back of her throat. Ibram shifted in his chair, and turned his head to look at her instead. At least one member of his family seemed pleased.

"Is there anything in there about who has charge of the heir, in the event of his death?" Ibram asked.

She cut her eyes in his direction. "Did you not read this?"

Ibram leaned back in his seat. "I did when I discovered it," he said. "Only we were interrupted."

"I read it," Ahksell said, "but I don't remember any passage detailing who was in charge of the child's affairs. There were several on

Mistress Savoldyn's widow's portion, and the list detailing her dowry at the time of her marriage. Mistress Dolman—"

"That being the housekeeper," Ibram said.

"She gets a nice set of her former mistress's clothing, which is being kept in storage, and a small sum of money should the household close all together," Ahksell continued.

Ibram moved closer to Ama and began to read over her shoulder. The will had been carefully burnt into the thin wooden slats in a deft, but blunt hand. There were few of the crisp drag marks or mistakes that showed the charcoal writing guides beneath which characterized work done by apprentices. The sigil marked below where Savoldyn had clumsily signed his name was for the house of Gruba, a family of lawyers in South Lityen. Savoldyn had clearly paid dearly for quality scribes and legal work.

"But nothing on who runs the business while the child is below her majority," Ibram muttered.

"It seems his post-death planning wasn't as thorough as he boasted," Ama said.

"No, he seems a most reactionary man," Ibram said. "He didn't tackle a problem until it happened."

Ama shook her head. "No need to plan for a siege if you simply keep the doors open."

"Surely that doesn't make sense," Ahksell said.

Ama began rolling the scroll back up. "What doesn't?"

Father continued to eat, neatly removing the mixtus from his stick with his teeth. "It seems to me," he said after swallowing. "That Master Savoldyn had much on his mind. Perhaps he simply knew that if he died, his heir would remain under the care of his former daughter."

Ibram blinked. "You...believe it's possible he deliberately kept any directions concerning a—a neutral regent out of this will so his daughter would regain control of the business through *her* daughter?"

Father shrugged. "Rage in haste, repent in leisure."

"Or a taste of her own medicine," Ama said. "Trying to wrangle a child and run a business."

The intense argument Ibram had interrupted told him Savoldyn wasn't the type to ask forgiveness, because he wasn't the sort who ever believed he needed to, but he didn't like to contradict Father in company. Ibram rather thought along the lines of Savoldyn merely not believing he would die as soon as he had. He nodded instead and sat back in his chair. Ama handed the will back to Ahksell, who tucked it away again.

"I don't like to think of it," Ahksell said. "A daughter murdering her own father?"

Ibram nodded. It fit a pattern, but what a mucky one. Crime and coin usually met to some degree or another, but did it fit? He cast his mind back to Mistress Ignalle as she had been inside her father's office. Her clothes had been in fashion, the southern styles favored by folk who were involved in Her Gracious Majesty's government. Apart from her glass bracelets, her jewelry had been just as nondescript as Mistress Savoldyn's, actually. Somewhat expensive, but the style was older. Perhaps the jewelry she had run away with upon her marriage. He sighed and wiped his palms off on each other.

"Suppose we should pay our respects to the grieving daughter," he said, and drank down his cider. "Perhaps we can see what's to do."

"But what about the body?" Ahksell asked. "If it's too far gone in the funereal process, I won't be able to get a sufficient reading."

From the corner of his eye, Ibram saw Ama cock her head in sudden interest. He cleared his throat. "It's not too far in the day to do both," he said. "We'll...have to get permission from someone in the family to examine Savoldyn in any case."

"Do you not have permission?" Ama asked in far too casual a tone of voice for Ibram's liking.

"A charge was uttered," Ibram said.

No need to let anyone else know who had proffered the charge, since it was only himself at this point. Once he had gathered the facts, Ladyship would doubtless understand. Father and Ama exchanged amused glances.

"I am sure Master Kalmar appreciates your taking an interest in this business, while the elder agents are otherwise occupied," Ama said.

Ibram stood up from the table and kissed her on the temple. "We had best be off," he said. "Thank you for your help."

He supposed it was the kind of favor Yilka the Green excelled at, showing all three of her faces and supplying both opportunity and work, with the appearance of luck on the horizon. Fact one being that Master and Mistress Ignalle lived in a respectable but nondescript home attached on either side to their neighbors, but near enough a bakery-mill, and a draughtshop not to notice the lack of a courtyard to grow anything. The buildings clustered behind the Bureau of Currency, a popular area for lower government officials. Fact two being that they had not been at home to visitors, and fact three resulting in that their maid-of-all-work was forced by sheer dint of courteous obstinacy to linger on the doorstep beneath the rather plain portico and speak with Ibram, while Ahksell stood tall in his best impression of an eager soul by his side.

"Lady Azadiya wanted us to pass on the condolences of the sect, you see, Mistress Agapito," Ibram said with a smile.

The maid was older than either of them, but not by much, and her red hair and tunic were neat as pins in a seam. Her wrapped trousers were grey, and her tunic matched in a finer cloth than most maids could afford. She had big dark eyes and a familiar chin. Ibram couldn't quite place her, but she matched her surroundings rather well.

She stood in the doorway and looked at Ahksell from the corner of her eye, before smiling politely. "Lady Azadiya? Mentor Hobon up the living mountain?" she asked. "Why—I mean, thank you. I will pass the message along to my mistress."

"We know, well, we all know about the problems in the family," Ahksell said, "but Mentor has had a relationship with the Savoldyns for a very long time. I mean, a father is a father, is he not?"

The corner of her upper lip curled; it was very slight, but Ibram made note of it. Beyond that tiny derisive slip, she nodded quite appropriately, and touched her hand to the back of her low bun. Servants were often a good barometer for the health of a household.

"I suppose you're right, Attendant Solari," she murmured. "But if you—"

"And it's not as if we could pass them on to Mistress Savoldyn,"

Ibram said. "With the rushes tied and all."

Remarkable how that little lip curled in derision, like Mistress Agapito couldn't control the expression, nor the sullen gleam in her eyes. He should crack an egg to Yilka the Green after all; she brought the most interesting folk into his life, to be sure.

"I suppose you aren't acquainted, though," he said, and leaned on the doorway. "What with this trouble I keep hearing so much about."

"Well, no, not as such," she said. "It's none of my business, but I wasn't such a cracked stone to inquire."

"Been with the Ignalles long, then?" he asked, and peered over her shoulder. "It seems a neat room, must be easy to clean."

She moved right and blocked his view. "Since they married," she said. "It's a good position."

"Hard work, though," Ahksell said. "Are you the housekeeper?"

A faint smattering of red bloomed across Mistress Agapito's cheeks. Ibram made a face at his boots, and shook his head. The portico was white, as was the stairs, almost too small for he and Ahksell to stand abreast, but neat; the smell of fresh paint lingered in the air. The threshold and door were a bright yellow, but the buildings around them showed the marks of age and use. He tilted his head back up with a smile.

"There's no room for a title such as that in a house this size," she laughed. "No, Attendant, I am merely the maid. I attend Mistress Elene and Master Ignalle has his own servant. We do what's necessary. Nothing too bad, really, a bit of cooking and cleaning."

"Cooking?" Ibram repeated. "You've a price above pearls, to be sure, Mistress."

She cleared her throat, and took a step back. Her elbow hit the door; it wavered on its hingers. "I thank you, Master Ucalegon," she said with a chuckle. She rubbed her elbow. "But it's nothing like that. Mistress Elene is good with coin and the staff, so having a few different talents under my belt stood me in good stead."

"It must have difficult, though," Ibram said, and took a chance, based on their surroundings. "The sort of parties a bureaucrat must have to throw to get ahead, and on such a little salary. You and your mistress must be run off your feet!"

"We manage, young master," Mistress Agapito said, with a sniff. "I won't say we haven't had our setbacks, but we've had our triumphs as well. You know how it is."

Ibram nodded. She was a very loyal young woman, to claim Mistress Ignalle's success and failure as her own. She must have started young. A thought bubbled at the back of Ibram's mind, but he set it aside to let it ferment.

"Indeed I do," Ibram said, and made a show of sighing. "I am sorry not to be able to properly pass on Ladyship's condolences, though. I can tell that I'll be in trouble, when I get back up the living mountain."

"Oh no," Ahksell said. "I'll put in a good word, don't worry."

Ibram didn't step on Ahksell's foot as he stood away from the door, but it was a close race. Trust Ahksell to go along well enough, but stop halfway up the hill for a rest. He lifted his hands.

"I—thank you, Attendant," Ibram said. "But I am mindful that Lady Azadiya is very particular about her wishes, especially as it concerns her business. You know how it is, and—just between yourself and the window, now—" he leaned forward and Mistress Agapito drew closer. "—Ladyship does want some kind of assurance that her family's contracts with the Savoldyns will continue apace. No telling with that widow, to be sure."

A sly twitch of her high forehead and that betraying curl of the lip slid across Mistress Agapito's face. She nodded.

"Well, I know it," she said. "But I think it safe to tell your employer that Mistress Savoldyn will set the business to rights, no matter what her father has done with it in the meantime. That's her way, you see, she sees what must be done, and she does what's needed. She's even taken charge of the disbursal of Master Savoldyn's corpse, you know."

"Now that's what I call proper behavior." Ibram leaned back and smiled. "They're at the Navigator's Ark, then?"

Mistress Agapito stopped moving just long enough to be noticeable, and but then nodded. "They are," she said.

Ibram bowed, hands at his sides and stepped back onto the road. He raised a hand up to the sky, and nodded. Ahksell stepped down from the small portico and into the street as well.

"Then we shall leave our condolences with you, and the Ignalles to their funereal duties," Ahksell said. "Thank you for your time, Mistress Agapito."

She placed her hands on her stomach and bowed; Ahksell waved her up almost immediately. "Oh, no time for that," he said. "It looks like rain. Best get inside."

Mistress Agapito smiled and closed the door without bothering to so much as wave in Ibram's direction. He shook his head and sighed, and then looked up. It did, in point of fact, look like rain, but then so did nearly any day. True, the wind was a bit much for the hour.

"Well now what?" Ahksell asked. "If we cannot—"

Ibram placed his finger diagonally over his lips, and jerked his head at the closed door. The window to the right of it was shuttered, but that didn't mean she wasn't still lurking. Servants and gossip were like ale and pie. Ahksell rolled his eyes, but obligingly fell silent. He pointed back up the street and then opened his palm to the sky. Ibram nodded. Together, they walked back towards the main street.

ཛཛ

"It could be said," Ahksell remarked from his side of the lillia tree where they had taken shelter. "That now, we have a convenience of both suspects and corpse all in one place."

On his side of the tree trunk, Ibram thrashed a dripping purple bloom out of his face, and then swiped his soaked hand on his already damp gambeson. "Yes," he allowed. "But we are stood outside the temple, and they are most definitely inside of it."

Ibram frowned at the entrance. There were guards behind those Spiny Orange bushes, he was sure about it. He could see their boots. No doubt, they were seeking shelter from the rain while at their posts.

A properly dedicated pilot with even a lay crew of devotees to the Navigator didn't need much to create an Ark in any area in which they chose to settle. In his travels, Ibram had made use of the smaller waystations, where for a few copper faunts and a test of patience, you could eat a solid meal while listening to a sober sermon on the bonds of family and "pulling together." It was a warm room, if not a soft bed, and they welcomed travelers in search of work. Ladyship had in her possession a rather amusing map he'd drawn of all the Arks down from the river Gyl to the Golden Fortress, with a key to show which withheld any drink stronger than small beer, and which demanded guests bath in salt water before being allowed to eat.

In Lityen, crammed as it was with merchant caravans using the only viable path up the Emerald Mountains, they had deep coffers. They'd settled their giant two-tiered bullock carriages in a rather lush grove on the outskirts of the village. A large manor built from Garappa wood sat in the middle of towering Jolek's pine trees they'd brought up from the south, fat with purple cones no matter what time of the growing season. The spaces between the trunks were stuffed with thornapple bushes, thick with inch-long thorns to keep out gawkers.

Ahksell hunched his shoulders and peered at the front gate. He sighed. "If only we were nearer the river," he said.

Ibram snorted. "Oh, would climbing up the side of a ship be more your style?" he asked. "Ever seen the chains they hang around the prow of their sea-going Arks? Tear the flesh straight off you."

Ahksell smacked his shoulder without looking. "Would you stop complaining?" he asked. "This was your idea."

"I told you to get back up the living mountain, and I would see to the body," Ibram said. He sneezed; lillia had such a heavy scent.

"You can't use a Hessele's Cage."

"You can't be caught invading a sacred grove!"

Ahksell turned to him then, and rolled his eyes so heavily, Ibram feared they'd be stuck in that manner. "As if you could?"

"I am an impetuous arm-for-hire drunk with festival wine," Ibram said, and sneezed again. "I can be excused my actions with a quick dunking. You? Not only could they never find a barrel large enough, but the shame of it would drown your chances for advancement before the mentors even have time to judge your gewgaw."

"It's not a gewgaw, and this is ridiculous." Ahksell frowned and dug a handkerchief out of his belt pouch. He shoved it into Ibram's chest and held it there until Ibram took hold of it. "You see those bushes? We'll never get through those thorns."

Ibram wiped his nose. "Servants' entrance," he said.

"They don't have servants, they have lay crew," Ahksell said. "Like the Runner has helpers."

"I know that." Ibram wiped his head and neck with the same hand-kerchief. The rain was still pattering down over their heads; only the dense foliage kept them from becoming soaked to the bone instead of simply down to their underlinen. Ibram crossed his arms over his chest and hunched his shoulders against the cold and damp.

"Still, it worked before."

"No, it won't," Ahksell said, and flung his hand out in the direction of the Ark. "I told you this was a fool's run."

"You did not!"

"How are we to get in?" Ahksell asked. "Neither of us can pretend to be dedicated to the Navigator without some serious questions of our devotion being asked. Nor can we pretend to be mourners because how would we have known where the man was taken in the first place?"

Ibram cocked his head, and shook his wet hair out of his face. "We could pretend to be mourners," he said.

Ahksell shook his head. "I would need more time with the corpse than is allotted to pay my respect to the dead's spirit. We should go back up the living mountain. If we present our suspicions to Master Kalmar again, he might allow us to include them in our report to Third Mentor Nieminen."

Ibram clicked his teeth together and rocked on his heels. That wouldn't do. Amota Viran thought he was being reckless—or at best over-cautious in light of past mistakes. There was also the question of whether or not he had known of Savoldyn's money troubles, and their cause. There had been no crop disasters or flooding in recent years. Why all the trouble in trade? Answers lay within that temple, and Ibram hated unanswered questions.

"We're soaked through," Ibram said, abruptly enough to startle Ahksell. "We should seek aid and shelter."

He stalked out of the tree line and towards the Navigator's Ark. What else was there to do?

"Ibram—no, wait!"

Footsteps rumbled behind him as Ahksell hurried to catch up.

"What are we even to say?" he whispered furiously as they approached the twin pines the marked the entrance to the Ark. "We live here, we're known!"

Ibram nodded, sneezed, and wiped his nose with Ahksell's handkerchief again. "Like Ladyship says, 'when faced with the unexpected: swerve'."

"That is not a plan!" Ahksell hunched sideways to speak into his ear.

Ahead of him, Ibram saw someone detach themselves from behind the nearest pine tree and stand in the middle of the woodland gate, arms folded. They were cloaked from head to toe against the rain. It made Ibram think wistfully of his own cloak, but he couldn't remember where he'd left it.

"Good day!" Ibram called out as they approached.

"Finally made up your minds?" The figure pulled back their hood far enough that Ibram saw her face, a youngish woman with wisps of blond hair stuck to her forehead. Her cloak was soaked at the shoulders; she must have been guarding the front for some time. Ibram bowed in hello and then gestured to Ahksell.

"Be known to Attendant Solari of the Preceptory of Yseult," he said in as cheerful a voice as he could muster. "We two were caught in the downpour, and now the relay stations back up the living mountain are shut. I thought we might seek shelter in the hold of your Ark? Just until the weather passes fair."

The guardswoman glanced from his face to Ahksell's without much expression. She had a tattoo on the hand facing them, of a compass with an anchor as its needle. She nodded slowly.

"Travelers are welcome," she said. "Non-dedicants pay a fee."

"Of course," Ahksell said quickly, glaring at Ibram as he opened his mouth. "I have money for myself and my agent."

Ibram sealed his lips shut. If Ahksell was going to pay there was no need to negotiate. The guardswoman nodded.

"Ten faunts for your arm-for-hire, and a silver picaio for yourself," she said.

Ibram felt his eyes widen. Ten faunts was high; he'd never paid more than eight and that was a bribe not to get dunked. "A picaio for the Attendant?" he exclaimed. "What, does your Ark have cargo it wants gold-plated?"

She frowned, and Ahksell patted the air. "No, no," he said. He felt in his nearest belt pouch. "That's a good sum. I have it."

"It's city rates in a village, that's what that is," Ibram said. "To be sure, I've never paid so much for an hour's visit, even in Kandrilat."

Her stern face did not budge. "An Ark which serves a place the size of Lityen requires a certain amount of coin, Master Agent."

"Lityen is a village," Ibram said. She must have been quite recently arrived to mistake the place for anything else.

She raised her eyebrows. "Never seen one so far spread, then," she said.

"Cities and towns are not for the likes of us here in Vanima province," Ibram said. "It's true the villages of South Lityen and Old Lityen —and even Lityen-by-the-Blue-Hole—are a bit closer by than they might be in other parts of the empire, but that is the price of life in a valley."

"And this is the price for travelers to enter the Ark."

"Here we are," Ahksell said, and held out his left hand.

The guardswoman accepted the coin, and stood aside. Ibram lifted his chin as they passed within. He tucked his handkerchief up his sleeve. The bullock carriages were spaced inside, bereft of their animals, but clearly still in use. Short steps led up to their open doors, and Ibram could see a people moving about in the upper tiers. He heard voices, the sounds of movement, and lowing coming from off to his left; the oxen being cared for in their pen. A manor for the pilots and crew stood tall on one side of the clearing, and on the other were a series of one-story buildings which seemed set up for travelers. In the center loomed a high weather vane, fashioned in the shape of a man pointing with his entire arm into the distance, and draped with yellow flags. There was a stables, and a small kitchen garden, and a fire pit below a wooden canopy where a man in a yellow tabard was stirring something in a great cauldron.

"Strictly speaking," Ahksell said as they crossed the damp, muddy field towards the outbuildings which lined the back of the Ark. "This is the most permanent looking temporary encampment I've ever seen.

Aren't Arks supposed to be moving ever forward as the Navigator wills?"

"They are ever thus," Ibram said. "Have you never stayed in one?"

Ahksell shook his head. "There was always a nicer inn when I traveled about the province."

Ibram huffed a chuckle. "Indeed, little lordship."

Ahksell poked him in the back; Ibram jumped. He peered around the nearest bullock carriage and spied a dainty two person carriage pulled alongside, with a well-dressed servant sitting atop the driver's bench beneath a small awning. That must have been the Savoldyn's conveyance, though the gleaming carriage and the plush beauty of the horses driving it were a surprise, considering their living space.

All around them were men and women in the Navigator's yellow, some in full dress and other with a mere strip of cloth wrapped around their arms. Ibram sniffed the air. They applied resin of rosemary and rue on a body when it was first arrived, and the heady bitter combination was seared into his memory. The closer they came to that smell, the closer they were to the body. He sneezed.

"Where do you think they've put Master Savoldyn?" Ahksell murmured.

"Hopefully, under a roof," Ibram said. "Maybe that house over there, the one with the double chimney."

It was the furthest building away from the front, built almost into the tree line, and had no windows. The structure was built to off angles, as if the carpenters had been more familiar with prows and forecastles than a good solid six-sided building. It rather resembled what might happen if an enormous sword had sliced off the back half of a bullock carriage and then the owner simply boarded up the hole.

They hurried to the closed front door. Under the eaves, Ibram made an attempt at wringing out his hair, while Ahksell brushed droplets from his own shoulders. Ibram stepped in front of Ahksell and knocked on the threshold. He paused, but heard nothing, and so knocked again. He sniffed, and wrinkled his nose.

"I think this might be it."

The door crashed open; Mistress Ignalle, Savoldyn's daughter, stood in its place. Her brown curls were covered by a flat white cap, with silver temple rings to either side, and she wore a yellow robe over her blue gown. She held the same sneer on her face as Ibram had seen when they'd first been introduced, but her eyes were reddened. Well, that was surprising; he hadn't thought of her as a mourner, truthfully.

She gripped the door in her hand, obviously prepared to slam it shut at any moment. "What?"

"Good day, Mistress Ignalle. How pleasant to see you again, even in these dark moments," Ibram said, and bowed shortly. "Are you known to Attendant Solari?"

She went rigid, flushed red all down her cheeks and collarbones and then turned pale. Ibram clasped his hands behind his back, and waited her silence out. Courtesy was important, after all.

"I am not," she finally said, biting out each word.

"Then may I make such an introduction?" Ibram said and began to turn left. "Be known to—"

"My father is dead," she interrupted. "I have no patience for your interruption."

She went to shut the door, and Ibram struck his foot against it. He stepped forward, almost into her, and Mistress Ignalle hurriedly got out of his way. Ibram raised his hands before him as he came further into the room.

"You are both soaked through," she exclaimed. "What is the meaning of this intrusion?"

"I apologize for the distress," Ahksell said behind him, "We would never barge in on your grief without good cause."

She sniffed and touched the back of her sleeve to the skin underneath her eyes. "I'm sure my father would be delighted at your concern, Attendant," she said with stiff courtesy. "I confess, I find your appearance confusing. Surely, our contact with the Sect of Seven Fires was in the name of business only."

Ibram hummed lightly in response, and looked past her. Master Savoldyn lay on a table in the center of the room, with twinned torches clamped to iron stands braced at his head and feet. He was covered with a yellow felted blanket, decorated with a thick black embroidery of small sailing vessels and caravan trains. The air was rank with the smell of the funerary unguent and Mistress Dolman sat at a small cauldron before a burning fire, with a pile of bandages at her feet, stirring, no doubt, more rosemary and rue and whatever oil they used to stick to the body. The old woman did not seem impressed at their intrusion, not that Ibram could blame her. The line of her back was stiff as a board.

"Exactly so, Mistress Ignalle," Ibram said as he walked closer to examine the corpse. "Though your contract was with Lady Azadiya, and not the sect as a body."

He leaned over Savoldyn's face; it had been cleaned already. He sighed. Should he have taken a portion of the man's spittle? It seemed disgusting, but if it had been poison, and the poison hadn't been in the shay, then... It couldn't be helped. He had to move forward before he could return up the living mountain.

"I am aware," Mistress Ignalle said, very much on her dignity. "Our family has always felt the honor greatly."

Ibram hummed in agreement, and nodded. "It's a high one, to be sure," he said. "And his only important customer, it seems. Why is that, do you think?"

Mistress Ignalle's lips thinned. "Father's attention has become a touch fragmented at his age. He was still managing quite well, from all reports."

"Managed well," Ibram said. He nodded. Someone in the household must have kept her apprised. "Kept up on his records, have you?"

"I naturally take an interest," she said. "My child will run the business someday."

"Indeed," Ibram said, and stood away from the corpse. "Hope to be in business with the family long after this, too. Are you ready to examine the body, Attendant Solari?"

"What do you mean you want to examine him?" Mistress Ignalle asked. "There's nothing owed to either Baran or Salacia in my father's will! His soul has no need of delving."

Ibram glanced away from the corpse. Savoldyn and his daughter had been arguing at the time of their first meeting, long enough for Mistress Savoldyn to try and use himself to restore quiet. He studied the signs of strain at the corners of her eyes, and the furrow in her forehead. It could simply be grief, but it could also be a murderer's natural inclination to keep the body out of inquisitive hands.

"I am of the Preceptory of Yseult, as you may see, Mistress," Ahksell said, and gestured to his collar tab. "As far as I am aware, your father had no contracts outstanding to any other personage within the sect but my own Mentor Hobon."

"And it's she who wishes my father's corpse..." Mistress Ignalle's thin mouth twisted disagreeably. "Researched," she settled on the word sourly.

Ahksell cleared his throat, but Ibram spoke first. "Lady Azadiya wished us to extend our condolences to your family," he said, because he was certain that would eventually be true once Ladyship was informed. "You must understand that—as a patron of your late father's—she feels a debt of care towards him and your family."

"His heart stopped," she said, and touched the back of her hand to the thin skin below her eyes. Her voice faltered. "No doubt due to an excess of drink and his own bile."

"How did you know that?" Ahksell asked gently.

"What else could it be?" she asked. "We argued no less than ten minutes before he died, I—Do you truly need to examine him?"

Mistress Ignalle turned away with her hand over her mouth. Her shoulders shook as she wrapped her other arm over her middle. Her glass bracelets clacked against each other. Ibram stood away from the body. He rubbed the back of his neck with his right hand. Ahksell eyed him, and spread his hands with a shrug. Ibram shrugged in return and chewed on his lower lip. Mistress Dolman stirred her cauldron, pointedly disinterested in their goings-on. Ibram studied the tense bend of her neck. A most devoted servant, to be sure.

"Mistress Ignalle," he said. "I believe it is important to relay all the facts to Lady Azadiya before your father is laid to rest. In case there were any irregularities which much be explained away."

Ibram tapped the table on which Savoldyn lay, and Mistress Ignalle turned with a gasp.

"How do you mean?" she asked.

The Navigator was a God of direction, specifically in the mundane achievement of Point Z when starting at Point A, but also quite keen to achieve righteousness through following the correct path. Of course, the 'correct path' varied from practitioner to zealot, but they all of them tended to appreciate a certain directness in manner.

He had to word this correctly. Too far in the realm of truth, and it might betray the oncoming storm about to envelope the Savoldyn household. Too much of a lie, and he'd have to retract at some point, which was always embarrassing.

"I mean," Ibram said, ignoring Ahksell's wide-eyed look of alarm. "You are Master Savoldyn's only living blood relation—he has no other protection before his soul is directed to the Crossroads. We here in Lityen know how eagerly Her Gracious Majesty's administrators take an interest in our day-to-day lives, our comings and goings. I've often made such a report to Lady Azadiya, have I not, Attendant Solari? About some poor deceased person whose animus has returned to the natural resonance of the world, but whose soul remains in abeyance?"

Ahksell nodded slowly. "Yes," he said.

Ibram waited a breath, but Ahksell didn't elaborate, so Ibram moved along. "Just so," he said and spread his hands. He attempted a solemn, but sympathetic smile while Mistress Ignalle stared at him blankly. He lowered his eyelids and looked at her sideways.

"There are always questions," he said. "With a dead body in a household. Not that you would know to answer them, but your father's widow certainly might."

The thought went through her entire body like a bolt of energy; Ibram watched how she wriggled on the hook he had baited. She swallowed, pressing her lips together tightly. There was no love lost between those two, to be sure.

"Very well," she said with a quick gasp of inhalation, as if she had forgotten the need for air for a moment. "Do what you must, but I—I can't watch."

She fled the room with a stiff gait that reminded Ibram of nothing so much as a horse who sees the stable door after a hard day's work. He frowned after her. What exactly did she think they were going to do to the body? The door shut; Ahksell jumped.

"Well," he muttered. "At least we have permission."

"We're well within the law now," Ibram said, with a glance in

Dolman's direction. He tugged on his gambeson. The heat from the fire was doing its work to dry him off, but the smell of the funerary unguent was working itself into the fabric. He grimaced.

Ahksell opened his mouth as if he were going to debate the point, but he too remembered Mistress Dolman by the fire, and subsided. He came to stand at the foot of the corpse, and opened his carry-all. He withdrew the Hessele's Cage and held it in both hands. He wasn't comfortable, but being at a complete ease with a possibly murdered corpse seemed impossible. Ahksell narrowed his eyes in thought as he observed the length and breadth of Master Savoldyn. Ibram obligingly raised up the yellow blanket so that Ahksell could examine the body beneath.

"Are these the clothes he was wearing?" he asked.

Ibram shook his head. "He had on a velvet tunic and hose, I think. I would expect this silken traveler's attire is for the funeral."

"Of course it is," Mistress Dolman muttered, almost unwillingly.

Ahksell raised his eyebrows; Ibram shook his head. Master Savoldyn did look like a fancy merchant—which was what he had been, of course—but he'd been dressed as if he were going out on one of his own caravans. If that caravan had taken place in an evening courtyard's theater. His clothes were silk and fine cotton, and a large enameled fibula brooch had been pinned over his heart to hold closed the thick cloak upon which he lay. Jewels glittered on his fingers and in his hands was a small pouch. Ibram would bet that it contained wood-biscuits and a bit of dried meat for the journey.

"Put that over there," Ahksell said, pointing nearer the fire. "I need room to maneuver."

Ibram did as instructed; he folded the blanket in thirds and lay the bundle on a side table he noticed hidden in a corner of the building. Mistress Dolman continued to stir her cauldron. She seemed quite at home, and so Ibram left her to her business.

Ahksell unwrapped the red and yellow yarn which held the Hessele's Cage closed, and then opened the thin metal frames which made up the structure. For such a small bundle, it was a dramatically long and wide thing, a framework of the finest metal threads connected by tiny hinges. Ibram thought even his own father, master craftsman that he was, might have struggled to accomplish so delicate a task as making it.

"Hold one end for me," Ahksell said. "I need to rewind the strings around it. Really, Attendant Dakreia is very hard on her tools."

Ibram licked his lips. "Are you certain? It seems to be glittering a bit."

Ahksell shrugged. "It can't hurt you," he said. "It's just happy to be waking up."

That didn't make Ibram feel any better, but he held up his hands anyway. "I just don't wish to be shocked again, that's all."

Ahksell winced. "Yes, well, don't worry about that," he said.

"You say that now, but if I develop a tic or some such from your continual jolting, then I demand you take responsibility for my care."

"I've got the tricky part," Ahksell assured him. "Just go back to his head, maybe a little further."

Ibram grasped the furthest metal threads which Ahksell held out to him, and then walked backwards the length of the table. Ahksell quickly drew up both ends of the yarn dangling to the floor, the red and the yellow strings. He raised them up by their copper capped ends, took a deep breath, and then removed his hands. The yarn dangled in the air, and Ahksell extended both of his first fingers.

He began to move them over and under in the air, left and then right, and right and then left, as if he were listening to music only he could hear. A feeling like chafing rose up Ibram's spine, as though a prickling cone was being curled against his skin. It was like watching Lady Azadiya doing her meditations, rolling and unrolling her hair into braids, up and over her combs and hair sticks. Only in this case, Ahksell had his eyes open and carefully watching; he almost seemed to be holding his breath as the yarn wound itself precisely through the metal wires until the copper ends dangled an inch from Ibram's hands.

Ahksell coughed and took a deep breath. "That should do it," he said. "I'm getting better at that."

"Any time to practice is a good time, I suppose."

Ahksell rolled his eyes. "Just put the cage over the body, please."

Ibram did so with his corner of the Hessele's Cage, laying it over Savoldyn's head, and then stepping back from the table. Ahksell, after a moment, did the same by the corpse's feet. He stepped back and wiped his hands on his gambeson. The cage sparkled a little, a small flickering brightness at the hinges.

"It's old," Ahksell said. "I'm sorry about the bleed through."

"Can it tell us what we need to know?" Ibram asked.

"Of course," he said, "it isn't broken."

Ibram shrugged. "Well then, let's examine Master Savoldyn's fibers."

"That's not—never mind," Ahksell said, and then took out his introrse pendant.

He slipped the end loop over his middle finger on his right hand and let the braided copper wires drop down. Ahksell closed his eyes, and took a deep breath. He held out the pendant so that the trimstone arrowhead dangled at the top hinge of the Hessele's Cage, and then covered his right hand with his left. Ibram leaned against the back wall, and crossed his arms. Mistress Dolman had left off her stirring, and now watched, unabashed.

"An alchemist's work is quite a sight to behold, don't you think, Mistress?" he asked quietly.

She nodded without looking at him. "But the plane of reality is as nothing to the direction of the Navigator," she told him, in a creaking voice.

"Just so, just so," Ibram said. "Still, whatever gets you there, don't you agree?"

She sniffed audibly, and deigned to give him a stern look from the corner of her eye. Ibram grinned. He was only a harmless young man, after all.

"Did the meddlers send you?" she asked.

Ibram chuckled, but softly. Ahksell was following the path of the lights glimmering along the yarn twisted among the wires; he was at Savoldyn's knees now. His face was serene, but intent, and Ibram had no wish to break his concentration.

"No meddlers up the living mountain," he said, and craned his neck towards her direction. "Only helpful folk."

Mistress Dolman sniffed. "They focus too much on where they are, and not enough on where they are going."

"Such are the demands of reality," Ibram said. "Its perfection requires focus."

He watched her observing Ahksell at his trade; not many folk had the chance to see real technical alchemy. On player's stages at some of the evening courtyards they often played the ancient romances, where alchemists held very high offices and struck terror into the hearts of evil Isconians before dying in the arms of their beloved, but the alchemy was mostly sketched in. Honestly, it was often just folk waving their hands in the air and muttering about 'feeling the earth move,' as fake as magic. Still, it seemed to have distracted her from her past irritation at Ibram's sheer existence. He sensed a strategic opportunity on the horizon.

"I feel I should apologize, Mistress," he said. "My actions in your house were not me at my best."

"It is not my house," she said, a tad automatically. She seemed then to realize what he had said, and deigned to glance up at him from her seat on the hearth. "But you were quite rude."

"Then I apologize," Ibram said, with a short bow. "I allowed my concerns to overtake my common sense."

She nodded. They both spent a few moments watching Ahksell frowning at the lights on the Hessele's Cage. Ibram tilted his head. She seemed content to sit there until they left her alone with the body. Did familiarity breed such loyalty? If Ama or Father died, he couldn't imagine their own housekeeper, Kholdo, keeping such a vigil; it was generally a family duty. He paused. Well, he might bake rose cake for the altars.

"How long have you been in the Savoldyns' household? Only it's not often that I see a worthy such as yourself attending at a death. I thought this was the journey undertaken alone."

His nights eating dinner beneath the droning of a lecture hadn't left him completely underprepared, after all. The Navigator was very impressed by teamwork, but even more delighted with independence. In Vissilia, stubbornness was a celestial trait. The Savoldyns' falling out would have been socially upsetting, but religiously permissible.

Her mouth pursed in thought. "I have been their servant since Mistress Ignalle's own mother still lived," she said, after a pause. "I came with her into her new household when she married Master Savoldyn. Her father was a welcome visitor to the Ark."

"And Mistress Ignalle?"

Mistress Dolman snorted, and went back to stirring her cauldron. Ibram fought not to sneeze. He could see several open pots by her feet, clearly new ingredients to be added.

"Her husband is for the Advisor," she said. "Mistress Ignalle comes but rarely these days."

Ibram resettled himself against the wall, and raised his eyebrows. It wasn't unheard-of. His own parents had had a doubled wedding, in the forge for Father and under the stars for Ama.

"But she did before?" he asked, watching as Ahksell moved up the body.

Was the Hessele's Cage seeing something? Or did Ahksell read the little lights shining off the framework. Ibram didn't see much difference in one light to the next, they weren't even different colors. At least with the stickums and the automatons, you could get a show in as well as call a bit of luck to yourself. They desperately needed a bit of luck now. If Savoldyn really hadn't been poisoned, Ibram would throw himself on Mentor Nieminen's mercy and try to keep Ahksell out of it. If he couldn't...well, he had better hope Ladyship's recovery was swift and left her in a forgiving mood.

"Mistress Ignalle is a sharp one," Mistress Dolman said with a tired chuckle. "She knows how the wind blows."

"Is that why she showed up the morning I arrived for Lady Azadiya's order?" Ibram asked. "Ladyship is a pretty important client."

Mistress Dolman shrugged one shoulder. "That, I could not say," she said. "She simply came to the door, just after breakfast, and asked to see her father."

"And you admitted her?"

"Master Savoldyn never gave instructions to bar her from the manor," she said. "I admitted her, and they spent the time much as you witnessed."

Ibram nodded slowly. "Just in time to share a cup of shay and screaming."

"The screaming happened," Mistress Dolman said, as she stirred her pot. "But not the shay. When Master Savoldyn sent for his next drink, there was only one cup."

Ibram tilted his head to the side. "Only one? A bit pointed, wouldn't you say?"

"I'm sure Marit merely hadn't realized two were required," Mistress Dolman said. She shook her head suddenly, and huffed a laugh. "If she had, there would have been bread and butter as well. Our cook is proud of her skill, and Mistress Ignalle appreciates a good meal."

"Oh?"

"Almost as much as getting her way—In that, she resembles her father. I remember, once, when her lady mother was still on the path, she ran away with a caravan sent to the Red Coast to take ship to Orlinda."

Ibram smiled. "All that way?"

Mistress Dolman looked amused; her eyes turned inward. "She sent a note by runner, telling her parents they needed a full accounting of the cargo, and she had appointed herself deputy."

Ibram shuffled his feet against the floor, and laughed quietly. "Your young mistress sounds like a handful," he said.

"She always knew her own mind," Mistress Dolman replied. "Even then."

"Was she as good at the business as her father?" he asked.

"They worked well together," Mistress Dolman said, "when her mother was alive to mediate. They got so that they could anticipate each other's..."

She swallowed and shook her head. Ibram watched as Ahksell moved around Savoldyn's head; he bent over, almost as if he were listening to something. Mistress Dolman leaned forward to fit another small log on the fire, and then resituated herself. Ibram rubbed his eyebrow with his thumb.

"I suppose you must have been around, when she ran away to be married," he said.

She snorted. "Of course, I was," she said. "Don't you remember the ruckus? The shame of her rejection nearly killed him, then. I felt sorry for him."

Ibram shook his head. "I'm afraid I was out and about when every-thing happened," he said. "It's the first I ever heard of it."

"She cast off the expectations of her family, all the work she put into the business..." Mistress Dolman pressed her lips together. "I would not say his response was just, Master Ucalegon, but anyone could have told her the outcome of her rash decisions."

"Too much alike, as you said," Ibram said, and watched her care-fully. Grief did many things to folk, made them talkative, made them quiet. Some got angry and then let it burn through them. Mistress Dolman seemed tired.

"Where is Mistress Savoldyn?" he asked.

"At home," Mistress Dolman said. "The terms of the master's will requires an inventory be taken of the household goods and stores."

"Surely that's a job for the housekeeper," Ibram said.

"Mistress Savoldyn feels more at ease with a task at hand," she said, "Now that he's not there, she has a greater degree of latitude."

Ibram leaned forward; he felt the urge to grin, but refused to let it show. "Ah, one of those folk, was he?" he whispered, as if they were in confidence. "I had an uncle like that, you know. Had to be in control of every little aspect of our work, almost never let me get a word in edgewise."

"I find it difficult to believe anyone could stopper your tongue, Master Ucalegon," she said.

Ibram waved his right hand in the air. "Oh, we always find ways around a difficult man, don't we?"

Mistress Dolman might have been tired enough of her responsibili-ties, but she wasn't stupid. Her face returned to that pinched expres-sion which Ibram was so familiar with. She took up the ladle in the cauldron and stirred its contents.

"Master Savoldyn was a man who demanded respect," she said.

"A man can demand all he wants," Ibram said with a shrug of his left shoulder. "I don't know if it changes what he receives."

Ladyship once told him, during that unfortunate incident with the portable forge and the linen chest, that everyone in the world had a story they wanted to tell someone about. Sometimes the story changed, and sometimes they never told more than part of it, but if a good agent tapped that rich vein, there was no telling what might spill out.

He glanced up at Ahksell, who was rounding the table again, this time following the red thread. Whisps of smoke rose up from beneath his hands, but Ahksell seemed sanguine about the matter and Ibram let it pass without question. Mistress Dolman made a noncommittal noise in the back of her throat. Ibram considered what he knew—which was little enough—and what had been bothering him, which was plenty. He considered the quality of Mistress Dolman's yellow gown; it was old, but finely made.

"May I ask you something, Mistress Dolman?"

She leaned back quickly, as if surprised, and peered up into his face. "Like what?"

"I have no wish to embarrass you," Ibram said, and she raised her eyebrows at him. He stood away from the wall and crouched before her, spreading his hands to show his palms. "Why do you have so few servants? A man who can import glass cloth to Lady Azadiya can run a full household."

Mistress Dolman sighed and looked out over the body. Ahksell glanced up; he was winding his introrse pendant around his first two fingers, pointing the arrowhead at Savoldyn's heart. Ibram shook his head quickly, and Ahksell returned to his work.

"When Mistress Ignalle—the young mistress Elene as she was—ran away from home to be married, it was her maid who helped her, and a groom who covered their escape," Mistress Dolman said, while she laced her hands in her lap. "Master Savoldyn turned them out in a rage, and most of the household with them. It has just been myself, Hilo, and the kitchen staff ever since. Until his marriage, of course, when his wife brought her own maid."

An entire household of servants released in such a manner as that. Ibram chewed the thought over in his mind. That was quite a number of resentful people to keep track of, whether they were upset at the impetuous young mistress or her father, or more likely, both. They would have knowledge of the house and grounds, as well.

Ahksell stepped away from the table with a sigh that swelled and deflated his entire chest. He looked down at his pendant, now pooled in the cup of his palm, and then shook his head. Ibram stood up while Ahksell put his tool away, and then began to gather the Hessele's Cage together.

"Mistress Dolman," Ahksell said with a frown at the body. "I feel I must ask you an impertinent question."

"That seems to be the fashion with you boys," Mistress Dolman said.

Ahksell cleared his throat, and ducked his head. "Well, yes, I suppose so."

"I don't know about that, to be sure," Ibram said at the same time.

They both paused, and then Ibram waggled his fingers for Ahksell to continue. Ahksell bit his lip; his eyes narrowed in thought.

"Master Savoldyn was a drinking man," he said, and continued at Mistress Dolman's nod. "What did he drink the morning of his death?"

"No more than his usual," Mistress Dolman said. She struggled to her feet, leaning one hand on the hearth to propel her upwards. "A glass of tolnic with his morning meal, and shay throughout the day."

"Nothing else?" Ahksell said. "Something one of the other servants might have given him?"

She clasped her hands together, worrying her thumbs over the knuckles. "He has been feeling ill," she said. "So he reduced the amount of tolnic he drank, from two to one mug a day."

"A mug of tolnic?" Ibram asked. "Goodness."

"Our cook's herbs and spices make it more beneficial to the body than you'll find in some draughtshop," Mistress Dolman said, regaining some of her previous sharpness. "She fortifies it herself."

"Spices *and* fortifies?" Ibram asked. That hadn't been what she'd told him.

"Why are you asking me this question?" Mistress Dolman stepped forward towards Ahksell. "Have you found something?"

Ahksell gathered the Hessele's Cage into both of his hands, and turned to face her more fully. His jaw was firm, but Ibram could see regret writ in the corners of his eyes. Ahksell nodded. "Mistress Dolman, would you please go and retrieve the pilot of this Ark, and Mistress Ignalle. The Preceptory of Yseult in the Sect of Seven Fires must make a formal request to remove this corpse for our inspection."

✤ *9* ✤

mota Viran pinched the bridge of his nose and bowed his head. In a normal hour, Ibram would have already been half-way towards a twelve-day patrol rotation around the glasshouses where the medicinal corps grew the plants for their foul ointments. As it was, his superior's dismay would have to wait. Third Mentor Nieminen had been summoned immediately upon his and Ahksell's arrival with, in order, one corpse, two distraught family members, and no less than the pilot and bo'sun of the local Ark. They had not been a happy party on their journey up the living mountain, and sadly, Ibram had found no glad tidings upon their arrival.

The corpse had been taken to a chillier location while its party had been ushered into a hastily erected gaudy pavilion with shay and snacks, and made comfortable. Ibram and Ahksell had been marched to Amota Viran's command tent, and made to explain themselves. Well, they would have explained themselves, had not it been for Third Mentor Nieminen's yelling. Really, she had no cause for such alarm, they had discovered a murder, after all.

He glanced at Amita Sarrha, who had invited herself into the meeting on the strength of no one being willing to cast her out of it. She seemed amused as she sat in her chair, rolling a fat cabochon of green and white serpentine rock along her knuckles as if it were a coin trick. When she caught him staring, she jerked her head in the Third Mentor's direction; Ibram refocused on the lecture.

"—out even a word to your superior agent," Mentor Nieminen was saying. "You might very well have caused a serious incident amongst the clerics! You are not at liberty to abscond with every dead body you find yourself curious about! Hasty, slipshod work undertaken in secrecy in defiance of your own chain of command is no replacement for due obedience to the authority of those your own mentor chooses to represent her interests. You both have shamed your preceptory, and your division, and when Mentor Hobon, wheelmaker willing, is released from her tower, I will absolutely be recommending your immediate censure."

Ibram straightened up while she paused to draw breath. "I take it this means you are not censuring us yourself," he said.

Amota Viran's entire body heaved in a soundless sigh. In front of him, Third Mentor Nieminen stared fixedly at him, a monument to disdain in every angle of her face and posture. She leaned back in the chair she had taken from Amota Viran, and placed both bony hands on its curved arm rests. She was an unusual sort for an alchemist, most of them tended to keep on looking as if they were in the prime of their years no matter how old they actually were. Lady Azadiya, for instance, looked just as she had since Ibram had first been formally introduced to her at the age of ten. The Third Mentor, however, appeared much older, with long wispy grey hair and a soft neck. She wore her hair long and free in the northern fashion, and her green quilted gambeson was embroidered at both shoulders in heavy gold curlicues, with her mongoose collar tag done in silver. A thick chain of jellied gold links entwined with opals lay along her neck, and jeweled rings lay heavy on all her fingers; clumsy work, but expensive looking. He supposed she must have begun her studies late in life, which either argued for her native talent or her persistence.

"I," she said in dire tones, "will be fully acquainting Mentor Hobon with the disastrous, insubordinate behavior of her agent and her Attendant. This division is a disgrace."

Around the table, agents Ibram did not recognize looked down at their hands or nodded in support. He supposed them to be a part of Mentor Nieminen's party. Amita Sarrha raised her eyebrows, but said nothing, and Amota Viran, who Mentor Nieminen had not invited to sit down, finally looked up from his boots.

"None the less," he said in heavy voice, "the news they bring is serious."

"And preposterous," Nieminen scoffed. "You already told me Attendant Abele ruled out any kind of poison in the shay this one—" she flicked her hand towards Ibram, "—brought back from the merchant's house."

She frowned in irritation, and then twisted in Amota Viran's chair. "And stand up here, Kalmar," she snapped. "You'll make me get a crick in my neck. As for you, Attendant Solari, never in my life have I been witness to such callous disregard for the work of your superiors. You have taken time away from their work in the name of your own studies and then wasted the opportunity granted to you in childish defiance."

Ibram dared a glance in Ahksell's direction; he stood stiffly and stared into the space above Nieminen's head, ignoring Ibram entirely. It wasn't often Ahksell got dragged over the coals, as it were, in their corner of the preceptory. At least, not for anything more serious than being found wandering in the laundry after hours because he'd rolled an inkpot over his blanket in his sleep. Ibram gripped his right hand by the wrist behind his back, and rested his weight on his heels. He'd not had the pleasure of the Third Mentor's company very often, usually when he was young enough to run messages between the divisions. He couldn't say he was enjoying the experience.

One of her agents jumped suddenly, and slammed his elbow on the table. The room flinched at the noise, and he cleared his throat. Awkwardly, the man rose up from his seat at the table, and stepped away towards the waxed woolen wall. Ibram noticed he was favoring his left foot when he bent in a half-bow and drew his hand out to the chair, offering it to Viran. Amota Viran nodded at the other man as he passed, and then took the recently vacated seat held out to him, at Mentor Nieminen's right. Amita Sarrha smiled at him from her seat directly opposite.

Ibram bit his lips together to keep from laughing. He and Ahksell remained standing, but at least now they didn't have to keep shifting their attention too far. After all, a crick in the neck was a sore subject.

Mentor Nieminen sighed, and rested her back against her chair. "You will explain to me again, Attendant Solari," she said. "Why you felt it necessary to observe the dead man's body through Hessele's Cage."

Ahksell swallowed, heavily enough to be visible, and nodded. He stepped forward, but Ibram came alongside him as well. It wasn't just that Ahksell should take the blame.

"I requested a further inquiry," Ibram said. "Master Kalmar knew of my suspicions, and when Attendant Abele revealed that she had found nothing in the shay Master Savoldyn had drunk, I knew I needed to present further evidence to you, Mentor Nieminen."

"I asked Attendant Solari a question," Nieminen said. "I do not recall seeking your opinion."

It wasn't an opinion, it was what happened, but Ibram kept his mouth shut. He noticed Amita Sarrha had her flat rock out on the table; she was rubbing her thumb along the white stripe at its green center. She caught his eye, and tapped the stone twice, as if coming to a decision, and then looked away. He frowned.

"And don't look so sour," Nieminen snapped. "You'll get your turn soon enough, young man."

Ibram straightened his posture, and nodded briskly.

"Mentor Nieminen," Ahksell began, and then cleared his throat.

"What were you doing in a house of mourning, anyway?" she asked.

"Searching for evidence," Ahksell said. Ibram could see his hands flexing into fists at his sides, but he didn't know if anyone at the table noticed. "When someone dies in a house suspected of a grave crime, there can never be too much care taken or suspicion too outside the realms of possibility."

"I suppose your Mentor told you that," Nieminen said. She shook her head. "Azadiya might think it educational to let you run wild amongst the commonfolk, Solari, but I will not have the honor of the sect besmirched by such illicit behavior. Indeed, Pilot Joundir tells me you and your agent sought entry to the Ark under false pretenses!"

"Not so," Ibram exclaimed. "We came in out of the rain, did we not? And paid our fee. It isn't our fault a murdered man entered first."

"Don't speak unless you are spoken to," Mentor Nieminen said.

"Of course," Ibram said, and bowed. He saw Amota Viran wave him up again, and stood to find Nieminen focusing her gimlet eyes on Ahksell.

"And the cage?" she asked, tapping the fingers of her right hand on her armrest.

"It was tied with yellow and red yarn," Ahksell said. "A standard array for work with organic matter."

"Why not white, if you suspected poison?"

Ahksell glanced over his shoulder at Ibram, apologetically. "Well, I—"

"If Attendant Abele found no poison, we did not wish to contradict her, to be sure," Ibram interrupted. No need to let her know they'd left the living mountain unprepared as well as with intent to meddle. "Better to have a bird's eye view, than an ant's."

"I grow very tired of your interference," Mentor Nieminen said.

"Enough, Ibram," Amota Viran said with a sigh.

"Very sorry," Ibram said. "I only mean to be helpful."

He smiled at Mentor Nieminen, and leaned forward, just a titch, onto the balls of his feet. Ladyship hated interruptions as well, but that was why she always interviewed folk separately. If Nieminen didn't want his and Ahksell's stories to match, then she should not have allowed Ibram to stay in the tent. He could do very well just listening behind the cloth tent, after all.

She sniffed and turned her cheek. "The yellow was spun from alfrin powder, I suppose? And the red?"

"Dyed with Malbiscus," Ahksell said.

Ibram cocked his head. Ahksell had explained the alfrin powder to him once, as there was little he could do with the information beyond knowing it. Something about a sliding transmutation, where alfrin powder, mashed from rocks that glittered like gold ore, was gold's lesser twin. Since souls were uniformly gold the alfrin reacted to... whatever it was in the body that the powder didn't find familial, like spotting a cousin across a lake and then getting close enough to realize it was merely a girl with the same hair color.

"What does that do?" Amita Sarrha asked in a bored tone, but with sharp eyes. "A healer tied red malbiscus yarn around my bad knee, but I never noticed much difference."

"Malbiscus flowers are one of the lesser balances of blood," Ahksell said. "The flowers are good to eat—you can even make a shay with them—but when you dye the yarn, it calls forth impurities, darkening the fibers." He paused and then straightened his shoulders. "Which is why when the yellow yarn lit up as I delved with my introrse pendant, the red yarn blackened. Master Savoldyn's soul was materially harmed by something which caused his body—his very blood and bile—to turn against him, almost like an acid."

"And you discovered this with his daughter's permission?"

Ahksell nodded. "She allowed me to examine the body."

"A disgraced daughter's atonement, perhaps," Mentor Nieminen mused, with her fingertips tapping on the armrest. Her eyes sharpened. "The widow was not also present?"

Amota Viran jumped, only slightly, but Ibram caught it and so too did Amita Sarrha. Ahksell glanced back at him, and Ibram nodded.

"I've never been introduced to her," Ahksell replied. "Ibram?"

"Mistress Savoldyn is at work protecting her husband's interests," he responded. "She is in deep seclusion, taking inventory, until the rushes on her gate are lit."

Ibram thought it more likely she was enjoying her time alone, but he kept the thought back. The Third Mentor had not spoken to him, after all. All he had heard of her through her division's agents and assorted servants was proving itself rather more fact than fiction. Her work revolved around keeping the Great Houses apprised of their cadet branches' goings on, really. A delicate balance of diplomacy and salacious gossip, but very rarely bloody.

Mentor Nieminen looked as if she had swallowed something nasty. "I had hoped to be able to present this mess to Mentor Stadat for his supervision," she said. "Azadiya finds the puzzle worth lowering herself to this level, but I do not."

Ibram stiffened, and clenched his hand around his wrist, digging his fingernails into the skin. Ladyship considered nothing and no one beneath her station, merely allowed that there were some folk she wanted to work with and others with whom she must merely deal. Amota Viran's face was perfectly composed as he watched the Third Mentor speak, but Ibram noted how still he and Amita Sarrha kept themselves in their chairs.

"And yet this is how matters stand, Mentor Nieminen," Amota Viran said. "We seek your guidance."

She sighed audibly, and shook her head. "And at festival time as well," she muttered. "Very well. Let us hear what this clerk and his wife have to say on the matter. Touran send the body to the medicinal corps. Perhaps they have some white yarn in their possession."

The agent who had been standing by the wall of the tent bowed, and left. None of the visiting agents had spoken a word as of yet, but they might have been ordered to only observe and remember. Ladyship did that often as well. Ibram switched his weight from his left to his right foot and then back again; his stomach rumbled. Amita Sarrha wrinkled her nose in amusement at him.

"Has Lady Sebbina been informed that one of her clerks is here?" she asked.

"She will be apprised of the facts as soon as is needful," Mentor Nieminen said shortly.

"Then with your permission," Amita Sarrha said, with an emphasis on her flowing Merrilian accent that made Amota Viran's eyebrows shoot all the way up to his hairline. "I'd like to take Ucalegon and Attendant Solari to get something to eat whilst I go fetch the family Ignalle. Young men, you know, they can only run on spit and vinegar for so long."

"Indeed," Mentor Nieminen said after a pointed lack of response. "You may remove yourself."

Amita Sarrha stood up from the table with no difficulty. She snapped her worry stone up in her hand, and then stumped around the side of the table toward the exit, waving at Ibram as she went. He turned and bowed shortly to Mentor Nieminen, stood when she curled her right hand carelessly upwards, and then exited after letting Ahksell take the lead. Once outside, he opened his mouth and was loudly shushed by Amita Sarrha.

"There'll be none of your prattle," she said, sternly and loudly. "And don't bother the Attendants, they're busy with real work."

Ibram shut his mouth, and followed her and Ahksell away from Amota Viran's commandeered tent. They stepped back out onto the road which led to Ladyship's tower, but turned left instead of right. Ibram cast a look backwards over his shoulder. He could slip away once Amita Sarrha had escorted them back to the food, and then see if he could get the catapult working again. He frowned. If she was still in her tower, anyway. But if she was, and he couldn't work the catapult, then he could at least shout at her. Or throw the rocks! They could not be that heavy; it was only a little war machine.

He walked quickly, catching up to Ahksell and standing between him and Amita Sarrha. She was a tall woman, who walked with her chin faced forward into the wind, invincible, one of the seafolk direct from the Red Coast where Ladyship's family resided. He glanced down at her dusty boots.

"Aren't you tired?" he asked. "You look dressed for patrol, and then to have to listen to that badosh talk must have taken the stuffing out of you."

Amita Sarrha flicked him in the ear without a change in her stride. "Keep a civil tongue in that mouth, or I'll make the rest of you run up and down the eastern field."

Ibram flinched and grabbed the side of his head, cupping his ear. Ahksell snorted, and knocked their elbows together. Ibram angled his face towards him; Ahksell's mouth was crumpled at the edges. His eyes showed strain.

"Do you think it's enough to work with?" Ahksell asked. "Do you think they'll call the warders out and blockade the Savoldyn house? How do—I mean, what's going to happen to them?"

Ibram shrugged. "No idea. I suppose they'll have to be examined in some such fashion. They stood to gain in the terms of the will. They're about the only ones to benefit, but I don't know all the particulars like Amota Viran does."

Amita Sarrha marched forward in silence for a few steps with her back straight as a fireplace poker. She squinted across the training grounds on their right, and rubbed her thumb along her forefinger.

"I gave you a body," Ahksell said. "So we could start there."

"You didn't give me—the murderer gave me a body," Ibram said. "You merely...did whatever it was you did with that pendant of yours."

"I examined the weave of Master Savoldyn's remaining connections to the corporeal plane," Ahksell said.

"I am at a loss as to how you believe that to be an explanation."

"And it's not exactly true," Ahksell continued as if Ibram hadn't spoken. "You know enough to know who profits from Savoldyn's death."

Ibram tugged his hair at the nape of his neck. "That is true."

Amita Sarrha snorted. "Finding someone of that sort," she said, "is as much a matter of asking the right questions as it is keeping the ears sharp and the eyes open."

Ibram thought that must be the other way around, but didn't mention it. He nodded to his aunt instead. "Have you done so before?"

She nodded, a quick up and down jerk of her chin. "There's nothing you won't do in Lady Azadiya's service, if you manage to stick around long enough," she said. "Look at me, fifty miles from the prow of a ship and on dry land. There used to be a man lived down by the imperial border, had a lively business transporting the unlawfully dead in fish barrels. Almost had to contract with the Abyss to keep him contained."

"That's terrible!" Ahksell exclaimed.

"Comes of dishonest dealings, Solari," she said. "You air your ill humor in the street, and it gets mud on your boots."

Ibram turned his grin down at his boots as they walked further along the road, so that Amita Sarrha wouldn't smack him for frivolity. He cleared his throat and raised his head to gaze at the sky, feeling the corners of his mouth twitching upwards. Ahksell knocked into him again, and he poked him back.

They were coming up on the bend in the road just beyond the last rise. Ibram could see the pointed peak of the central pillar holding the guest pavilion up. They stepped off the road to avoid an oncoming hand cart, and onto the soft grass.

"Anyway, the principle need is the same," Amita Sarrha said. "What did you find in the study?"

"Ledgers and bad poetry," Ibram said.

She nodded. "Bad poetry? Whose?"

"Savoldyn's," Ahksell said. "There was a small fortune in wooden slat scrolls on his shelves."

"And he'd been losing money on his journeys," Ibram said. "It was the strangest thing. He kept applying for permits to shorter and shorter trips."

"His wife in good clothing?" she asked.

"Expensive fabric, nothing worn," Ibram said. "The castoffs her servant wears aren't very old."

"Loss of business, a household to maintain," Amita Sarrha mused, "and an expensive hobby. Not many can afford that." Amita Sarrha stopped walking; she smiled lopsidedly. "But there is no poison in the shay."

"Ibram didn't watch him drink everything he might have consumed during the day," Ahksell said quickly. "He could have had it at any other time."

"So we must ask them who would profit most from the death," she said. "Now, you see, this is how you catch a man with something to reveal. What's the first lesson, Ib-la?"

Ibram swallowed heavily. "A body wants to talk, especially when being complimented."

"A truth as solid as water in the north," Amita Sarrha said.

"But that's just a trick!" Ahksell exclaimed.

She shrugged. "We're but arms-for-hire, Solari, making our way in a deceitful world. Tricks are dead useful."

"How can I help then?" Ahksell asked.

"No need for aid," she said, and eyed him carefully. "It's an agent's job, not an alchemist's."

"He's already involved," Ibram said. "Why can't he keep his ears open?"

"He butted in without Ladyship's permission," Amita Sarrha said. "Which none of us ought to do if we can possibly help it."

"Well, you can't run a Hessele's Cage by yourselves," Ahksell said.

"Though we still need him because what if they explain something about his humors or the animus?" Ibram asked quickly. "I never paid attention at the Bedris school, everyone knows that."

"What I care about," she said, holding up one hand, "is finding out the correlation between the body, and the current debacle. Now, we shall escort the Ignalles back down to Viran. Consider this practice, Ibram. I want to know more about these two by the time we return to the command tent than they do about themselves."

"And after that?" Ibram cleared his throat of the rock lodged within it. "What are you going to tell Amota Viran?"

"What would I need to tell him?" she asked. "Do I work for him? No, I do not. I merely make my own way."

She waved them both forward to the pavilion and began walking on her own. They hurried to catch up. It was a short distance, not even fifty feet away, but Ibram's racing mind skipped from his pleasantries to the Ignalles and their clerics, to his own predicament, to Ladyship still up in her tower, and then to Amita Sarrha.

"Yes, of course," Mistress Ignalle was saying. "We are only too happy to have this sorry circumstance explained to us."

"Right this way, then," Ibram said. His attention caught on the velvet flower sewn above the bow on Mistress Ignalle's shoulder. Her loose yellow robe was also velvet, and still done in the southern style, but it lacked the fasteners for sleeves. Most southern dresses that closed at the shoulders were pinned by golden hinge brooches or filigree clasps, not cheaper fabric ties. Perhaps the shoddy house was not the only place the Ignalles saved money.

The whole party—husband, wife, pilot and bo'sun—accompanied them back down the hill. Ibram didn't have much time, if he wasn't to fail Amita Sarrha. If she thought he was slacking on the job, running in circles would be the least of his worries.

"I didn't get the chance before, Mistress Ignalle," Ahksell said, and Ibram forced himself to pay attention. "But may I express my deepest sympathies for the loss of your father?"

"I thank you, Attendant," Mistress Ignalle said, and touched the white cap on her head. "I confess it was a surprise."

"It always is, when a parent dies," her husband spoke up beside her.

He had a pleasant, smooth kind of voice. They were dressed in a similar style, as was the fashion for monied couples. His yellow coat was of the same crushed velvet, and beneath it, his blue robe brushed leather boots. "I found myself quite shocked, even though the old man had been drinking since before I ever knew him. I take it, however, that something is amiss?"

"Why would you say that?" Ibram asked, and tucked his hair behind his ears.

Master Ignalle turned his head to blink in surprise at him. "Why else would we be here?" he asked, and lifted one hand to the air. He had a studied manner about him; Ibram narrowed his eyes. "I would never presume to think the Sect of Seven Fires would disturb a corpse's journey to the pyre without good reason."

"And it had better be a very good reason," Pilot Joundir interrupted. He was a peevish sort, with a bald head beneath his square yellow cap. His silent bo'sun trailed at his elbow. "Master Savoldyn's wishes upon his death were very clear to us at the Ark. I will not have his soul's journey derailed on an alchemical whim!"

Amita Sarrha dropped a step behind to keep pace with the clerics, leaving Ahksell and Ibram to bracket the Ignalles. She smoothed her hand down her sect brooch. Her eyes rested on Ibram; at her side, her hand revolved in a clear gesture to get on with it.

"Hardly that," Ibram said, keeping the Ignalles in the corner of his vision. "Are you well acquainted with his wishes, Pilot Joundir?"

"I am," he acknowledged. "As a dedicated soul, Master Savoldyn placed his will into our keeping, with the particulars to be dispensed after his death. We held it in trust once it had been duly recorded in the Hall of Records in the Bureau of Commerce."

"So when his widow comes out of seclusion, she'll be joining the family for the pyre?" Ibram asked.

Mistress Ignalle's face twisted briefly, as if she had scented something foul. "I suppose she must," she said. "Though the world knows nothing good will come out of it for her."

"All the better," Pilot Joundir said with a heavy tone. "To bind oneself to another without hope of reward, but in true feeling."

Her lips pursed very tightly together; her cheeks flushed. Ibram had a feeling that if circumstances had been different, Mistress Ignalle's tongue would not have been so firmly held behind her teeth. Her husband sighed faintly, and looked out over the training fields to the lightly cloudy sky overhead.

"I suppose that's so," Ibram said, and tilted his head upwards a bit. "I'm afraid I was away when the business occurred, but you might be a finer example of that, eh, Mistress?"

"I?" Mistress Ignalle startled, and then ducked her head with a pleased smile. "I suppose we must be, are we not, Dima?"

Her husband's polite smile turned indulgently in her direction. "Indeed so, Elene," he murmured, and then he glanced up. "You weren't here for the scandal, then, Master Ucalegon?"

Over both their heads, Ahksell opened his eyes wide and shook his head. Ibram pressed onward, conscious of the shortness of the road before them. There was a chance they would be allowed back into the tent, but it was far more likely that the Amota Viran would order them away again.

"I was not," Ibram said. "Though my younger sister was in raptures about it upon my return. I feel I missed quite the adventure."

"They chased us all the way to the river crossing," Mistress Ignalle said, with a laugh. "but I tossed a basket out of the window of the carriage. It startled the riders' horses, and we were able to get across the north bridge with no one to catch us!"

Master Ignalle shook his head, grinning. "And then it was a seven-day of hiding under assumed names until her father's arms-for-hire stopped watching for us."

"They told Father I must have already taken ship!"

They really were quite proud of themselves. The entirety of their demeanor had changed, from a studied mourning to a bright and eager recounting. Ibram watched the way their bodies turned inward towards each other as they linked arms, the luster in their eyes as they spoke. Ibram looked over to Ahksell, and saw his own surprise echoed there. An elopement begetting a disinheritance no doubt fathered further humiliations, yet there they walked, blithely unconcerned about what this death meant for their next round of friendly village inspection. No one blessed with their full complement of wits was that much in love.

Ibram whistled lowly, and kept his own smile as charming as he could make it. Which was fairly charming, in his own estimation. He felt a little more solid on his feet now.

"What a to-do," he said. "I congratulate you on your success."

Mistress Ignalle turned her head at that, all easy smiles, and then suddenly sobered. She coughed and squeezed her husband's arm. "Yes, well," she said. "It was years ago now, and I don't regret it a moment. Only...only what followed."

She sniffled, and removed a handkerchief from her husband's sleeve, and then pressed it below her nose. It sounded true enough, though her sudden turns of feeling felt a bit abrupt. But then, again, people couldn't only be unhappy during their grief. There had to be room for the rest of life as well, as it continued. He glanced down at her shoes as Mistress Ignalle kicked a stone from her path. They were made from fabric, and the right side of the sole had been previously mended. Ibram nodded and let his smile turn sympathetic.

"It was quite a fight I interrupted," he said, leaning forward as if there was no one else to hear.

"Such a stubborn man," she said, a real trace of impatience in her voice now. "When Mother died there was no padding between us, and it simply got worse whenever he refused to listen." She dabbed her face with the handkerchief again, and then wrapped it in her hand. She wistfully eyed the training fields and the Learners twisting through their meditative poses. "I used to come up the living mountain as a child, you know. Such a beautiful place"

"I had heard you visited," Ibram said. He hadn't until just now, but it still counted.

She smiled at him. "Mother had no other family, and the sect has several of her family's glasswork. She used to come and advise the artisans...allowed me to follow along and learn to negotiate." She shook her head. "Father never seemed to think much of my lessons."

"But you kept trying," Ahksell said. "That's what I—that's what's important."

Ibram's eyebrows drew together, but Ahksell had turned his face suddenly, and all he saw was the edge of his jaw. He made note of the slip, and set it aside for a later time. The Ignalles were nodding along, after all.

"Yes, indeed," Mistress Ignalle said. "There's no such thing as a closed negotiation."

"You were negotiating?" Ibram asked.

She stumbled a little. "Oh, a rock—my apologies, Master Ucalegon, I didn't hear that?"

"You said there was no such thing as a closed negotiation," he replied. "I did not know you were still involved in your father's trade." He laughed. "Rumor proves us wrong again, to be sure!"

Master Ignalle shook his head. "No, Master Savoldyn never allowed my wife to regain her responsibilities in the family business."

They walked down past the first row of tents and the fire pit where some of the other sect agents were gathered. Stories were clearly being told in the proper fashion, with a handheld drum and a small set of bells. A group of tiny Learners—young enough to still be housed in Bedris—sat at their feet, rapt.

"That must have been very difficult," Ibram said to keep their attention. "Mistress Dolman spoke quite highly of your dedication, Mistress Ignalle."

"Did she?" Master Ignalle spoke for his wife again. "Dolman's always been a silent support."

Mistress Ignalle's smile had more of a wince in it. She sighed. "I had hoped she would come with me, when Father turned the servants all out, but he kept her, so she stayed."

"Did you retain many of the servants?" Ahksell asked.

"No," she said. "The needs of our house are—quite different."

Ibram took another look at their clothing. It was of good cloth, but the embroidery was only thread. Mistress Ignalle's jewelry was fit to her previous station, but nothing new. Ibram had seen the set at their first meeting. Someone as particular of their appearance as she seemed to be would more likely take care to switch out her pieces along with her clothing. A woman capable of paying her own marriage fee in full would have a chest of jewels and clothes—especially one attached to a fabric business. Perhaps she had blown the lot on that wedding in

Delbrite, or sold an heirloom, if she didn't have money of her own. Hilo Kenes had mentioned that some of Mistress Ignalle's mother's glass had come to her after the woman had died, perhaps those glass bracelets were all she had left.

"Did you know him well, Master Ignalle?" he asked.

They were approaching the open awning of Amota Viran's tent. Ibram could see several sect agents he didn't recognize standing guard outside it. He frowned.

Ignalle sighed and shook his head. "I did not," he said. "We had some few dealings with each other, when I was commissioning fabric for my investment robes in the Bureau of Commerce."

"That was how we met," Mistress Ignalle said, and resettled her arm woven through her husband's. He patted her hand.

"What office do you inhabit?" Ahksell asked.

"I hold a small position in the office of market rights."

"Oh, well," Amita Sarrha said with a laugh. "So it's you we have to thank for all the little stalls crowding Lityen at the moment."

Ignalle smiled politely, but Ibram saw no answering pleasantry in his eyes. "As to that, Mistress," he said. "I am afraid that is beyond my level. I am attached to the head clerk for travel."

Ahksell's eyebrows shot up so high they met his hairline. He opened his mouth, and Ibram shook his head quickly. He smiled at Mistress Ignalle, hopefully the exchange was too quick for her notice.

"He has a most elegant hand," Mistress Ignalle said. "The clearest in the office. I can only hope our daughter has his skill when she grows up."

"May all the bells ring out for it," Ibram said.

She seemed a little unsure, but nodded pleasantly. They had arrived at the tent. Ibram moved forward to the front. The two agents on either side of the opening frowned at him.

"As instructed," Ibram announced. "Master and Mistress Ignalle, Pilot Joundir and, er, his Bo'sun to see the Third Mentor."

He could see past them into the tent, and felt his mouth drop open a bit before he recalled his dignity. Third Mentor Nieminen worked quickly. Second Mentor Stadat now sat tall at the head of the table, flanked by herself on the left. Amota Viran was nowhere to be seen.

Ibram caught the Second Mentor's steely eye, and froze for a crucial second, before bowing with his hands on his stomach.

"Not to worry," Stadat's voice boomed out from the tent, loud as a clap in an empty room. He seemed as overly friendly as ever with his smile just lingering on the far side of manic. His hair stuck out at angles around his head, framing his gaunt face and staring eyes. "Duty done! That will be all, Agent. Take our wayward Attendant back to his duties, and let these good people in!"

Ibram straightened immediately, and stepped back without turning his back. He moved to the side, and let the Ignalles, Joundir and the Bo'sun pass him by. He breathed in quickly as Amita Sarrha also went into the tent. She was a great one for Ladyship's standing orders on asking forgiveness, rather than requesting permission.

"Find Viran," she ordered quietly before she had crossed the threshold and the strange agent dropped the tent door between them.

Ibram glanced at him up and down. He was of middle-age with lank curls for hair and a thin mustache. His loose pants and tunic made him seem like a lost plainsman after a missing mouflon. The man opened his mouth as if he had something to say, and Ahksell cleared his throat. Ibram smiled tightly.

"Back to your duties, now, Attendant," he called out. "Job done, after all. Let me show you the quick path."

Ahksell's face was a courteous blank as they walked away from the tent and back onto the road. Ahksell opened his mouth, but Ibram shook his head. He led Ahksell to where the agents and Learners were telling stories, and then ducked down the opposite side of the group.

"Ibram!" Ahksell hissed.

Ibram twisted briefly to look behind himself and shushed him. They took the path through the tents set up close to each other, the servants with the mending and the Attendants piping some kind of concoction directly into the eyes of an overly trusting patient. They wove their way around and backtracked to the command tent; its canvas sides ruffled in the wind. Ibram sidled between it and the tent closest next to it. There was enough room to walk through, but as long as the wind didn't pick up and press the canvas against their bodies, there was more than ample space for an interested ear, or four.

Ahksell sighed at a dangerous level. Ibram looked left and then right. He ducked back out between the tents, and grabbed Ahksell by the sleeve. He tugged; Ahksell was unmoved. He raised his eyebrows; Ahksell's own eyebrows refused. He jerked his head and widened his eyes. Ahksell wrinkled his nose, and with a look like a man about to pitch off a short pier, stepped between the tents. Ibram led him to the middle and they paused between two guy ropes. He placed his finger sideways across his lips, and then leaned down, putting his ear right up against the tent. Behind him, Ahksell covered his face with one hand, but crouched down as well.

❦   10   ❧

Ibram paced the length of the garden wall from the entrance to Ladyship's kitchen garden to the first corner; he kicked a rock in the shell path down the hill and stalked back up again. The shells ground beneath his feet. Ahksell, standing tall by the garden gate, frowned at his approach.

"I know you're disappointed," Ahksell said.

Ibram clasped his hands behind his back, and kicked another rock into the hedges. Ahksell sighed, and shuffled his feet. The sailing lights attached to the outside of the gate wavered in the wind, making their mooring chains clink against one another. Ibram turned his nose up to the tree cover.

He shivered as the damp cold twined up his legs from the ground. The sky over Lityen was dark and littered with spinning stars following the rain, the clouds having passed down to the numerous other valleys and peaks that dotted the landscape at the foot of the Emerald Mountains. In the dim orange glow of the sailing lights, Ibram could see the wind dragging through the branches higher up. Ibram frowned, and flicked his thumbnail against the fabric wrapping the hilt of his sica. He whirled around to make another lap.

"We should have expected it," Ahksell said, and hid a yawn behind his hand. "It's one of Mentor's tents after all. Why wouldn't she have placed some kind of muffling weave within the canvas?"

Ibram twisted back to face him on one foot; he staggered slightly as he pointed his finger at Ahksell. "All that running to and fro, and we heard nothing!" he snapped. "A moment's conversation with two important and suspicious folk, and then Mentor Stadat sticks his fingers in our pie."

Ahksell held his gambeson more tightly against his frame as a sudden gust of wind blew down the path. "We heard enough, surely," he said. "You got the Ignalles talking about themselves."

"Oh, yes, their much beloved scandal." Ibram shook his head. "Who cares?"

"It's romantic."

"A man marries a rich girl against her father's wishes," Ibram said with a shake of his head. His hair had caught in his eyes again; it curled into frizz during the rains. "There is nothing to amaze in that. I can list six traveling plays all with the same story in their greedy hands."

"And it brings us no closer to figuring out who in that house is responsible for a murder," Ahksell said.

Ibram held his hands up to the night sky, and groaned.

"Where could the murderer have obtained poison? Did they make it? Or had it brought into the house, for that matter?" Ibram asked. His belly gurgled unpleasantly. They had had no chance of food after spending the rest of the day in a vain search for Amota Viran. He had not been in the tents, nor the makeshift dining hall, and no one had seen him at the relay stations either departing the living mountain or traversing more deeply into the sect. But Amita Sarrha wanted Amota Viran found, and so he would be. Amota Berac had seen him marching towards the stables, but Amota Lakum had been alone with Ladyship's aged destrier. At one point, they had even split the work between them and searched the length of every single training field in walking distance. By the time the servants had lit the torches, and the glow-bulbs had begun to shine out, nighttime had been well and truly under-way. If Amota Viran had slipped out, then he'd done it in the morass of Attendants running off to enjoy their leisure. No one could have kept track of that river of humanity.

They had given up searching the surrounding tents when Ahksell had caught sight of Attendants Dakreia and Zorion parading down the road carrying a box. All thoughts of a quick dinner had fled. It hadn't been the work of two moments' thought to figure out where they might be headed; all else could wait.

Ibram turned away from the hedges and jerked his head at Ahksell, who raised his eyebrows. Ibram crossed his arms over his chest, and ducked his chin. He waited for a moment, but neither a thought, nor an action strayed into his mind.

"Worst thought?" he asked, for want of a better option.

Ahksell shrugged. "The Second Mentor will decide there is nothing to the investigation and set it aside, which will leave us with nothing better to do than study."

"Or patrol."

Over the garden wall, Ibram heard a dim banging noise. They ducked their heads past the open gate. A man in a green smock passed by the broken window panes carrying something; lamp light beamed down from the upper levels of the tower. Ibram glared at the lonely catapult sitting in the middle of the garden with its small pyramid of ammunition. The bell tent in the center had been taken down, taking away any chance of scrounging up writing supplies without questions being asked. He leaned back out and shook his head.

"Still talking or some such," he muttered.

"And the warders will botch the thing," Ahksell resettled himself and continued their conversation. "Because all they're seeing is the division of the Savoldyns' goods and property, which shall carry on according to the law, and that means a murderer might go free."

Ibram dug his bootheel into the dirt. Murder was a question of property and authority, a crime against Imperial order. If the warders did become involved, they might do no more than confiscate the Savoldyn business, and deny the entire family their inheritances in penance for the insult against Her Gracious Majesty's peace. Ama used to tell Ibram tales of Merrilian justice, of punishment by single combat where the guilty could be redeemed through acts of valor before the Vissilians had outlawed the practice. Ibram didn't know which he preferred, but it seemed to him that a crime demanded a personal punishment, rather than a communal one. A warder's jail was a cold place to be alone, after all.

"How long does it take to make a—a what did you call it, a filtering mask, anyway?" Ibram asked.

"It takes as long as it takes," Ahksell said. "If they come out again, we'll ask for Hilbert and see if we can hear good news."

Ibram shook his head. "Attendant Zorion had better be nothing but cheerful, then. I grow very tired of this."

"Imagine how Mentor feels," Ahksell said.

Ibram groaned and dug the heel of his left palm above his eye. "She will not be best pleased."

Ahksell nodded. They stood there, for a moment, while the wind blew the scent of greenery and displaced earth about them. The entirety of the problem was that Ibram could only go so far without instruction. He hadn't the authority for his own legitimate investigation, and with Lady Azadiya stuck up the tower and Amota Viran off doing whatever he thought he was doing, then anything he did find ran the risk of becoming ignored as the ravings of an impertinent young man. An agent for the Sect of Seven Fires acted under the aegis of the alchemists, not beside them.

"You believe waiting around for the Second Mentor's judgement is futile?" Ibram asked. He felt his throat tighten.

"I do," Ahksell said, and tension Ibram had not before noticed flowed out of his body. "Mentor always says the worst mistakes are made in delaying the inevitable."

Ibram grinned. "But he could tell us to be done with it, and then you could go back to your gewgaw."

"True, but then what happens?" Ahksell said. "Do you inform the warders and let them run the roost? It's not even their village."

Ibram laughed under his breath. "True enough."

"I think if the empire wanted only the warders to handle affairs in this province, then it would say as much in the sect's charter," Ahksell said. "So, if one of our neighbors is murdered, are we not bound in law to appear before the next visiting judge and explain ourselves?"

Ibram tapped his foot on the ground in thought, and nudged his boot against a hand-sized shaped rock. "Indeed so."

"And what better way to keep the peace, then by providing both cause and culprit?" Ahksell asked.

Ibram laughed, and glanced at him. "Careful," he said. "You begin to sound like me."

"Better to say we both sound like Mentor," Ahksell said. He grew pensive just then, and bit his lips together. "What has you so out of sorts, anyway?"

Ibram shook his head. "Nothing much. Poor sleep."

Ahksell scoffed. Ibram turned and leaned against the stone wall. He raised his hand to his shoulder and flicked his finger at the man's back. The trees on the opposite side of the path bobbed in the wind; it ruffled Ibram's hair and sent a shiver down his spine.

"Worse thought?" Ahksell offered.

"Evil thought," Ibram said.

"What about?" Ahksell crossed his arms over his chest. "About the poisoning?"

"About——" Ibram cut off and looked about them, which was ridiculous since they were alone. Nonetheless, he felt prickles of uncertainty run up and down his spine. "About Amota Viran," he said in a quiet voice. "Is he a cautious man? Yes. Does he usually worry about the feelings of someone wholly unconnected to Lady Azadiya? No."

Ahksell stood before him, just beneath the nearest lantern, quietly at a loss, and then shook his head. "I see the bend of your thoughts, and I tell you now, I don't believe it."

Ibram frowned. "Why?"

"Because that would mean that Master Kalmar knew for a fact that Mistress Savoldyn had murdered her husband, when he barely admits you had cause to worry the man died unnaturally."

A miserable knot, half-hope of being talked out of it and half-certain of Ahksell's future failure, tightened in Ibram's chest. "He could be concealing her crime for her."

"For what reason?"

Ibram shrugged. "Love?"

"You merely said he *liked* her!"

"But then why would he not act on my suspicions?" Ibram snapped, and then flinched as bird suddenly took flight from a leafy bush on a rock outcropping.

Ahksell shook his head and opened his arms to turn his palms up to the sky in a helpless gesture. "Because he has so many demands on his time? Because he gave you a chance with Attendant Abele and she found nothing strange?"

"Because he is concealing a murder?" Ibram leaned in close.

Ahksell paused, and the slow rejection of Ibram's misfortunate thoughts rippled across his face. "He is too smart for that, surely."

Ibram narrowed his eyes. "How so?"

Ahksell looked up into the air in thought and then to the bushes and trees and the shell path. He met Ibram's eyes squarely at the end of his perusal and tightened his mouth. Ibram cocked his head; the knot in his chest pulsed.

"Who would be stupid enough to align themselves with a woman foolish enough to kill her husband when she could simply divorce him and be free? Especially if she could count on such a protector as Master Kalmar," Ahksell said. "And if she did, what could be the object of such a relationship but being victim number two when she inevitably meets the third?"

Ibram sank back on his heels and rubbed his hand around and up his neck into his scalp. He hiccupped a laugh. "That is the sum of your argument? The Vissilian love of divorce without compensation?"

"Is it better to go through the court of chancery like they do in Orlinda?" Ahksell asked. "She could have lived out of the house for a year and a day, and never had cause to worry again."

Ibram shrugged. There were many reasons for murder over divorce. The expense of finding another place to live, the lack of title and property if the marriage contract was not in their favor, a fear of reprisal... Ibram breathed out and watched his breath curl like smoke in the air. Night in the mountains was still chill compared to the valleys. It wasn't the worse thing in the world that Ahksell didn't have such thoughts as plagued him.

"Master Kalmar is a man of reason and caution and planning," Ahksell said. "We know him, Ibram! We have known him since our childhood. Would he truly put such a plan in motion? How?"

"Some alchemist's poison," Ibram muttered.

"Which would have immediately been identified by even an Attendant from Baran like Abele," Ahksell said. "And then no one would have been able to ignore it because it would implicate the sect."

"Not if no one knows Savoldyn was murdered!"

"Which is why he sent you?" Ahksell asked. "If he knew Savoldyn was to be murdered, then he knew when the man would die, did he not?"

Ibram swallowed. "It follows."

"Oh, thank you," Ahksell said. "My classes were not spent in futility. Because he didn't discover the body, did he?"

"I did," Ibram sighed.

"Because he couldn't," Ahksell said. "Because Mentor drank—"

"The potion Amota Viran handed her," Ibram said.

"See?" Ahksell jabbed him in the shoulder. "Proves he could not have done it."

Ibram frowned up into Ahksell's shining face, and scoffed. "How? I have slept on this—or not as the case might be—and it is hard to think that Amota Viran could have done such, but—"

"So he somehow adulterates a potion he would have no chance to interfere with unnoticed. He engineers Mentor and himself out of the way, leaving you to discover the body and thinking you will simply ignore every single oddity you find?"

Ibram's jaw set. He ground his teeth together and looked out over the expanse of trees and rocks to their right. He heard Ahksell sigh.

"Do you really believe it?" Ahksell asked. "Master Kalmar is a man of lists and rules. Does such a man leave behind his entire life and cast his fortune on you not doing your job? Would he betray all the trust Mentor has in him?"

"The thought is...unpleasant," Ibram said through a tight throat.

"No!" Ahksell answered himself.

Ibram dug his heel into the ground, feeling shells crack underneath his sole. "I would never have thought he would betray Lady Azadiya. She's his aunt."

"He's your uncle," Ahksell pointed out. "He wouldn't have done anything to damage Ladyship's reputation."

"And yet here we are."

Ibram flexed his hands in the cruxes of his elbows and shifted his weight on his feet. His mouth twisted to the left. Every division had its manners and customs, the paths to employment. The First Mentor favored clever folk with pasts in the Bureau of Information's offices of diplomacy. The Second Mentor was inclined to former soldiers. Third Mentor Nieminen provided a haven for a particular flavor of displaced nobility. The Fourth Mentor's domain was no different in that, perhaps, or at least, only in specifics.

"But he is truly her nephew," Ibram said. "She's his father's sister."

"See? You prove my point for me." Ahksell pointed at him, and then stopped. His mouth opened and closed. "That's not allowed, though," he said finally.

"Don't tell anyone, besides it doesn't come up much."

"The Proclamation of Incorporation clearly states alchemists are not allowed a household. That includes having an adult blood relation in their employ."

Ibram shrugged one shoulder. "You all still have families," he said. "Attendant Kivi has six siblings, all living close enough to celebrate the Feast of the Sundered Legion in their parent's home."

"That's different," Ahksell said. "She only has a brother in Govan, not—why didn't I know about this? Do the other Attendants know? I was raised in the tower!"

Ibram glanced around and behind himself, even though there was no need for it. The path was empty, and so was the garden. The folk up in the tower wouldn't be able to hear him. On his return swivel, he poked Ahksell in the chest, right over one of his shield buttons. "Stop it," he said. "It's not such a big revelation as all that. Ama says that Ladyship has always been allowed her peculiarities, and the number of Merrilians in her division is, as you might say, a concession."

"From who?" Ahksell asked. "Are you all actually related?"

Ibram shook his head. "If we are, I have some cousins about to be married who need a stern talking to."

Ahksell crossed his arms over his chest. "No one ever told me this. I just thought she had a way of siphoning new hires from the pool."

"I don't know," Ibram said. "My mother told me never to speak of it."

Ahksell leaned back against the wall of the garden, and frowned at his boots. He nudged his toes against a loose stone in the mud, and took a deep breath.

"Well, if this is what comes of hiring relations, then I'm glad I have none to support," he said.

Ibram clapped him on the shoulder. "That's the spirit."

"It doesn't leave us anywhere helpful," Ahksell said. "What are we supposed to be doing? Finding Master Kalmar solves nothing."

Ibram sighed and let his head fall back a little on his shoulders. Ladyship's tower loomed to his right. He bit his lip.

"You are, unfortunately, right," he said.

"And it's not like we can go to Mentor Nieminen and ask to help."

Ibram shook his head. "She's not best pleased with us, to be sure."

"Mostly you," Ahksell said. "Because you wouldn't stop answering for me."

"Well, did you wish to speak with her?"

Ahksell snorted.

"An agent is ever helpful," Ibram said, and spread his hands. He tilted his head downwards to the ground, the rocks used to line the shell path were pointed at all angles. Some of them were out of place entirely. "We're not allowed to use the catapult."

He glanced at Ahksell, whose eyebrows slowly came together. "No, we are not," Ahksell agreed in a reluctant tone of voice.

"Don't have anything to write with."

"No, we don't."

Ibram nodded. "We shall have to make do."

Ahksell's eyes widened immediately. "Oh no, no, Ibram, we can't go in!"

Ibram swooped downward and grabbed the nearest fist-shaped rock from the path. His fingers squelched in the mud as he twisted it free. He pushed past the garden gate and strode into the center of the path. The broken window sat high up before him.

"You can't throw that in there!" Ahksell said, running up.

Ibram paced backwards to the catapult, and sized up the angle. He would have to throw it quite hard if he wanted the lift. He closed one eye to judge the distance. Ahksell frowned.

"You are not a catapult," he snapped.

"Exactly!" Ibram said. His heartbeat kicked up, shaking blood down his arms and legs. He bounced on his toes. "Otherwise, I would use it!"

Ahksell looked up at the tower and then back to Ibram. His shoulders fell. "What if you hit someone?"

He rather hoped it was Zorion, then, for causing all the trouble, but Ibram chose the politic path and merely shrugged. "Then it's well that the healers are up there, eh?"

'Oh, my small gods,' Ahksell muttered, and pinched his temples.

"Now, I will throw, and when someone comes to the window, you tell them that Lady Azadiya is urgently required," Ibram said as he wound up his arm for a practice throw. He clenched the stone carefully as he revolved his arm up and over in slow motion. "Then I will do the talking."

"We won't even get the chance—no wait, don't!"

Ibram threw the rock with all his might, skipping forward a few steps for momentum, and the rock sailed upward, tumbling end over pointed end. Ibram held his breath as he watched it go. Clumps of muck flew off it as the rock climbed upwards. He pumped both arms in the air and drew in a breath to shout.

And then the stone began to arc before it had reached more than the second level of the tower. Ibram dropped his hands to his knees and groaned. The rock sank lower, clearly heading for the battered remains of Lady Azadiya's Sleeping Rose bushes.

"Runner's damned corns," Ahksell swore. He clenched his left hand into a claw, sucked in a deep breath, and flung his arm underhanded. A heavy wind blew up from the ground, scattering new blossoms and bright green leaves from the spring shoots high into the air, ripped free as if caught in an explosion. The stone launched itself straight upwards, and fired directly through the open window, smashing what little remained of the glass pane. Shouts rained down from the tower.

Ibram gasped with laughter, his heartbeat thudding against his ribs, and stumbled back a pace. Finally, some actual proof of life in the blasted tower! His ears popped in the displaced air. He bowed deeply to Ahksell, who flicked his middle finger at him, direct from the shoulder. Ibram beamed at him.

Attendant Dakreia appeared at the window with a scowl so fierce Ibram could see the force of it crackling like flames. The little staked lights they used for pathways in the kitchen garden did nothing for her complexion. She leaned out into the air, and threw the rock back outside; it smashed apart on the shell path.

"What is the meaning of this!" she yelled.

Ibram cupped his hands around his mouth. "Attendant Solari to speak—"

"This was not my idea!" Ahksell insisted.

Ibram rolled his eyes. "We need to speak to Lady Azadiya!" he called out.

Attendant Dakreia's rather wide-spaced eyes were as hard as chips of flint. "Mentor Hobon is indisposed," she shouted. "How dare you interfere in her recovery!"

She twisted around and disappeared from the window. Ibram heard loud talking—a man's voice and another woman's—but no words. Ahksell put his hands on his hips and shook his head. Ibram shrugged.

"Her recovery will go much more quickly when she learns what all we've been up to while she has been away!" Ibram yelled back. "Zorion can tell you!"

The voices in the tower paused, or grew quiet enough that they could hear no more of it. Ibram brushed his muddy hands off on his trousers' leg. He glanced up when Ahksell coughed, and saw Attendant Zorion framed in the window. He leaned out, braids dangling off his shoulders. "She says you're to come up!"

◈

They took the stairs up to the third level two at a time, winding around the empty open center of Lady Azadiya's tower with its burbling fountain. The glowbulb torches were lit to guide their path, but the cleverly angled mirrors and faceted glass ceiling had been covered. Their footsteps echoed around them; Ibram's back tensed with unease.

Ahksell reached the third floor landing by virtue of his longer legs, but Ibram quickly maneuvered himself in the lead to where one of the healers in the medicinal corps stood outside Lady Azadiya's office door. It was half-way closed, which seemed additionally wrong in the midst of all the damned quiet. The man wore a green smock that brushed the tops of his soft shoes, and his hair was cut short to his scalp. He crossed his arms at their approach and shook his head in disapproval.

"You will be quick," the man said, "and you shall be mindful of your tone. She has only just stabilized her external control."

Ibram sank his weight onto his heels; the muscles in his shoulders tensed. "What's wrong with her?" he asked.

"No one will explain," Ahksell said. "There's all sorts of rumors."

The man sighed through his thin nose. He wiped his lined forehead and measured them both, in turn, with his eyes. "The problem is one of filtering, as you might have guessed by now," he said finally. "In an attempt to aid the eyes' ability to focus, Attendant Zorion has instead widened Mentor Hobon's usual range of sensory input. The result is that she is perceives all physical stimuli at once, both what is visible, and those facets of reality which can be observed only with aid and practice. Until this potion wears off, her brain receives all this information at once, and the result is…"

"Painful," Ibram said.

"Extremely," the man said. "Her normal acute abilities on top of those enhanced functions are overloading her usual fine control. She is, in a sense, relearning how not to see."

"But that's a first year Attendant's lesson!" Ahksell protested.

"And am I so high that the basic tenets of my discipline no longer apply to me?" Lady Azadiya snapped from within the room. "Ibram, what is the first principle of physical transmutation?"

Ahksell looked mortified. Ibram winced. "To adapt is to seek perfection," he mumbled.

She cleared her throat. Ladyship was ever the most impatient of invalids.

"To adapt is to seek perfection," Ibram said louder. "To seek perfection is to know that adaptation is a ceaseless task."

"I knew that," Ahksell said under his breath. Ibram nodded at him.

"Indeed so," the healer said. "But care must be our watchword, nonetheless. Now, keep your voices at a level before we enter. She has her hearing under control, but loud noises can be upsetting."

Ahksell raised his eyebrows. "How far was she hearing before she had it under control?"

"All the way to Oblivion," Lady Azadiya said.

Ahksell winced. Ibram patted him on the arm.

"They don't help?" Ibram asked, and pointed up to the charmed silencing ceramic tiles inlaid above the lintel.

"Her megrims have been severe and debilitating," the healer said. His voice barely stirred the air between them.

Behind Ibram, Ahksell hissed under his breath. "It's that bad?"

"Tincture of withybane can only do so much. I fear a setback if we are not careful." The healer stepped into the room, making space for Ibram and Ahksell to step through. He raised a restraining hand, chest-high. "Make certain you keep this quick."

"We will," Ahksell assured him as Ibram brushed past him.

All the windows except for the broken ones had been covered with bedclothes, messily hung on floor-length candleholders and a few experiment clamps from the laboratories. A pile of neatly stacked catapult stones lay beneath them. The room was illuminated by a single glowbulb descending from a delicate chain attached to the high ceiling. Ibram grimaced. Its twin hung in a twisted blob of metal and glass, as if a giant hand had melted the entire lamp in their grip. It sparkled but very dimly.

He walked to the center of the room, past the desk where Ladyship usually worked, to where she sat in one of the comfortable low chairs in the center of the room. She was surrounded by two healers in green smocks and Attendants Dakreia and Zorion. Ladyship leaned her head on her left hand, dressed in a soft-looking red felt kirtle with her dark hair loose about her shoulders. Her eyes, centered in deep bruised circles, were closed. She looked pale.

"Well, Ibram," she said. "You have my attention."

Ibram bowed with his hands on his stomach. From the corner of his eye, he saw the healer at the door stride past; the man had a line of small diamond-shaped crystals picked out in heavy red thread down the length of his arm. So, he was a doctor instead of simply an alchemist with an interest in poultices.

"Don't just stand there," Dakreia snapped. "Answer the Mentor."

Ibram straightened just in time to see Ladyship's head tilt in Dakreia's direction. She had her eyes firmly closed, but seemed to have no trouble at all finding the other woman in the room. He cleared his throat, and glanced over to see Ahksell step up beside him.

"Attendant, while I am pleased you have come in person to rectify your junior's mistake," Ladyship said, "you will refrain from berating my agents at their work."

Dakreia's face flushed; she twitched her nose and looked away. "Of course, Mentor," she said.

"Very well," Lady Azadiya sighed and turned towards Ibram. She flinched, and squeezed her eyelids even more firmly shut. "You may continue, Doctor Berot. Ibram, why are you throwing rocks at the tower?"

"Because Amota Viran forbade us the use of the catapult," Ibram said.

"I have a splitting head," Ladyship said, and cracked one eye open long enough for Ibram to see it was bloodshot. "What have you been up to when you are supposed to be patrolling?"

Attendants Dakreia and Zorion went to a thin workbench Lady Azadiya usually used to store wood oil for her gar, with Doctor Berot in tow. Ibram frowned at the small wooden box lying open on the table. Ladyship seemed unconcerned, and the two healers remaining to hover over her, merely recorded their thoughts with charcoal sticks on their wooden tablets.

"I see Amota Viran has already spoken with you," Ibram said, wincing.

"And why should he not?" Ladyship asked. She adjusted the embroidered clasp at her waist which held her kirtle closed.

"It's not that we believed he would keep anything from you, Mentor," Ahksell said in a rush. "It's simply…"

He glanced about the other folk in the room and then looked to Ibram, spreading his hands out before him. Ibram nodded. He cleared his throat and took a deep breath.

"Master Savoldyn was murdered," Ibram said.

Lady Azadiya's eyes flew open. She groaned and slapped her hand over them, squeezing both temples. "What?"

Attendant Zorion opened the wooden box with a small scrape of its hinges, and pulled out something in both hands. He turned and offered the object to Attendant Dakreia, who took it and placed it on the table near the portable furnace. Her back was to Ibram, but he could see her shoulders and arms flex, almost as if she were twisting something into place.

"And we think one of the family did it," Ahksell said.

The entire room froze in shock, and then Attendant Zorion whipped around to face Ibram. "That's why you kept asking me if I knew how to kill a man!"

Lady Azadiya snorted and then quickly turned it into a cough. "How murdered?" she asked. "I thought the man had a bad heart."

"I believe it to be poison," Ibram said, "and the body has been sent to the medicinal corps for further testing."

She raised her eyebrows, and then waved her hand irritably in the direction of the healers. "Well? Is this filtering mask you've come up with ready?"

One of the healers, a stout woman with short red hair, jumped. "Yes, of course, only—Attendant Dakreia has some concerns over the frame of the lenses."

The Attendant in question grunted and bent over the worktable. Something that sounded thin and metallic snapped with a twang like a spring. Doctor Berot put his hands at his waist.

"Another moment, Mentor Hobon," he said.

"Riant," Ladyship muttered and then sighed deeply. "What caused you to think poison, Ibram?"

Ibram swallowed, and called up the sight of Savoldyn angrily complaining from behind his desk. "He spoke out of turn when his wife introduced me. I could have ignored it, because he was arguing with his daughter only a moment before, but it wasn't the sort of speech one gives a wealthy client unless he wanted to lose your patronage."

She seemed amused beneath the strain. "He'd also lose his trading right to the market towns up the Savin river," she said. "Continue."

Ibram's mouth twisted; he glanced at Ahksell. "And then," Ibram obeyed. "when Mistress Savoldyn ran out screaming, I went into the office to examine the body. I felt sure that I would need to make some sort of report."

"Which you did, to Viran," Ladyship said.

Ibram paused. "Yes, Ladyship."

She rubbed her fingers together, and then held out her right hand, flat enough that Ibram could see the red notched scar in the center of her palm. A pomander that Ibram had not noticed before rose up from her feet and into her hand. She brought it up to her nose for a sniff, and nodded.

"Savoldyn's behavior had been irrational when we met, but he had also been sweaty, blurry of vision, a tad too uncoordinated for sobriety—"

"We've been informed he was a sot," Ahksell interrupted.

Ibram pointed in his direction as he continued. "And when I smelled the body, the odor off him was strongly alcoholic. He was also clutching his stomach."

"How strong was the smell?" Doctor Berot asked.

Ibram startled. The doctor had moved away from observing the table, and now stood a little in front of Ahksell. Ibram looked to Lady Azadiya, who nodded.

"If I'd lit a match, Savoldyn's breath could have started a fire," Ibram said.

"And when I performed a study with Hessele's Cage," Ahksell said, "the red string proved that something had interfered with his organs. It was almost like an acid."

"But even a sot knows not to drink poison," Attendant Zorion said.

"The point of murder is typically that the victim doesn't realize that's what they've drunk," Ibram said.

"And Savoldyn was exceptionally picky about his choice of drink," Ladyship mused. "Our payment has often been half in mulling spices."

"The cook said she makes it herself," Ibram said.

Lady Azadiya made a noise of agreement. Doctor Berot cleared his throat. "Mentor Hobon, if I might?" he asked.

"Proceed," she said, with a wave of her hand. She sniffed the pomander again. It most probably contained mint; Ama pulped that for a paste when she got headaches.

"What did this man drink? Did he have anything in your presence?" Doctor Berot asked.

"Only shay," Ibram said. "He'd had a pot with his daughter, and then the housekeeper brought in a fresh one as I watched. That's what Attendant Abele tested when I brought it in."

"Attendant Abele tested the dead man's shay?" Ladyship asked. "Why did you go to her?"

"Amota Viran took me to the tent the remaining Attendants had set up in your kitchen garden, Ladyship," Ibram said. "We were looking for someone to test the shay—and the still pot I found which turned out to be natron—and she was there."

"A still pot?" Ladyship asked. "What about that?"

"I thought it might have been connected to the death at the time," Ibram said. He shook his head. "It seemed suspicious that a decorative item would need to be cleaned inside and out, but it came to nothing."

Ladyship nodded. "And the shay?"

"Abele said the shay held nothing but what you might expect."

"Oh, that means nothing," Doctor Berot said. "If it's what I suspect, then Master Savoldyn could have imbibed hours previously and died as a result."

"What do you suspect, then?" Lady Azadiya asked.

"Years ago—I don't know if you remember, Mentor, you were only an Attendant at the time—but a man in the preceptory of Govan was found dead below the stargazing ridge," Doctor Berot said.

Ibram hummed in surprise. Doctor Berot had been working when Ladyship been an Attendant? He stared at the streaks of grey in Berot's hair, and then at Lady Azadiya. It hardly seemed credible, Ladyship had been in residence since...well, for at least two imperial corona-tions. Ibram had been teaching himself not to be surprised at what alchemists got up to, but he always caught himself stumbling when it came to their specifics.

"Neck broken?" Lady Azadiya asked.

Doctor Berot shook his head. "No, he'd fallen, but only to roll down the grassy side of the hill. At most, the corpse had a twisted ankle. He hadn't been encouraged to go up there, because his fellow Attendants assumed he had caught a summer cold. He exhibited signs of discomfort, and had appeared confused at times. What we discovered upon examination was that he had been in the habit of taking a flask of spiced perry up with him on cold nights, and they had opened a new cask two days prior."

"Sounds perfect," Ibram said.

"I confess the event remained a mystery until four others had fallen ill." Doctor Berot glanced at him in clear dismissal. "Upon our investigation, the common element in all three cases turned out to be the perry. When we tested the cask, we found it to be adulterated," he said.

Lady Azadiya leaned forward in her chair. "What do you mean?"

"The peri had been fortified with wood alcohol," Doctor Berot said. "By mistake, naturally, but it was enough to kill him."

"Wood alcohol?" Ahksell repeated.

"Oh, we have to keep that up high on the shelf," Attendant Zorion said. "Sometimes the unwary get it and strong akvavit confused in the laboratory."

Ibram restrained his urge to scoff. Only an alchemist would keep imported Northern liquor in the workplace. The rest of the world simply drank it.

"Just as you say, Attendant," Berot said. "It's distressingly easy to make, and confuse with drinkable spirits. It was this that killed the man of which I spoke."

"How did he not die the first time he drank it?" Ibram asked. "If it's such a strong poison."

"The toxicity of wood alcohol can be ameliorated by the introduction of drinking alcohol," Berot said with some severity in his tone. "The perry itself diluted the concoction enough that he doubtless did not notice, but once he kept drinking it..."

Berot shook his head; his words stopping on a thin sigh. Lady Azadiya nodded. "It would fit, seemingly," she said. "In the morning, go to the Hall of Medicine and see if your suspicions bear fruit."

Berot stared at her for a moment and then shook himself. "Mentor Hobon that is quite impossible!" he protested. "I am attached to your care, and cannot leave my post."

"No one is more attached to my care than myself, to be sure," Ladyship said. "And I have an entire room of people who can watch me put on spectacles as if I were being crowned in a traveler's play. What I need, at this moment, is your suspicions confirmed as fact, and to speak with Viran Kalmar. Where is he?"

Ibram stepped forward. "We don't know, Ladyship," he said. "He turned over our reports to Third Mentor Nieminen who—"

Ladyship cut him off with a groan, and rubbed her forehead. "She sent for Stadat, didn't she?" she asked. She turned in her chair. "Dakreia, what is the wait over there? I can possess myself in patience only so long before I begin to think Afsoun is conspiring to give me an unwanted rest from my labors."

Attendant Dakreia turned from the table with stiff shoulders. "We are ready now, Mentor Hobon," she said. "If you will sit back and look forward in the chair? You may leave your eyes closed for the moment."

Lady Azadiya resettled herself in her chair with her chin held high and her eyes shut, but Ibram noticed the way her first two fingers on her left hand drew a twisted circle upon her knee. In response, the lower half of a lock of her hair was braiding and unbraiding itself.

Ibram cleared his throat and looked away. He watched Zorion approach with his filtering mask instead, carefully holding it in both hands. It seemed such a small device for such a very large problem, more spectacle-shaped than the full face mask he had been picturing in his own mind. From his vantagepoint, the octagonal front glass lenses had been smelted green with iron in the sand, but they were surrounded by smaller oblong-shaped smoked glass pieces. The frame was metal and wood.

"This will work, yes?" Ibram asked.

"Of course it will," Attendant Dakreia snapped.

"It stands a good chance," Zorion said at the same time.

"Go look over the notes Viran has sent to me," Ladyship said, and waved them away.

Ahksell took his elbow, and Ibram allowed himself to be led to the desk, but could not help watching as Zorion handed the filtering mask to Dakreia, who placed it solemnly on Lady Azadiya's face. Immediately, the mask slipped far down her nose, revealing her eyelids. A hiss like a bubbling kettle escaped Dakreia's mouth. Zorion winced.

"I fear the ear rests need to be adjusted," Lady Azadiya said, and removed them. She ran her fingers over the curved metal, and then tried them again. Once more, the mask slipped down. Ladyship sighed. "The nose guard."

"We can make a new frame," Dakreia said, "or add padding."

"No no," Lady Azadiya said. "I thank you, they do seem to be working, regardless."

Ibram turned away from the desk; Ladyship had braced the mask over her eyes with her hand, and nodded. The feeling of pressure in the room lessened. One of the healers leaned against the workbench in relief.

"The frame does let in too much light," Ladyship said. "As if lightning bolts were striking before my eyes."

"A side effect of the ash wood's interaction with the enamel pastes," Zorion said. "Glue would invalidate the beneficial aspects of the work, so we decided to fit them together in a kind of groove."

Ladyship nodded. "Never the less," she said. "A bit heavy on the face. Ahksell, jump up and fetch me that length of crystal spider silk. It's next to my wardrobe."

Ibram swallowed and glanced up to the wooden ceiling above him. Ladyship's bedroom was more of an exaggerated loft landing. Ibram had seen it from the door when he glanced up, but never anything past the carved wooden screens near the edge. No one was allowed up there; no one could even reach it without alchemy as there were no stairs.

Ahksell's mouth opened and closed for a moment. He glanced at Ibram, face bright with shock and not a little embarrassment, and then stepped out into the room. He flexed his shoulders, cracked his neck to the side, bent his knees and then jumped. The floor shuddered beneath Ibram's feet. Ahksell shot up like a fish from a waterfall, with his arms outstretched and his feet dangling. He caught the ledge between both hands, swung, and then backflipped up and over. A gigantic rolling thud shook the ceiling; dust drifted down onto Ibram's head. He sneezed, and rubbed his nose.

"Well enough," Doctor Berot murmured.

"Hush," Lady Azadiya said. "He's still growing."

Ibram hoped she meant in talent and not in form; Ahksell was already quite big enough. Any larger, and they'd have to raise the roof back home. He shook his head, and then bent down to look over the notes as Lady Azadiya had told him to, while Ahksell thumped about above them all. They were seven in total, all in Amota Viran's careful, blunt hand. He flipped quickly through the ones detailing the decampment and the changes to the patrol rotation—nothing surprising there, the world knew Gravayne needed a day off that bum leg—and then the copy of the letter sent to the other mentors concerning Lady Azadiya's unfortunate accident.

"The Savoldyns used to come up the living mountain for feasts under a harvest moon," Ladyship mused behind him. "When First Mentor E'garcid handed out gifts of thanks for contracts of long-standing. He stopped coming around the time his daughter ran off, if I recall correctly. I remember the first mistress of that house, but not the second. What is she like?"

"Overwrought," Ibram said over his shoulder. He frowned down at the note Mentor Nieminen had attached to Amota Viran's missive. She was truly unhappy about being pulled from her other duties.

"A pity. Her predecessor was a born mediator," Lady Azadiya recalled. "We were sorry to lose her at the sect's table. Unfortunately, her family's business went to a distant cousin, and E'garcid lost the glass factory entirely."

"The glass factory?" Ahksell called down from the landing. "Did you say it was on the bench, Mentor?"

"Near the wardrobe," she answered.

"You have three!"

"And the silk is near all of them," she said. "And to your other question, Master Savoldyn's first wife was the last of a glassmaking family.

Upon her death, the business went outside the imperial boundary, and we had to seek other sources. It was a pity, to be sure, they made solid laboratory pieces."

"Suppose that explains the goods littering the manor," Ibram muttered. "Poor Mistress Ignalle, finagled out of a fortune on both sides."

He frowned, and put down the inconsequential papers. The last two he held before him in either hand. The left was Viran's report of Ibram's trip to the Savoldyn's household, which reported his death. The right was his determination that Ibram had too much time on his hands, and Amota Viran's rather pointed request to send Ibram back to Amota Evren to lug chests around the archives until he learned discipline. His suspicions of murder were not mentioned, though Attendant Abele's aid in a "small matter of intent" was commended.

Ibram slapped both papers down onto the desk and faced Lady Azadiya. He leaned back on the desk, rocking a little as Ahksell jumped down from the landing. Ahksell paced forward with the length of bright yellow spider silk held out before him; its tapered ends fluttered in the air. Ibram rubbed the back of his neck, and grit his teeth.

"I don't mind being thought a fool, Ladyship," Ibram said. "But I do hate being made to look one."

"Or perhaps, he wanted to avoid your embarrassment," she replied. "I shall have to ask."

Ahksell glanced over his shoulder as he moved to the side. Lady Azadiya wrapped the length of spider silk twice around her eyes before knotting it securely behind her head. She patted her sleeves, and then withdrew four iron pins from her left wrist; she pinned the silk in place behind her ears. When she stood, the folk arrayed about her automatically stepped back. Ibram rather thought they were holding their breath; he was, after all.

She looked about herself slowly. She might have been seeing him, and she might have been peering through him at this point. Ibram had no clue, but Lady Azadiya seemed quite satisfied. She shook out her skirts, and nodded briskly.

"This shall work very well," she announced. "The experience is, admittedly, a little blurry, but perfectly functional. You are to be commended, Attendant Dakreia."

Attendant Dakreia bowed with her hands on her stomach. Without rising, she noticed Zorion taking notes and smacked him on the side until he, too, bowed. Ibram noticed he was also still writing.

"Thank you, Mentor," Dakreia said. She rose as Lady Azadiya waved her up, and yanked Zorion with her. "It was the least we could do."

"Spider silk for the depth perception," Zorion muttered.

Lady Azadiya hummed politely. The healers approached her from the work table, but halted when she raised her hand. "Tomorrow is well enough for an examination," she said. "I've had my fill. Everyone out again, and leave me to rest. Berot, I shall expect you for breakfast in the central training field. Ibram, have them set up a pavilion, and then find Berac and Sarrha and tell them to attend me at that hour as well." She brushed her hands together, and then paused. "Ahksell?"

"Yes, Mentor?" he asked.

"Why aren't you up in Afsoun?"

Lady Azadiya's idea of breakfast was entirely Western, a communal affair with her guests surrounding a giant circular table beneath the largest open pavilion Ibram could scrounge. Word had spread like rot in a barrel when Ibram had relayed Ladyship's orders to the cooks, and so the rest of the field was full of folk eating their own meals with an equal measure of gawking to sauce the feast. She sat in her comfortable wooden chair, which the servants had piled high with thick colorful rugs, in full view of anyone who wished to walk by, and so very many of them did. At least the weather was dry enough for the show.

The Learners had been driven wild by both the appearance of Mentor Hobon and a chance for a late morning's feast. The Attendants not seated at the table were all aflutter to determine how Dakreia and Zorion had done it. In the meanwhile, Lady Azadiya sat and drank caffa from a cup which the kitchen staff never allowed to be empty. To her left and right were seated the Third and Second Mentors, while the rest of her elder agents and Attendants made up the surrounding places at table. Attendants Dakreia and Zorion had been invited, and were bent over their soft-boiled eggs on toasted rolls. Forks had been provided for them. Ahksell was seated next to Doctor Berot, across from Amota Berac and Amita Sarrha and Amota Lakum. Amota Viran was not in attendance.

Ibram stood behind Ladyship on her right, watching the crowd beyond the pavilion. The servants could barely keep up, as soon as one platter of flatbread or ancasis or mouflon pies was carried out, another was sent for. The pitchers of small beer were no sooner poured than emptied. An entire cauldron of quash hung from a trivet in the field, where a cook ladled bowl after bowl.

A maid, clearly dragooned from the washerfolk, ran by with steaming pots of shay in both hands. Ibram breathed in deeply; he'd had time for no more than a stale bun and a quick drink of water back home before he'd had to be up the living mountain before the sun rose. He glanced over to his left, where Mentor Nieminen had left her own agent to gaze wistfully after a platter of thickened quash cut into cakes. The other man—Ibram had not been introduced—turned back and their eyes caught briefly. He shrugged with his face; Ibram quirked the left side of his mouth.

"Now then, Azadiya," Second Mentor Stadat said in his booming voice. "How's the eyesight? All healed up?"

The Second Mentor had made an effort for this event; his gambeson was velvet edged with gold and silver work at the high neck and long cuffs. His heavy signet ring glimmered with jewels which threw their own light.

Ibram twitched back into attention, stiffening his spine with his eyes forward. He stood between them both, quite able to see the side of Lady Azadiya's head, as well as Mentor Stadat's. He had the long face of a man from the middle of the empire, and a way of speaking as if charging past on horseback. Ladyship had chosen to braid her hair around the length of yellow spider silk that morning, no doubt to further support the mask Zorion and Dakreia had made her. Her dark bronze green gown and sleeves exposed her rich blue shift; her finger-less mitts matched the scarf wrapped around her eyes, embroidered with bluecaps. She looked, in Ibram's estimation, as if she were about to be presented at court, or possibly like the lead in a play about the Advisor. Wisdom was not blind, but a good politician made it so, as the saying went.

"I'm well enough, Ortwin," Ladyship said, and drank her caffa. "I thank you for the concern." She set down her drink, and smiled. "And I thank Mentor Nieminen for her aid while I was indisposed."

Nieminen raised her eyebrows, and delicately spooned quash out of her bowl. She chewed and swallowed before answering. "You are most welcome," she said. "One should always stand ready to aid one's fellows after all."

"Indeed, indeed," Stadat said. "I've been called down here on a nasty business, I'm afraid. Thought that eye problem of yours would be an interesting case. Never thought I'd have to weigh in on one of your investigations."

"Your agents seem to wriggle out the worst worms from the muck," Nieminen said. She adjusted the heavy gold chains she had twisted around her neck. Her gambeson was shot through with heavy blooms of bronze embroidery. "The merchant's daughter and her clerk were quite overwrought about the prospect of a murder in the family."

"Happens in the best of them, though," Stadat said.

A faint bang resounded from the eastern training fields. Ibram squinted; a plume of mauve smoke drifted in the air. Some of the younger Attendants had grown overenthusiastic in welcoming Lady Azadiya back from her tower by showing off how delicately they maneuvered the wobbling pink bubbles through the air. They had been directed further away from the feast to work off the excitement. Another bang, close enough that Ibram felt the ground tremble beneath his feet. One of the servants on the far end of the table caught a shaypot as it toppled, and returned it to its tray.

Ladyship laughed politely. "The Vo Wolly affair?" she asked. "Really, that was simply a matter of poor negotiation."

"You are the best judge of that amongst us, I suppose," Nieminen said, and then dropped her eyes from whatever expression was on Mentor Stadat's face.

Ibram frowned and leaned his weight on his heels. Lady Azadiya sat back in her chair. She raised her hand with her thumb and two fingers extended and plucked a sweet roll from the pyramid near where Ahksell sat. The bun drifted through the air and down to her plate.

"I do wonder," Nieminen began. "If you feel up to finishing your portion of the examinations. It's no trouble to me, of course—"

"Oh, no ceremony, Lamy, to be sure," Ladyship interrupted. "We're all overtaken with examinations during the Festival of Sangrin. Your willingness to take on my lot is commendable, but as you can see—" She spread both hands in front of herself "—I am recovered."

"Well, I do have a full laboratory waiting on me, so if you are feeling recovered, perhaps it is better to keep the schedules as they are." Mentor Nieminen appeared unwillingly pleased at the compliment. She lifted her palm to the sky and a small jug of cream came to her elbow. She inclined her head with a smile.

"Bit of a waste calling me down here, then," Stadat said, as he chewed on the braided crust of a pie held at one end by his fork. "Don't see us having much to do, in fact."

Nieminen's nostrils flared. She leaned back in her chair. Ibram saw her agent visibly wince from the corner of his eye.

"Did Master Savoldyn's daughter request the aid of the sect?" Lady Azadiya asked quickly.

"She did not," Nieminen said, and added a splash of cream to her quash. "Nor would I have allowed her to. It's no business of ours if a man dies in his own study, and she has no standing. I am informed by your own Master Kalmar that she is no longer his heir."

"Viran is usually correct in these dealings, to be sure," Ladyship said, and tore a bite-sized piece off her roll. "I hope he was of help to you."

"You were not absent long enough to cause any further problems but a delay in the examination schedules," Nieminen said. "I directed Kalmar to take on the more mundane of your tasks; he seemed capable."

"He always does," Stadat said. "Pity he wasn't available when I arrived. Talks sense, that man. A good head on his shoulders."

"Just so," Ladyship said. "Where is he?" She turned her head to Mentor Nieminen. "Did you send him on an errand?"

"He requested the evening to apologize to the Savoldyn widow," Nieminen said. "He showed a remarkable amount of loyalty to maintaining your ties with their house."

Ladyship continued to eat, delicately wrapping bread around a bite of mouflon sausage. "They have been supplying me with goods for most of the time that Viran has been with the sect," she said, and chewed. She licked her fingers, and began peeling a glass apple.

"No doubt, he wishes to smooth over the trouble your young agent's meddling put her through."

Nieminen lifted her chin to fix her stare on Ibram; he bowed slightly. Her eyes narrowed, before she sniffed and looked away. Ibram chewed the inside of his lower lip. Viran had been down the living mountain all night, then, and with permission to approach Mistress Savoldyn. On the first foot, it was a stretch to think Mistress Dolman would follow one outrage of impropriety with another. Yet, on the second, Ibram no longer knew what to think. Amota Viran and a married woman? Amota Viran and a widowed murderer?

"Yet we may have to trouble her further," Ladyship said. "After all, the man was murdered. How did you find the corpse, Doctor Berot?"

"Suborning one of my folk, are you?" Mentor Stadat asked.

From the other side of the table, the good doctor looked up at his name. He had made some attempts to lay flat his shorn hair for the morning's meal, and he had changed from his green smock to the standard gambeson and grey wrapped trousers, though his gambeson had red crystals embroidered on its sleeves as well. The table quieted as he cleared his throat.

"Indeed he was, Mentor," Berot said. He picked up his wooden goblet of small beer, and drank quite deliberately. "It was as I thought."

Lady Azadiya nodded and sighed. "The charge has been laid," she said, "and most definitely proved."

"Who made the charge?" Stadat asked.

"Her agent," Nieminen said. "The one standing behind you there."

Stadat turned briefly in his chair. "Quite the precedent," he said. He had sharp pale eyes and a face too young for grey hair. He faced the table and again, and Ibram's breath stuttered in his chest. "What killed him, then?"

Ibram clenched his fists behind his back. He rose up on his tiptoes and, from across the way, Amita Sarrha nodded at him. He settled, but couldn't help the bubble of excitement from expanding in his chest.

"My agent, Ibram, was present at the death and noticed the irregularities with the corpse," Lady Azadiya said and flicked her right hand over her shoulder. The glass apple peel slipped from her fingers, paused mid-air, and then returned to Ladyship's trencher. "He laid the charge before my—"

She paused and touched her fingers to her temple delicately. The table slowly quieted as she breathed in and out, an obviously calming pattern. Ibram tensed, and took a step forward. She was still apt to turn pale and waver on her feet. Doctor Berot began to stand from his chair, but Lady Azadiya came back to herself and waved him down.

"Apologies, Ortwin," she murmured, but by then all at the table were so quiet, everyone could hear her clearly. She smiled thinly. "While these goggles of Dakreia's are very effective, there is still a touch of vertigo involved if I move too quickly. Now, as I was saying, Master Kalmar was notified that Ibram feared a murder had been committed. He of course brought the matter to me, and then to my temporary replacement."

Here she gestured to Mentor Nieminen, whose smile grew a touch fixed. Ladyship took cut out a sliver of glass apple. She chewed and swallowed.

"Attendant Abele rather helpfully ruled out the usual poisons," she said. "And then Ibram reported his and Ahksell's findings to me later on. Really, I am grateful for Mentor Nieminen's assistance in this matter. It takes a great leader to understand when one must meddle, and when one must stay above the fray."

Mentor Nieminen drank from her cup of shay. "I am always happy to help another alchemist, of course," she said.

"As should we all," Stadat said in a very bland tone. "Guardians of the Emerald Mountains, aren't we?"

"At least this portion," Nieminen said. "What shall you report to the Imperial Commissioner? Surely with the Fourth Mentor back on her feet, this matter doesn't reach the level of warder intervention."

Ibram felt his eyebrows threatening to raise, and schooled his expression. His stomach rumbled as a servant darted past bearing a tray of bread fresh enough to make his mouth water and a crock of herbed oil. Amota Berac glanced at him, and then turned his head to mutter into Amita Sarrha's ear. She laughed, and stabbed a pear to bring onto her plate.

"Oh, we shall always have need for the empire's peacekeepers," Lady Azadiya said. "But I believe we can handle the matter ourselves before turning the culprit over to the proper judiciary."

"Feeling equal to it now?" Stadat asked.

"Entirely," Lady Azadiya said.

Stadat finished eating his mouflon pie, and then washed the remains down with the contents of the mug on his left. "And who will handle the rest of your examinations?"

"I believe I have enough information to score Zorion's results," she said, and laughter rippled down the table. Zorion glanced up from his food, still chewing, and looked confused. "But the limits of this device impel me to call upon the services of a scribe. I shall complete that report, and then review the rest of the cohort assigned to my division. I believe they were released back to Afsoun?"

"They were," Nieminen said.

Ladyship shrugged one shoulder. "Then they can resubmit their proposals. If I cannot adequately judge their competency, I will inform their teachers in Afsoun. I highly doubt it will be necessary, but in the interest of fairness I should give the matter its due attention."

"More than fair," Stadat declared, and waved his hand at a servant carrying a large platter of steaming beef broth. "You'll drink this," he said over his shoulder. "It fortifies."

"Of course," Lady Azadiya murmured.

Ibram frowned. Behind his back, he began to tick off the remaining Attendants to be examined. Rumin, Frumari, Ences... The tally came to about six in number, or seven if the twins decided to break up their duo and be critiqued separately. That left precious little time for Lady Azadiya to determine who amongst Savoldyn's exiled relatives or moderately beloved household had murdered him.

❧

The breakfast party decamped quickly enough after Lady Azadiya had been shown off to half the sect, even though the cook staff remained hard at work, preparing for the rest of the day's meals. Ibram had tried to melt into the crowd streaming back to the makeshift dining hall for a bite to eat, but Amita Sarrha had intercepted him before he'd even stepped foot off the field. She had him firmly by the back of the gambeson as if she'd caught him trying to climb the walls for freedom.

Ahksell smiled encouragingly next to him, as they followed Ladyship and his amitai down the road to the tower. He removed a glass apple from his bundled handkerchief and handed it over. Ibram snatched it from Ahksell's hand and bit into the apple immediately; the tart juice burst out and dripped on his hand. He wrinkled his nose, and licked his palm, and then chewed.

"It's like all your lessons in courtesy slid out of your ears as soon as Verena stuffed them into your head," Amita Sarrha said, and shook her head.

"Ama hasn't thrown me barefoot into the street," Ibram said, still chewing. "I must be doing something correctly."

Ahead of them, Ladyship had taken Amota Berac's arm for balance. Amota Lakum kept dividing his time between watching where he was going, and making sure to keep Lady Azadiya in his sight. She seemed to be walking all right, but at moments her head wobbled. Other times, her normally brisk steps slowed and Berac's back muscles bulged as if he were bearing up a sudden weight. Doctor Berot had attached himself to Lady Azadiya's orbit, and was patently observing her every move. Amota Lakum kept up a steady murmur of all the events Ladyship had missed in her absence.

Ibram swallowed his mouthful of glass apple. "Some of us had no breakfast, you know. I'm hungry."

"And you never found Viran," she continued as if he hadn't spoken. "Which I recall ordering for you to do. Is there a reason I was ignored?"

Ibram bit another chunk of apple off, and shrugged. Ahksell looked pained. "He didn't ignore you," he said. "We were waylaid by certain events."

Amita Sarrha frowned. "It's just as well Ladyship found out where he went, since you made no attempt."

At this, Lady Azadiya turned her head to her right shoulder. "Do I hear myself talked of?" she asked. As always, when amongst her division, her accent came through the strongest, burbling like a clear water stream. "I am an ill woman, make light of my faults."

Amita Sarrha rubbed her upper lip, and shook her head. "Just Ibram's inability to follow orders," she said.

Ladyship held her head still for a moment, and then turned back to face the road. She hummed in thought. "And yet do I censure a boy for what benefits me?" she asked. "If he had sought Viran, would I then know he is missing?"

Ibram had the strangest urge to both puff out his chest and hunch his shoulders and hide behind Ahksell at the same moment. He looked over at Ahksell instead, and found his discomfort easily echoed. Ahksell shrugged; Ibram returned the gesture. Amita Sarrha tsked as they turned down the sight hill cut through the stand of withy trees that led back to the tower.

"Better to have a fugitive in hand and then explain why he was gone," Sarrha said.

"A sensible thought in less urgent times," Ladyship said.

"If only there existed a method of informing others without telling them personally," Amota Lakum mused to the bright green canopy overhead. "Some kind of servant who could, perhaps—"

"Lakum," Ladyship said. "Save your humor for the stables."

Amota Berac laughed, though at a fraction of his usual volume. Ibram finished his glass apple and tossed its core into a bush; he licked his fingers clean and Ahksell handed over his handkerchief. They continued down the path, and Amota Lakum pushed open the front stone doors of Ladyship's tower. She had ordered the lamps be lit, but the windows and mirrors be kept covered. The dark wood beams and whitewashed walls seemed closer without the bright, encompassing light, but their footsteps echoed on the floor as they all trooped inside. Ibram shivered; it felt wrong for such a lively place to be so silent. Ibram wiped his hands clean, and handed the cloth back to Ahksell.

"Down here, I should think," Ladyship said, and pointed down into the open space around the fountain. Long couches had been placed there, and enough room without the tables that there was no fear of tripping. "I have had enough of my rooms for now."

She allowed Amota Berac to lead her down the small set of stairs and into the wide open space. He guided her to the nearest couch and she settled down onto the central cushion. Ladyship resettled her clothing about herself, and flipped her long braid over her shoulder while holding her mask steady with her left hand. They all stood before her, the amitai in front and Ibram in back with Ahksell. Doctor Berot lingered to one side of the couch.

"Send for Evren, Lakum," she said. She pressed both hands in parallel along the column of her neck and then up under her chin, and wiggled her shoulders in a stretch. "He has the best hand of all of you, and the clearest voice."

"Yes, Ladyship," Amota Lakum said. He bowed and stepped quickly up the stairs. Ibram heard the doors open and close behind him.

"Now, if Viran has been in charge of his usual duties as well as mine," Ladyship said, and leaned back. "What have you all been up to?"

"Tending the stables and keeping the most junior of the Attendants away from the kitchen garden," Amota Berac said. "We've had most of our agents out in the fields making sure the Learners and the Attendants not under examinations were kept out of trouble."

"And you, Sarrha?"

"I've been keeping busy," Amita Sarrha said, and leaned her weight on her good leg. She scratched the underside of her chin with one finger. "There's a heavy load of work when you take a tumble, to be sure. When Viran disappeared with the Third Mentor's permission, I took his place in her conferences, just to make sure our interests were represented."

"What conferences?" Ladyship asked.

"To the purpose at hand," Amita Sarrha said. "The Ignalles, the Pilot and Bo'sun of the local Ark, and then the Second and Third Mentor having a polite disagreement on the proper disposal of a body they don't want to deal with."

Lady Azadiya played with the mongoose signet ring on her finger. "Anything of importance?"

"The Pilot holds the will in trust for the Savoldyns," Amita Sarrha said. "He will be executing Savoldyn's demands after the body is burned. That won't happen, of course, until it is removed from the Hall of Tranquility, where Berot has the corpse captive. The Ignalles aren't happy about that, but they didn't seem overly concerned. It's probable that they need the money, but it's also likely they won't see a faunt until the circuit judge from the Courts Civil makes it up here to determine who has control of the business while the heir is so young."

"They'll likely get the regency, though," Ahksell said. "Since they are the only remaining family."

Ibram frowned. "Wouldn't it be a case for the Court of Chancery, then?"

Amita Sarrha shook her head. "If the child were still in infancy, then yes," she said. "But there is no freeholding in the will, so the land isn't an issue."

"How old is the heir?" Ladyship asked.

Amita Sarrha shrugged. "From their talk, the girl's about five."

"A perilous age," Ladyship said.

"Mistress Savoldyn seemed to believe that her husband's daughter would take over as the child's regent," Ibram said. "She admitted it readily."

Lady Azadiya thought for a moment, and then sighed. "Is it certain, when he left, that he would go to Mistress Savoldyn? Might it be otherwise?"

Of course, she would ask about Amota Viran. Ibram cleared his throat, and picked at the skin beneath his thumb nail. It wasn't certain that Amota Viran was complicit, merely... Ibram wrinkled his nose. Merely possibly having an affair with a woman who possibly murdered her husband. There were unwelcome images playing across his mind.

Amita Sarrha shrugged. She shifted her weight from her braced leg, and Ladyship frowned. She gestured to the room.

"Sit, Sarrha. Berac, fetch her a chair."

Amota Berac lumbered to his feet, and lifted one of the taller, sturdier wooden chairs from beside the fountain. He set it down by Amita Sarrha. Amita Sarrha sighed and patted his hip as she sat down, and he returned to his former spot.

Amita Sarrha made herself comfortable, but shook her head. "He's been acting like a fenek who smells a wolf on the wind for days."

"He doesn't like shocks," Lady Azadiya said. "My sudden removal is a rather large one, you must admit."

"I'll allow, Viran also hated that," Amita Sarrha said. "But usually, this time of the season, all we have to do is send him down the living mountain to a nice welcoming evening courtyard and then cart him back up the next morning. Last night, he went down and did not return."

Ibram winced. The morning after the night before was typically the responsibility of the more junior agents. He had never yet managed to avoid it.

"Did you know the Savoldyns, Mentor?" Ahksell asked.

Ladyship cocked her head in his direction. "Not personally," she said. "Viran handled all of the orders, and we approved the samples together."

"So he alone would have had contact with the joyous widow," Amita Sarrha said. "You had no chance to take her measure."

"We don't know if she's happy," Ladyship said. "No one has seen her since the rushes have been tied."

Ibram cut his eyes directly towards Ahksell; Ahksell stared right back. They broke eye contact almost immediately. Ibram's scalp tightened. Amota Viran had not told Ladyship about his breaking into the Savoldyn's home. He hadn't told her anything, really. He frowned down at his leather boots and coughed.

"Not strictly correct," he said, and then cleared his throat. "Ladyship."

"What?" Lady Azadiya asked, and leaned back in her couch cushion to turn her face in his direction.

He shivered. Ladyship had a way of looking at a man like she knew his character down to the last breath of animus, but now it made Ibram's scalp prickle. It was uncanny how Lady Azadiya could see through the mask, with no holes cut into the cloth. She could probably see six feet past his very blood and bones.

"Well, you see," Ahksell said. He swallowed heavily. "Ibram had forgotten one of your packages, and—"

"I prevailed upon the household staff to let us into the house and searched the office for evidence of foul dealings," Ibram said. "Ahksell delved for him."

"He did what?" Ladyship frowned.

Amita Sarrha's bark of laughter was sharp and immediate. She shook her head, grinning. "Ladyship, I take back my harsh thoughts."

"As to Mistress Savoldyn's disposition, I would call it distressed," Ibram said. "She spoke plainly of their differences in the marriage, but seemed...understanding of Savoldyn's problems."

"His problems?" Lady Azadiya repeated.

"The drinking you are already aware of, Ladyship," Ibram said. "He was a bad poet but spent money on expensive scrolls to record his work." He began ticking off items as he recalled them. "Kept a barely useful staff of servants after he tossed the rest of them away in a fit a few years ago. His wife's jewelry is fancy but of middling quality, and all his most recent expeditions for profit show that he reinvested much of it back into his business. When he could, that is. He registered some decidedly purse-flattening losses." He turned to Ahksell. "We should have stolen the ledgers."

"Our mistake," Ahksell said.

"So far," Ladyship said, and rested one arm along the back of the couch. "I wonder Savoldyn had time to acquire my cloth."

Her forehead furrowed. Doctor Berot stepped forward with his hands out before him. "Mentor, is your headache becoming worse?" he asked. "It may be that you need to limit the use of the filtering mask."

She waved her hand at him, and shook her head. "Well and good," she said. "I'll have Ibram's report, before I let you peer into my ears or what have you."

"If the bookcases were anything to go by," Ibram continued, "when he wasn't composing odes to spring, he must have been applying for permits to trade with villages all around Vanima province."

An additional problem, Ibram soon discovered, was that when Ladyship's eyes were covered, he had no clue when to stop speaking and let her think. He could no longer simply notice she had stopped looking at him, in favor of staring into the middle distance. With her eyes bound up in spider silk and behind those lenses, he had the unnerving sensation that everything he said and did was under her intense focus.

"Permits to trade?" Amita Sarrha echoed.

Ibram nodded. "I did not see them, but judging by the expeditions written in his ledger they were going from village to village. It's a wonder he managed to transport goods at all; half his caravanners must have been weighed down with warrants."

"Whence to where?" Ladyship asked.

"Incredibly short trips," Ibram said. "Lityen-by-the-Blue-Hole to Othy, and such like that."

"Odd," she said.

Ibram nodded. "I thought so. It makes no sense to purchase so many permits, when one large regional warrant will do."

Lady Azadiya hummed in agreement, and then winced. She put her hand up to her forehead again, and relaxed against the back of the couch with a sigh. Ibram pressed his lips together tightly. The room stilled, while the sound of Ladyship's breath came slowly and evenly. Finally, she cleared her throat lightly, and put her hand back in her lap.

"What warders are stationed nearby?" she asked.

"Talsconis has returned from his sojourn to Delbrite," Ibram said. "He's the most senior now that Vainamonien was promoted outside the imperial boundary."

"He should have no more than three of his fellows," Amita Sarrha said. "Dibra and perhaps Claes."

Lady Azadiya nodded and adjusted the side of her silk wrap where the fabric twisted into her braid. "It should be easy enough to send for Talsconis," she said. "Prepare a short message inviting him to my evening meal, Sarrha. We shall welcome his return with word of the death and notification that it will soon be resolved."

"Will it?" Ahksell asked. "Soon be resolved, I mean."

Ladyship seemed surprised. "Of course, it will," she said. "There have been charges laid, two mentors involved...it's all a bit too much to leave it in the hands of imperial officers."

Ahksell nodded. "Yes, Mentor."

"I would like a full report, Ibram," Lady Azadiya said, and turned her head in his direction. "Berac can continue his duties with the rest of my agents, and Sarrha, I will expect you to take over for Viran while he is away."

Amita Sarrha sighed deeply. "I suppose that's my due reward for initiative."

"The spoils of war are more work," Ladyship said. "Find Viran's daily ledger, if you would."

Amita Sarrha bowed from her chair and stood with a groan. She clapped Ibram on the back as she passed by on the way to the doors. Amota Berac laced his hands over his stomach and smirked into his beard.

"What about me, Mentor?" Ahksell asked as the doors opened and shut.

"Take a seat next to Ibram," she said. "I want to hear everything you have observed while I have been indisposed."

Doctor Berot cleared his throat; she sighed and leaned her head back against the couch. "Very well," she snapped. "We shall kill two feneks with one snare. Berot, do your worst. Ahksell, you may begin."

The good doctor removed a long hollowed horn from his belt purse, and a pair of wooden slides inset with glass lenses. He moved to stand next to Lady Azadiya on the couch. Ahksell cracked his knuckles and looked about the room. Amota Berac smiled encouragingly.

⁂

When they were finished untangling their comings and goings for Ladyship's approval, she had Ibram read out Savoldyn's will in full. At the end, Lady Azadiya sighed long and low, and shook her head. The heavy fall of her braid over her shoulder rustled against the silk of her clothes. She laid her fingertips on the web of delicate chains that comprised her necklace, and then tapped one of its roundels of golden amber. Ibram glanced at the burbling fountain and then to Ahksell. Doctor Berot had taken Amita Sarrha's seat, and engrossed himself in making detailed notes on a bound sheaf of paper he had pulled from his belt purse.

"For the moment we shall keep this between ourselves," Ladyship said finally. "Viran's involvement with the Savoldyns is unfortunate, but at my instigation, and I shall not fault a man for climbing into a lonely bed." She considered the air for a moment. "Well, not until the moment serves, to be sure."

Ibram winced. "Lady Azadiya," he said and jerked his head in Ahksell's direction. "There are innocent ears present."

"I'm fine," Ahksell said.

"He and Viran had that talk when you were on your travels," Amota Berac mentioned.

"Disturbing," Ibram said.

"Perfectly natural," Doctor Berot muttered in distraction.

"And as such we must move on," Ibram said. "Obviously, we must find Amota Viran and have him explain his actions."

"Indeed," Ladyship said. "Though I think he will turn up by himself, if we merely ensure Mistress Savoldyn comes for a visit. Ibram, you must return the will. If she does not have her own copy, it has no doubt been searched for already."

"How do you know that?" Ahksell asked.

"There is no husband nor wife alive who wouldn't secure such a document when the family relations are so consistently fraught," Ladyship said. "Ibram, go to her home. Use the pretext of inviting her to my tower."

Ibram's eyebrows rose without his express consent. "To visit you?" he asked. "What for, shay and scandal?"

"I am convalescing," she said. "The company of a potential murderer cannot help but aid in my recovery."

"How?" Ahksell asked.

"Excitement keeps the heart beating," she said. "While you are delivering this message, Ibram, you will find your way back into the kitchen and speak to the cook. I want to know where she gets her fortifying spirits."

Ibram nodded. "She told me she merely spices it, not fortifies." Ahksell questioned him in a glance; Ibram shrugged. "It's a telling omission."

"Ah, he can be taught," Ladyship said. "Bring back the ledgers he reviewed, and see if he has stored copies of the permits themselves. I want to see these shortened trips for myself. If not, Ahksell will go to the Bureau of Commerce and look at the Savoldyn's most recent paperwork. Find out who has been in charge of his travel authorizations."

Ahksell nodded, but hesitated a moment before speaking. "How am I supposed to get that information?" he asked. "Isn't it private?"

Lady Azadiya pulled gently at her left mitt, and tucked her clan bracelet away from an embroidered bluecap stem at her wrist. "You'll think of something," she said.

Ibram frowned. "The terms of the will say that Mistress Savoldyn has nothing to do with the business. I can't sneak an entire ledger out in Ahksell's carry-all."

Ladyship nodded. "You are allowed to use my family's contract with the Savoldyns as leverage," she said. "It should have some import."

"Yes, Ladyship," Ibram said. He opened his mouth, and glanced about himself. He cleared his throat; there were words lodged in his throat and suspicions in the back of his mind. He didn't like to think on them, but it was his job. Amota Viran had helped teach him that. If it were found out that Lady Azadiya's nephew was involved in a murder, the consequences would rain down on her head like rocks in a mountain pass. The entire situation left a sour taste in the back of Ibram's mouth, and a tightness in his belly.

"She gets a house in Itol, which Amota Viran knew about," Ibram said. "And we must allow he would know of what he speaks."

Ladyship sighed, but bobbed her head in a slight nod. Ibram pressed forward. "It's my recollection that he handed you Zorion's potion," he said. "Which rather neatly removed you from daily life, and placed him in charge. Well, in charge more than he usually is, anyway."

Lady Azadiya tilted her chin upwards. "Yes, he did," she said. "And naturally he would assume such duties in my absence. But he did not poison me, if that's what you worry about."

Ibram's hands clenched and unclenched at his sides. "How do you know?" he asked. "It fits neatly."

"It does," she allowed. "But he had no time to adulterate the potion between retrieving the bottle from Zorion and handing it to me. It was stoppered, if you recall."

Ibram leaned backwards. "What if he got to it before he handed it over?"

"You mean when it was in Zorion's carry-all?" she asked. "No, I think not."

"But what about—"

"Of all of us in the room, I have had the greatest amount of time to go over the events that led to my current state." He opened his mouth; she held up her hand. "We may go further and further back in the timeline of Zorion's concoction until we find a point where all circumstances align for Viran to have been crowned king of Merrilia, Ibram. Think back, were his hands occupied?"

Ibram sighed, but brought the image of Viran walking to the table where the Attendants from Afsoun had laid their materials. Attendant Zorion had his bag on the table, a scroll in his right hand. Viran walked easily over the uneven ground; his arms at his sides.

"No," Ibram said. "Not until he touched the vial."

Lady Azadiya nodded. "The fact remains that it is beyond his knowledge to affect a potion in such a way that aligns with the stated purpose of the potion and explodes its boundaries.

If Viran wanted me poisoned, there are a thousand easier ways for him to have done it. While I reluctantly admit Viran might be involved with Mistress Savoldyn, and may yet be proved a disastrously foolish accomplice to murder, of this—" She pointed to the spider silk wrap covering her eyes. "—he may be fully acquitted."

"What luck," Ibram muttered.

A thin smile graced her face. "It runs in the family. A more pressing concern would also be to find out how the wood alcohol was added to the man's tolnic."

"It wasn't the tolnic that killed him," Berot said, as he looked up from his notes. "It was whatever he drank following the tolnic."

"But I thought you said the tolnic was adulterated?" Amota Berac asked.

Doctor Berot shook his head. "I said he had died from wood alcohol poisoning," he said. "I make no statements concerning where it was imbibed. In point of fact, the tolnic itself would have slowed the poison's progression. It would have made him ill, but that could have merely been taken for a drunk man's comeuppance."

And so a quick murderous inclination became a torturous affair. Ibram tilted his head back slightly. "His handwriting deteriorated," he said. "It started off quite accomplished in his ledgers, but then it got worse and worse. And Mistress Dolman mentioned he'd been abstaining from his usual volume—from two mugs down to one."

Doctor Berot nodded. "Master Savoldyn could very well have confused poison for illness and sought to cure the symptoms without knowing the danger he was in."

Ladyship tsked. "The housekeeper would have access to both tolnic and shay."

"That's Mistress Dolman," Ibram said. "She hasn't looked upon me favorably, but she's been helpful."

"And Master Savoldyn kept her in his service, even when he tossed out most of his other servants," Ahksell said.

Lady Azadiya hummed lightly, and nodded.

"I thought there was nothing in the shay?" Amota Berac asked. "That's what Viran told us."

"Yes, but," Ibram started and then stopped. He glanced at Ahksell and found him staring at his boots.

"Yes," Lady Azadiya echoed. "You both had the presence of mind to ask what the victim drank the morning of his death. Tolnic and shay. Do you remember in what quantities?"

"I do," Ahksell spoke up. "A mug of tolnic and two pots of shay."

"So one would not have killed him outright," Lady Azadiya said, "and the latter held nothing deadly, but the middle drink was never tested, nor seen."

"But he drank it with his daughter," Ahksell said.

Ibram blinked rapidly. "No," he said. "She didn't. Mistress Dolman said when the kitchen prepared Savoldyn's shay, they only included one cup on the tray. The cook didn't know Mistress Ignalle was there, she said."

"How would she have known?" Ahksell asked.

Ibram shrugged. "Mistress Dolman could have told her."

Lady Azadiya hummed in agreement, and a silence fell over the group. Ahksell looked unhappy. For his part, it wasn't Ibram's job to judge the guilty or the innocent, only to lay facts at Lady Azadiya's table so that she might pick out the choicest morsels. Still, the thought irked him. If the murderer was connected to Viran, if it was even as remote as an ill-judged affair, she would still have her share of social embarrassment. Ladyship never appeared to care much about that, but the other mentors definitely would. It made Ibram wonder what might happen when she inevitably sent someone off to the warders for disposal.

$$\text{❧ 12 ❧}$$

In Lityen, there were always six streets barely large enough to claim the description crammed almost but not quite up to the gates of the moderately wealthy, and beyond those straggled the manors of the rich or merely mighty. The Savoldyns might not avail themselves of the street vendors with their constantly boiling vats of stew, but they all of them bought bread from the bakery-mills or sent out for the freshest brace of fenek swinging from the butcher's hook. The festival enlivened daily life, but did not eclipse it. You could still lose a foot if you didn't mind your step in traffic.

Ibram maneuvered through the street by the Kilk clothiers without much thought, letting his feet dodge the cart wheeler and traveling players with their viols. Uncertainty bubbled in his stomach. On the first foot, Lady Azadiya was returned and had made her orders quite clear. On the second, Amota Viran was involved and even such experience as Ibram had told him the combination was unstable.

"Why is it that only one man is murdered and it causes no end of trouble for a score more of the living?" he asked.

He scratched the hinge of his jaw, where he had missed a patch of stubble in his haste to get up the living mountain that morning. A pair of children with their faces sticky from sugar candy ran past with their mother. So Ladyship didn't believe Viran was guilty of poisoning her, for reasons Ibram could understand, but no great pleasure lurked in his thoughts. He didn't want Viran to be a murderer, nor party to one. Who could? Viran was Ibram's uncle, too. Or, at least, one of them, and even if they were no ties of blood, the obligations were still in place. Most of them had had a hand in his education or training, and some of them had made it their business to invent games for his amusement as a child. Ibram nudged Ahksell in the side.

Ahksell startled, and looked down at him. "What?"

Ibram rolled his eyes. "I said, why is it that only one man has died and now at least six people must be heartily inconvenienced?"

"You did not say that."

"How would you know?" Ibram asked. "Since you were not listening?"

Ahksell sighed. "I was thinking about how we are supposed to get anything of use out of the Bureau of Currency, if there's nothing in the study."

"I don't have to do anything," Ibram said. "Ladyship said that was your problem."

"What, you won't help me?" Ahksell exclaimed. "After all I did for you?"

Ibram shrugged.

Ahksell jabbed him in the side with his elbow, using the crowd cover as his ally. Ibram elbowed him in return, and then quickly stepped back into his proper place, a little to the side and behind the noble alchemist. He smiled and Ahksell rolled his eyes.

"I can't go to the Bureau of Commerce and ask for paperwork that doesn't belong to me," Ahksell said, moving aside for a group of Attendants with Baran's badges on their necks. "They'll refuse. And they'll send a runner up the living mountain to tell Mistress Pariamua that I'm fiddling with official documents. Which means it's a warder problem, and I thought we were supposed to be avoiding those."

"Worst thought," Ibram muttered.

Ahksell held his hands to the air and looked up at the sky. "I just said it!"

"Light a candle about it," Ibram said.

"I have no more left," Ahksell said. "I used them all up asking forgiveness for your thieving ways."

A passing chandler suddenly swerved out their path with a heavy frown. Ibram groaned. "All right, all right," he said. "I'll help! If Savoldyn didn't keep copies of his past travel permits, then after we speak to Mistress Savoldyn, I will go with you to the Bureau of Commerce. I'll tell them you have a question about the next, ah—" He quickly counted to six on the knuckles of his first two fingers. "The next Haldrix's Festival. They always forget to sign the permits for the fish market, and then I am sent for eels on the dock in Preserved Corner."

Ahksell grinned. "Such a quick wit when you want to use it."

Ibram pointed down the street to the mouth of the alley where the Savoldyns lurked. They cut their way through the busy street until they came to the quieter avenues, now with their gates open in anticipation. Bedris alchemists attended all sorts of parties and dinners during the Festival of Sangrin, and not all of them were in a noble household. A few hay-strewn carts were in the roads, topped with barrels and the men to off-load them. Ibram chewed the corner of his mouth.

"What dramseller might sell a rich house their fortified spirits?" Ibram asked as they passed by one such cart, reeking of old beer.

"Any number," Ahksell answered.

"Yseult alone contracts with five for Ladyship's tower," Ibram said. "And that is merely her personal cellar." He frowned. "The houses in the village make their own ales, but Savoldyn preferred tolnic."

"Marit, the Savoldyn's cook, said she got it from the Tarsis."

"But if it was from a reputable seller," Ibram said, "then we would have heard of more such deaths in our corner of the province."

"And there has been no such rash of deaths," Ahksell said. "Or unexplained ones, either."

Ibram nodded slowly. "Mistress Dolman said Marit spiced and fortified the tolnic herself."

Ahksell shook his head. "But a cook wouldn't poison someone," he said. "Even if it was ruled an accident, who would ever eat their food again? They'd be turned out of the house!"

Ibram laughed. "Like the rest of Savoldyn's servants were," he said.

"Still, perhaps we detour to the Tarsis' festival stall before the Bureau of Currency."

"The question becomes," Ahksell said, as they walked down the alley that led to the Savoldyn's kitchen door. "How do we get a nip of the tolnic and take it back for a closer look? We have to prove at least something is adulterated in that kitchen."

"Easy enough. Just...when I ask for your bag, make a distraction."

"Why do you need my bag?" Ahksell asked.

"Trust me," Ibram said. "I have the shape of an idea."

"That's not enough, Ibram," Ahksell said. "Ibram—"

Ibram knocked on the door, and then stood back with his hands clasped behind his back. "I'm feeling rather thirsty, to be sure."

This time, Liepa answered the door, rather than Jara, the kitchen maid. She wore the same blue gown with mouflon collar, and her hair was neat beneath its net. Her long eyelashes fluttered decisively in Ahksell's direction, when Ibram re-made their introductions.

"Please, come in Attendant," she said, and swept back into the kitchen to allow room.

"Thank you, Mistress..." Ahksell said, as he stepped across the threshold.

"Otero," she said with a smile.

Ibram's eyebrows rose and fell. Surely, his own invitation to enter was implied, after such a welcome. He followed Ahksell and stepped to the right so that Liepa could close the door behind them all. He clapped his hands together and bowed to the room in general. Jara Whaite was at the big fireplace, turning a spit of four tiny hortulanas. Lover's birds, they called them, small enough to feed one on their own, but always served in sets of two. Seemed like an odd time to be cooking, so soon after breakfast. Perhaps Mistress Savoldyn had woken late. The cook was at her worktable again, though she was sitting down now, and had a small ledger in front of her. Across from her sat Mistress Dolman.

"Mistress Dolman. Mistress Marit," he declared. "Every time we meet my joy increases."

"Does it indeed, Master Ucalegon?" Mistress Dolman asked.

"Why else should I come through the kitchen?" Ibram asked,

undeterred by the weariness of her tone. "The smell of the food alone can sustain me for hours."

Mistress Marit looked up at that, and smiled tensely before she returned to ticking figures off on her ledger. She squinted at the pages, and bobbed her head closer to the paper. Her hair was coming out of its neat bun, as if she'd tied it poorly in haste. He looked into the corner of the kitchen where the barrel of ale was propped up against the wall. If his memory served, the little clay jars hadn't been moved from their perches on crates next to it. Savoldyn must have gone through drink like a sieve. Ama stored her tolnic in the furthest corner of their cold room, in a clay urn with a bowl for a stopper. Naturally, they would want the food and drink stored in a cool spot, but in a space like this it would be an undercroft either reached through the kitchens or very close to it. How to find it?

"And where is Master Kenes this fine day?" he asked. He walked idly forward, keeping one eye on the vegetables piled on one end of the table, the picture of a young man with an empty belly. "Don't tell me he's still abed."

"Hilo is upstairs with Mistress Savoldyn," Liepa said. "They're running through the accounts."

Ibram nodded and made an acknowledging noise in the back of his throat. That corner of the room was a little oddly shaped, with perhaps room for a downward passage. What was more likely to happen...that he would be offered a glass of tolnic to quench his thirst while he waited on his Attendant to return from visiting the lady of the house? Or that he could sneak past all these servants to the under-croft and find the very bottle Lady Azadiya wanted to examined? And what was he to do, just take any bottle that smelled of alcohol? Surely, as careful a murderer as this must be would have disposed of the poison by now.

He turned back to the room, and saw that Liepa had drifted near Ahksell. She stood to her advantage in the light from the fire and lamps, and smiled as Ahksell noticed her standing at his elbow and jumped a foot. Ibram let his upper body sag briefly, as if in sudden dismay.

"Attendant Solari," he said, shaking his head. "You really must let me have my carry-all back."

"What?" Ahksell asked, and grasped the strap of his bag.

"The Attendant is kindness itself, Mistress Otero," Ibram said. "He knows about my old trouble, you see." He hunched his right shoulder and rubbed his hand down and up his biceps. "And seeing as I have been known to him since he was only a child—"

Ahksell frowned. "Oh," he said. "Yes, are you sure? It's not still troubling you?"

"Not at all," Ibram said. He held out his hand, and Ahksell unslung his carry-all. He passed over the bag, and Ibram set it over his left shoulder. "See? I shall just use the other one."

"How good of the Attendant to help," Liepa said. "It's a kind master to hold his own servant's bag."

Ahksell's smile was more like a wince, but he managed it. "I...try to be helpful," he said. "Tell me, Mistress Marit, uh, what have you planned for your meal today? I still remember the smell of that sauce!"

Mistress Marit jumped, and then looked up from her little booklet. She laughed. "Young men are the same in all stations of life, I suppose."

"Surely it's not simply young men who enjoy good cooking," Ahksell laughed.

The cook smiled and shook her head. "I'll admit my own daughter has hounded me for the recipe more than once! She has no one but her mistress to cook for, of course, but every little bit helps."

"Ah, a small household, then?" Ahksell asked.

Mistress Marit paused, and tucked her reddish hair behind both ears. "Indeed so."

Ibram stepped back from the table, and turned to Mistress Dolman. "Time and pleasure wait for no one, to be sure. Would it be possible to speak with Mistress Savoldyn? I'm afraid there's been news of her husband."

The entire room looked to him at that pronouncement. By the anticipatory looks on their faces, he had no doubt the removal of the body from the Ark had been spread about as soon as Mistress Dolman returned home, and Catha the Grey only knew what Viran had whispered in the lady of house's ears. Ahksell crossed his arms over his chest, and raised his eyebrows. Ibram ignored him.

No one was going to allow him access to their undercroft without a solid reason, and most probably an order directly from Mistress Savoldyn. The empties were still stacked against the wall, and he deliberately paid them only the thinnest slice of his attention. Who was more likely to give him tolnic? The servants, led by Mistress Dolman, who was perhaps not completely thawed by his charms? Or Mistress Savoldyn, who even now might be cherishing Ibram's lost uncle? He considered the thought, and the images it led to, for an uncomfortable moment, and then shook his head. Decision made.

"Is she at home to visitors now?" he asked in a quiet voice. "I confess, the Attendant didn't have me check to see if the rushes had been burnt."

Ahksell cleared his throat. "Well, I was just so anxious to relay our news," he said.

Mistresses Dolman and Marit shared a quick, but telling look. Then, the housekeeper rose from her chair. "I am afraid Mistress Savoldyn is busy with funereal affairs, as Liepa mentioned before," Dolman said, and smoothed down the front of her gown. "I don't think she should be disturbed."

"Oh, but this news is grave, Mistress Dolman," Ibram said.

"Is it true he's up the living mountain?" Jara Whaite's voice burst out. She clapped her hands over her mouth with a gasp.

"Jara," Mistress Marit snapped.

"I'm afraid to say he is," Ahksell said. "He's been murdered."

Mistress Dolman sat back down with a decided slump to her shoulders. "Attendant Solari," she said. "Mistress Savoldyn did not want that information shared amongst the servants."

"Better they hear it from friendly voices than the neighbor's gossip," Ibram said. "We both saw the stall being prepared outside, they're quick to seize an opportunity."

Mistress Dolman sniffed, but said nothing, and so Ibram continued. He took a step towards the opposite wall and made a show of looking about. "Where's that boy you had?" he asked. "Tawrit?"

"His mother is ill," Mistress Marit said. "I sent him home with some leftover broth from our meal."

Ibram twisted briefly to smile behind himself, and rested his hand over the clasp that held Ahksell's carry-all closed. He touched the metal carefully, wary of any warning tingle, but his fingers remained unsinged; he slipped the metal tongue free.

"Mistress Marit, kindness flows from your very fingertips," he said.

Mistress Marit coughed like she was swallowing a laugh, and stood up. She clapped her hands together, and turned to where Jara Whaite was neglecting her birds.

"Turn the spit, girl!" Marit exclaimed. "I can smell the skin already burning!"

"Sorry! Sorry, Marit!" Jara gave a little jump, and then bent down to her task.

Ibram saw Ahksell clench his hand down by his side; his expression turned vague. Jare wrenched the lever on the spit, but the handle refused to turn under her power. She grabbed it with both hands, and pulled again.

"Marit, it's stuck!"

"Honestly, step aside, girl!"

Mistress Marit strode to the fire, and Jara gave way before her. She reached down, and clasped the wooden handle. Ahksell's hand relaxed, and the hortulanas revolved again.

"There, do you see?" Marit asked.

"I...we think we know how it happened," Ahksell said. "But we'd like your help in discovering who did it?"

"You do?" Liepa asked.

"Oh definitely," Ibram said, and jerked his chin slightly towards the fire and spit. "Something he ate."

"Something he—absolutely ridiculous!" Mistress Marit exclaimed. She whirled around with her hands on her hips. "There's nothing in this house that doesn't go past my table, nor that doesn't cross my lips as well!"

Ahksell immediately raised both hands and stepped in front of her, blocking her view of the rest of the room. "Now, Mistress," he said, soothingly. "No one is accusing you—"

"Then you mean me?" Jara asked, with a tremor in her voice that threatened to become a quake. "But I'd never kill anyone! Mistress, tell him. If the house closes like she's threatening, then where will I go? You know—"

"Now is not the time for this, Jara," Liepa said, and came over to stand too close to Ahksell's side. "We must help the Attendant by answering his questions."

"Well, you've been helping serve," Jara snapped. "Maybe you smeared something on the fish!"

"How many times a day do you help with the food, Liepa?" Ahksell asked. He pointed at her, and she stared at him, wide-eyed. "Have you ever noticed a funny smell?"

"My food always comes out just as it ought to!" Mistress Marit exclaimed. "And keep turning that spit, girl. I can smell the coin going up in smoke with those birds."

"Oh, let them crisp to oblivion," Jara said. "I'm no murderer."

"You're certainly no cook," Liepa muttered.

"I fear that there may have been a misunderstanding," Ahksell said. His hand clenched again. "It simply might have been an undercooked bird."

"So we're in no danger now," Marit said. "If the mistress only eats one side of that hortulana."

"Girls, I won't have this," Mistress Dolman said, and jumped to her feet.

She strode forward into the angry circle surrounding Ahksell, where old slights amongst the staff burbled up like bubbles in ale, and Ibram ducked back to the far wall. Up close, the corner of the room smelled of old beer, and there was indeed a narrow wooden door, sealed with a heavy iron lock. That most probably led to the undercroft, or something very like one. Ibram took note, but left it alone; there was no time for that. He scanned the little clay jars that lined the crates next to the ale barrel. Each was a solid thing, with a sturdy plug, and no doubt had seen many boiling washes for reuse in their time, but these had drips and drabs of old liquor tracks down their sides. At the base of each neck, Ibram recognized the square stamp of stylized vines the Tarsis used to mark their wares. Ibram grinned briefly. The death had disrupted the household routines. Food deliveries, to be sure, and probably the necessities of collection as well, but nothing so frivolous as the bottle boy or rag and bone man.

He reached his hand out over the rows of empties and lifted the flap of the carry-all with his left hand. If he were a poisoner, he'd hide such an bottle in plain sight, near enough its more innocent siblings to make no notice. He frowned. But he also might rearrange the bottles and put the offender in the furthest part of the batch on the crate. He heard Ahksell's calming voice start to take precedence. It was too dark to see a pattern of dust on the bottle tops. He squinted, and leaned in closer. There at the very back against the wall was a line of bottles, squat vessels that stood a little lower than the others, and without the Tarsis' stamp. The back of his head throbbed; this was no time to belabor thought. He held his breath, and grabbed two from the back row.

"It's not my fault," Liepa said loudly. "That milk was old when the cold charm cracked in half!"

"Fresh as anything," Mistress Marit insisted. "Master Savoldyn knew the difference between a properly curdled posset and a cup of whey."

"Is that what he had for his morning meal?" Ahksell asked with a high note of incredulity in his voice. "I think perhaps we should have a list of everything Master Savoldyn ate and drank on the day of his death."

Ibram stuffed both bottles into the carry-all, and drew down the flap. He turned back to the room, and held the bag against his side, careful not to let the bottles clack against each other. He glanced down at the leather; it didn't look too different from before he'd stuffed the evidence inside. When he looked back up, Mistress Dolman was watching him.

He smiled immediately, letting his lips stretch back to show his teeth, and sunk his shoulders away from his neck. Ama always taught him that the best defense was congenial behavior; if you believed you had done nothing wrong, then of what could you be accused? He walked over to the end of the table, by the vegetables, and rested his hip against the wooden planks. He picked up a tidily cut stick of carrot, and stuck the end in his mouth. He chewed deliberately.

"What a wonderful idea, Attendant Solari," he called out, and made sure he was wide-eyed in admiration. It was, in point of fact, a good idea.

Dolman's eyes raked the side of Ibram's face, but he said nothing and neither did she. He finished his carrot. He tilted his gaze in her direction, and waited. That she suspected something of him didn't mean much in the long run, she was an intelligent woman after all. But the question of what she did with those suspicions was more immediately interesting.

She looked over his shoulder to the corner of the room, and breathed in deeply. She pursed her mouth, and settled her hands, folded, at her waist. Then, Dolman faced him completely. "I believe Mistress Marit can supply the Attendant with such a list," she said, cutting through the talk behind her.

Ibram quirked his eyebrows, but bowed, dipping his head. "The Sect of Seven Fires appreciates your aid," he said.

Jara and Liepa's argument had crumbled into a sneer and an unpleasant face as Marit separated them. Ahksell put his back to the fire with a poorly concealed look of relief. The cook returned to her table, and sat back at her ledger.

"As to an interview with Mistress Savoldyn," Dolman continued, "I fear she is—"

"In the family courtyard with Master Kalmar?" Ibram asked.

Ladyship had often despaired of his lack of patience, but Ibram could admit to his own faults while still enjoying the effect he had on a room. Besides, he needed to get up the stairs. He smiled, and Mistress Dolman's lips thinned so quickly they nearly disappeared.

"I fear an ulterior motive has been exposed," he said. "Attendant Solari is not to blame, of course, but I am tasked with returning my uncle up the living mountain. He missed breakfast, you see."

Jara Whaite hiccupped a laugh, and then ducked her red face and began turning the spit so fast Ibram feared the birds would fly free again. Mistress Dolman smoothed the front of her kirtle and nodded sharply.

"Well enough," she said. "If you will follow me, Attendant."

"Of course," Ahksell said. "Ibram, come along."

⁂

Mistress Dolman took them from the smaller servants' courtyard and up into the main rooms. The Savoldyn's private family apartments were above their wares, but no less expensively appointed than any rich merchants. Their footsteps puffed dust into the air—Liepa clearly didn't stretch to cleaning—but they barely made any noise on the thick carpets fixed to the floors. Dolman knocked briskly on a closed door past the dining room, and then strode inside without waiting for an answer. Ibram would have followed, but Ahksell lingered on the threshold, politely, and he bounced off the man's back.

"Dolman!" Mistress Savoldyn said from inside. "What's happened?"

She sounded nervous, which was as it should be. If Amota Viran had let spill half of what had been said up the living mountain, then even a fool would know they were in trouble. And Mistress Savoldyn, while silly, did not strike Ibram as foolish. He went up to his tiptoes and peered into the room over Ahksell's shoulder. He caught sight of Amota Viran sitting next to Mistress Savoldyn on a low couch, and dropped back to his heels with a heavy sigh.

"Good day, Mistress Savoldyn," Ahksell said. "Master Kalmar."

Ibram pushed Ahksell in the back; Ahksell barely rocked forward.

"May we come in?" Ahksell asked.

"Oh, yes," Mistress Savoldyn said. Her voice trilled like a startled bird's. "Of course, I apologize for keeping you waiting, I…"

"This is Attendant Solari," Amota Viran said. "And where he is, doubtless there is another. Come inside, both of you."

"Finally," Ibram muttered, and pushed Ahksell again. This time, Ahksell obeyed, and they both of them entered Mistress Savoldyn's sitting room. It was well lit, large enough for two windows to grace the furthest wall, and for glowbulbs to make up the rest. The walls had been whitewashed. The low couches in brightly patterned blue and orange fabric surrounded a wide table, where a tray of food and drink lay plundered. Hilo Kenes was also in the room, seated on the couch opposite. His long thin tail of hair looked scraggly, as if he'd been pulling at it. A sheaf of papers sat near the food tray, now that Ibram had a closer look, he could see a wax seal at the bottom of the topmost page.

Kenes and Mistress Savoldyn stood to make their proper bows, which Ahksell waved back up, and then retook their seats. Mistress Savoldyn smiled tightly as she resettled herself next to Amota Viran. Mistress Dolman closed the sitting room door and then drifted to stand behind her employer. Ibram remained where he was, in easy distance of the door and not too far to block a run for the windows, if needed. He nodded to Amota Viran, who frowned in return.

"Please Attendant," Mistress Savoldyn said, "have a seat. I—" She laughed a little. "—I think I must be some kind of oddity, a widow with so many visitors! It's...really not the custom, you know."

Ahksell sat on the couch opposite her, and nodded stiffly. "I am sorry to intrude on your grief," he said.

"Please, may I offer you something to drink?" she asked, and gestured to the shaypot.

"No, I thank you," Ahksell said.

She nodded tightly, and returned her hand to her lap. She was dressed in her white mourning cap, still, and the only jewelry she wore was her wheel-shaped pendant; her tunic and hose were the same simple pale grey-green. The carry-all and its stolen loot tugged on Ibram's shoulder; he readjusted the leather strap and settled his hand on top of the closed flap. If the bottles held no poison, the odds were likely that the tolnic had never been the problem. She could have done it; slipped poison in her husband's shay when no one was looking.

He looked to Dolman, whose stony eyes glared back. She had stayed in the house, when most of the servants had been let go and managed without for years. Would she have helped her mistress murder her husband? Why wait that long, if it was the case? It seemed possible, but not probable now he was faced with the pair of them.

"What brings you to see Mistress Savoldyn?" Amota Viran asked.

"Same as you, Uncle," Ibram said. "We bring important news."

Amota Viran cleared his throat sharply, and frowned. He was fully dressed, gambeson buttoned to his throat, and the leather strap with its bronze sect badge attached on his chest. He was missing his leather bracers, however. They lay unbuckled on the table nearest his half-empty cup of shay. Well, *he* didn't think her a poisoner, then.

"Mistress Savoldyn, do you drink much shay?" Ibram asked.

She frowned. "Not really," she said. "I prefer water or wine, if I am honest."

"Not even in the mornings?"

"Small ale suits me best," she said. "Better for the digestion. This is for Hilo and Master Kalmar, really."

"I wonder if I might trouble you for a moment?" Ahksell asked.

She patted the bottom of her white cap. "Yes, Attendant?" she asked.

Ahksell looked across the table firmly, but his gaze twitched away from Amota Viran's glower. "I'm sure I don't need to tell you why your husband's body was detained by the sect. Master Kalmar has no doubt informed you of the trouble I discovered," he said, and waited until she nodded her head. He nodded as well and pressed a smile between his thinned lips. "It would help us greatly if we could see the contracts and planning of your husband's caravans for the past few years."

Hilo placed his left hand on top of the papers on the table. Ibram stepped forward and pinched the corner of the stack. He smiled; Hilo's face paled.

"Thank you, Master Kenes," Ibram said. "No need to stand up; I'll take charge of these."

"Those are Master Savoldyn's private records," Hilo blustered.

"Victims of murder, to be sure, cannot afford such niceties," Ibram said.

He slowly pulled the papers out from under Hilo's heavy hand, and stepped away from the table. The room remained quiet. He ruffled through the top half of the stack. The official language was dense, but the handwriting was quite fine. At first glance, it seemed like a common charter for travel-in-commerce.

"Something like these would be quite handy, Amota Viran," he said without looking up. "He did keep his travel permits after all."

"Indeed so," Amota Viran said. "Which is why I asked to see them."

Ibram glanced up, and then back down to the papers. "I stand ever in your shadow."

Mistress Savoldyn sniffled. "I never thought—he wasn't always healthy, but I never dreamed he could be murdered. Do you think it might have been a competitor?"

"I think we all in this room know that Master Savoldyn was troubled, but not by his professional competition," Ahksell said.

"Einar often thrived as much on quarrels as he did on meat," Mistress Savoldyn said.

"And you preferred a quieter household," Ibram said.

"As do many of us," Amota Viran replied sharply.

Ibram shrugged. "As you say."

"Is that why you have a bag with you, Master Ucalegon?" Mistress Savoldyn asked. She retook her seat on the couch, and smoothed her clothes over her knees. "Has—I mean, it's a little irregular to just take someone's household records like this. Isn't it?"

Amota Viran's face tightened at the jaw; his nostrils flared with a sudden inhale. He wasn't a fool, after all. Ibram turned his back to the group, and opened the carry-all. He folded the papers, and stuck them between the two empty bottles, and then closed the bag. He spread his hands as he faced the room once more, and a curl of his hair swung past his face; he tucked it back behind his ear.

"Lady Azadiya merely wants to make certain opaque facts clear again," he said. "Before she sends the reports to the Cohort of Peace. You know how it is, Mistress, in a village such as ours, there's always more paperwork to feed the imperial bureaucracy's belly."

"And Lady Azadiya wishes these reports?" Viran asked with a deep frown. "You are here on her orders? Because when I left last night—"

"Mentor Hobon has left her tower," Ahksell interrupted, and Amota Viran's head jerked like he'd been slapped. "She requests your presence at the preceptory."

Mistress Savoldyn stood abruptly. "You must go!" she cried out with a smile. "At once! Oh, Viran—"

Mistress Dolman coughed loudly, and Mistress Savoldyn winced. She looked down at Amota Viran, and something passed between them that made his shoulders slump. He shook his head fondly, and then began to buckle his bracers onto his arms. Ibram tsked, and looked away.

"Do you have something to say, Ibram?" Amota Viran asked.

Ibram tugged on the hair on the back of his head, and shrugged. "I am merely here to pass on the good news," he said. "And extend Lady Azadiya's invitation to Mistress Savoldyn to meet with her up the living mountain."

Mistress Savoldyn whirled to face him. "She wants to see *me?*" she asked.

"The very same," Ibram said. "Would a little past midday be all right with you?"

"Oh, but I shouldn't leave the house," Mistress Savoldyn said. "Not with everything still to do."

Amota Viran stared at him from over her shoulder, and then shifted his attention to her. His face softened, even his eyes seemed sympathetic. Ibram saw Mistress Dolman frown, but she didn't put much force into the expression.

"I think it would be a good idea to meet with her, Yanna," Viran said.

Ibram nearly whistled aloud. It was *Yanna* now, was it? Caution was just tossed to the winds, it seemed like. He bounced on the balls of his feet and raised his eyebrows toward Ahksell, who shrugged back at him.

Mistress Savoldyn sat down again, and stretched out her hand to Viran. He took it, and held it between both of his palms. She swallowed, peering up at him, and nodded.

"Perhaps you're right," she said. "After all, Einar's business is still— there's still a contract to be maintained. It's what I can do for him, now."

"I'll go up first," Viran said, as if he had a choice in the matter. "You gather up the will and the old contracts. If you bring them with you, then no one will say you aren't giving Savoldyn his due."

Mistress Savoldyn smiled, and pulled her hand from Viran's grasp. She touched her pendant, and looked down at her lap. Ibram pursed his lips. He could let her take the paperwork up the living mountain, but without seeing them in their entirety first, there was no way to know if they had been given them all. Yet, if he asked…

"Do you have your own copy, then, Mistress Savoldyn?" Ibram asked. "Of the will, I mean."

She turned her head towards him. "Of course," she said. "I keep it with my marriage contract in the wedding box."

"Sound thinking," Ibram said. "Do you like Itol?"

She shrugged. "It's a nice little village," she said. "Not bad for mouflon, but the—how did you know about my farm?"

Viran frowned at him. Ibram shrugged. "My father shared a guild with your first husband. He was awfully talkative."

Mistress Savoldyn snorted softly; her eyes watered, but no tears fell. Mistress Dolman tapped her hand on the wooden back of the couch. "Master Savoldyn left the guild some time ago," Dolman said.

"Strange how things stick in the mind," Ibram said. "I only wondered. Itol's such a change from Lityen."

Mistress Savoldyn shook her head. "Not really," she said. "It's close enough by carriage, and the farm has a deep stream round the back." She paused and looked wistful. "I miss the river, you know."

Ibram clicked his teeth together. "Indeed," he said.

"If that is all, Ibram," Viran said. "I believe you and I might escort Attendant Solari back to the preceptory."

"Oh, there's no need for that," Ahksell said. "But I'll accompany you nonetheless. Shall we all go?"

"Mistress Savoldyn would need time to prepare before visiting Mentor Hobon," Mistress Dolman said quickly.

"We can certainly wait," Ibram said. "I'll take Attendant Solari down to Master Savoldyn's office. I know the way."

"I can show you," Hilo said, and stood.

"That would be fine," Ahksell said. He got to his feet with a sigh, and then straightened his gambeson with both hands. "I'll go down with Ibram. Are you…will you join us, Master Kalmar?"

There was a searching tone to his voice, and an intensity to the way he looked to Amota Viran that urged Ibram to swallow the comment on the tip of his tongue about Amota Viran's interest in lingering. He sniffed and rubbed the end of his nose instead. Lady Azadiya said he had not blinded her, and that was all very well. Ibram was delighted by that news. But Amota Viran was supposed to be up the living mountain, going about his work, and not down in Lityen, coming to the aid of distressed widows. It upset a balance Ibram hadn't realized they had all been depending upon.

"I will," Amota Viran said slowly. "I want to see Ladyship up and about with my own eyes, to be sure."

Ibram snorted. "She's in a fine, rare mood. I'm sure you'll have much to talk about." He bowed shortly to the room, and left without waiting for Ahksell, or Mistress Savoldyn's permission. It would be short work to get the rest of the ledgers—or note that they were missing, if he had to—and it was best they get on with it.

☙ 13 ❧

Freed from her office, Lady Azadiya signaled her clear determination not to be trapped there again. The tent city still reigned outside her tower walls, and the rest of her division was scattered within it. Amota Viran had been fending off runners from all three of the upper divisions within Yseult from the moment he had stepped out of the relay system, trailing urgent messages and requests from aides on both sides. The little crowd of functionaries now loitered outside by the front doors, unwilling to barge inside, but not allowed to leave without his signature or approval, or some such nonsense. Ibram closed the too-light stone doors on them with no little sense of satisfaction.

Amota Viran led Mistress Savoldyn down the short staircase to the open area in the middle of the tower, while Ibram carried a bag of ledgers and Ahksell floated two crates more off Savoldyn's bookshelves. The whole place was on display, even though it remained empty. Someone had lit a censor of ermite paste, a soothing mash of medicinal plants and fruit oils, most probably on Doctor Berot's orders. The giant covers had been taken off the faceted glass roof, the glowbulbs had been shaken into luminescence, and the burbling fountain was flowing happily. Even the snapping euphorbia on their little shelves seemed to bristle with delight. Ladyship sat in the middle of it all, at the same couch she had ensconced herself before, with a full tray of shay and a plate of vivekas on a table before her.

"I am glad to see you, Lady Azadiya," Amota Viran said. He bowed deeply, but kept his head raised to study her face. His eyes caught and held on her yellow silk blindfold; his forehead grew deep lines.

Mistress Savoldyn bowed as well. "I thank you for the invitation to meet you—to meet with you," she said. "Your family's contracts with my husband's business are of the highest priority."

Lady Azadiya waved them up, curling the fingers of her right hand loosely. "I am simply glad to be out of my office," she said.

"The Savoldyns' business has been with us for some time," Amota Viran said. "I'm sure—"

Lady Azadiya tilted her head to the left, and Viran's mouth snapped shut. She smiled politely, and touched her thumb to the face of her signet ring. "The Savoldyns were indeed a business partner of long-standing," she said. "But I invited Mistress Savoldyn here not simply for a reassurance as to my yearly linen order."

"You did not?" Mistress Savoldyn asked.

Lady Azadiya shook her head. "Work can so often get in the way of living, don't you agree, Mistress Savoldyn?"

The other woman stood there, blinking, for a moment, and then shrugged slightly. "I find work...directs life, Ladyship," she said. "If there is no work, there is nothing to do. It's rewarding."

Lady Azadiya smiled and draped her long dark braid over her shoulder. "When well-regulated, I might agree," she said. "Although I have found there's always something to do, especially in the absence of duty. Or in its escape, for that matter. Don't you agree, Vir-la?"

Amota Viran flushed; he ground his teeth. "Kwod doan Di sekwate nu, Damita?" he spit out. "Doan Di burzj meke?"

Ibram cleared his throat, and set down the bag of ledgers. Ahksell lowered both hands as well as the crates. He rubbed the back of his head. "What did he say?" he asked.

Ibram waved him off. "Sometimes they go too fast for me."

Lady Azadiya tilted her head. "Di pluone anmavarde, nacht bo giel-lan. And let us not be rude to my guests. Vissilian, if you please."

"As you say, Aunt," Viran said.

Lady Azadiya held out her right hand, and crooked her first two fingers; the shaypot lifted from the tray. "Sit down, the pair of you. Boys, array yourselves."

Ibram sighed, and took up a place leaning on the stack of crates Ahksell had just set down. Ahksell, for his part, sat on the opposite end of the low couch with Lady Azadiya, across from Mistress Savoldyn and Amota Viran. The shaypot tilted and poured its contents into the three cups placed on the tray. Ladyship lowered the pot and curved her middle finger and thumb into an open circle. A delicate porcelain cup rose and floated towards Mistress Savoldyn, who took it with a trembling hand.

"I—I am very glad to see you so recovered, Mentor Hobon," she said, and settled the cup in her lap. She had dressed in a rose damask silk gown to meet Lady Azadiya, belted at the waist with a multi-colored tassel from which hung bronze dress hooks. It was what rich ladies from the riverlands wore, easily adjusted to save their hemlines when onboard a family ship. "Master Kalmar has always spoken so well of you."

"He has a way with words," Lady Azadiya said as she sent Amota Viran his own cup. "Is that why you wish to marry him?"

Amota Viran sputtered into his shay, and jerked his head up to stare at Lady Azadiya in abject and dawning horror. "Damita—"

Lady Azadiya snapped her fingers; the sound reverberated in the empty room. Amota Viran glared at her, while Mistress Savoldyn clapped one hand to the side of her head. Ibram winced and wiggled a finger in his ear. Ahksell touched a button on his gambeson, and a little purple light winked out. He settled more comfortably in the couch.

"I suffer from headaches," Lady Azadiya said into the heady quiet. "I would prefer not to also suffer interruptions."

Amota Viran and Mistress Savoldyn glanced at each other. She leaned over her knees, and opened her mouth as if she had something to bring to the conversation. Lady Azadiya observed her, Ibram was sure of it, just as if she had two unharmed eyes. Ladyship's thumb touched her signet ring.

"I have a conundrum, Mistress Savoldyn," she said. She raised first her left hand, and then her right, palms to the ceiling. "Here is my nephew, who has been at my side since his youth, and there is a man murdered, a circumstance which I find he has neglected to inform me. You perceive the turn of my thoughts?"

She closed her right hand and Amota Viran jerked forward. His shay sloshed in his cup. "That's not what I intended!"

"He didn't know!" Mistress Savoldyn said at the same time.

"Did he not?" Lady Azadiya sat back and dropped her hands into her lap. "Did you?"

Mistress Savoldyn flushed and laid her shaking hand on her collarbones. "No," she gasped. She shook her head, overcome, and then dragged in a breath. "Neither of us knew Einar—and neither of us thought of marriage, or murder or anything like it."

"When Ibram laid out his suspicions I gave them due consideration," Viran said. "What else could I do? You were sealed away relearning how to walk three steps without tripping, and the entire division was running about dreaming up more and more elaborate tragedies being enacted in the tower. The cooks lost an entire day's supply of duck eggs to Lakum and Evren's shrines!"

"I had not thought—I am newly widowed, Mentor," Mistress Savoldyn protested. She gestured to her white cap as if Lady Azadiya could have missed it. "He was being *kind!* He's always been kind to me."

Amota Viran looked down into his shay, and pursed his lips. Ladyship nodded slowly. "Grounds for friendship, indeed," she said.

"When I married Einar, we both understood it was not for love," Mistress Savoldyn said. "I have been in love before, and found a comfortable home more profitable in the end."

"Come now," Lady Azadiya said. "I might have my little aches and pains of late, but what kind of aunt would I be if I did not recognize facts as facts?"

"There are no facts!" Mistress Savoldyn declared.

"You don't like Viran?" Lady Azadiya asked. "That's disappointing. I've always found him good company."

"No, of course I like him!"

"He has nine other siblings, you know, and I can't stand most of them. Pity he's not the heir."

Amota Viran cleared his throat. He looked like a man caught on a rock in the ocean while the tide turned. He put down his cup of shay, and leaned forward.

"Really, there's no need for this," he said. "I am well aware that I made a mistake. Master Savoldyn's death is suspicious."

"Murder is very suspicious," Ibram said.

"It could very well be a mistake from the draughtshop," Viran snapped.

"And it only affected one house?" Ibram asked.

"Perhaps Master Savoldyn stocked his larders so well, he bought out the seller?" Ahksell suggested in far too hopeful a tone.

Mistress Savoldyn turned her attention to him, hunched with discomfort. "It can't have been a mistake," she said. "I only wish it were! Einar wasn't the sort to lay in more than a limited store."

"Not even for his favorites?" Ladyship asked.

"Not even then," Mistress Savoldyn said. She touched her white cap again. "We were comfortable, but I was raised in such economy, and our comfort was becoming...stricter. The most he ever paid attention to the larder was to tell us we had spent too much."

"Why would a merchant of your husband's caliber worry himself about expense?" Lady Azadiya asked.

"He expected everything at hand when he wanted it, but he thought...he thought a limited household budget would take up more of my time. Keep me busy, as if his daughter had run off because she was bored. He always used to say the rich only kept their wealth because they guarded it well," Mistress Savoldyn said. "And paid attention to where they were going."

"Hence his love of the Navigator," Viran said, a touch sourly. "They always follow the golden path."

Ibram touched the carry-all still on his left shoulder. The bottles moved softly inside, but he didn't want to pull anything out while Mistress Savoldyn was present. He quietly set it down behind the crates instead.

"Oh, it takes all kinds to steer the ship," Mistress Savoldyn said. It seemed a familiar argument between the two of them, for they both relaxed a little and smiled at each other. Ibram hoped Ladyship was well enough to see that little exchange.

"Whereas Kivan the Red and the Wheelmaker both find joy in effort," Lady Azadiya said. "But come now, this is nasty talk, isn't it? Ahksell, take a viveka and then past it round. I want to hear how you became acquainted with Viran, Mistress Savoldyn."

Ahksell did as he was told and ate one of the diamond-shaped cookies. Mistress Savoldyn looked briefly confused, Vissilians decided who ate by hierarchy of rank, but people of the west chose by age. Ibram had it both ways at home, he snagged a cookie from the air as Ahksell flicked one in his direction, before he passed the plate across the table to the guests. Ibram popped the entire thing in his mouth, crunching through the sugar crust to the tart jam beneath.

"It's not like what you suppose," Amota Viran interjected quickly. He returned the cookies to the table. "Mistress Savoldyn and I are friendly, to be sure, but we're both perfectly aware of our places in the world."

"That's just what I thought," Ahksell said. "And who would be foolish enough to marry a—"

Lady Azadiya cleared her throat, and Ahksell subsided. Mistress Savoldyn took a sip of her shay. Ibram scratched his jaw as he swallowed, and crossed his arms over his chest. Amota Viran caught the movement, and frowned at him. Ibram shrugged slightly. A bit late to worry about his posture, was it not?

"I did not kill my husband," Mistress Savoldyn said. "He wasn't a kind man, but you don't kill someone for that."

"Freedom is a wonderful commodity," Lady Azadiya said. "I have often bet on its future and am never surprised at the result."

"The future of freedom?" Mistress Savoldyn asked. "I suppose so. I'm familiar with that, at least, if not—" she cleared her throat, "—love. Einar was many things, but not a lover. At least, not with me. Our relationship was different, and his losses pained him. His first wife, you know, they wrote poetry together. They met at some family recital."

"And how did you meet?" Lady Azadiya asked.

"My family's freeholding was a part of one of his caravans, shortly after the whole affair with his daughter."

"The romance of the road?"

Mistress Savoldyn laughed, and seemed to surprise herself. "No, I... thought him clever, which he was, and strong, which was only partly true. I was at loose ends at the time, doing nothing but portage my family's goods to markets and come back. Life seemed...I needed a change." She took another sip of shay. "It wasn't the best of reasons, but I got what I bargained for."

"Which was?" Lady Azadiya asked.

Mistress Savoldyn glanced sideways to Amota Viran, who grimaced, but nodded. "The farm in Itol," she said. "I was granted the running of it in my marriage contract, with the deed to pass to me as part of my widow's portion. Our marriage allowed Einar to divest himself of a property while still keeping control of it in his lifetime. It's turned a profit these two summers. I thought the experience and the reward worth the time."

Lady Azadiya nodded. "Which you would not receive if you divorced."

Mistress Savoldyn shook her head. "He wished to aggravate his daughter, and I wished to become independent from my family in a more comfortable manner than I might afford on my own. In this, our terms seemed agreeable."

"He wasn't an old man," Lady Azadiya said.

"No, he wasn't," Mistress Savoldyn said. "But at the time, I thought if all went well, we would both get what we wished. I wanted to see what all the fuss was about your living mountain. The way he described life within the imperial boundary...houses that glowed under their own power, and caffa in the streets and automatons flying in the air—festivals on every corner..." She shook her head. "To live with the freedom of my own house and in such a place seemed like magic."

"And if Master Savoldyn turned out to be a horrible husband?"

"Which he was," Viran muttered.

Mistress Savoldyn sighed. "It did not all turn out as I had wished. We were...allies and not friends." She dabbed the corner of her eyes with her knuckle. "But it wasn't anything so bad as to make me abandon our bargain. The farm's money was my own. If I'd wished, I could return to my family. They're not bad folk, there are just too many of us in too small a space."

"Something I know about," Viran said.

Mistress Savoldyn pressed her hand against one of his, and smiled. "A year and a day and it wouldn't matter. Perhaps I would be worse for wear, but if there was one thing I learned on those endless caravans, Mentor, it was that life is not without risk."

"She could have come to me," Viran said, and sat up in his seat. "I know you wouldn't have cared, and I—I did tell Yanna that, once."

Lady Azadiya hummed in agreement. Ibram slouched against the crates. Mistress Savoldyn might not be a murderer, but underneath all that crying lurked a brain. She could have just as easily decided to run away to be a traveling player as marry a rich man like Savoldyn, but she hadn't done so. He frowned down at the tops of his boots. Savoldyn had exhibited signs of sickening from the wood alcohol poisoning beforehand, and she had just proven that she had the patience for a long-term plan.

"It's in my mind that you would have to wait an awfully long time to get that farm," Ibram said. "Begging your pardon, Ladyship."

Ladyship shrugged one shoulder. Viran licked his lips and coughed. "You're always jumping from suspicion to suspicion," he said. "Part of the reason, I recommended Evren take you back to the archives."

"So you admit you tried to get me out of the way!" Ibram stood away from the boxes, and jabbed his finger in the air.

"I admit to thinking you were once again attempting to get out of your normal duties at a time when I needed every hand to the plow!"

Ibram shook his hands out in front of him. "A man had died!"

"And when I did as you asked, Attendant Abele quite firmly stated that she found nothing noxious in Master Savoldyn's drink," Viran pointed out. "I believe the fact that I held her findings more highly than your opinion weighs more heavily on your heart than you would like to believe."

Mistress Savoldyn inhaled deeply and sighed over her cup of shay. "Einar was murdered, though, Viran," she said.

Amota Viran sagged back on the couch, and rubbed his hand down his face. "Yes, he was," he admitted.

Ibram tsked, and Amota Viran's head twisted in his direction. He glared, and Ibram sagged back against the crates, feeling the slats bend under his weight. The wood creaked.

"We all try to help our friends, when they are in need," Ahksell said, with a sideways glance in Ibram's direction.

"I should have brought the matter to you, Aunt," Viran said as he finally turned his head to look at Lady Azadiya. "At the least, it should have been your order to dismiss Ibram's suspicions and not my own, once you had recovered."

"That is true," Lady Azadiya said, "but you had no knowledge of when I would recover." She sighed through her nose, and adjusted her fingerless mitts. "I believe you should show Mistress Savoldyn the delights of the preceptory, Viran. For someone who wished to know more of us, I do not recall her visiting recently."

"Oh, no," Mistress Savoldyn protested. "I shouldn't, Mentor Hobon. Leaving my house without burning the rushes—"

"Has already taken place," Ladyship said. "There's no stoppering a broken bottle. I would have you learn more of us. Viran, take her to see Berac and Lakum. Between the three of you, no corner of Yseult will remain unexamined."

"Damita," Viran said. He stood and looked between the two women; his eyebrows pinched in the center of his forehead. "If Yanna does not want to stay, I don't think we can stop her."

"I would..." Mistress Savoldyn got to her feet, setting down her cup as she did so. "My husband's body is here, is it not?"

"It is," Ahksell said. "We took it to the Hall of Tranquility after Doctor Berot had finished examining him."

"Then I would like to see him," she said. "Elene whisked him away so quickly, I had no time to make my good byes."

"Mistress Ignalle took him up?" Ibram asked. "I thought Mistress Dolman had ordered the Ark to take charge of the body."

Mistress Savoldyn shook her head. "No, it was his daughter. I think she wanted to make up for their estrangement, in the end."

A thought occurred. "Is that why she came by the house, the

morning when we met?" Ibram asked.

"In a way," Mistress Savoldyn said. "She kept an eye on the business, you know, through Dolman. I don't know if Einar knew of it, but the rest of the household certainly did. She would arrive at the house and they'd upbraid each other about, oh, shipments lost, or the price of damasks, that sort of thing."

"What was the argument on the day of Savoldyn's death?" Lady Azadiya asked.

Mistress Savoldyn tilted her head upwards in thought. "Oh...a trip Einar was planning," she said. "Woolens, I believe. Or, at least, that was the beginning of the argument. I've found when you truly know someone whatever the point of the fight was to begin with is often distracted by old business."

Lady Azadiya smiled slightly. "Indeed so. How old?"

"The will again, of course," Mistress Savoldyn said. "Einar gave the business to her child with the expectation that Master Ignalle would never amount to much as a clerk." She shrugged. "He hasn't, you know. They live very simply."

A wavering image of the Ignalle's little house near the bakery-mill flashed in front of Ibram's mind, that neat front entrance, freshly painted. "Indeed, they do," he said.

"The thing of it is," she continued, with a wrinkle in her brow, "that Einar gave the business away, but he never stated who he wanted to run it, if he died before she reached adulthood."

"Seems an odd detail to omit," Ahksell said.

Savoldyn shook her head. "Oh, but he didn't," she said. "He told me so the...oh, it must have been after their last great clash. He left that bit out purposefully, because it will go to the Courts Civil, you know, and the circuit judge might take years to deliberate. He wanted me to fight the will and try to keep control until his grandchild was old enough to take over."

Amota Viran stood up from the couch, and cleared his throat. "Is that—did you agree to that, Yanna?" he asked.

Surprise heightened the corners of Mistress Savoldyn's eyes and mouth. She stood as well. "Of course," she said. "I didn't want him to break the terms of our agreement, after all."

"Farms are a lot of work," Ibram said. "Or so I am told."

She swiveled to face him, and nodded. "They are," she said. "But..." She paused, and then glanced at Lady Azadiya from the corner of her eye. "Ladyship," she said, and faced her. "I lied to him."

Lady Azadiya nodded. "Did you? How so?"

"I was aware—how could I not be with that great loud bellow— that Einar had told his girl why he refused to set down who had control of the business. He told her about my promise. I went to her on the next market day."

"Are you friends, then?" Lady Azadiya asked.

"Not at all," Mistress Savoldyn said. "But I know my right from my left, and I told her so. I promised her that when Einar died, I wouldn't fight for the business. I never wanted it in the first place."

"It's a fair amount of coin," Lady Azadiya observed.

"I want my life," Mistress Savoldyn said. "I want my farm in Itol and I want—" She stopped talking and looked down, blushing. Amota Viran cleared his throat again, and stared off into the distance above Ladyship's head.

"I don't suppose you put that in writing," Ibram said, and picked dirt out from under his fingernail. "It's a legal-minded family, after all."

Mistress Savoldyn shook her head. "No," she said. "I swore to it, though."

Lady Azadiya hummed, deep in the back of her throat. She turned her face towards Amota Viran; her mouth quirked to the left. Amota Viran stood up from the couch, and held out his hand to Mistress Savoldyn. She grabbed hold.

"Lovely to finally meet you," Lady Azadiya said. "Viran, the path from the south field should be dry this hour. Attempt a stroll."

They bowed, and Ladyship waved them away. Amota Viran led Mistress Savoldyn from the area; he caught Ibram's eye as they passed, but Ibram couldn't figure out the expression in his face. Pity that, it might have helped him name the reason behind the knotted thud of his pulse in the back of his head. Ibram turned as they mounted the steps, and watched as they exited the tower. The stone doors thudded closed behind them.

14

Ibram groaned, and sat back against the edge of the couch, splaying his legs out along the floor. He leaned his head back against the molded cushion, and dropped the open scroll into his lap. Across from him, Ahksell glanced up from the open crate and shook his head.

"I know there was a reason you ordered I be taught to read, Lady-ship," Ibram said, "but I can't remember what Ama thought about it."

"Your sufferings are great, to be sure." Lady Azadiya drank from her cup of shay, and then floated the porcelain cup back to the tray. She adjusted her yellow silk binding. "Read on, and stop mumbling."

He stared across the piles of unrolled wooden slat scrolls and opened ledgers with a bleak and hollow heart. "Even the poetry?"

Ahksell snickered under his breath; Ibram kicked a stack of the offending works into his lap. Ahksell yelped, and threw his hands out. The papers flew backwards on a great gust of wind. Ibram ducked awkwardly sideways, and curled his arm over his head. A rattling scroll hit his elbow and folded itself on top of him.

Lady Azadiya sighed loudly. "Some potgirl in an evening courtyard will no doubt be all sympathy once you've finished with the past summer's taxes there."

"Yilka the Green protect me from petty clerks," he muttered, and stared down at the ledger held across his knees.

Most of the task of going over Savoldyn's ledgers and written effects came down to Ibram and Ahksell reading each list and ledger out loud while Lady Azadiya made approving noises or asked pertinent questions, as needed. Ladyship's head twitched in his direction.

"What was that?" she asked.

"Petty clerks," Ahksell said, as he curled both hands in front of himself. The loose papers ruffled and began to raggedly collect themselves. "Ibram thinks he's funny."

Ibram tsked. Lady Azadiya frowned, more in thought than an expression of displeasure.

"Read over the last three travel permits," she said. "Those were for a chain of travel from our perpetual wheels thence to Othy, correct?"

"Believe so, Ladyship," Ibram said.

"Oh," Ahksell looked about himself, and winced. "I think I might have—"

"Sent them into the fountain?" Ibram asked, and pointed to the burbling offender.

Ahksell straightened in alarm and glared at the water feature. "*No.*"

Lady Azadiya pinched the bridge of her nose. "Well, find them," she said. "As well the charters from the previous seasons' travels."

"Those," Ibram said, as he shifted position and dragged a stack of papers out from under his thigh, "I retain, Ladyship. What do you want to know?"

Ahksell groaned as he leveraged himself to his feet, and began to pick through the paperwork he had disturbed. Lady Azadiya shook her head.

"First you skip your examination, and then you drown my evidence," she muttered.

Ibram startled, and glanced up. "You missed it?" he exclaimed. "I thought you said you switched places in the lists!"

Ahksell's shoulders hunched as he continued to hunt through the loose paperwork. "I did," he said. "I simply forgot to do it again when my place was called."

Ibram groaned. "I cannot—"

"I only have to put my name in again next festival," Ahksell said, and whirled around. Papers slipped from his grasp and floated to the floor. "Is this not a little more important?"

He gestured towards Lady Azadiya and then the tower at large. Ibram winced and tugged the hair at the nape of his neck. His shoulders drew taut beneath his gambeson.

"You're an alchemist," he said. "Not an agent. You are here to learn."

"Well, if we're so far apart then why did you need me to run Hessele's Cage for you?" Ahksell said.

"If you do not prove yourself to be learning, then you run the risk of being sent on assignment," Lady Azadiya reminded him. "An alchemist at loose ends is no aid to the empire."

Ahksell's jaw clenched; he frowned. "I wasn't at loose ends," he insisted. "I was helping Ibram. This is my *home*."

Lady Azadiya touched her signet ring again, and nodded while Ahksell took a series of soothing breaths. Ibram scrubbed the back of his head again, pressing his fingers into the sore spots on his scalp. He picked up the travel permits again.

"Remember that when writing your report for me," Lady Azadiya said, with a trace of satisfaction.

"Ladyship," Ibram protested.

"Reason must come from within, Ibram," she said. "Just like a defense against charges of wrongdoing. Now, the permits."

"I found them," Ahksell said.

"Ibram first," she said, and pointed.

"What part did you want to review?" Ibram asked.

"What does the handwriting look like?"

"It's dense," Ibram said, "but it's a fine, clear hand. Seems rather standard, if you ask me."

"Standard?" she asked. "Look more closely, if you will." She sighed in dissatisfaction. "I cannot think with the distraction of my own senses! I miss the most obvious things."

Ibram raised the top paper and angled it into the light for a better look. "The lettering is even and the spaces between the words is uniform. It's ordinary." He picked up the next paper to the light and compared the two. "Oh, I see, yes."

"Do you?" she asked. "Riant."

Ibram snorted. Ahksell brought up the papers he held, and looked at them, side by side. He raised them high to the light, and then brought them down. "An ordinary man with extraordinary spite," he murmured.

"Petty, yet methodical?" Ibram asked, and held out his hand. Ahksell came over to the couch, and handed them down. He sat while Ibram read the papers over.

"What is the chance that the same clerk in the Office of Market Rights writes out every permit for Master Savoldyn's entire business?" Lady Azadiya asked the ceiling above her head. "I think it small indeed."

"It's not a very big section of the Bureau of Currency," Ibram said.

"Possibly," she said, but then shook her head. "Does a signature make a murderer?" she asked, with her face tilted to the ceiling.

"Savoldyn knew all these years his son-in-law was hindering his business," Ibram said, "yet he stayed silent."

"Or it's another reason he refused to assign a regent in his will," she said. "Revenge begets revenge. Still, it must be confirmed. Ahksell, I task you with this."

"Me?" Ahksell asked. "Mentor, why?"

"You did not go to them as I said to, before, did you?" she asked. "For copies of these same papers. There must be old refusals, times when Savoldyn applied for his same old regional charters and was rejected. Find them, and get confirmation by this same supervisor who allowed his clerk to wield such power."

"Yes, but you have these," Ahksell said. "Do you really need me to inquire any further?"

"I do," she said, and smiled. "These are only the most recent working seasons. I wish to firmly establish a pattern." She gazed up to the glass ceiling, briefly. "It is just past the middle of the day, is it not? I am sure they'll not be too busy. Go and inquire, and then seek out Warder Lieutenant Talsconis."

"He's a captain now," Ibram reminded her. He rubbed his collarbones with one hand and stretched out his shoulders.

Lady Azadiya shrugged one shoulder. "Make certain he has accepted my invitation to visit and celebrate his promotion."

"Why me, and not Ibram?" Ahksell asked.

"Because I have several other jobs which need doing," she said. "Ibram has another task. Now, off with you."

She waved her hand and Ahksell stood with a groan. He stepped over Ibram's legs. "I suppose this means you'll have to clean up the mess," he said as he crossed to the little stairs.

Ibram rolled his eyes. "May fortune ring out over your quest," he called as Ahksell left the tower.

Lady Azadiya snorted, and he turned back to her with a grin. He settled back against the couch, and shifted position on the floor. Lady Azadiya floated her shay back into her hand, and drank.

"I suppose you have a special occupation for me, Ladyship?" he asked.

"I do, as it happens," she said. "There are several factors to consider here," she said. She rubbed circles against her right temple and lay back against the couch. "How did the wood alcohol enter the house? Where did it come from?"

"Easy enough to make," Ibram said. "That's what the doctor said, anyway."

She nodded. "Yes, by pyrolysis."

Ibram blinked. "As you say, Ladyship."

"And you say Savoldyn turned out all his staff when his daughter absconded?" she asked.

"Most of them," Ibram said. "Mistress Ignalle said she wished for Dolman to come with her, but that she decided against it out of loyalty to the house."

"It must be finely furnished," Lady Azadiya said. "So who do they employ? Family servants? Temporary folk from the village?"

He shook his head. "A small bunch. The kitchen maid, Jara, and Marit, the cook. Dolman and Hilo Kenes, who worked for Savoldyn himself, I think. There's a small boy who comes in and serves at table, and Mistress Savoldyn's own maid, Liepa."

The light shifted behind clouds, and a pressure Ibram had not noticed bearing down upon him before left him so suddenly that he gasped. He watched as Ladyship's hands flexed into claws in her lap and then relaxed. Lady Azadiya dropped her hand to her lap, and tsked. "Damned potion," she grumbled. "Damned *students*. Bedris should have the running of the lot of them."

"It would be a sight easier to patrol without them," Ibram said.

"And yet if they were not here," she sighed, "what would the rest of the day be taken up by?"

"Dueling?"

She snorted. "Outlawed since before either of us were born, but I'll grant you points for a surprising grasp of history."

Ibram shrugged. "Battles liven up those lectures down the Bedris school."

She hummed in agreement. "Something had to."

Ibram grinned down at the papers in his hands. The handwriting was remarkably close, even to his unenhanced eye. He held up the stack before him.

"Would you like to look?" he asked. He didn't ask Ladyship if she felt equal to the task. She didn't, clearly, or he and Ahksell would not have read out reports until their throats rasped. But if Lady Azadiya was capable of a limited amount of reading, it was best to find out now, and worry further about recovery at a later date. Ibram supposed Amita Sarrha would be in charge of dividing up the new chore, if it came to that, since Amota Viran's attention was so thoroughly diverted.

Lady Azadiya held out her hand, pinched middle finger and thumb together, and tugged the permits out of Ibram's grasp. The travel permits came to her and settled in her lap. Ibram flexed his hands; his fingers tingled.

"I shall," she said. "While you pick up the mess you two made. When we return these papers, I want no allegations of tampering. The Ignalles seem pugnacious."

Ibram rocked to his knees and put his hands on his hips. "They are certainly feisty," he said.

He rolled up one of Savoldyn's poems, and tied the strap to hold it closed. There was no spot to place it, but where it had been before. Ibram looked about himself, and then leaned over to grab hold of the nearest wooden crate.

"I'll take the bottles to Doctor Berot, if you would like," Ibram said. He tugged on the crate, and it snagged against the woven carpet laid down on the floor. He winced, and tipped the crate forward instead. "He would know how to find out if they held wood alcohol, would he not?"

"I would like, yes," Ladyship said. "Might as well make full use of the man. He'll be difficult to unstick from the second mentor's side, but not impossible."

"They're unmarked," he said, "which is in our favor. The rest of the refuse bore the Tarsis' stamp, but these ones were pushed to the back."

"Hmm, we shall have to check the bottoms for a maker's mark," she said. "At least we'll know the potter."

Something rustled inside the box. Ibram frowned, and craned his neck to look into the crate. A handful of smaller bundles lay at the bottom, they looked like old bills tied together. Ibram tossed the scroll inside, and pulled out four of the little stacks. The first page of names and tallies was written out in a deft hand, all loops and slashes, in faded brown ink.

"I think we must have taken every inch of paper in the house," he said, as he dropped the bundles to the ground. He picked up the closest one, and rifled through the first three pages. "Even from the bottom shelves, which held more dust than I thought possible."

He frowned down at the paper, and then brought it up to his nose. He sniffed: dust and a little mold. He wriggled his nose, and then squinted down at the list of folk written down next to their figures.

"Dolman, mistress' maid, four dresses and a cloak, twelve picaio, thirty faunts at the summer season," he muttered.

"What do you have there?" Lady Azadiya asked.

"It looks like a bill," he said, and pulled out his sica. He sliced through the old bit of twine holding the papers together, and shoved his dagger back into its hilt. "A very old household account, actually. Going by the number of folk employed."

"What names stand out to you?"

Ibram drew his eye down the list of folk who used to be employed in the Savoldyn's household. He slowly shook his head as he checked the back of the page, and then moved on to the second. "It's a lot of folk who might bear a grudge," he said, and he dragged his finger down the paper. "I've found one name I recognize, and from this...oh, yes."

"He was a scandalous old man, was he not?" Lady Azadiya asked. "How many are we speaking of?"

"Porters, to be sure, though I've never spoken to them. The old wife had a maid, the housekeeper—who was not Dolman—had six, the kitchens had their full complement, and the young lady of the house was equally and properly attended."

Ibram frowned. He rocked forward, braced himself on the crate, and stood. He picked up Ahksell's carry-all and slung it over one shoulder, and then walked to the couch. He held out the little pile of papers.

"I would say a bustling old manor used to stand in that relic's place," he said, and tapped the list. "Can you see that, Ladyship? It's a recipe for misbehavior."

"For brief periods." Lady Azadiya took the sheaf from him, and paused a moment, tilting the words back and forth as if she were trying to get her eyes to focus. She took a slow, deep breath, and then nodded.

"Even a relic may speak," she said. "I want you to write out a new note for Captain Talsconis. Deliver it today, and make certain of his agreement."

"All right," Ibram said. "Shall I catch up to Ahksell before he gets there?"

Lady Azadiya shook her head, and rested the papers against her chin. "No," she said. "Best he becomes accustomed to all of us. Now then, the Ignalles. You know where they live?"

"I do."

"To produce wood alcohol might require many things," she said. "A fire, a pot, a spoon, those are easily sorted, but certain aspects require more specialized equipment. I believe you will know how to identify them." She smiled at him. "Bring back knowledge."

Burglary was illegal. In the Grand Empire of Vissilia, it came right beneath kidnapping and murder in the Code of Enyabi I under denial of property. As every subject of Vissilia owned their own bodies, never to be serfs again, so too did their goods and services become intrinsically theirs. Steal a man's jewels and lose a finger for every bauble.

So, as a good subject, Lady Azadiya would never command Ibram to steal. He was an agent of the Sect of Seven Fires, and such acts were beneath him. Bringing back information, on the other hand, was a wonderfully legal pastime and one in which Ibram indulged frequently, including those circumstances when he gained temporary custody of lost items before returning them to their owners. It was all wonderfully above suspicion.

In the spirit of helpfulness towards his ailing employer, Ibram wandered down to Lityen as fast as he could. The smell of ripe clingstone dumplings fried in honey distracted him for only as long as it took to gobble up his full portion on his way through the village. He then took a moment to observe and record the various comings and goings of the Savoldyn household, just in time to let Mistress Dolman know that her mistress was unavoidably detained. And, because he was alive and awake with the possibilities of advancement and achievement so celebrated during the Festival of Sangrin, he doubled back from the Savoldyns' emptying house, passed through the courtyards demarking the borders between the residential manors and the working split houses, and the open courtyards where the caffa sellers and the cook shops were prepping for the night's revels, and then into the imperial corner of Lityen, where the warders tended to flock when not on assignment. Captain Talsconis had no time for him, of course, but after re-reading Lady Azadiya's message several times—interspersed with Ibram's detailed explanations—resigned himself to her respectful demands. Ibram counted it as a victory; his predecessor usually required far more campaigning.

The sun was high enough in the sky by the time he reached his destination that it was about to roll down the heavens on the opposite side. Shadows lengthened where Ibram walked. The Ignalles lived on the opposite side, where the living arrangements all shared walls and chimneys, and sometimes a small courtyard to dry laundry or plant food. Ibram skirted around the bakery-mill and into the narrow trench cut between the houses as a drainage ditch, jumping the wooden gate. They were difficult areas to enter, uncomfortable by design and hard to navigate. Every so often the Bureau of Sanitation paid work crews to dump chalk and vinegar on top of any detritus that couldn't—or wouldn't—decay to get rid of the smell, or very rarely, to clear it out. The nicer streets ran a subscription to pay for one of Afsoun's contraptions that got rid of odor; this was one of them. Yilka the Green deserved a rose cake the size of all three of her heads for that blessing.

Ibram stepped carefully, and aimed his feet where the muck looked solid. In a way, his task was simple. All he had to do was figure out if Master and Mistress Ignalle were wise or foolish. If they held tent poles up in lightning storms, his job would be made easier. If they knew enough to come inside when it rained, then his job would be made harder. Either way, he would know how to proceed.

He tried to angle himself higher on the grassy slope rather than the mucky dirt in the middle, sticking close to the homes on the right. A crooked line of snapped clay pipes and broken bowls lay at the bottom of the ditch, as well as clotted mud of a variety of colors. He wrinkled his nose, and breathed through his mouth; the inlaid tiles must have been losing their strength. The soured prickle of mold spread across his tongue. Ibram closed his jaw with a snap, and tried to breath the air nearest the buildings instead.

A sapling withy tree was growing in the drain that led down to the stone sewer system. He could hear children playing somewhere, but no one came out to dump refuse from the shuttered half-doors. The air smelled as good as it ever did in these back areas, musty and sharp, but the sun was out, for a wonder, and so Ibram could take care with how he stepped. No unmentionable splatters to disgust his family with later on.

He counted to himself as he walked, soundlessly moving his lips as he passed down the line from house to house to house. The clerks and minor officials who lived in these places weren't poorly off. The wood frames and slabs of daub were good and solid, and the roofs had their proper amount of gutters to direct the rain. Back in the drainage area, they were just stone mounts, but in the front Ibram knew he would find all sorts of fanciful characters. How else to tell who lived where than by the tarmap spitting water down to the ground, or the spindly trumpet spraying rain off the porch?

Master and Mistress Ignalle and their rebellious household sat ten homes away from the bakery-mill, at the end of a long line of smashed cosmetics bottles and broken sticks and sponges, and whatever else folk tossed when it wouldn't fit down the indoor sewer access. Ibram paused, and then rubbed his arm across his clenched mouth. Yilka's megrims, if they'd tossed anything down to the sewers, he was sunk. The entire system was massive—not to mention, disgusting—and pride of the sect's founder or not, Ibram had no wish to be anywhere closer to it than he stood now.

He shuddered, and resumed counting out the buildings. At the tenth, he stopped, and put his ear to the half-door. He heard voices, muffled but relaxed. Most probably that was Mistress Agapito, the maid, and the carriage driver Ibram had seen at the Ark. He stared down at the space where a door handle should have been. The back half-doors never featured them, of course, but it would have made Ibram's life so much easier if he could have hung on to it for balance. He glanced about himself; the drainage ditch was free of watchers, except for the wildlife. Something skittered two houses down; Ibram grimaced.

He took a deep breath, and crouched down as quietly as possible. A cloud passed over his head, darkening the ground. He waited for it to pass, and then the sun shone down upon him. Amidst the unidentifiable glop, the refuse glittered.

15

It was good to have a proper occupation again; Ibram did a lot of work for the Preceptory of Yseult that bored him. When Lady Azadiya had no tasks requiring his full attention, there were dozens more in a busy division like hers to keep his idle hands occupied. Patrolling, inventorying, yanking alchemists young and old out of places that should not be randomly generating mists, smells, or strangely colored fires, and reporting on which caravans had requested permission to ride the perpetual wheels up the Emerald Mountains to the west were not beyond the scope of his mission. Thus, a better, more joyful Ibram went back up the living mountain and entered Lady Azadiya's tower. By that time, signs of life had returned to the place. Dihya, Ladyship's housekeeper, had returned to the upper floors; Ibram could hear her calmly directing servants up and down the hallways, clearing away what little mess had been left behind when Lady Azadiya had swept everyone out. The servants' footsteps echoed comfortingly downward.

Lady Azadiya herself had chosen to remain in the common area, and a sphere of serenity had enveloped the low couches within her circumference. The medicinal paste was still burning from a large open brazier. It wasn't her office, to be sure, but the scurrying Attendants lining up by her couch to report on their day's tasks was certainly a start in the correct direction. Amita Sarrha sat next to her with Amota Evren on the opposite couch. He had a traveler's writing desk balanced on his bony knees.

"Ladyship," Ibram said, and bowed. He bobbed up again and held out Ahksell's carry-all. "I think you'll enjoy this."

"Is it what we supposed?" she asked.

"To be sure," he said. "I was a poor example of a Bedris student, but even I know my way around such as this."

He crouched down by the little table leftover from Ladyship's meal, and opened the bag. Ibram dug into the carry-all, and grasped the canvas bundle inside delicately; a piece snapped with the tiniest screech. A bright, sharp feeling of something giving sliced through his palm; he winced, and pulled the thing out, and then laid it on the table.

"What have you there?" Amota Evren asked.

"You're bleeding on it," Amita Sarrha said.

"Dihya!" Ladyship called out. Her voice echoed. "Ibram's hurt himself again! Send for the medicinal kit!"

Ibram switched hands, left to right, and flipped open the canvas. Glass shards tinkled out. Lady Azadiya clasped her hands, and rested her sharp chin, briefly, on her long, interlaced fingers. The color was back in her tanned cheeks, and Ibram thought he read a certain amount of smug approval in the set of her mouth. She smoothed both hands outward through the air. On the table before her couch, the cloth stretched itself flat to more fully display the reason he had run all the way back up the living mountain.

Attendant Zorion appeared by the low couch, holding the small chest they used in the tower as a medicinal kit in both hands. "The bottles have come back with Doctor Berot, Mentor Hobon," he said. "He's getting settled in his room now."

Ibram raised his eyebrows. "What are you doing here, Attendant?" he asked.

Zorion readjusted his glasses. "I've been reassigned for remedial studies," he said. "Mentor Tikari says she won't have me back until I can balance myself on my head or step sideways out of a tree."

"She has no idea what we do," Lady Azadiya muttered. She was slowly stirring her finger over the glass shards; they rocked and waved against each other, delicately seeking their familiar edges. "All the control of a drunken—"

"Lady Azadiya," Amita Sarrha interrupted, as she yanked the medicinal kit open. She tossed a bandage roll onto the couch, and then shut the top of the kit. "Is it enough? Stick out your hand, Ib-la."

Ibram obeyed. Amita Sarrha pulled tightly on the bandage she was wrapping around his palm; he yelped, and leaned back.

"What was that for?" he asked.

Amita Sarrha shook her head, and yanked again. "That is for bringing things back from unclean places, and managing to get yourself cut."

Ibram flinched. "I was more than careful, to be sure. It isn't my fault that there were delicate pieces."

Amita Sarrha sniffed audibly. "It could be an empty bottle of scent."

"It might be, but I doubt it," Ibram said. "Too many pieces."

She wrapped the trailing edge of the bandage up and around his palm, and then tied the end off against his knuckles. "There."

"If it turns purple, don't wait until your hand falls off to go and see one of the healers," Amota Evren said.

"If you insist," Ibram said. He leaned further to the left, and eyed him. "You're not here to drag me back to the archives, are you?"

Amota Evren smiled thinly. He was a sharp sort of man, with shoulders that jutted out from a body that seemed cobbled together out of wire and wooden planks, and a crooked chin. He wore his thinning hair long and braided down the back, and never deigned to leave the living mountain unless Lady Azadiya ordered him personally. He also never had to patrol, corral, or otherwise fetch and carry, so it was entirely possible that he was the smartest of Ladyship's entire coterie of agents.

"I think with Viran leaving us for a time, we'll need all hands on deck around the tower," Amita Sarrha said.

Ibram jumped. "Amota Viran is leaving?" he asked, and hated how his voice squeaked on the final word.

"Only for a little while," Lady Azadiya said, as she sat back. "He has carried a heavy duty for me, and a reward's as good as a rest."

"But this is both," Ibram said.

Lady Azadiya's mouth quirked up at the side. "It shall be, indeed," she said.

Ibram frowned, and looked at his amitai, but Amota Evren and Amita Sarrha appeared neither strained, nor anxious about this outcome. He glanced up at Attendant Zorion, who had wandered to the opposite end of the couch and was peering down at the glass with a brightly interested gleam in his dark eyes. His hair dangled down, and he tried to push it behind his ears without much success.

"Do I smell paint?" Zorion asked, and sniffed.

"In a way," Lady Azadiya replied. "You'll test the residue on this when I'm finished." Her filtering mask slipped down her nose; she readjusted the tie woven through her hair. "Lieutenant Talsconis?"

Ibram nodded. "*Captain* Talsconis should be here by dinner, he said."

"Riant," Lady Azadiya said, and clapped her hands. "When Ahksell returns, take him home and feed him. Dihya is much too busy to lay out more than quash and ale, and good work deserves recompense. Bring the Ignalles and Mistress Savoldyn up to me tomorrow."

"You have those twins up for their examinations in the morning," Amita Sarrha said.

Lady Azadiya grimaced, and flicked her hair over her shoulder. Ibram got the impression she was rolling her eyes. "Transactional properties of orderless ambulation, I well recall."

"What's that?" Ibram asked.

"They want to walk upside down," Attendant Zorion said.

Lady Azadiya tsked. "We shall settle for a midday conference," she said.

"Shall I bring up anyone else?" Ibram asked.

She shook her head. "The housekeeper, if she insists. Other than that, I'm sure Talsconis will be more than adequate to rounding up whoever else we need for our later reports." She leaned forward and held out both of her hands, palms down. Her fingers spread out and curled. "Now, to put this back together."

It was the work of a full morning to convince all the requested guests to come up the living mountain. Firstly, he had to present them in order of precedence—which according to Ladyship, meant the folk they most wanted to speak with were invited only when they saw no reason—or way—to refuse. Secondly, Lady Azadiya's invitations were well-known in the province, and Ibram suspected there was no one living—and possibly dead—who didn't realize some kind of sharp, short shock lurked in their future when they received one. Only Mistress Savoldyn seemed resigned to her fate, but that might have been due to Amota Viran's taking up residence in her home, and the decidedly burnt remains of the rushes previously tied to her front gate. Ibram took note of the events, but firmly pushed any conclusions far from his mind. Ahksell could worry over the proprieties well enough for the both of them.

After extracting firm promises from all parties concerned, Ibram returned up the living mountain in time to help Amota Berac rearrange the low couches in the common area of the tower. Lady Azadiya had had the chair from her office placed in front of the fountain, and now required that her guests be able to see her as well as each other. A familiar wooden crate, filled with papers, sat near the chair. Ahksell was stolen away by Attendant Zorion as soon as he popped his head in the door, and left Ibram to the tender mercies of a plotting employer.

"How go the examinations?" he asked Amita Sarrha as she stumped past with an travel writing desk and an anxious messenger in tow.

"Went all right," she said, "until the twins' boot braces failed. They've been put to bed until they can see straight again."

"It's catching then." Ibram ducked his head out of the way of Amita Sarrha's admonishing swipe, and shoved his end of the couch down across the carpet. He stood up and away. He touched the pouch on his belt where he kept his bells and dice. "May their recovery be painless," he said.

She muttered something uncomplimentary as she sailed off into the tower, and Ibram surveyed the arrangement of the couches. Amota Berac sighed, and nodded. He walked over and clapped Ibram on the shoulder.

"Seems in order now," he said.

Ibram nodded. The couches were, at the very least, spaced well enough away from each other that Ibram would be able to intervene if someone got rowdy. Not that Lady Azadiya needed the help, but it was far easier to excuse his own disorderly conduct than a tribunal of Yseult mentors weighing in on Ladyship's use of force. The rest of the tower was noticeably quiet. He saw a few of the other, more junior agents standing in doorways, but nothing like the usual bustle of folk. He supposed they must all be breaking down the camp set up outside.

"Will you be here?" Ibram asked.

Amota Berac shook his head. "Patrol suits me better," he said. "I'm for the south wall."

Ibram nodded. "Good luck then," he said.

Amota Berac clapped him on the shoulder again, and departed. Ibram put his hands on his hips, and surveyed the common area. The fountain burbled away, and someone had angled the reflecting mirrors on the third and second bannisters so that sunlight shone down from the transparent roof instead of the glowbulb torches Ladyship had had lit before. It was a pretty scene, to be sure.

He twitched his head toward slight movement on the stairwell, and saw Ahksell bounding down to the common area. He came to a stop at Ibram's side, and grinned.

"All prepared?" he asked.

Ibram quirked his mouth to the left. "To be sure," he said, and waved his hand at the couches. "It's a pretty place for an interrogation."

"Or a confession," Ahksell said.

Ibram nodded. "That, too."

It was a distinct advantage to Lady Azadiya, surrounded by every aspect of her authority and not a small reminder of her personal power, even in the midst of her unconcealable personal trouble. The tower soared above them, three levels of wood molded together with alchemy and strung with enchanted tiles and expensive gewgaws. The sort of place that looked like a gilded cake, easy in and easier out, but only if you weren't paying attention. Typically, they used Lady Azadiya's office, but this wasn't a bad alternative.

Ibram stretched his sore back. "Hopefully, we can leave the furniture where it lays, afterwards."

Ahksell snickered, and Ibram elbowed him in the side. Ahksell shook him off, and then cleared his throat. He frowned.

"Do you think she'll get one?" he asked. "A confession, I mean?"

Ibram shrugged. "Ever stolen a bun from the kitchen?"

Ahksell stared at him, flatly.

Ibram waggled his head from left to right. "And didn't it weigh on you? Think of what murder does. Makes a body nervous as a soul in Cangsa."

"But that's only when they regret it," Ahksell pointed out.

"Everybody regrets something."

The weightless stone doors thudded open behind them; Ibram wheeled around just in time to witness newly-made Captain Talsconis swagger into the tower, bracketed at one end by Warder Claes. Ibram smiled and bowed politely at their approach. Talsconis grunted as he marched down the stairs, and Ibram raised himself up. There was no profit in waiting for the warders to answer his courtesy, they knew each other of old, after all.

"Good day, Attendant Solari. Still here, Ucalegon?" Captain Talsconis asked.

"There's the wit that won you your promotion, Captain," Ibram said. "You have the heartfelt congratulations of Mentor Hobon's entire division."

Ahksell stuck his fingers in Ibram's side; he flinched, but kept smiling. Warder Claes was too professional to roll her eyes at the pair of them, but Ibram marked the way her face twitched, distinctly. Talsconis had no such niceties. He was as tall as he was wide, the sort of bluff and hearty type, who looked like he'd stepped off a farm and wandered into the Cohort of Peace by mistake. But he had a way of catching folk who thought him slow or dull, and a hard grip on the comings and goings in their corner of Vanima province. Life was going to be more interesting under Talsconis than it had under Vainamonien.

"Two days up the living mountain is too many," Talsconis said. "Isn't it enough I have to clear up after all your blasted festivals?"

"Oh now," Ibram protested. "I hear you don't do to badly with the evening courtyards these days. They even set aside the more interesting drunks especially for your perusal."

Talsconis grunted, and stared at him with his hard, dark eyes. "Keep on laying this out," he said. "I'm here on business, but I've no problem mixing it up with the pleasure of putting you in a room for a night."

Ibram shrugged. "All right, all right. To be sure, I've no complaints against the accommodations in the Cohort of Peace besides the poor air, worse food, and impolite company, but we can reserve the discussion for a later time."

The captain snorted, and made a show of looking about the tower from the ground floor on up. "Where's the lady?" he asked.

Ahksell wrinkled his nose, but shrugged. "Mentor had her hands full with the Attendants this morning," he said.

"I'm sure she'll be out in a shake of a mouflon's tail," Ibram added.

"I'll sit down, then," Talsconis said, and pointed behind Ibram towards the couches.

Obligingly, Ibram stepped aside. Talsconis settled down on the couch nearest the empty chair where Lady Azadiya would take up residence, and Claes stood at her leisure behind him. Her bright blue eyes made quick note of the area; she caught Ibram looking, and they exchanged cautious nods. Claes was in Talsconis' old job now, he figured, operating as her captain's second in command. She was quiet, but fierce, and the sword at her hip was not to be ignored any more than the bundle of rope she'd hog-tie him with if so ordered.

Dihya appeared with a tray of caffa and snacks as if summoned from the heavens by a mentor of Baran, and disappeared just as quickly. She had no interest in Ladyship's goings-on, and less desire to see the outcome. Talsconis helped himself to a cup and a handful of roasted treeka nut cookies. His predecessor had enjoyed similar privileges; Ibram sometimes wondered if Ladyship's table advertised as a benefit of life as a warder captain in the area. She wasn't stingy with food, Merrilian hospitality would never allow it.

Talsconis tossed a cookie behind himself; Claes caught it and ate it. "What's this about a murder?" he asked.

Ibram came down to the low table, and shrugged. "Best to let Ladyship tell it," he said. "I'd hate to repeat rumor."

"Mentor Hobon told me a little of what you've gotten up to with the Savoldyns last night by way of our helping you all this morning. What part of trouble do you avoid, Ucalegon?" Talsconis shook his head. "I've certainly got enough."

"I am merely a concerned subject of Her Gracious Majesty," Ibram said, and smiled. "Doing my duty for employer and empire."

Ibram spread his hands, palms out, and Talsconis snorted. He shook his head again and drank down his caffa. Ahksell took a seat on the couch opposite, and helped himself to caffa in a double-walled glass bowl. He dosed it with cream and drank it down with barely a wince for the steaming heat.

The stone doors thudded open again. Ibram turned back to his duties, and left the warders to amuse themselves. After Talsconis, Amota Viran arrived escorting Mistress Savoldyn and Mistress Dolman, whose face could have clapped back at a thunderstorm as she marched inside. The Ignalles came some moments later, breezing past Ibram all politeness and smiles. Ibram made sure the doors were shut firmly, and then raised his hand to Ahksell, who ran up to the third level.

Ahksell disappeared into a private laboratory. Lady Azadiya emerged onto the landing with Attendant Zorion and Doctor Berot in tow. Ibram watched as she made her entrance into the common area. She still wore her filtering mask with the wrap of yellow spider silk over her eyes and braided into her hair. Her dress was orange silk, cut wide and low at the neck, and her open-fronted surcoat was emerald shot through with embroidery in the same color. A belt of silver metal disks hung at her waist; Ibram recognized several incredibly nasty shield buttons of Ladyship's own construction hidden among them.

Warder Claes walked quickly to her, and extended one hand to Lady Azadiya to lead her down the small staircase that led into the common area. They spoke briefly, but too quietly for anyone to hear. At her chair, Lady Azadiya removed her hand from Warder Claes' grip, and settled down with all appearance of great satisfaction. Ibram bounced on his toes, and then settled back before anyone noticed. As the others sat down on the couches, Ibram took up space behind Lady-ship's left shoulder, while Ahksell stood at her right. Ahksell smiled at him, and nodded slightly. Ibram dipped his chin in return.

Once bows had been exchanged and introductions made, Lady Azadiya took a moment to adjust herself more comfortably. The amber beads in her filigree and chain necklace shivered as she breathed.

"Thank you for coming," Lady Azadiya said. "I know how all-consuming it can be to bury someone and get him to the Crossroads in a timely fashion."

"We're only happy to help, Mentor Hobon," Master Ignalle said, after a quick glance at his wife. "And may I express how sorry we both were to learn of your injury."

Lady Azadiya smiled. "Thank you," she said.

She pointed two fingers at the caffa tray. The glass pot lifted itself up from its wooden frame, and poured caffa into a small double-walled glass bowl. She lowered the pot and coaxed the bowl to rest in the palm of her hand. Mistress Ignalle cleared her throat, and shifted ever so slightly in her seat on the couch.

Lady Azadiya took a polite sip, and patted the clean corners of her mouth. "As you know," she began, "I dislike dramatics, and I find the disruption of my work intolerable."

Ibram didn't snort aloud, but it was a near thing. Ahksell wavered briefly, but recovered; neither of them looked at each other. Amota Viran narrowed his eyes in Ibram's direction.

"Of course, Damita," Amota Viran said.

"Which is why when Einar Savoldyn is murdered while my own agent is visiting his house, I find myself discomfited," she said, and Viran closed his mouth. "After all, what if my agent was wounded in this attack? What if others were hurt?"

"Surely not," Mistress Savoldyn protested. "No one else—I mean to say—"

"It's a lax mind that doesn't see the threat of escalation in any act of violence," Lady Azadiya said firmly.

"I'll drink to that," Talsconis muttered, and poured himself another drink.

"But no one else has been hurt," Mistress Ignalle said. She frowned.

"Does that not speak to some kind of accident? My father was a cantankerous man, and he liked a drink. Captain Talsconis, I hate to say this, but haven't you seen cases where a man may drink himself to death and not know it until it happens?"

Talsconis nodded slowly. "I've seen it," he said. "Usually in the winter months. They wander out and don't turn back from the cold."

"Pulled three out of the Blue Hole last spring," Claes added.

"And we all know strong drink can hasten a man's death," Mistress Ignalle said. "Would this not account for my father? We were never close—I don't like to think it—but it seems obvious."

Talsconis grunted. Mistress Dolman pressed her hand to her stomach and turned her head away. Though, whether it was at the thought of all those bodies, or the way Talsconis kept sharing his snacks with Claes by tossing them up and over his shoulder, was a thought process for another time.

"Accidents come in lots," Ibram said, "but murder tends to string them along."

Ah, there was the glare that blocked a thousand contractmen at the gate. Ibram nodded at Mistress Dolman, and settled back on his heels. Ladyship hummed in agreement, and drank her caffa. She leaned her elbow on her chair, and tilted her head.

"Let us consider my position," she said.

"Your position?" Captain Talsconis scoffed.

"The law requires that offenses are resolved either by local mediation or imperial determination, and there is very little more offensive to me than murder," Lady Azadiya said. "We're a sleepy little corner of Vanima province, to be sure, nothing like what goes on in Delbrite, nor further south. The ripples in this pool seep into every corner."

And if the Sect of Seven Fires could not control the lands they had been confined to by imperial decree, then the Empire of Vissilia in its wisdom and imperial authority would restrict their borders until they diminished to a plot of land the sect could control. Most probably, the areas without the perpetual wheels or the mineral rights or income from the farms, and then bang went the coin for all those lovely, expensive ingredients the alchemists loved to blow up.

"So a man is dead," Lady Azadiya continued. She glanced left. "How was it done, Doctor? Refresh my memory."

"Master Savoldyn died of poisoning," Doctor Berot said. He looked uncomfortable with the attention. "I examined his body thoroughly, and found extensive damage that could only be made through ingesting wood spirit."

"How examined?" Master Ignalle demanded, and beyond him, Mistress Savoldyn shuddered. "You cut into him?"

"Of course," Berot said. "His organs were beyond repair. His blood was acidic."

"Where did you get such authority?" Ignalle leaned forwards and stabbed at the air with his right hand. "My wife said no more than that Attendant Solari could examine him with a—ah—one of those wire contraptions!"

"Which I did," Ahksell said. "And discovered the evidence of poisoning following Ibram's own observations on the day of the death."

He gestured to Ibram, and Ignalle transferred his glare to him. Ibram grinned modestly.

"What horrible thoughts you must have to come to such a conclusion," Mistress Ignalle snapped.

"Only as necessary," Ibram assured her. "Most days, I barely think at all."

"I'll believe that," Talsconis muttered, but as he had once spent a solid month digging Ibram out of a variety of ditches and shanty gambling halls—purely for recognizance on Ladyship's orders—Ibram let it slide.

"That's as may be," Lady Azadiya said. "But apart from the duty every loyal subject owes to the empire, I must say I felt a personal stake in this business."

"Personal, Mentor?" Mistress Ignalle asked. She played with one of her bracelets, turning it around and around her wrist.

"Your father was in business with me for quite a number of years," Lady Azadiya said. She smoothed her hand down her overdress. "This fabric came from him, as did many other pieces of clothing I've had made. Is it not good quality?"

Mistress Ignalle nodded. "Yes, very good quality."

"And your father's business interests often coincided with my own business in the west, did they not?"

"Yes, they did," she agreed. "I remember the contracts drawn up when I was still his heir."

"Then is it not in my best interests to find out who is disrupting not merely my own affairs, but also that of *my* family?"

"Which you have no legal hand in, of course," Master Ignalle said, "considering our full understanding of the law."

"Of course," Lady Azadiya said. She sipped her caffa. "My position in life has divested me of so many traditional commitments. It makes me even more anxious to advance those common causes I have left to me."

She smiled, and lifted her bowl of caffa up to the air, just as if she could admire the play of light through its doubled walls. "This cup, for instance. It's from my own personal set, a gift from the first Mistress Savoldyn. What do you think of it, Captain?"

"It's nice," Talsconis said, and frowned down at his own caffa.

"To be sure," Lady Azadiya said. "I was so disappointed when your mother's rights to the glass making business passed out of the province, Mistress Ignalle. Your uncle lives so far away that it makes no profit to continue ordering from him."

Mistress Ignalle, to her credit, never fluttered an eyelash. "Yes, I agree," she said. "Mother was devoted to the business, but she died before she had a second child, who would have taken over after her."

"Such clarity and strength," Lady Azadiya said, and brought the bowl back to her lips. She sipped, and then rested the glass in her lap. "I still have many pieces."

Mistress Ignalle fiddled with her bracelets. "I wish I could say the same."

"Oh? Does Mistress Savoldyn still hold them in the house?" Ladyship asked.

"No!" Mistress Savoldyn exclaimed. Amota Viran put his hand on her wrist, and she settled. "At least, I will not for much longer. I told you, I have everything I want or need."

"Told who?" Captain Talsconis asked.

"Told, well, I told Mistress Ignalle," Mistress Savoldyn said. "And Mentor Hobon, when she asked."

Ignalle stood up from the couch, and drew himself up tall. "What you do mean when she asked? What business is it of hers who has my wife's mother's glass? It belongs to her!"

Ibram took a step forward. "Have a seat, Master Ignalle," he said. "Where's that imperial courtesy all you clerks like so much?"

Ignalle clenched his jaw. Ibram shrugged and hooked his hand around his belt, just before the hilt of his sica. "If you want, we can practice bowing and scraping together."

Mistress Ignalle set her hand on her husband's elbow, and pulled steadily downward until the man had regained his former position. Ibram settled himself back on his heels, and crossed his arms over his chest. From the corner of his eye, he saw Ladyship pinch her thumb and forefinger together and tug, but since he felt no answering yank on his ears, Ibram figured he was behaving with proper decorum. Ahksell took a step away from the group and disappeared back up into the tower.

"Well, again, it all comes back to business," Lady Azadiya said. She drank her caffa and then tossed the bowl back towards the tray. It spun through the air, and landed gently as a feather next to a plate of pepper crackers. "Master Ignalle, you work in the Office of Market Rights in the Bureau of Currency."

Ignalle looked confused. "I do, yes."

"I am informed it is in regards to travel."

"Yes, that's right."

"So you were in a rather perfect position to impede your father in law's business dramatically."

Ignalle flushed from the roots of his hair to his neck. "I don't know what you mean."

"Warder Claes," Lady Azadiya said, and turned her head. "The top stack of papers in the box by my feet is for Captain Talsconis, would you mind handing it to him?"

Warder Claes cleared her throat. "Of course, Mentor Hobon," she said.

She stepped around the side of the couch, retrieved the bundle of paperwork, and then handed it over to Talsconis. He thumbed through the first three layers of paper, and then eyed Lady Azadiya.

"Travel permits around the province?" Talsconis asked. "What is this about?"

"Consider it a token of my regard in the hopes of a long relationship," Lady Azadiya said. "You'll note the signatories at the bottom?"

Master Ignalle's flush deepened. He sat forward and banged his knees on the caffa table. "What of it?" he snapped.

"Dima," murmured his wife.

"It's your name on these permits," Talsconis said. "What do you want me to make of it?"

"I write many such permits," Ignalle said. "It's my life's work."

"Funny that a man with such extensive business interests all over the empire suddenly couldn't move out of Lityen with a bolt of cloth in tow without individual permits for every village and freehold he might wander past in the dead of night," Lady Azadiya said.

"Typically, they apply for regional licenses," Ibram said. "Saves time."

"And coin." Talsconis narrowed his eyes in Ignalle's direction. "You have an explanation for this?"

"There's a sworn letter from his supervisor as well," Lady Azadiya said. "My dear Ahksell took it down. Does he not have an able hand?"

Ignalle and his wife exchanged a quick look, but Ibram couldn't put a name to the expressions on their faces. Finally, with an obvious swallow, Ignalle wrapped his hand around his wife's, and faced the assorted party with an upraised chin.

"It's no secret that Elene and I were treated horribly by her father," he said.

"Well, you did run off with his only living heir," Ibram said.

"We had no intention of staying away forever!" he flared up, and Ibram raised his hands at his chest. "It was ridiculous. I have a good job, prospects, I was a perfectly acceptable choice."

"And then you ran away, and cost him money," Lady Azadiya said. "And no little embarrassment as I recall. The whole village talked of nothing else."

Mistress Ignalle lowered her head and shook it firmly. "If he hadn't taken such an obstinate dislike of Dima, then none of this would have happened."

There was a ring of truth in what she said, and the sound resounded about the common area. Talsconis set the bundle of papers aside on the couch, and watched the pair of them with a deceptively placid look on his face. Ibram put his hands behind his back, and clenched his right hand around his left wrist. Then, he thought better of it, and let his hands hang loosely, just in case.

"He wasn't a man who could stand embarrassment," Mistress Savoldyn said, gently. "Is it so shocking?"

"I was his *only* heir!" Mistress Ignalle's head jerked in her direction; her frown carved slices down the sides of her mouth. "Casting me out was as bad for the business as it was for any connection we had as a family!"

"And his lack of approval stunted your own opportunities," Lady Azadiya said. "The Bureau of Commerce is a busy place, but they all have to live here with us, do they not? And are subject to the same requirements inside the imperial boundary."

Master Ignalle nodded stiffly. "I admit..." he swallowed and cleared his throat with a grunt. "I have not risen as high as I might have hoped, when I first arrived. And we both know why."

"A man who is not respected by the guilds, often finds himself at loose ends in the imperial bureaucracy," Lady Azadiya said.

"And if he could afford to be obstinate with his own daughter, then he could afford to pay in like kind!" Master Ignalle declared. "See how he liked it!"

"Not at all," Mistress Savoldyn murmured. "It made him drink more."

"All he had to do was apologize to my wife," Ignalle said. He picked up their clasped hands, and kissed Mistress Ignalle's knuckles. "And he could have had his regional permits again, and all the savings therein."

It appeared likely they were all in danger of witnessing a love scene. Ibram glanced in Lady Azadiya's direction; she nodded slightly.

"And then he remarried," Ibram said.

Both Ignalles stiffened, and then pointedly relaxed against the couch. Their hands remained clasped together. Mistress Ignalle nodded.

"Now, we all know what the will stated," Lady Azadiya said. "Whoever had a child first would inherit the business. Yourself, Mistress Ignalle, or his new wife. What assurances did your husband leave you with, Mistress Savoldyn? Were you to have a child?"

Amota Viran stared out across the tower, blank-faced. Mistress Savoldyn touched her white cap, and took a deep breath. "That if we were to have a child, then it would inherit Einar's business—and if Elene had one first, well, then he would settle a sum of money upon the child, and it would be tied up with my family's affairs."

"That was in your marriage contract?" Lady Azadiya asked.

"Yes."

"He enjoyed his loopholes, did he not?"

"He did," Mistress Savoldyn said.

Lady Azadiya leaned back in her chair, and tugged thoughtfully on the end of her loose braid. "Did you mind that your husband so clearly married you in order to bedevil his estranged daughter?"

Mistress Savoldyn shivered, and pressed her lips together. Amota Viran wrapped his arm around her shoulders. By her side, Mistress Dolman turned pale. The housekeeper stood up, and pressed her hands to her stomach.

"That is unfair," she snapped. "Master Savoldyn was difficult man, but he wasn't a cruel one."

"She can answer the question herself," Captain Talsconis said, and waved his hand. "Sit down, there, Mistress. Sit down."

Dolman sat. Mistress Savoldyn shook her head. "He had a temper," she said. "It got away from him once in awhile."

"Cruelty is for the victim to judge," Mistress Ignalle said. "And he *was*. He lied to me! He lied to my mother! It was in their marriage contract that their first born child was his heir, and to make a mockery of that promise because I had the temerity to displease him was a punishment too far."

"Too far from what?" Lady Azadiya asked.

Ibram heard a step from above. He angled his head to the right, and spied Ahksell walking down the stairs from the second floor to the first. He was carrying a small box in both hands. Ibram recognized it as one of the specially made crates the sect used to transport delicate equipment. Ahksell waggled his eyebrows at him once, and then moved to Lady Azadiya's side; he placed the smaller crate on top of the box filled with papers from Savoldyn's office.

Mistress Ignalle took a deep breath, and then raised a hand to her white cap; the temple rings clinked against each other. She pressed her fingers to her collarbones; her face crumpled at the mouth, as if she were holding back tears. Ibram made note of the fact that she couldn't quite get her eyes to glisten accordingly, however.

"I knew he would be angry," she said in a tight voice. "We were often angry at each other. I knew he might be angry at the servants who helped us, or even the priest who married us. I never expected he would be so—so *petty*. So vengeful as to put the business in jeopardy. After my mother passed, I thought it was the only thing he loved."

Lady Azadiya adjusted the yellow silk around her temples, and pressed lightly at her hairline. A soft feeling of light pressure waved across Ibram's shoulders, like a moment's pause before a storm. Ibram frowned, but she only dropped her hand to her armrest, and hummed in agreement. The feeling dissipated.

"And yet you overcame that obstacle rather handily," she said.

Mistress Ignalle sniffed and nodded. A bitter smile curdled her face. "I did."

"How old is the child?"

"She's a babe," Mistress Ignalle said. "It will be some time before she's able to handle the running of the business."

"Then who will?"

The Ignalles and Mistress Savoldyn looked at each other in discomfort. Mistress Savoldyn shook her head and breathed outward. "I have already told them that I have no interest in running the business," she said in a controlled voice. "I am perfectly happy keeping to the agreements Einar and I previously reached when we wed."

"Sounds healthier," Ibram said.

Master Ignalle jumped to his feet and clenched his fists. "What do you mean by that?" he yelled.

At the noise, Esti, one of the other junior agents, came out of the reading room on the second floor, and leaned over the railing to watch; he waved. Ibram grinned and resisted the urge to wave back. "I love that new paint on your front stoop," he said. "Mistress Agapito is a credit to your household. She never let me past the steps."

"You have no right to enter my home," Mistress Ignalle said.

"Ah, yes," Lady Azadiya said. "I was cheered to learn you retained a greater loyalty to your servants than your father, Mistress Ignalle. I respect that."

"Oh, is that why they made the wood alcohol?" Attendant Zorion suddenly spoke up from his seat by Doctor Berot. "To thin the paint?"

Ibram didn't laugh, but it was a near thing. "Too proud to whitewash?"

"How dare you," Mistress Ignalle gasped, and her husband took a step forward. Ibram cocked his head, and kept his shoulders loose; his hands free at his sides.

"Mistress Ignalle, I'm afraid my agents dare very much and entirely too often," Lady Azadiya said. "It is my constant goal in life to corral their impulses."

"I should think you'd be better at it, then," Master Ignalle snapped.

Lady Azadiya tsked, and shook her head. "It's in my mind that you cost your father in law quite a bit of coin, after all, Master Ignalle. He had to restructure his business, according to his ledgers."

"And he'd been poisoned a long time," Ahksell said. "If his handwriting was anything to go on. Had he been losing his eyesight, Mistress Dolman?"

"I..." Mistress Dolman sounded nervous. "Yes, he had—he had been."

"A man who loved tolnic is a man who knew quality," Lady Azadiya said. "I myself keep it in my stores for any special occasion. I even offered Captain Talsconis a cup in congratulations for his promotion."

Talsconis cleared his throat abruptly. Warder Claes looked amused.

"Indeed so," Amota Viran murmured. "I suppose a man who wanted for a lost fortune might turn to a familiar comfort."

"How clever of you, Viran," Lady Azadiya said. "You have hit on the point exactly. Ahksell, the bottles."

"Yes, Mentor," Ahksell said.

He turned to the small crate near her, and reached inside. Captain Talsconis leaned forward on the couch. Master Ignalle wavered on his feet.

"This is an outrage," he said. "Painting our house does not make us criminals!"

"No," Lady Azadiya agreed.

"Nor do either of us have anything to do with the making of spirits!" Master Ignalle cast a wild eyed glance in his wife's direction. She shook her head excitedly.

"Again, all true," Lady Azadiya said. "I concede your every point."

Slowly, Master Ignalle's shoulders creeped down his neck. The bottles, plain clay jugs, clinked in Ahksell's grip as he set them on the table near the tray of caffa. Captain Talsconis eyed them, and tapped his thumb against his lips.

"Then what— Why would your servant bring up our house paint?"

"My agent," Ladyship stressed the word delicately, "and my attendant merely made polite comment, Master Ignalle. I'm afraid such stress as a death in the family has unsettled your mind."

Someone from high above squeaked, and was swiftly muffled. Ibram glanced up, and saw that Esti had been joined by Bels and Arix. He frowned and jerked his head. Bels unwrapped his arm from Arix's mouth, and shrugged. Ibram sighed, and returned his attention to the group. Master Ignalle looked about himself, suddenly unsure, and sat down in a slump by his wife.

"Mentor Hobon," Captain Talsconis said, "I do have other duties today."

"Ah, and I should hate to keep you from your work," she answered. "A few moments more should suffice."

Talsconis grumbled, but resided into the couch. Lady Azadiya poked the air, and one of the bottles wavered on the table. Mistress Dolman gasped, and put her hand to her mouth.

"Mistress Dolman," Lady Azadiya said. "How long have you worked for the Savoldyns?"

Mistress Dolman swallowed. "Too many years," she said.

Lady Azadiya nodded. "When the deceased turned out most of his household, he kept you, did he not?"

"He did."

"Why?"

Mistress Dolman looked at her lap, and clenched her hands together. "I was his former wife's maid," she said. "He let the old housekeeper go—she had looked the other way when Mistress Elene made her escape—but he asked me to stay on and promised to raise me to her position. He said—" she took a deep breath. "—that he wanted a reminder of my old mistress about him."

"Poets are often romantics," Lady Azadiya said, "even bad ones. He did keep a few of you, yes?"

"Yes, that's true," Dolman said. "I will say this for him, he didn't stint on our pay. Master Savoldyn kept to the terms of his agreements with us."

"The ones he kept," Ladyship said, quite at ease. She shook out her sleeves and touched her thumb to her signet ring. She nodded.

"What are these bottles, Mentor?" Talsconis asked. He frowned.

"These are from Master Savoldyn's kitchens," she replied. "I believe they held a mulling solution for Master Savoldyn's tolnic."

Mistress Dolman frowned and squinted. "They are not," she declared.

Lady Azadiya paused. "Oh?" she asked. "Why not?"

"Our household's spirits are supplied by the house of Tarsis," Mistress Dolman said. "These bottles do not bear their stamp."

Ladyship smiled. "And so my own Ibram told me, to be sure," she said. "Where did you find these bottles, Ibram?"

"In the last row of empty bottles," Ibram said, "next to the ale barrel in the Savoldyns' kitchen. Mistress Dolman witnessed me picking them up."

Mistress Dolman turned pale. "Yes," she said. "I thought you were up to something there."

Ibram nodded. He settled back on his heels. Captain Talsconis reached over and picked up on of the bottles. He looked it over from top to bottom.

"Where did they come from then?" Talsconis asked.

"From the maker's mark you are observing," Lady Azadiya said. "We believe they come from the draughtshop near the bakery-mill near the Ignalles' home. Lovely establishment, I am informed. Very helpful to wandering Attendants when they get lost."

Ahksell grinned. Lady Azadiya took a deep breath and continued speaking.

"Attendant Zorion has confirmed that they contained a healthy dose of wood alcohol. Odorless, of course, and quite prone to evaporation, but bottles are terribly difficult to clean." She sighed. "It does horrible things to people, you know, who come in close contact. It gets through the skin...you might even breath the fumes in."

Captain Talsconis slapped down the clay bottle and sat back on the couch. He wiped his hand on his trouser leg.

"Causes eye problems," Attendant Zorion said, and adjusted his glasses. "Especially with repeated exposure."

Mistress Dolman appeared to be doing some very rough addition in her mind; it didn't appear she liked her sums. Her mouth thinned to a white line; her face flushed and then turned pale. Mistress Savoldyn lay her hand on Dolman's back.

"She murdered him?" Mistress Ignalle asked. She gripped her husband's arm with both hands and turned horrified eyes towards Mistress Savoldyn. "I knew you were happy he was dead! I knew you just wanted to get free of him, and I never blamed you, but this? *Why?* Why not just run off with *him* and free yourself?" She shook her head; her temple rings clinked. "Was it just the money?"

Mistress Savoldyn shrank back; her mouth opened in alarm. "I never! I wouldn't!"

"Who else could it be?" Mistress Ignalle demanded. "You went to that draughtshop to—to make it seem as if we had procured it! Do you think I'm going to the kitchen and poisoning my father's drink? He wouldn't even let me see my mother's old rooms."

"Ah that was the sticking point," Lady Azadiya said. She nodded. "How could poison be administered? How could it be made? You have an incisive mind, Mistress Ignalle. You see a problem, and you create the solution."

"I do, yes," Mistress Ignalle said. She covered her mouth, and let a sob escape from between her fingers. Her husband drew her against his shoulder, and put his arm around her back.

"The problem being, of course," Ladyship continued as if she had not spoken. "That Mistress Savoldyn had a great deal more to lose in divorcing her husband than in his death."

"No, no," Mistress Savoldyn murmured in a daze.

"And yet," Lady Azadiya said. "I pride myself on my abilities as a teacher, and I would be remiss if I allowed such a moment to pass. Ahksell, what have you observed?"

Ahksell tucked his hands behind his back, and stood tall. "That the Ignalles had much more to gain in Master Savoldyn's death than his wife did."

The Ignalles froze in place, mid-comforting; Ahksell kept going. As remedial examinations went, Ibram supposed this one beat climbing a tree and shining a little light.

"If Mistress Savoldyn divorced her husband, she lost all rights to the farm she has spent so much time working on, but if he died then she retained those rights."

"And?" Lady Azadiya asked.

"And she became an excellent suspect for his murder."

"But what if it was never suspected that he was murdered?" Doctor Berot protested.

"Then she was still a good-hearted woman who would return all the things her husband had withheld from Mistress Ignalle during his life. His business, his purse, and the glass pieces which were the only remaining items from her mother," Ahksell said.

The Ignalles drew apart from one another in the sudden silence following Ahksell's speech. Ibram caught his eye, and grinned. Ahksell rocked on his feet, just a little, and straightened his gambeson.

"Mistress Savoldyn lived with him, and they did not," Lady Azadiya said. "She has an overly intimate friend, and they are a couple, rich in love and stable enough to maintain their home and prosper."

"Yes," Master Ignalle said, and threw his arm out towards Amota Viran. "Your own agent. What embarrassment would you submit me and my wife to in order to protect yourself?"

Lady Azadiya smiled. "Oh, I like embarrassment," she said. "Keeps things lively. Don't you find that, Captain Talsconis? What would we do if not for the escapades of our deputies?"

Captain Talsconis grunted, and made himself more comfortable on the couch. Behind him, Warder Claes sidled over to the end of the furniture into the spot by Ahksell, between the couch and Ladyship's chair. Lady Azadiya smiled, and touched the side of the yellow silk across her eyes. She leaned on her left elbow. Mistress Savoldyn shuddered and sank back into Amota Viran's side. The Ignalles were coiled together on their own seats, and Ibram did not like the careful look they shared between them. He flexed his fingers at his sides.

"Now," Lady Azadiya said. "We have established how I feel about embarrassment, and how you feel about it, Master Ignalle. I shall return to a more comfortable topic. Mistress Elene, I remember your mother so fondly."

Mistress Ignalle watched Ladyship carefully. "You do?"

"I do," Lady Azadiya confirmed. "Such an artist. Like those bracelets of yours."

Mistress Ignalle's smile was a pathetic example, but it crossed her lips. She touched her bracelets, and nodded slightly. Ladyship continued, "Her glass business made such wonderfully sturdy laboratory equipment, as well. I could never bring myself to throw one out. Like this one was, which was recovered from behind your cottage. Ahksell."

Ahksell held his hand out over the small, specialized crate, flexed his fingers, and raised his arm. The repaired glass alembic that Ibram had so painstakingly collected from the drainage ditch rose up into the air. The light caught on its repaired cracks.

"I tested that as well," Attendant Zorion said. "The residue is unmistakable."

"It's not mine," Mistress Ignalle flared up immediately.

"Then you've got a public nuisance who smashes expensive glass equipment out behind your home, Mistress Ignalle," Ibram said. He lifted his bandaged hand. "I'd tell the warders."

Ahksell lowered the alembic carefully back into its protective crate. "It's not your father's," he said, and shook his head. "He had one just like it, small, but functional—a matched set. The only thing it contained was natron."

"And, of course, the problem remains," Lady Azadiya said. "That a need for paint thinner does not make one a murderer, it merely provides opportunity for it."

"It does not," Mistress Ignalle said.

"You tried and tried to be patient," Lady Azadiya said, and shook her head. "You aren't made for it, but you gave it your best effort. You beat him to a marriage, you bested him over the child, you curtailed his business—except for mine, and you have my compliments—and yet the man just would not die of old age."

"Indecent of him, to be sure," Ibram said, and watched Master Ignalle's face grow ugly.

"This sounds like work ahead of me," Talsconis said. "Am I to understand they dosed this dead man with wood alcohol in his tolnic?"

"Oh, several times," Lady Azadiya said. "It's the drinking alcohol where they made their mistake. When you add it to wood spirit, it softens the effects. Drags the business out to appear to be a sickness. Loss of feeling, of appetite, of sight."

"I have never made tolnic for my father," Mistress Ignalle said.

Lady Azadiya nodded. "But on the day he was murdered, you didn't drink the shay," she said.

"I don't know what you mean," Mistress Ignalle said.

"You show up to the house uninvited," Lady Azadiya said. "As you have before, but that only means you are unremarkable—which I presume was a happy accident. You quarrel with your father all the time."

"Exactly so."

"Mistress Savoldyn, do you drink shay in the mornings?" Lady Azadiya asked.

Mistress Savoldyn shook her head and swallowed heavily. Her lips moved; her voice failed her. She cleared her throat and said more clearly. "No, I—I prefer small ale."

Lady Azadiya nodded. "And as such the cook was in the habit of bringing only one cup for her employer's shay. Is that not so, Mistress Dolman?"

"It is," Mistress Dolman answered.

"Lucky things, habits," Lady Azadiya said. "They can hide all sorts of interesting coincidences. Mistress Ignalle shows up to fight with her father on the day he dies. Master Savoldyn is the only one served shay throughout the day. The wood alcohol comes in bottles from a common draughtshop..."

"Nearest the Ignalles," Ibram pointed out.

"That means nothing," Master Ignalle said. "Anyone can purchase spirits from there!"

"Yes, but no one is buying wood alcohol," Ibram said. "Else so many other folk would be ill."

"The public health is always in my mind," Lady Azadiya said. "And, since we had eliminated it, my mind flew to other worries. Again, your mother provided the solution, Mistress Ignalle."

It was clear that thought had not gone over well with her. Mistress Ignalle clenched both hands into fists. *"What?"*

"After the strain of believing such horrible things, you really must consider the methods used," Lady Azadiya said. "And Mistress Savoldyn very generously offered us free reign over her husband's study. He kept excellent records, dating all the way back to the household bills your mother wrote out." Lady Azadiya leaned over towards the warders.

"Did you know, Captain, in their famous flight to marriage, the Ignalles kept the servants who helped them? The ones they could afford, of course, though the shame of it all has rippled through the community much like this murder. Servants, you know, who get turned out for disloyalty often find new employment difficult."

"So I have observed," Talsconis said.

"Well, but they were grateful folk," Lady Azadiya said. "To their credit. They kept the maid who helped them, and the stable boy. We have the lists, here, of all the old familiar faces at the Savoldyn house-hold. Einar Savoldyn kept a few, himself, out of sentiment. Included among them are Tethna and Marit Agapito."

"That would be Mistress Ignalle's maid, and Master Savoldyn's cook," Ibram said.

"Warder Claes," Lady Azadiya said. "When you escorted the Agapitos to the Cohort of Peace did you find them cooperative?

Warder Claes cleared her throat. "I did, Mentor," she said. "After a few hours conversation, they've been very helpful."

"I thought I saw you on my rounds this morning," Ibram said. He turned to the party assembled. "Lovely folk, to be sure. Mistress Marit makes her own tolnic, and shares her recipes for an excellent dressing with her daughter."

"Shaming two sets of daughters all over one hasty marriage," Lady Azadiya tsked. "It's a bad business."

Dima Ignalle lunged out of his seat with a roar, knocked his wife to the side, and sent the low table skidding across the carpet. Someone screamed. Ibram tackled him, wrapping his arms around the man's torso; they slammed to the floor. Ignalle drove his doubled fists into Ibram's back, and kicked out. He managed to lift them both up, but Ibram got his knees under him and braced, hard. He let go, and Ignalle immediately tried to wriggle backwards. Ibram grabbed his wrists, and pushed them with all his weight against Ignalle's chest. Ignalle rocked beneath him, teeth bared, and Ibram bore down.

"Now, settle!" Ibram barked directly in his face. Ignalle squirmed, and got his heels underneath him. Ibram let him wriggle until there was nothing for it; he knocked their heads together and Ignalle went limp. "I said, settle! You think you have any place to go?"

Ignalle's red face turned mottled. He shook his head. Ibram cracked his neck to the side, and promised himself a dose of withybane at the earliest convenience. Headbutting was always a remorseful event.

"Dima," Mistress Ignalle called for him. "Dima, calm down! We can't—oh, let me go!"

Ignalle rocked against Ibram, more out of pride than strength, and then slumped all at once to the floor. Ibram braced himself above him, and watched Ignalle's eyes carefully. He sniffed and cleared his throat, and then flexed his grip on Ignalle's arms.

"Are you finished?" he asked. "There's a whole room of armed folk waiting on you."

"I expect so," Ignalle replied, and Ibram loosened his grip.

He leaned back on his knees, and watched Ignalle scuttle backwards to freedom, right into Amota Viran's shins. Ibram raised his eyebrows. Amota Viran nodded. He swatted Ignalle on the back of the head, and took a firm grip on the neck of his tunic.

Ibram got to his feet, and brushed off his clothes. He rubbed the back of his neck, and looked about himself. Warder Claes held Mistress Ignalle by the arms; she had somehow made it as far as the staircase in all the struggle. Mistresses Savoldyn and Dolman, Doctor Berot and Attendant Zorion had sensibly remained in their seats. Captain Talsconis was on his feet, glaring indiscriminately. The three agents from the landing were now standing in the common area, carefully spaced to run after anyone who tried to leave without Ladyship's permission. Lady Azadiya sat in her chair, with Ahksell protecting the crates of evidence the warders would need to peruse for themselves.

"I'm afraid it's true, Captain Talsconis," Lady Azadiya said. "We've made more work for you once again."

❧

When Ibram returned from escorting the Ignalles to the Cohort of Peace's charterhouse, the sky was clear for a wonder, gentling towards nighttime with a smear of pink and orange sunset on the horizon. The glowbulbs and torches were lit all over the preceptory, gilding the walkways and fields in light. He found Ahksell sat on the split rail fence.

"Think quick!" Ibram called out, and tossed the jug.

Ahksell caught it in both hands against his chest, and grunted over its weight. He looked down at the plain brown glaze, and sat forward. "What's this?"

Ibram leaned against the railing, and shrugged. "Ama's tolnic," he said, and Ahksell snorted with laughter. "She said we had earned it!"

"I don't know if I ever want to drink it again," Ahksell said, as he uncorked the top.

Ibram leaned his weight on his elbows. "If I let every murder weapon cheat me of its use, I'd never eat meat again."

Ahksell shuddered. "Don't—don't put that image in my head."

Ibram chuckled, and then surprised himself by yawning. Ahksell took a deep breath, staring at the bottle, and then slugged back a healthy measure. He coughed as he came up, and passed the bottle to Ibram. He wiped his eyes.

"Runner's corns, that's spiced."

"Special occasions," Ibram said, and took a more cautious sip. The tolnic burned, but the spices bloomed warmly in the back of his throat. He licked his lips.

"Everything went well?" Ahksell asked.

"It was a production to get the Ignalles down the living mountain," Ibram said.

"Difficult to walk with your hands tied together," Ahksell said.

Ibram nodded. "But we got them to the cells in good order. Warder Claes' knots are impressive."

Ahksell shook his head. "They didn't seem so angry at first, but they must have been."

Ibram shrugged. "Impatient and angry. Amota Viran says it's a lethal combination."

Ahksell paused to consider. "I suppose it must be," he said finally. "Had the Ignalles left Savoldyn alone, they still would have gotten their reward and without any loss of profit."

"And if Tethna Agapito hadn't harbored resentment over her dismissal, she never would have agreed to pass wood alcohol on to her mother."

"And if Mistress Marit hadn't gotten frustrated dosing her employer's tolnic with wood alcohol and slugged it into the shay she sent up—"

"The first shay, which I was right to be suspicious of."

"Which you never got tested on account of its being drunk," Ahksell said. "But if he hadn't died just then, you never would have been in a position to know or mind that Savoldyn had passed on."

"Maybe we should all adopt Mistress Ignalle's policy," Ibram said.

"What?"

"Never drink anything you haven't served yourself."

Ahksell winced, and shook his head. "More like 'don't touch anything in a house you're deliberately poisoning,' I should think."

Ibram nodded, and drank his tolnic, a little more deeply this time. He licked his lips, and passed the bottle back. Ahksell rubbed the mouth clean, and then drank. He shuddered.

"Did Mistress Savoldyn return home?" Ibram asked.

"With Mistress Dolman and Master Kalmar," Ahksell said.

"I think Amota Viran might be taking up residence there," Ibram said.

"He might," Ahksell said. He nodded and gazed down at the tolnic. He sniffed and cleared his throat. "I missed my examination."

Ibram sighed. "I think you did. Ladyship isn't pleased."

"No, she isn't," Ahksell said, and scratched his cheek. "It might be some time before I can get my shield button tested."

"I thought it worked all right in the trials," Ibram said. "All the flashing lights, and such. I have to make my report," he groaned, "Amota Evren will have me writing until my hand cramps."

He turned around and gazed out on the empty training field. All the tents and such had been stored away, leaving small divots in the ground where the stakes had been driven. The air smelled like mountain trees and cooking fires, still. Ibram rolled his neck on his shoulders.

"Here," Ahksell said, suddenly. "For times of trouble."

"What?" Ibram lifted his head.

In front of him, Ahksell's experimental shield button hovered in the air. Ibram blinked at the enameled front, and the way the center glimmered with an icy blue light if he concentrated on it. The button bobbled and Ibram snatched it out of the air. He stood up from the fence, and stared at Ahksell.

"What's this?" he asked. "You're just handing out shield buttons now?"

Ahksell grinned. "You had a hand in testing the gewgaw, did you not?"

"Yes, I remember the pain it caused me," Ibram said. "What am I to do with this?"

"I figured since you seem to be in the habit of tackling folk," Ahksell said, "it might be a good thing to have in hand in case you meet someone bigger than you."

"To blind them?" Ibram asked. "Because I remember how strong that strobe effect of yours was."

Ahksell shrugged. "It's a thought," he said. "But you know us alchemists, I'll get distracted by the etheric movements of the local

Abyss, and forget all about my rescue light in time for the next Festival of Sangrin. Best you hold onto it and see if it gets some use."

Ibram snorted, but grinned. He tossed the gewgaw into the air and caught it. His gambeson had a button that just might fit the shield.

"Well, if you're so bored with it, I might as well keep it," Ibram said.

Ahksell took another swig of tolnic, and grimaced. "Might as well."

Ibram cleared his throat, and glanced down the road. "Best get to my reports."

"Might as well," Ahksell said again, with a long sigh. "I think I have to write one, too."

Ahksell jumped down from the fence, and plugged the bottle of tolnic. Together, they walked down the road to Lady Azadiya's tower. All in all, Ibram couldn't say it had been the worst festival he'd ever worked.

AUTHOR'S NOTE

Thank you for reading my novel! I hope you enjoyed reading *The Elixir of Inheritance* as much as I enjoyed writing it.

If you've left a review for my work, thank you again! Reviews help others find my book.

ABOUT THE AUTHOR

E. M. Burnham likes fantasies, mysteries, and stories of all shapes and sizes, which is why she's decided to write them all at once. She's been a Jedi, a Fellow of The Ring, a Trekker, and even a Newsie, raised on Agatha Christie with a shot of Dorothy L. Sayers and a chaser of Margery Allingham.

She has lived and worked on three continents (and somehow earned two masters degrees in the midst of all that moving!) but settled down to be near her family in the United States. Check out her other work at emburnham.com

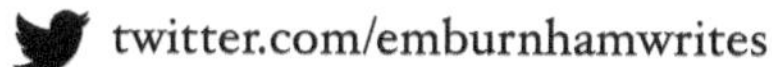 twitter.com/emburnhamwrites

ALSO BY E. M. BURNHAM

THE ALCHEMIST'S AGENT SERIES

Cursebird On A Wire

The Gilty Party

The Elixir of Inheritance